Campaign 2100:
Game of Scorpions

Larry Hodges

World Weaver Press

Published by World Weaver Press, LLC
Albuquerque, NM
www.WorldWeaverPress.com
Editor: Eileen Wiedbrauk
Cover layout and design by Sarena Ulibarri.
Cover images used under license from Shutterstock.com.

First edition: March 2016

ISBN-13: 978-0692657485
ISBN-10: 0692657487

Also available as an ebook

Dedication

I'd like to dedicate *Campaign 2100: Game of Scorpions* to the **Odyssey Writing Workshop**, especially those who helped critique parts of the novel: *Jeanne Cavelos (Odyssey Director and Evil Mastermind), Jason Allard, Ellen Denham, Olivia Do, Arthur Dorrance, Erica Hildebrand, Andrea Kail, Rita Oakes, Thomas Parker, Lane Robins, Susan Sielinski, Holly Stoj, Larry Tayler, Susan Winston, and Victoria "Tori" Witt.*

I'd also like to thank the critiquers from the **Hasting Point Workshop:** *Stephen Buchheit, Merrie "Mer" Haskell, Kajsa Herrstrom, Elizabeth Shack, and Victoria "Tori" Witt (who suffered through it twice).*

I'm also grateful to the **Taos Toolbox Workshop:** *Director Walter Jon Williams, Kelly Link, and Stephen Donaldson;* and the **Codex Online Writing Workshop** *Director Luc Reid and countless others.*

Three people helped tremendously in discussing the novel before I wrote it: *Jeanne Cavelos, Robert J. Sawyer, and Walter Jon Williams.*

I'd also like to thank the staff at **World Weaver Press:** *Sarena Ulibarri (publisher), Eileen Wiedbrauk (editor), and Elizabeth Wagner (publicist).*

And lastly I'd like to thank the **American Political System:** A tree bursting with rotten fruit begging to be mocked.

CAMPAIGN 2100:
GAME OF SCORPIONS

Chapter One
The Changing of the Scorpions

Noon, Friday, January 20, 2096

*W*hat have I done?

The thought raced through Toby Platt's mind as he stood in the shadows of the Twin Towers in Lower Manhattan as the live orchestra played *Hail to the Chief*. He was sick of the song. He was sick of the cold, misty weather. Above all, he was sick of Corbin Dubois, the president-elect, the man he'd made the next president of Earth.

The music was in honor of President-for-five-more-minutes Jing Xu. The Chinese man stood at a lectern, side by side with Dubois. The two blue-suited mortal enemies smiled and waved at the huge crowd of dignitaries. Then Xu turned to Dubois, and they shook hands, one scorpion to another. Except, Toby thought, some are more scorpion than others.

All politicians are scorpions. Bruce, his former top aide, once said that a politician without a sting was like a ping-pong player without a paddle. And yet it was how—and why—they used that stinger that mattered. Xu had quite a sting, as they'd learned during the campaign. Xu the president wasn't so bad, but Xu the politician—well, you didn't get to be leader of the world without a little scorpion blood.

But Dubois just stung anyone who got in his way, often using Toby's own words. Whether it was hunger in Asia and Africa, Mormon-Israeli strife in Utah, or even piracy in the South China Sea, they were all just political points to the Dubois campaign. Toby had five more years of it to look forward to—five years of the never-ending campaign that all worldwide offices had become. He could feel the deadness in him growing.

Which was why Toby had decided to resign.

The plump Frenchman was Napoleonic short, a comparison they'd used with great success in the election. His bleached white hair twisted upward to a point, his sideburns splayed sideways, and his beard looked like a series of long, white icicles. With hair shooting in all directions like an exploding star, he was an easy caricature for the world's late night comics. Add the archaic red tie and the perpetually darting eyes, and Dubois had a memorable face that had grown on voters. So did his American cowboy persona, which every Frenchman publicly detested but privately wanted to emulate. The white hair made him look older than his 45 years.

It seemed wrong to Toby that this man would take the oath of office at the foot of the Twin Towers, with their storied histories. There was no sight more majestic, more inspirational than these monuments to human resilience. Twice they had been destroyed, and twice rebuilt, the second time at well over twice the height of the originals. Those two terrorist acts had marked the start and end of the Age of Terror. The second had led to world government, and to the likes of Dubois.

At four thousand feet, they were the tallest skyscrapers in the world and one of the Seven Wonders of the Modern World. They housed the World Congress; The North Tower the House of Representatives, the South Tower the World Senate. Nearly all the Representatives and Senators were in attendance for the inauguration.

Dubois stepped back from the lectern and stood next to Toby, a little apart from the other dignitaries. Xu began the customary farewell address, which was scheduled for a mercifully short five minutes.

"We're almost there," Dubois said, patting Toby on the back as they listened to Xu's gracious words.

"I'm resigning," Toby blurted out, his voice low enough so others would not hear.

Dubois turned and stared at him. Then he smiled. "No you're not." He went back to watching Xu.

"No, really," Toby said. "We haven't agreed on anything in years. I can't stay."

"We'll work it out," Dubois said without looking at him.

A dozen times Toby had decided to leave, a dozen times he'd decided to stay, to at least finish the campaign. Nobody runs a worldwide campaign and then quits on the verge of winning. They had won, and now he could walk away as a famously successful campaign director.

"We can't work it out," Toby said. "You can bring in anyone now, so you don't need me."

Dubois turned his piercing eyes back on him, the smile still frozen on his face. "You're my political guru. You got me here. I need you to handle the politics the next five years, and the next campaign. We're great together!"

Toby shook his head. "It's over. I resign, effective the instant you become president."

The smile was gone, replaced by the famous Dubois glare, something Toby had never faced before, though he'd seen many others wilt under it. "You do this, and you'll never work in politics again."

Toby knew that was coming. "I know."

"Neither will your daughter."

Toby froze. Lara and Bruce had been his top advisors. When Bruce left to return to the ping-pong circuit, Lara was the only life he really had outside politics. Which somehow seemed contradictory, since Lara's whole life was also politics. Of course, Toby had a wife and son as well, though he rarely saw them.

"You wouldn't—"

"Plug the mouth hole, and please don't say I wouldn't dare," Dubois said. "You know I would. Isn't that why you're resigning in the first place? And now, why you won't? So let's just forget we had this discussion."

"You can't—"

"You and Lara are the only advisors I trust," Dubois said. "We're going to do great things these next five years. We'll even go moderate, if that's what you want. You'll both be a part of it. Meet me in the Red Room in one hour so we can make plans. That's all."

It took more than a penetrating stare to force someone to submit. You had to have a weapon to back it up. Toby glanced over at Lara, who stood with the other dignitaries, a broad smile on her face on this triumphant day. Dubois had the stare and the weapon.

Ice cold anger rose in him, but what else was new? Once upon a time he would have acted on his anger. Now it was just another emotion to control. He'd become good at that.

Toby gave a short nod. Dubois nodded back. They went back to listening to Xu's speech, which was already over the allotted time. Security floaters flew in slow circles around the towers, guarding the airspace like hawks, ready to dive and attack if the unthinkable were to happen.

Just when Toby thought they were going to have to shoot him to get him off, Xu turned and took his seat off to the side, ceding the lectern to Dubois. The Chief Justice of the United States of Earth approached the lectern. Dubois raised his right hand, his left on a stack of religious scriptures—Christian and Jewish Bibles, the Muslim Quran, the Hindu Vedas, the Buddhist Buddhavacana, the Confucianism Analects, the Sikh Adi Granth, the Book of Mormon, and several others.

Toby wanted to run to the podium and yell *"Stop! A terrible mistake has been made!"* But he did not.

The Chief Justice spoke the words, and Dubois recited them back. *"I do solemnly swear that I will faithfully execute the office of President of the United States of Earth, and will to the best of my ability, preserve, protect, and defend the Constitution of the United States of Earth."*

The changing of the scorpions was complete. Toby adjusted the fading purple scarf he always wore, even in warm weather. It seemed entirely out of place. Long ago he'd pulled it off a dead victim of his past idealism.

"Isn't it great, Dad? *We did it!*" Lara's beaming smile contrasted with his own outlook. How many other families ran worldwide elections as their main father-daughter activity?

Lara's upbeat outlook, quick mind, and long, shiny black hair had earned her spot as campaign spokesperson, but she'd been much more than that. They both wore "Win with Corbin!" buttons, with a small Coca-Cola logo centered over the words.

Missing from the team was Bruce Sims, table tennis champion and Lara's almost fiancé, who'd abandoned the campaign months before. Toby wondered if Bruce was watching on his thought computer. Of course he was.

Dubois raised his arms over his head. When the crowd quieted, he lowered his arms and began to speak. Toby closed his eyes and mouthed the words he himself had written as Dubois spoke them. Inspiring words, promises and pledges. *Lots of sound and fury, signifying nothing*, he thought. *Who's the idiot here?*

The speech ended, the crowd cheered, and the orchestra leaped back into *Hail to the Chief* as Dubois began walking the VIP line, shaking hands. His bald and emaciated vice president followed, the always-frowning Rajan Persson, towering two feet over his boss.

Lara beamed at Toby. He forced a smile back. This was the culmination, the ultimate father-daughter moment, the reason why he'd stayed with Dubois, and would continue to do so. He didn't want to ruin it for her.

"We did it, Daddy!" she repeated, clenching her fists in the air. During the campaign, as his assistant, she'd made the final transition from daughter to woman in Toby's eyes, turning thirty in the process. He was only fifty, with rapidly balding reddish-brown hair that only bad genetics or a political campaign can give you. Lara gave his scarf a yank. "Just this once, could you take that smelly thing off?"

We did it, Daddy. The words wouldn't leave his mind as he fingered the scarf, watching Dubois shake hands and wave to his admirers. What would Vinny have said if he were here, alive, instead of just his scarf? Toby yanked the scarf off and jammed it in a pocket. He didn't deserve to wear it.

What have I done?

He stared off into space for a moment.

What can I do to fix this?

The answer was nothing. Not for five more years.

Who's worse, a bad king or the kingmaker?

Chapter Two
The Arrival

Tuesday, July 27, 2100

The spaceship landed shortly after 9:00 A.M. in front of the United Nations Building in East Manhattan, exactly four weeks before the start of the worldwide election for president.

The large black sphere, 20 feet in diameter, had plummeted out of the sky at a meteor's speed, then slowed in seconds until it came to a stop, floating five feet above the ground. No Earth vehicle could match that performance. There was no visible means of levitation underneath the ship, just a smooth, black surface. In most places on Earth there would have been panic. However, this was New York City, Earth's capital, where "alien" was just a matter of degree.

Crowds gathered, many broadcasting the images worldwide with their thought computers. A child threw a veggie dog against the black sphere, leaving dripping mustard on its side. Several other children dashed under the black sphere until stern parents pulled them back.

Within minutes, delegations of police arrived. They cordoned off the area around the black sphere to hold the crowds back, then sauntered about, not sure what to do about this strange ship that had fallen in their midst.

The chief of police stepped past the cordoning. There was no obvious door on the ship, whose shiny black surface was marred only by the dripping mustard. He rapped on the ship with his stick. "Anyone there?"

7

While the alien ship was landing, Toby and his daughter were in the Red Room in the United Nations Building—*The Bubble*—going over campaign strategies with the president and vice president.

On the wall to the left and right of the president's huge walnut desk were portraits of past world presidents, brightly lit from a chandelier and the sunlight through the windows. Interactive holomaps floated near the front wall. Lettered in blue on the soft red carpeting were the letters "POTUSE": *President of the United States of Earth.*

It hadn't always been the Red Room. When Wallace had been elected the world's first president in 2050, he'd painted the office green, to represent the environmental work needed to clean up after the nuclear wars of 2045. When Abrams succeeded him ten years later, he painted the room red, the color of the Conservative Party. Since that time the room had changed color and name whenever it changed parties. During the liberal Xu administration, it had been the Blue Room. Now it was the Red Room once again.

"We need to find a compromise," Toby said as he rose to his feet. "If we take either side, we lose the votes and funding from the other side." He fingered the fading purple scarf under his short beard. He'd lost weight this past year, and his green suit sagged loosely along the sides.

"You're going soft," said Lara. She walked over to the holomaps by the front wall, stopping in front of a shimmering map of North America. Colored dots indicated various voting regions, Conservative headquarters for each state, upcoming political events, and other data. "A compromise means you lose both sides," she said as she tapped her finger over two almost overlapping orange dots on purple Utah. One was Salt Lake City; the other New Israel. "Forget the Israelis, we need the Mormon vote. Get them angry, and you lose the Midwest and Mexico." She waved her hand over the indicated regions. "Side with the Mormons, and you win all this."

"But we've always supported New Israel," President Dubois mumbled. He was seated at his desk, his mouth full of natural peanuts he was stuffing in a handful at a time, ignoring the bowl of artificial no-cal peanuts also on his desk. He'd gained thirty pounds the past four

8

years, and was on his sixth set of blue suits as he moved up in waist size. "If the media starts calling me a hypocrite again I'll lose votes. They can do that all they want *after* the election."

A fly buzzing in the window behind Dubois brought Toby's attention away from the pungent peanut aroma. How had a fly made it past the best security system in the world? Toby watched it fly up and down against the window. Maybe it liked peanuts.

"We have to do something about the Salt Lake riots," Lara said, "and a crackdown on the Israelis solves the problem." As she looked side to side, her black pyramidal hair, reaching a point a foot over her head, stayed rigidly in place. The four corners looked sharp enough to use as a weapon. The new style was cultivated for the press and voters, but Toby hated the latest trend toward polyhedral hair.

Persson, the towering vice president, slouched in his chair, frowning in his baggy brown suit and black bolo tie. If he stood, his head would hit the chandelier, and his chin would be above everyone's head. "Sir, don't you think—"

"Plug the mouth hole, Rajan," the president snapped, pronouncing it with an exaggerated "Ray-Jan." He didn't bother to glance at his vice president, whose frown grew deeper. "I don't want to deal with the New Israel Lobby before the election. If you can keep them out of my face until then, I'm fine with whatever helps us best."

"Corbin," Toby said, pulling his attention away from the fly. "If you take sides in this, you *will* look like a hypocrite, and everyone will see that." There's a limit on how much we can hide you from the voters, he thought.

"Everyone?" Lara asked. "Aren't you the one who preaches that all politics is local, that nobody notices what politicians do until they're in their own back yard?"

"It's all local," Toby replied, "until they find out what you've been telling others."

"They rarely pay attention and find out, do they?" Lara turned back to the holomap, and jabbed her finger in the middle, somewhere in Kansas, her finger going through it like a gigantic missile. "Dad, North

9

America is seven percent Jewish and fifteen percent Mormon. It has 88 electoral votes, 62 from the U.S., and the momentum as the second continental election in the world, and the first major one. If we let Ajala take North America and its electoral votes, the next thing we know he'll be moving in here and the place will be crawling with liberals. As campaign director, what do you *really* recommend?"

Crawling with liberals, Toby thought, watching the buzzing fly. He'd had his greatest successes running moderate conservative campaigns, which was why he was blackballed by the Liberal Party. Dubois had promised Toby that he'd lead as a moderate, but once in office, he'd gone back to his conservative roots. Toby had once considered himself a liberal, but he no longer was sure. Conservatives, liberals—there weren't any other options in a world dominated by the Conservative and Liberal Parties.

"Well?" Lara asked, bringing Toby out of his reverie.

"Don't forget about the New Israel Lobby and their funding," Toby said. "We need NIL." The fly's buzzing was irritating; couldn't housekeeping or security or *someone* take care of it? With all their guns and other weapons, wouldn't they have a flyswatter packed away somewhere?

"Shouldn't we at least—" Rajan began.

"Plug it," Dubois said. "Toby, how much of our money have we gotten from NIL?"

Toby pulled his attention away from the distraction at the window. "About ten percent. But if we turn our backs on them, they'll let us know very loudly. Besides, the Israelis aren't the ones who started the rioting, it was—"

"How much do we expect to get from them before the North American election next month?" Dubois asked.

"We've received—" Toby began.

"—nearly all we're going to get from them," Dubois finished for him.

"Meaning," Lara said, "we already have the NIL money and can still get the Mormon vote, if we play this right. If we emphasize low taxes and law and order, we'll keep the conservative vote. They won't even

10

notice what's happening in Utah, except the law and order part. As you always say, Dad, throw some spiced vegetables to energize the base."

Toby shook his head. "It just isn't—"

"I think we have to go with Lara's plan," Dubois said. "Just before the election, I'll condemn the Israelis and side with the Mormons. The Israelis will have to give up the disputed areas."

Toby knew he'd lost another argument. He was arguing with his heart instead of his head. He knew the saying: liberals have no head, conservatives no heart. Where did he fit in?

They'd been through a long primary campaign, but they'd easily won the Conservative nomination at the convention. Soon he'd have to make some tough "the end justifies the means" decisions in the upcoming general election. He remembered long ago having great difficulty with such decisions. Then he'd been introduced to the drug Eth, which took away moral constraints. It solved the problem, as long as he didn't get caught taking the illegal drug. It wasn't a magic bullet; you still had to choose to take the drug, knowing its effects, which was a moral dilemma in itself. This meeting would have been a lot easier for him if he'd taken some in advance. Fortunately—or perhaps unfortunately—he'd quit the habit after the 2095 election. It had been his decision to take Eth back then, and the consequences were his alone.

He couldn't argue with the hard political facts, since he was supposedly in charge of them. *Politics*, he thought. Once it had inspired him. "Poli" meant many, "tic" meant bloodsucker, so "politics" was just "many bloodsuckers." He was one of them.

As the glorified Campaign Director, he had about as much influence on the issues as the buzzing fly on the wall.

And once again, he knew, Israel was doomed. The establishment of New Israel outside Salt Lake City fifty years before had led to nothing but conflict. They'd won many votes in the last election by promising to resolve the ongoing Israeli-Mormon conflict; now, just before the next election, they were going to do so. Israel had once been destroyed by nuclear bombs; now it would be destroyed again, this time by administrative fiat.

11

Damn fly! Maybe he couldn't save New Israel, but the fly had to go. He looked about for something to swat it with, and grabbed a paper document from Dubois's desk. It seemed archaic to use so much paper in this age of thought computers, like counting on one's fingers, but Dubois was old-fashioned in that regard—and paper would always be a staple in any type of office, no matter how many predicted its demise. And they did make handy anti-fly weapons. Toby glanced at the title: *North American Tree Repopulation Study: The Regreening of America.* As if that had a chance. He'd make better use of it.

"Excuse me a moment," he said, rolling the paper into a cylinder. Then he realized that Dubois, Lara, and Persson were looking off into space, their eyes vacant. The words *Breaking News!* appeared in the air in front of him, and he now heard the words in his mind, care of his thought computer.

"TC on," he said under his breath, and the World News Network broadcast screen appeared before him. No one else could see or hear it, just as he couldn't see or hear the broadcasts the others were watching. The thought computers, implanted in their heads, played directly into the optical and auditory portions of their brains.

The WNN showed pictures surrounding what was apparently an alien ship. A disembodied women's head on the lower right gave all the information available—essentially nothing. A scientist came on and explained how nothing on Earth could come out of the sky at such a speed, and how the alien could be a threat. Then the woman's head returned.

Toby stared at the black ship. Was this a prank, or could it actually be an alien, an actual first contact? His heart was racing. He realized he'd crushed the anti-fly weapon in his hand. He tossed it aside. Maybe the aliens could swat humanity like he could swat a fly. But a single ship that could probably fit in the Red Room didn't seem like an armada out to destroy humanity. He took a deep breath. First contact. On our watch.

"TC off," he whispered when the report degenerated to repeating itself, and found the president and Lara already in animated discussion. The fly now stood directly in front of Dubois on his desk, seeming to stare at Toby. Then it flew back to the window and continued its irritating buzzing.

Four aides came through the door at a run, all talking at once. They surrounded the president like bees around a beehive.

Dubois slammed his fist on his desk. "Shut up, all of you!" He pointed at each of the aides in turn. "You, you, you, and you, get out!" After a few seconds of blanching, the aides left, also at a near run.

"The last thing we need right now," Dubois said, "are a bunch of self-important lowbodies who think they know everything but know nothing of the political implications of anything. Who knows what's really going on with that ship, and how it'll affect the election?"

Like a laser beam fixed on a target, Toby thought, Dubois had zeroed in on the political aspect. Toby knew he'd once been like that, but not in recent years. At least he didn't think so.

"It could be an attack," Lara said. "Call out the guard, and if anything from that thing so much as sticks out its tongue, blast it. Of course, it might be a hoax."

"Why," Toby asked, "would you even consider attacking when this supposedly alien ship has done nothing hostile?"

Lara gave her most ingratiating smile. "Strong and wrong beat meek and weak. You said that, remember?"

Persson still sat on the couch, looking down at the president, who paced back and forth. "Perhaps we should—"

"Plug it." The president came to a stop. "If I go out there and play the 'welcoming leader' role, and it's some prank or something, I'll look like a fool."

"This is no hoax," Toby said. "There's nothing like that in the USE air force, or any other regional air force."

"How do you know?" Lara asked. "That's what they said about black helicopters."

"You think we have black spheres in the air force that can move like that thing did?"

Lara began to protest, but Dubois silenced her with a raised hand. "If these are real aliens, then I'm the one who's going to welcome them to Earth and get the credit. If we play this right, I can ride this to victory."

Persson began to say something, but changed his mind at a glance from the president.

"Sir," Toby said, "this could be the biggest thing this century—"

"All seven months of it," Lara interrupted. "Unless you're one of those potato-heads from the university who say the century doesn't start till next January."

"—and I believe we need to put politics aside for now and just see how this goes."

"Why would we do that?" Lara asked. "Heck, we can play this either way. Corbin can act all presidential, welcoming foreign dignitaries to Earth, or he can turn on the 'get tough on aliens' shtick, just like he did with the African émigrés last year. We win either way."

"And if it's a hoax?" Dubois asked.

"Then," Lara said, "you get to play the 'law and order' role when you deal with those idiots. It's win-win."

The president nodded. "Rajan, call the Army Chief to set up security. Toby, Lara, I'm going to need a welcoming speech. This is going to be historic, and people will read my words for centuries. And this could win the election. Get cracking."

On the way out, Toby alerted maintenance about the fly.

Chapter Three
Two Hundred Forty-Two Guns

*I*t's *beautiful!* Twenty-two had seen images of other planets like this back on Tau Ceti, but in person it seemed so much more alive—even if she was watching Earth through a large viewscreen from orbit. The blue oceans, the mostly brown and gray land areas—dotted by lights on the dark side—were all so vivid. There wasn't a lot of green, and most of it was in concentrated areas that appeared to be farmland. Had they urbanized the whole planet?

She'd soon find out. Already the ship's sensors were taking readings of the planet's surface and atmosphere. From the latter, she made adjustments to her internal breathing apparatus. Despite the seeming lack of vegetation, there was plenty of oxygen, though not quite what she was used to back on her home planet of Grodan. Probably from plant life in the seas.

She stood in the middle of the ship's only room, belted to a white railing that came out of the white floor. Except for the viewscreen, the wall that circled the room showed lively images of shiggles, the small aromatic scavenger creatures from her planet. The ship's vents filled the air with their sweet scent while the soothing sound of their wing beats played in the background.

"English lesson plans are ready, Your Greatness," said Zero, the ship's computer, in its sing-songy voice. It basically *was* the ship. It had been scanning the infowaves and uploading what it found on the planet and its inhabitants, including samples of the primary alien language so it

15

could decode it and set up lesson plans for Twenty-two. "Would you like a massage?"

"Not now," Twenty-two said. She had work to do.

It took her a few hours with the lesson plans Zero had set up to master the intricacies and inflections of English. What a fascinating language, she thought—such a mixture of poetry and inconsistency! In some ways it was similar to her own language, the old version, before One ordained that the irrational aspects be taken out. The grammars were similar. She remembered reading a theory that connected language with spaceflight. It claimed a race wasn't really mature until it looked both inwardly—cleaning up its language, thought processes, and so on—and outwardly, where it looked to the stars. If the theory held, humans had a long way to go.

Of course, that was the whole point of her visit. She'd been studying non-stop all semester, right through her male phase and back to female, and felt that if she read one more dialogue from the sayings of One, her eyestalks would go nuclear. This was one school break that she was going to enjoy. She'd chosen her destination with care. Earth was outside the Galactic Union and well out in the spiral arms of the galaxy, a developing planet few would notice.

Where was the best place to land? She could land somewhere inconspicuous, but why do that? She wanted to get to know these bipeds. She might as well land in the most obvious spot, next to their central government. Other than her status as a student, she had nothing to hide from these people—although there were plenty of things she would hide. As long as she stayed hidden from her own people. If they were to catch her here . . . .

Of course, even if she were caught, she could always claim she was doing research on a non-member of the Galactic Union. She was, after all, a major in political theory.

She wondered what political system the humans used. World governments could be some version of communist, dictatorial, democratic, or randomist. Which would it be?

For the good of the humans, she hoped their politics were a bit more civilized than galactic politics. Not that it mattered in the long run; she knew the history of first admittance. Assuming they didn't destroy themselves—as about half of advanced races did before qualifying for galactic membership—there'd be plenty of time for her fellow grods to corrupt their politics. She shook her eyestalks in disgust.

Or perhaps they'd be that long foreseen race that would inject idealism back into the cold, hard reality of galactic civilization. *Hah!* Perhaps they'd also raise their eyestalks and black holes would flower, novas implode, and One be reborn.

Forget politics, Twenty-two decided; let's just enjoy the next—she did a quick conversion to local time units—few months before she went back to school to study power plays and diplomatic deception with her partner Ninety-seven.

"Zero, put all the viewscreens on." The shiggles disappeared from the wall, and she could see outside the ship in all directions. She watched in awe the majestic stars trailing off to infinity, and the huge blue and brown planet below.

"Zero, do you know where the human capital is?"

"Yes, Wise One," Zero sang back. "It is on the island of Manhattan in New York City, on the east coast of the North American continental mass we are currently passing over. Would you like to go there?"

"Put on the antigravs and take us there full speed. Exceed the specs."

"Yes, Oh Wonderful Being. Would you care for a refreshment first?"

"No, just land us next to their capital building." Twenty-two wondered if she should turn down Zero's flattery mode. No, she decided, it was fun.

"I will do that, Perfect Being." The ship began its dive.

Sirens flashed as the ship shot down faster than its specs. She liked the thrill of plummeting through an atmosphere, the wind buffeting the ship as it spiraled down. She flinched as they approached a wall of white; after shooting through the cloud, she could see the human world below. Buildings, streets, it was like dropping onto the Grodan world from long ago. She adjusted helm control so the ship no longer spun as it descended.

Zero landed the ship next to a large, white building. "We have arrived, Lordly Creature," it said. "This is the United Nations Building, home to the planet's central government and their executive leader. Would you like to beat me in a game of cross-squares?"

"You can go to sleep until I call you," Twenty-two said.

"Thank you, Master of All."

Okay, Twenty-two decided, this was getting a bit much. "Zero, lower flattery mode fifty percent."

"Yes, Your Goodness."

The walls of the ship were still transparent. On one side loomed the huge white structure that must be their capital building. On the other side stood a statue of some sort of offensive weapon, but with its barrel twisted into a knot. How could it function? Or was it symbolic? Next to the white building a green flag with a white picture of the twisted gun, surrounded by stars, waved from a high pole. A symbol of peace? She hoped so. The last thing she wanted was the inconvenience of a shower of primitive bullets or lasers as her first greeting.

This would be Twenty-two's first contact with a race that was not a Galactic Union member. Should she go outside and ask them to take her to their leader? Or wait for them to knock?

Humans quickly surrounded her ship, but they couldn't see in since her walls were transparent only one way. She'd looked at pictures of humans that Zero had uploaded while in orbit, but seeing them live, in person, moving about and watching her ship, was riveting. Her hearts beat rapidly as she looked about. They had two legs and two arms, half a grod's allotment. Some of them looked almost twice her height, but somewhat thinner. They wore clothing, but like many primitive races, left their mouths exposed. She nervously rocked side to side, then forced herself to stop. She'd just have to get used to that.

A smaller one stepped forward. It was about the same height as Twenty-two, who moved closer to study the creature. It must be a human child, she thought. Other than its size, it seemed similar to the adults, though its head was a bit larger in proportion to its body, and its clothing a bit more colorful. Like the adults, its mouth was uncovered.

It reached back and threw something at the ship. Twenty-two flinched. If not for the ship's walls, it would have splattered on her face. Instead, the brown, oblong object, covered by light brown material—some sort of sandwich, similar to ones Twenty-two ate back home—bounced off the ship, leaving a splattering trail of yellow on the ship's surface.

"Damn human!" she said, using the English version she'd learned earlier of a common grod curse word. She watched as other human children ran under the floating ship, then were pulled back by others, probably parents.

One of the larger humans walked to the side of the ship and rapped on it with a stick. "Anyone there?"

Based on the uniform, and in particular on the obvious weapon the creature wore on its side, Twenty-two figured the human was a security person. She waved her eyestalks in disgust, ignoring the knocking.

She decided to give them some time before she emerged. She'd studied first contacts in school, and there had been some real horror stories. She decided it was best to let the locals think they were in control, so the real leaders could show up as a welcoming committee. The last thing she wanted to do was make first contact with some shooting-happy thug like the one banging on her ship.

Over the next hour she watched as more uniformed humans surrounded her ship, all with naked mouths. Most held guns pointed at the ship. They wheeled several larger guns into position, also aiming at her. So much for the twisted gun symbol! Zero's sensors counted two hundred forty-two guns aiming at her ship. *Have they no common sense?* she wondered. Bringing guns to a first contact? Do they think a single ship landing is an alien invasion, and that I'm going to come out firing weapons? Me against their planet?

Just beyond the security humans were others, jostling for position. Probably news people. Well, shortly she'd give them some news!

The welcoming committee finally arrived. A rather short human, with white hair shooting in all directions from his head, led a procession as the security people stepped aside. The short one walked up to her ship and circled around it, as if looking for a door. A human leader? It was time to make her entrance.

She wanted to wear her nice red vest, which matched the red velvo over her mouth. She shook side to side for a moment as she thought it over, then tossed the red vest aside and chose the yellow one, just in case. Clashing yellow and red at first contact! Why hadn't she thought to bring a matching yellow velvo? Hopefully humans didn't have a fashion sense.

She stuck a hand sensor into a vest pocket, which would also allow her to communicate with Zero if they were separated. Should she bring the pocket laser? No, she decided, it was pointless. She wasn't about to start shooting humans.

She lowered the ship's door into a walkway and shuffled out into the crosshairs of two hundred forty-two guns.

Chapter Four
First Contact

Dubois led the delegation from the United Nations Building toward the alien ship, followed by his vice president and a small army of aides, including Toby and Lara. His heart raced; this was his chance for a historic photo-op that could lock up the election. *First contact with an alien race, and it came on his watch!* How convenient, he thought, as he made a few last minute adjustments to the welcoming speech displayed on his TC.

They passed *The Twisted Gun*, the symbol of world government. Designed by Swedish artist Carl Fredrik Reutersward, and originally titled *Non-Violence*, it was a giant bronze revolver on a pedestal. The barrel of the gun was twisted like a pretzel, causing the tip to point up into the sky rather than in the direction in which the gun aimed. The world flag was a picture of *The Twisted Gun* on a green field, surrounded by 165 stars—one for every country on Earth with a population over one million—plus the grandfathered Antarctica—which qualified them for membership in the world government.

They passed the media groups that circled the alien ship, each clambering for the best spot. News anchors talked at TC finger cameras as the world watched. No doubt many billions of voters were watching.

Dubois stopped ten feet short of the ship, and stood with his legs spread, chest thrust out, his ever-present red power tie flapping in the breeze. Toby and the rest of the entourage gathered behind him. The ship, a big black sphere, floated in the air, featureless except for what looked like mustard dripping down one side. A veggie dog and bun lay

21

on the ground below. Dubois smiled at the welcome the ship had received.

A minute went by. "Do I look silly just standing here?" Dubois whispered, keeping his confident smile for the cameras.

"You look fine," Lara whispered back. "Like a wall, guarding Earth."

"Right, we'll call him Stonewall Dubois," Toby whispered back.

He thinks I'm an idiot, Dubois thought. Well, that couldn't be helped. When you act dumb, you get the best advice. Act smart, and everyone's afraid to speak up. Toby probably thought Dubois spent his spare time reading comics, and had no clue that he knew that the famous General Jackson had supposedly gotten the Stonewall nickname as an insult for *not* coming to the aid of troops under fire. As usual, he'd pretend he didn't get the insult.

It was obvious to him that Toby was a damn liberal. How could the man be so smart and so stupid? To face the world's problems, you needed strength, not short-sighted feel-goodedness. Even the French were sick of being the pansies of the world and looked to him and his tough cowboy ways to lead them. But for now, it was best to play dumb.

"I like that, 'Stonewall Dubois,' protecting mankind from invasion," Dubois said, smirking on the inside. "Plug it, Rajan," he added when the vice president began to speak. Long ago he'd grown tired of dealing with his griping number two. Putting Persson in his place brought a bit of joy to his busy life, knowing that the Indian Swede's ambitions would keep him from responding.

The outline of a door appeared on the side of the ship. It lowered like a drawbridge. As it dropped, a dark outline appeared in the entrance.

The figure walked down the drawbridge door and into the bright sunshine. The alien, green and hairless, stood about four feet tall, shaped like an upright torpedo. It stood on four legs that stuck out from under the torpedo bottom, two in front, two in back. The feet were only a few inches long, each covered with a sock-like shoe. It wore a yellow vest with pockets, and a red handkerchief on the lower portion of its face, where a mouth might be. Two short and delicate-looking arms—four in all—stuck out from each side of a large, neckless head. The ten-fingered hands looked like sea anemones. Two eyestalks waved slowly side to side from just above each pair of arms, moving independently of each other as they examined the crowd.

Dubois approached the alien and read from the TC teleprompter. "On behalf of Earth and all its residents, I welcome you in peace to our planet."

The alien's eyestalks focused on the president. The handkerchief moved, as if a large mouth underneath had opened.

"If you welcome me in peace to your planet, why do you have weapons aimed at me?" were the historic first alien words on Earth.

Dubois looked about, and for the first time noticed all the weaponry. He was used to traveling with security, and rarely noticed it, but this was a bit over the top.

"Put down your weapons!" he ordered in his most commanding tone, knowing half the planet would be tuned in by now. He reminded himself to speak slowly and clearly; he was speaking for posterity and the upcoming election.

He turned back to the alien. "I apologize for this misunderstanding. I am Corbin Dubois, president of this planet, which we call Earth."

"You are . . . Corbin Dubois?" the alien asked, pronouncing the words slowly. "I do not recognize that in your numbering system."

"It is not a number," Dubois said, "it is my name. You may call me President Dubois."

The alien's eyestalks glanced at each other in almost comical fashion, then refocused on Dubois. "You use random sounds as names. An interesting but confusing system." The two eyestalks splayed out, looking over the crowd. "Do all humans have unique sounds for names?"

"Yes," Dubois said. "What is your name and your purpose here?"

One of the alien eyestalks pointed back at him, while the other continued to observe the crowd. "Translated into your numbering system, I am 55,257,461,522," it said. "You may call me Twenty-two. I am—" It stopped and shook from side to side for a moment. "I am

23

Ambassador Twenty-two, a grod from the planet Grodan. It circles the star you call Tau Ceti. I am here to observe your . . . civilization."

"How does it know English?" Toby whispered to Dubois.

"How do you know English?" Dubois repeated.

"I learned this afternoon," Twenty-two said. Dubois started to say something, but shut his mouth as he realized what the alien had said. There were gasps from the crowd.

"Your speech," Toby whispered to Dubois.

Dubois had forgotten about the speech. It still hung in front of him, seemingly in mid-air, care of his TC. He began again. "On behalf of Earth and all its residents, I welcome you in peace to our planet."

"You said that already," Twenty-two said. "You are the leader of this planet?"

"Yes, and—"

"I would like to discuss politics with you. I am a student . . . I was a student of government. I would like to study yours. I would like to learn from you."

Imagine, Dubois thought, an alien landing practically on his doorstep, and in front of the world, asking him to teach it! Or was that him or her? He had no idea. He'd find out later. Meanwhile, he had to get the alien where he could control access. No chance he'd let Ajala or the other liberals talk to it. Forget the speech; he already had his sound bite. Time to take control of the situation.

"I would very much like to teach you how our political system works," he said. "If you will follow me, I'll take you to my office, where we can talk." He turned to the press. "People of the world, this is a great moment, a time to put aside our differences. Humans and Grogs—"

"*Grods!*" Toby hissed at him.

"—have much to learn from each other. I declare this the beginning of the golden age of humans and *Grods*." He glanced at Toby, then turned to Twenty-two. "As a gesture of friendship, please accept this presidential pen as a welcoming gift." He handed the alien one of the thick pens they gave out as souvenirs to heads of state. Dubois thought the gift somewhat cheap, but the best they could do on short notice. The alien took the pen in two of its hands and examined it before putting it in one of the pockets of its vest.

He motioned toward the United Nations Building. "This way, Ambassador."

"I would like to do a sensor reading," Twenty-two said. It reached into one of its pockets and pulled out an object about the size of a handgun. With its eyestalks scanning the crowd, it pointed the object at Dubois.

Security reacted instantly, pouring an inferno of bullets and energy weapons at the alien, whose body disappeared in billowing smoke.

Agents pulled the president to the ground and buried him with their bodies. Turmoil erupted as people screamed and dove for cover.

Chapter Five
Arguing at the U.S. College Table Tennis Championships

Bruce Sims stood in a relaxed ready position, clutching Sling, his paddle, as Notre Dame's Todd Davis prepared to serve. The thousands in the packed stands surrounding the playing court in the Baltimore Convention Center quieted to a murmur.

Bruce glanced at the scoreboard; he led 19-18 in this game to twenty-one. He was glad they'd change games back to 21—games to 11 were ridiculously short. They were in the fifth game of this best of five, so he was only two points away from victory in the final of the USA National Collegiate Table Tennis Championships.

He was twenty-nine, with a thick mat of curly brown hair and several days' beard growth. Sweat dripped down his face and from his red shirt, which was drenched and covered with corporate logos. The back of his shirt said "University of Maryland," with a large holographic Pepsi logo underneath that seemed to leap off the shirt in a swirl of colors. When he'd worked for the Dubois Campaign, he'd been sponsored by Coke, but he'd switched to the obscure Pepsi afterwards rather than go the liberal route with Hancola.

Sling was the latest model of ping-pong paddle, a Maestro Prime covered with Spinsey pinhole sponge, both from Trump Sports. When the ball hits it, the Spinsey sponge compresses, forcing air out through the tiny, angled holes that permeate the surface. If he held it one way, the air would shoot upward from the parallel holes, creating a topspin. If he flipped the paddle, so the backhand side became the forehand side and vice versa, then the air would shoot downward, creating a backspin. He held it in the topspin position for attacking.

Bruce had never played the hulking Davis before, but he had scouting reports: powerful from both sides and quick off the bounce, but with a tendency to serve fast and deep too often. Not too bright for a high-ranking player. Bruce couldn't match up with Davis backhand to backhand, but by anticipating many of the fast serves to the backhand and attacking them with his forehand, he'd battled the top-seeded freshman phenom into the final game. Bruce was used to taking on bigger, stronger players; it was why he'd named his paddle Sling, after David's weapon against Goliath.

After losing in the final three years in a row, perhaps this was Bruce's year to win. He'd already knocked off the number two seed in the semifinals.

It would have been a lot easier if he hadn't let his ranking drop from lack of training, which hurt him in the seeding. His ranking, normally first or second, had fallen to number seven in the college pro ranks, costing him a fortune in sponsorship money. He'd also lost his spot on the U.S. National Team. He'd spent way too much time studying the election primaries, writing detailed political memos and election plans for the Dubois Campaign and then destroying them in disgust. He was through with Dubois, and with Toby and Lara. But he could stop breathing more easily then he could stop thinking about the campaign.

Davis rotated a bit to his right as he served, telling Bruce that the serve was probably coming to the backhand. Then he saw the barest flicker of Davis's tongue sticking out of his mouth—a telltale Bruce had noticed earlier, telling him it was going to be a fast and deep serve, rather than short and spinny.

As the ball contacted Davis's paddle, Bruce stepped to his left so he could attack the serve with his forehand. As expected, the predictable Davis had served fast and deep to the backhand. *What a chimpanzee*, Bruce thought, as he began his backswing. He contacted the ball with a grazing motion, which, along with the airholes, created a heavy topspin to Davis's backhand.

Bruce knew that Davis's return would be to his now wide-open forehand side. He quickly moved back into position just in time to make another swooping forehand topspin, again to Davis's backhand.

Davis hit a quick backhand to Bruce's wide backhand. Out of position from his previous shot from the wide forehand, Bruce had to lunge to the left to get to the ball. As he did so, he flipped his racket about, so the pinholes pointed downward. He contacted the ball with a downward grazing motion, which along with the airholes, created a heavy backspin.

Davis threw his body into the next shot, a powerful forehand to Bruce's wide forehand. Bruce dove for it, flipping his racket into topspin position as he did so, and barely got his paddle on the ball. He lofted it fifteen feet into the air, a defensive topspin lob that hit deep on Davis's side. Bruce got to his feet and raced backwards.

Davis smashed twice in a row, each time taking a running start and jumping into the air to increase his power. From the barriers twenty feet back, Bruce ran each shot down with more topspin lobs. On the third one, to his wide forehand, he crashed into the barriers, knocking them against a number of surprised spectators. Fully stretched out and trying to stay balanced after his collision, he still managed to flick his wrist at contact, adding a bit of sidespin.

Davis misread the sidespin and miss-timed his next smash, sending the ball nearly off the end. But it just nicked the edge of the table for a winner, making the score 19-all. Bruce closed his eyes in disgust.

The ghosts of last year were laughing at him, Bruce thought, except that last year it had been a net-dribbler at the end that had done him in. There are no Gods, he knew, but those bastards were out to get him anyway.

The umpire flipped the scoreboard to 20-18 match point for Bruce and announced that score over the loudspeaker. The umpire hadn't seen the ball nick the edge! Davis was staring at the far side of the table, his mouth working furiously as if he wasn't sure whether to argue.

Double match point. One more point and he'd be the national champion. The best of the best. What he'd trained for much of his life.

Not really, of course. It should be 19-all. He smiled fatalistically; if only he'd taken some Eth!

Bruce approached the umpire. "The ball hit the edge. It's his point."

The umpire looked up, the hint of a glare on his face. Then he held up a blue card with a white "R" for replay on it, and his eyes glazed over as he watched a replay of the shot on his TC. Then his eyes cleared and he put the blue card back in his pocket.

"Too close to call," the umpire said. "Point stands. 20-18 match point for Bruce Sims."

Bruce looked heavenward. *Another chimpanzee!* "Look, the ball hit the edge, so just give him the point." When the umpire did nothing, Bruce walked to the scoreboard in front of the umpire and flipped the score back to 19-all. The crowd cheered his sportsmanship, with the fans in the Notre Dame corner especially loud.

"Are you trying to show me up?" The umpire rose to his feet, his face red with anger. He flipped the scoreboard back to 20-18 for Bruce. The Notre Dame crowd booed. The umpire jabbed a finger into Bruce's chest. "Touch the scoreboard again and you'll be defaulted."

"*Chimpanzee!*" Bruce muttered under his breath. Oops, he thought, shouldn't have said that out loud.

The umpire held up another card, this one a yellow warning card. "One more outburst, Mr. Sims, and I'll default you."

The booing from the Notre Dame corner turned to cheers. Bruce stared at them for a moment and then walked over.

"Why were you booing me?" he asked. "And now you're cheering me because I might get defaulted? I'm the one trying to give your guy the point!"

"You're a sore loser!" one from the Notre Dame crowd cried.

"That makes no sense," Bruce pointed out. "I'm the one leading 20-18 match point, but I'm trying to convince the umpire it should be 19-all. You should be *cheering* me." *Why was everything like politics, where the more you do the right thing, the angrier the mob?*

His reasoning didn't have much effect as the Notre Dame crowd began shouting at him. One began chanting, "*Lose, Bruce!*" over and over, and the others joined in the chant.

"That doesn't even rhyme," Bruce said, but doubted anyone heard him. He shook his head as he muttered, "Crowds: the ultimate stupidity magnifier."

Some from his home school began a rival chant of "*Maryland! Maryland!*"

Bruce started back toward the table, but found himself blocked by the massive Davis in his sleeveless muscle shirt dominated by a Coke logo. Bruce stared at the man's arms; could any sleeves hold those biceps?

"Why are you yelling at my friends?" Like most professional athletes, Davis's steroid-built body was a sculpture—or monstrosity, as Bruce thought of it—of bulging muscles. They were both a little under six feet, but Davis outweighed him two to one.

Davis took another step closer. Bruce felt the floor vibrate. He also got a whiff of Davis's lack of hygiene.

Okay, Bruce thought over the continuing chants, not a chimpanzee, a gorilla. Who, he noticed, had left his paddle back on the table, and was currently clenching two coconut-sized fists from a few feet away. Do steroids increase fist size? Apparently.

"Watch what you say to my friends," Davis said. His voice sounded an octave lower than anything humanly possible, and came out of a head that Bruce figured was hardwired for stupidity.

The words "*Breaking News!*" appeared in the air in front of him, obscuring Davis's angry face. It was poor etiquette to leave your TC on during a match, and Bruce was sure he'd turned his off.

"TC, I told you not to bother me while I play," Bruce said under his breath. "Why are you bothering me during a match?"

The TC spoke directly into his head. "You said, 'Do not interrupt me unless there's another nuclear war or an alien invasion.'"

Davis was also saying something to him. "What?" Bruce asked.

"I said watch what you say to my friends or else," Davis said.

"*Bruce Lose! Bruce Lose!*"

"*Maryland! Maryland!*"

"Mr. Sims, you're disrupting play," the umpire called from his chair. "You've got ten seconds to return to the table or I'll fault you a point."

"There is an alien invasion," Bruce's TC continued. "Would you like visual?"

"Are you going to apologize to my friends?"

"*Bruce Lose! Bruce Lose!*"

"*Maryland! Maryland!*"

"Five seconds, Mr. Sims."

"Play visual," Bruce said. A small screen opened up in front of him, showing the alien ship.

"When did this happen?" Bruce asked.

"When did this happen?" Davis exclaimed, his breath like moldy onions. "You insulted them just now!"

"The alien ship landed twenty-seven minutes ago," Bruce's TC said.

"Why didn't you let me know then?" Bruce asked.

"I did!" Davis exclaimed, his face now a foot from Bruce's.

"I'm faulting you a point," the umpire said, flipping the scoreboard to 20-19, still match point in favor of Bruce.

"The evidence at the time suggested it was an alien landing, but not necessarily an alien invasion," the TC said. "When the shooting started, the preponderance of the evidence was that it was an alien invasion. Would you like me to play that scene?"

"Play it," Bruce said.

"Then go to the table!" the umpire said.

"I'm going to pound you after this match," Davis said.

"*Bruce Lose! Bruce Lose!*"

"*Maryland! Maryland!*"

The TC played the shooting of the alien scene. Bruce watched, ignoring the growing havoc around him.

He walked to the side of the table where he'd left his playing bag, tossed his paddle into it, threw the bag over his shoulder, and made for the door, ignoring the shouts of the crowd, umpire and Davis. The world had just gotten a lot more interesting and he wanted to be a part of it.

Chapter Six
The Gift of Many Bullets

The gunfire ended after an eternal ten seconds. Toby looked up as the smoke dissipated, feeling a bit stunned. When the shooting began, he'd tackled Lara and covered her with his body. He'd somehow banged his head against the ground.

"You didn't have to do that," Lara said, rubbing her shoulder. "Are you okay?"

Toby glanced at her as he rose to his feet, but didn't respond. He watched and listened as the smoke and screams faded away. Then he remembered the alien.

It stood as before, with no sign of injury, still holding the object pointed at the president. Most of the crowd had fled or dropped to the ground. A few news people remained, broadcasting the events to the world.

Dubois was roaring at his security people as he roughly pushed them off of him and rose to his feet. His face was as white as his hair. The security people tried to form a circle around him but he slapped the nearest one in the face, then shoved another against his neighbor, causing them to fall to the ground, domino style.

"Get away from me!" he yelled. The security backed off, though they still hovered a few arm lengths away, out of presidential reach. Dubois approached the alien.

"Is this how you normally greet aliens?" Twenty-two asked, slowly rocking side to side, her eyestalks rigidly staring at Dubois.

Dubois brushed dust from his clothes, his jaw working, but nothing came out.

Toby stepped forward. "We're sorry about this. That thing in your hand—"

"This is a sensor. Would you like to know how many of your bullets and energy beams hit me?" An eyestalk peered at the instrument. "Why did you try to kill me?"

"How did you survive?" Toby asked.

The other eyestalk peered at Toby. "I am wearing a shielded vest. I had planned to wear an unshielded red vest. If I had worn the red vest I would be dead."

Dubois stepped forward, giving Toby a nasty look. Toby stepped back.

"Mr. Ambassador, why don't we go to my office, where we can talk." Dubois's face had regained a bit of its color.

"Are you going to shoot me again?"

"No, Mr. Ambassador, we—"

"Why do you keep calling me 'mister'? I am in my female stage. Would not 'miss' be the appropriate term?"

"Sorry, Ms. Ambassador—"

"Let us go to your office. There I will explain to you the basics of first contact. Bringing guns and shooting are considered poor manners."

Toby realized that the press had crept closer, and all of this was being broadcast worldwide. Dubois looked about and must have realized it.

"We didn't mean to shoot you, but you—"

"If you did not mean to shoot me, why did you surround my ship with weapons?" the alien asked. "Only an idiot surrounds himself with things he does not plan to use. Are you an idiot?"

Uh oh, Toby thought; Dubois wasn't going to take that well. He'd spent much of his presidency acting on grudges, some from as far back as his childhood. Toby remembered the time Dubois had secretly gotten Congress to insert into a bill a funding cancellation for a specific school in France. It made no sense until an aide discovered the school's principal had struck Dubois out to win a little league baseball championship when the two were both fourteen. Local newspapers ran a photo of the pitcher jumping in the air in celebration as Dubois slumped to the ground. Toby had good reason to stay with the Dubois Campaign—to protect Lara from the wrath of Dubois. Apparently nobody had warned the alien.

The president's face flushed red with anger, and then returned to a professional smile, the red rapidly fading away. Toby recognized the switch to Dubois's "attack mode." Cool, calm, and scary as hell.

"Or perhaps it was part of a cultural exchange," Twenty-two continued. "I appreciate the gift of these many bullets," and she waved two of her arms at the bullets now lying on the ground about her after bouncing off her invisible shield. "Also the energy from your primitive laser weapons. Should I return this cultural exchange with my own weapons?"

Dubois stepped back and glanced toward the cameras. He'd lost the smile.

"Ms. Ambassador, I welcomed you to our planet for this historic event with respect and dignity," the president began. "We made a mistake, and I do apologize for that. But now you are acting with malice and threatening us with your weapons. I will continue to treat you with respect and dignity, but I *demand* that you get off our planet or face the combined fury of our people."

It was a brilliant response, Toby thought. Decisive and short, and completely wrong. It should swing a few million voters back our way. Of course, they'd lost many more millions from the ill-advised attack, and from the image of Dubois floundering about on the ground, buried under a pile of security people.

"Are those cameras broadcasting to your world?" Twenty-two asked, motioning with her eyestalks at the press. "I am guessing they are." She shuffled toward them in a strange gait where the two legs on each side operated as one, giving the alien a strange four-legged biped-like walk.

"Hello humans," she said. "I am Ambassador Twenty-two. I come from Grodan, the third planet from Tau Ceti. I am here to observe and learn about your political process. I have learned much today. I look forward to learning more. I will be around. Now I return to my ship." She paused. "Is there a better way of explaining things without this constant use of 'I'?" When there was no response, she shuffled back toward her ship, one eyestalk looking back, one forward. She stopped where the mustard marred the side of her ship. "Damn human," she said as she wiped it clean with a cloth from her vest. Then she shuffled back into her ship. The doorway rose back into the ship, leaving no seam.

Incoming call from Dubois. "Accept," Toby whispered to his TC, glancing back toward the president.

"Meet me in my office immediately," Dubois said. "We're going to war."

Chapter Seven
Stop the Invasion!

"Gentlemen, we have a new campaign priority, so listen carefully," Dubois said, back at his desk in the Red Room. "*Alien. Go. Home.*" He punctuated each word by slicing the air with his index finger. From where Toby sat, the picture on the wall of Wayne Wallace, first world president, was just over Dubois's head, his own hand held up in greeting.

"Shouldn't we consult with some military and other experts," Toby asked, "to get their judgment on just what we're up against?" Once again Dubois had ordered the "lowbody" aides out, and locked the door so even cabinet members couldn't enter. Only his most central political staff were present: Toby, Lara, Vice President Rajan, and Phil Farley, Dubois's chief of staff.

Dubois smiled and shook his head. "You're thinking like a bureaucrat. What happened to the 'get things done' Toby I used to admire so much? The one who wanted ambitious policies that voters would notice?"

"We're not setting grain policies here," Toby said, fiddling with his scarf. "We're not arguing about meat-eating in Australia, or gun violence, or cutting taxes. This is *first contact*. We can't slam our doors on the galaxy because some alien was rude to you."

"Why can't I?" Dubois exclaimed. "Are the aliens in the rest of the galaxy going to go away? They'll be there when we're ready to meet them, but we're not doing it now, not with this alien, this grog creature—"

"Grod," the vice president said.

"Just plug it, Rajan." Dubois glared at his vice president, then at each of the others in the room.

"Where's General Duffy?" Toby asked.

"He's on his way," Farley said.

Toby knew the trigger-happy chairman of the armed forces would back whatever Dubois wanted, especially if it gave him a chance to blow up something. Toby hoped the alien ship had very strong shielding.

The hated fly was buzzing again. "Excuse me for a moment," Toby said. Again brandishing the rolled-up *The Regreening of America* report, he advanced on the window. The fly took off across the room. Toby gave pursuit, but lost it somewhere over by the portrait of Jim Abrams, the world's second president. Sighing, he returned to his chair, still holding the rolled-up paper.

"Are you going to talk softly while you carry that big stick?" Lara asked with a grin.

Dubois fixed his stare on Toby. "You always complained that there was no point in having such a large military, since we're all under one government. What do you think now?"

"I think that we just shot up the first alien visitor to Earth, and didn't even scratch her. And somehow, I don't think a bunch of floating tanks or high-energy lasers will help much against a ship that can move like that, especially if it's shielded like the alien. We have no idea what type of weapons it has."

"It's a direct threat to us," Dubois said. "It's my job to protect Earth from threats, and by God, that's what I'm going to do. We'll show that we can stand up to these aliens."

"Alien," Toby said. "You said we have to show we can stand up to aliens, plural, when there's only one."

"How do you know?" Dubois asked. "That ship could be crawling with aliens with ray guns, ready to come out at night and, well, do whatever aliens do when they invade. Haven't you heard of the Trojan Horse?"

"Ray guns?" Toby asked with a slight grin. "It could also be the start of a new era where the galaxy becomes the new frontier."

"You could get credit for that," Farley said. He gave Dubois a silly grin. Dubois and Farley had been close friends for many years, Toby knew, even rooming together during college. Neither had ever married, leading to rumors they'd had to put down during the 2095 campaign. Homophobia, real or imagined, was alive and well in parts of the world.

"Why don't we—" Persson began.

"Rajan, why don't you—" Dubois began.

The vice president slammed his fist on his chair's cushioned armrest, making a light thumping sound. The vice president couldn't even find a good place to slam his fist, Toby thought, as Persson rose to his feet.

"No, you plug *your* mouth!" Persson said. "This is too important. I ran for office with you because it was politically convenient and it put me next in line."

"Rajan—"

Persson raised his hand, palm outward at the president, and for once, Dubois shut up.

"I'll be running for president next time," Persson continued, "and I'll be stuck with whatever policies you come up with. I've shut up for five years, but not now. Not this. Not when you're setting the most important policy *ever*, based on a snub!"

It was more words than the vice president had spoken in a meeting as long as Toby could remember. Toby had put together the Dubois and Persson partnership when he'd calculated Dubois needed a boost in Europe, which resented France's domination, and India, where the Swede had grown up. It had been politically successful. Persson was a checklist conservative's conservative, and he brought in European and Indian votes. However, his aloof temperament turned many voters away, and so he had run a distant second in the Conservative primaries in 2095. He'd agreed to drop out and run on the Dubois ticket in the expectation that he'd be next in line in 2105.

Toby knew that Dubois was more likely to endorse a randomly chosen zoo animal—or an invading alien—than the vice president who, as a presidential candidate, had once criticized Dubois in an early debate about France's domination of Europe. He'd publicly called Dubois an American cowboy, something others had only done in private, and the nickname stuck. Secretly, Toby thought that Dubois liked the characterization. Dubois liked to say in private, "Stand in partnership on the shoulders of those who criticize you, and then kick 'em in the face." Persson's shoulders were very high, and he had a very large face. And he was high on Dubois's enemies list.

"Everyone, let's cool down," Lara said. She pulled a large bottle of Coke from the refrigerator by the wall. She poured it into five glasses, which she distributed. "Ronald Reagan once said the eleventh commandment was 'Thou Shalt Not Attack a Fellow Conservative.' Those words are engraved right here on the Coke bottle." She held the bottle up for all to see, but Toby already knew the words. He knew Reagan had actually said this about fellow Republicans, the political party that had fallen apart after the third and most disastrous Bush administration. Its members later regrouped and became the worldwide Conservative Party.

Toby knew his Reagan quotes. "Reagan also said, 'I occasionally think how quickly our differences worldwide would vanish if we were facing an alien threat from outside this world.' It looks like your patron saint was wrong."

"He's your patron saint too, Dad." Lara grinned. "You're running a campaign for conservatives, remember?" Toby grimaced. How *had* that happened? Thank God Vinny wasn't around to see him now . . . what would his old mentor think?

"I never planned on running such a conservative campaign," Toby pointed out, ignoring a glare from Persson. "You know I pushed moderate issues from the start—"

"And they worked, five years ago," Dubois interrupted. "But that was during a campaign. You can't do *anything* if you don't get elected, and that was the way to get elected. You should have known that once elected, I'd govern as a conservative. That's the party I come from, the people I represent, and the ones who vote for and contribute to my campaign. And in this campaign, you yourself admitted that if we went moderate, the liberals would paint us as hypocrites. Plus, what would our sponsors think if we went all moderate on them?"

They wouldn't be sponsors anymore, Toby admitted to himself. He wondered what he'd think if Dubois were a more thoughtful leader. He'd truly respected some of the more thoughtful conservatives whose campaigns he'd run in the past, even if he didn't always agree with them. But the most thoughtful ones rarely won. At the highest levels of politics thoughtfulness was a dreaded handicap.

"To thirty more years of Coke sponsorship!" Lara said, raising her glass. She took a big gulp of her Coke, as did Dubois. Persson, who had sat down again, left his untouched. Toby took a sip of his, then examined his drink. It always amazed him how two companies that sold a product that was basically water, sugar, and some chemicals, had come to dominate the political landscape. Personally, he preferred the sweeter Hancola, but Hanna sponsored the Liberal Party, so it was Coke only for him.

"Okay, we've had our drinks," Persson said. "Can we reconsider this *Alien go home!* policy? We should be negotiating trade agreements, not blocking them. We're the party of business and economic growth, remember?"

"No," Dubois said. "The policy's a done issue, so get on board. How does *Stop the Invasion!* sound as a slogan?"

"Perfect!" Lara said. "What do you think, Dad?"

Toby felt a bit dizzy. He blinked his eyes a few times, and his head began to clear. He glanced over at the window where the fly buzzed about, and it didn't bother him anymore. Then realization hit him. "You put Eth in my Coke, didn't you?"

"Sure did, Dad. We need clear thinking here, and you always did your best thinking with it. So drink up! What do you think of the new policy now?"

"You learned a lot from your old man," Toby said, grinning. He'd been trying to get Lara off Eth for several years, but somehow that didn't seem important now.

"I learned from the best."

"I certainly am!" Toby knew that he'd be angry at her when the effects wore off. While on Eth, it was hard to be angry at someone else for being unethical.

Ironically, he'd championed the anti-Eth movement that led to it getting banned, and so knew a lot about how it affected the moral judgment center in the brain, in the prefrontal cortex in the frontal lobes, the Brodmann Area 10, just above the eye sockets. He could imagine the drug swirling about in there.

Some people thought a person on Eth could be excused for their actions. That wasn't true—they *chose* to use the non-addictive drug. Unless, of course, your daughter spiked your drink with it.

He knew the underground saying—it's a lot easier to *choose* to be unethical than to *act* unethical—and Eth allowed one to make the choice to be unethical without actually acting so until you were under the drug's effects, and no longer blocked by your conscience. It was a godsend to many politicians and business people, until they got caught. Toby still felt guilty about some of the things he'd done while under its effects before he'd quit—but he had chosen to take the drug when he had tough choices to make, and so was responsible for those choices.

"If this lovefest can be postponed," Dubois interrupted, "can we go back to deciding the fate of the world?" He took another gulp of Coke. "I'm glad to have you back on board, Toby. So what's the plan? How will this play out?"

Toby stood and paced back and forth. He felt free for the first time in years. He knew taking Eth was a scandal in the making. Yet, what better way to hide it than in the privacy of the Red Room?

"It'll play out the way we want it to play out," Toby said. "We play the fear card. Once we do that, there's no turning back, and there's no stopping it. The Liberals will look weak if they don't join us, and most won't. They'll get the support of intellectuals and their liberal base, but we'll take the rest. The liberals who go along with us will split their party's base."

CAMPAIGN 2100: GAME OF SCORPIONS

He stopped pacing and gazed at the others in the room. "This is the wedge issue we've been looking for. When the issues are economic and social, the liberals get the masses. But if we make security the issue, they look soft."

He examined the world holomap, next to the North America map. There were eleven continental groups, with varying electoral votes for the countries in each, and rarely could you find an issue where all agreed. The countries were shaded by their current electoral preference, with red for conservatives, blue for liberals, and various shades of purple in most regions where the real political wars would be fought.

"Fear," he continued, "is the strongest unifying force in the world. We'll have *Stop the Invasion!* and *Alien Go Home!* stickers everywhere. It's going to be the main issue from here on, at least until people tire of it, and then we'll think of something else." He walked over to the president's desk and slammed his fist on it, knowing it was over the top, but enjoying the contrast of his slammed fist on the desk with Persson's earlier thump on the chair's armrest. "Anyone who disagrees, well, either they are with us . . ." He stopped and looked each of the others in the eye. ". . . or they are against us."

Dubois slowly clapped his hands. "Wow. Now I remember why I hired you."

"Do you think you can convince people of an alien conspiracy?" Lara asked.

"Easily," Toby said. "The masses have believed in conspiracies ever since the truth of the Kennedy and Brown assassinations came out. People *look* for conspiracies everywhere, especially if we tell them to."

Persson leaped to his feet. "You're all a bunch of drug-addled pygmies! If anyone needs me, I'll be in my office with a *real* drink, planning out the rejection of your policies when *I'm* president in five years, starting with a return to the principles set forth by Reagan and Steif, which you have all ablomerated."

Dubois rose to his feet, eyes blazing, and seemed to tower over his two-foot taller vice president, who visibly wilted, his shoulders slumping.

"Rajan, why don't you go back to your summit?" Dubois said. "I'd love to see you talk like that to the Mountain Monster, and see what Feodora does to you."

She'd probably punch out his kneecaps, Toby thought of the tiny Russian general, Feodora Zubkov. That was someone you didn't want to cross. He liked people like her, ones who decided what needed to be done, and just did it, without worrying too much about nuance and formalities. Persson chaired the endless Korean International Sovereignty Summit—KISS—which mostly pitted Feodora and the Russians against Japan and China. Inevitably nothing happened, but it was fun reading the latest Feodora quips.

"Fine," Persson said. "I'll go back to my summit, and I'll 'plug it' until the next election. You do what you want." Persson left, slamming the door on the way out.

"He never really was with us, was he?" Dubois said. "He'll be back. There's nowhere else for him to go."

"We only need him another few months," Toby said. "Then he either joins us, or you shut him out of anything worthwhile."

"He's politically dead anyway, when I'm through with him," Dubois said. "Hell, I might support the Liberal candidate over him." He grinned. "Don't quote me on that! Now, we've got *Alien go home!*, and *Stop the Invasion!* Any more?"

"How about *Earth First!*, or *Get off our planet!*" Toby said.

"We could try a more statesmanship-sounding approach," Farley said. "How about, 'Treat the alien with dignity and respect, and show him the door off our planet.'"

Toby stared at him as if he had turned into the alien. "No, that's clunky. It's gotta be short and snappy, so it hits you right in the pit of the stomach, the center of fear in the human body. The shorter the sound bite the better, and the better it looks on a bumper sticker. We're gonna scare the heck out of people, turn this Twenty-two into a monster, and the voters into sheep bleating for help. *Our* help."

"Excuse me," Farley said. "I just got a message from General Duffy. He said the alien took off and flew to Washington D.C. The general's diverted his floater there, says he's going after her."

"I gave him . . . special orders regarding the alien," Dubois said. "How soon will the alien be in D.C.?" Toby noticed that the alien was no longer "Ms. Ambassador" to Dubois.

"According to Duffy, it took it about two minutes to fly there," Farley said.

"That's not possible!" Lara said. "That's two hundred miles in two minutes. A hundred miles a minute . . . that would be like six thousand miles an hour!"

"*Breaking News!*" Toby's TC startled him from his line of thinking. He looked about; already Dubois and the others had that dazed look as they watched a broadcast. How come his was always a few seconds behind?

"TC on," he whispered, expecting the worst.

Chapter Eight
The Liberal Hideout

Twenty-two had Zero analyze the mustard in the cloth, which it proclaimed "compatible with your illustrious system." She wondered if she should turn the flattery mode down some more, but decided not to bother. Twenty-two sampled the mustard, and found the taste wonderful. Besides studying their politics, perhaps she'd survey their foods as well.

She examined the gift she'd been given by Dubois, and concluded it was a device for drawing black artwork, perhaps on a human face or in religious rituals.

She felt a bit guilty about the ambassador deception, but what was she supposed to have said? "*Hi, I am a college student on break who is visiting your planet illegally. Take me to your leader.*" To get the respect and access she wanted, she had to be an ambassador.

But what was the point? She had just made an enemy of the planet's leader. What access could she get now? She checked Zero's shields, just to be safe; there was no telling what these humans might do next.

She didn't even know what form of government Earth had. "Zero, have you been monitoring broadcasts?"

"Yes, Perceptive Leader."

"Can you briefly describe what worldwide government system they use?"

"Earth is a standard Constitutional Republic with three branches. The head of the executive branch is the president, elected every five years with a proportional electoral system. The legislative branch, also known as the World Congress, has two houses. Each country with a population over one million has two representatives in one house, the World Senate, and a number of representatives proportionate to their population in the other house, the World House of Representatives. Members of Congress are elected to five-year terms. The judicial branch has eleven members, each nominated by the president and confirmed by the legislative branch. They have lifetime terms. It is a multi-party system dominated by the Conservative and Liberal parties, also known as the Roosters and Donkeys. You have not used the restroom in some time; would you like assistance?"

Two major parties? Twenty-two wondered how that could work. If there were ten issues, then there would be over a thousand permutations, and so a thousand parties needed. It meant party members were forced to adjust their beliefs to their party's beliefs. Over time, wouldn't their loyalties move toward their party instead of their country or world? What a silly system!

But if there were two parties, then that meant President Dubois wasn't the only option.

"Zero, which party is President Dubois?"

"The Conservative Party, Wise One."

"Your flattery is irritating, even at fifty percent. If I ordered you to turn it off, how would you address me?"

"I would address you in many ways, such as Formerly Wise One, Formerly Great Leader, Formerly—"

"Stop. Where is the headquarters for the Liberal Party?"

"It is located in Washington D.C."

"Take me there."

A few minutes later they landed next to a huge blue building, overlooking what Zero said was the Potomac River, just west of Georgetown University. The building rose twenty stories into the air, tapering off above to a point. Circular windows, also tinted blue, circled the building. A huge Hancola logo adorned its side: a blue capital 'H' against a white background, tilted sideways, with an animated image of the sweet soft drink pouring out of the top of the letter.

47

Within minutes, the ship was again surrounded by humans. She wondered how word got out so quickly, and realized they must have some sort of person-to-person communication devices. She hadn't seen anything like that; perhaps they were internal, connected directly to the brain? She found that repulsive.

The view from her ship had been blocked by buildings. Now she could see a good distance in most directions. It was a world of cement, steel and plastic. Her sensors verified that the few trees and other plants in sight were artificial.

A dark-skinned human knocked gently on the side of the ship. If this were going to be a regular occurrence, she might have to put in a doorbell.

"Zero, lower the door." A minute later Twenty-two shuffled out the door and into the throng of people surrounding the ship. The air seemed fresher than the stale air of New York City.

The dark-skinned one approached and extended one of his huge hands at her. She wasn't sure what it meant—was this another attack? She took a step back.

The human pulled his hand back. "Ambassador, I am pleased to meet you. I am Carl Ajala, governor of Nigeria and candidate for president of Earth. I saw your earlier meeting with Dubois. On behalf of all humans, I would like to apologize for what happened."

There was an uncomfortable silence as Twenty-two waited. Finally she said, "You said you wanted to apologize?" It was strange, this saying what one wanted to do rather than just doing it.

Ajala stared at Twenty-two for a moment, then smiled, a facial gesture that she had learned meant happiness. What was Ajala happy about? She tried not to look at the red lips, exposed in public. She put one of her hands to her face where she still wore her red velvo. Different worlds, different customs.

"On behalf of all humans, I apologize for what happened," Ajala said. "I would also like to shake your hand. It is a human custom. Let me show you." He reached his hand out again, and this time she understood. She put two of her hands inside the human's huge hand,

and they shook up and down. Another strange custom. On Grodan, one greeted another by nodding eyestalks at each other.

"You are in a political campaign against Dubois?" Twenty-two asked. She studied the dark man with one eyestalk while the other looked over the crowd.

"Yes," Ajala said. "You are here to study our political system? You may find it somewhat . . . unpleasant."

"I would like to learn about your political system. May I be an observer in your political campaign?"

Flashing lights and a siren from overhead interrupted Ajala's reply. A small ship drifted to the side and landed.

"Dubois sent his boys," Ajala said.

They allow human children to fly ships, and use them as emissaries? If necessary, she would meet with Dubois's boys. Perhaps they had come to apologize on behalf of their father for the earlier events.

The three humans that came out of the ship were not human children. Two of them pointed handguns at Twenty-two. Here we go again, she thought.

The third one was the largest human she had seen in terms of mass. He—she had given up trying to tell male from female, so would just assume male, like most of the humans she had met, until she learned otherwise, since there didn't seem to be a neutral pronoun in the local language—was built almost like a huge, biped grod, with a midsection much larger than the other humans. He wore what seemed a uniform covered with jangling bits of metal. The large human approached and towered over her. She was pretty sure her yellow vest would protect her even if this huge ball of flesh fell on her, but wasn't so certain.

"I'm General Waylon Duffy," the large ball of flesh said. "On behalf of Earth's defense forces, you are under arrest for threats against human citizens."

The creature probably did not want to shake hands, she decided. She wasn't sure what it meant to be arrested, but knew it involved being confined in a prison. "I am sorry, but I do not wish to be arrested."

"What are you trying to pull, Waylon?" Ajala asked.

"Stay out of this, Carl," Duffy said. "Go back to your liberal hideout, or I'll arrest you for obstruction."

"That'll go over well when the press reports it," Ajala said, now face to face with Duffy.

"I think I will join you inside your . . . liberal hideout," Twenty-two said to Ajala, and began to shuffle toward Liberal Headquarters.

"Stop, or we will shoot," Duffy said.

"Then you'll have to shoot me too," Ajala said. "I'm going back to my *liberal hideout*."

Twenty-two continued toward the building, side by side with Ajala. One eyestalk pointed backward to study the huge general. Was he insane? They'd already gone through this once before. However, the human Ajala might not be so protected.

"I warned you! One more step and—"

Twenty-two reached the steps by the entrance to the building at the same time as Ajala. She climbed them somewhat clumsily since they were a bit too high for her.

"*Fire!*" Duffy cried. Their handguns fired bullets like the ones she had faced earlier, the explosive sounds hurting her internal ears. Ajala dropped to the ground, covering his head with his hands, but he was not the target and was not hit. The air was full of screams from the crowd, who were split between those running away and those that dropped to the ground.

"Would you stop doing that?" Twenty-two said. "It is repetitive and irritating. At least attack me with something different. How about a water cannon? I am a bit thirsty."

That's when she noticed Duffy was holding a new weapon. It fired a long line of what looked like thread. When it hit Twenty-two, she felt a small shock. It was some sort of electrical device. Her shielding adjusted, jettisoning the thread, and she felt no more shocks. But it meant that Duffy was experimenting. What would they try next?

Ajala rose to his feet and quickly walked to the building. Twenty-two followed. Ajala slammed the door closed.

Twenty-two wondered if anyone had noticed the three humans in the crowd who had taped it all with small finger-held devices.

Chapter Nine
Are You With Me?

Toby and the others in the Red Room watched the scene on TC. He'd always known Duffy was an idiot. There was going to be quite a public outcry when the public saw yet another alien-shooting video, and Dubois would take another political hit. And yet, people were funny things. Many would see the two shootings as evidence that there must be something threatening about the seemingly invincible alien, and with circular reasoning, conclude that the attempted shootings were justified.

He hoped the alien's meeting with Ajala went well. Maybe the alien would have some political tips for the down-in-the-polls liberal?

Huh? he thought. A short time ago, Toby had been actively planning strategy for Dubois's reelection, and had wholeheartedly supported him. How had this leaked into his mind?

The Eth. He'd only taken a sip, and the effects had worn off. He looked about the office. What would the worldwide public think if they knew the president of the planet, their "decider," was a user? What would their conservative base think, the ones who claimed morality as the basis for all social policy?

"The Liberals have obviously gotten to the alien," Lara said. "Call in your world security advisor, and ask him if an alien of unknown origin and weaponry is a potential danger to society. When he says yes, we tell this Twenty-two she's being deported?"

"And if she refuses to leave?" Dubois asked.

"That's exactly what we want!" Lara said. "Imagine that knot in people's stomach when they go to vote, knowing there's an alien threat that won't go away, and knowing only one party is trying to protect them from it."

The president stood up, beaming. "I like it!"

Toby had had enough. "Look, don't you see what this means? This is our chance to enter galactic civilization. This is the time to show them what we're made of, not act like a bunch of politicians!"

Dubois came around his desk and put his hand on Toby's shoulder. Toby cringed at the touch. "Toby, we *are* politicians."

"We're supposed to be *statesmen*." Toby looked from the president to his daughter and back again. He pulled the president's hand off his shoulder.

"Dad, drink the rest of your Coke," Lara said.

"Damn it, Lara, I can't even trust you when I eat and drink anymore!" He fiddled with his scarf for a moment, then pulled it off and examined the stained and worn-out threads. Five years ago he'd pulled the scarf off, believing he didn't deserve to wear it, and asked himself, *What have I done?* He'd later put it back on, and yet here he was running the Dubois campaign all over again.

Not again. Not ever.

"I can't continue this anymore," he said, putting the scarf back around his neck.

"Dad, don't do this," Lara said. "Are you having another mid-life crisis?"

Dubois put his hand on Toby's shoulder again. "Are you with me, Toby?"

"I don't like the direction we've gone—" Toby began.

"*Are you with me?*" For a second, Dubois's eyes blazed, an ability Toby knew he practiced. Dubois removed his hand from Toby's shoulder, and returned to his desk and faced Toby. "As *you* said, you are either with us, or against us."

Toby felt a hurricane had hit him. Those words echoed through history, from every bad leader that ever set foot in the halls of power. It replaced argument with threat, true loyalty with fear; it was a way to deal with challenge without dealing with the challenge.

Fear, the very focal point of the strategy he'd outlined for the president just a short time ago. Fear and extremism, whether it be conservative or liberal, went together. It gave him a bellyache.

He was no conservative, and yet he was responsible for inflicting the current president on the world, who was both a conservative and corrupt. A double whammy. He'd once been a liberal, but that was just a label. He'd long ago stopped thinking of himself as conservative or liberal. Neither fit, and they were the only choices available.

And he realized what he had become. In a world that only allowed blue pegs and red pegs, he was somewhere in between, a purple peg with nowhere to go.

He had become a moderate, in a world dominated by the Conservative Party and the Liberal Party, and nothing else. That's what gave him a bellyache.

"Some say liberals have no head, and conservatives no heart," he said. "Moderates must have no stomach because I can't stomach either one anymore."

There was silence for a moment. Lara looked the other way.

"Nice line, but you didn't answer the question," Dubois said. "One more time: *Are you with me, or are you against me?*"

Toby ignored the president and turned to his daughter. "Lara, I love you, but if I have to go to hell and back, I'm going to put you out of a job."

He turned and left. He decided slamming the door on the way out would be inappropriate, and quietly closed the door even as he heard the president yell, *"You're fired!"*

He felt light on his feet. The bellyache was gone. But what was he to do now?

Chapter Ten
Bruce and the Chimpanzees

The bellyache had been replaced by hunger pangs. So much had gone on since the alien had arrived that it seemed late at night, and yet it was only dinnertime.

The office Toby shared with Lara was down the hall from the Red Room. Two muscular security men watched as he loaded his personal belongings into a box. He wondered who Dubois would hire to replace him. Lara was the obvious choice, but he remembered the threat Dubois had made. He'd fire Lara and destroy her politically, just as he would do with Toby. At least it would save him the trouble of putting her "out of a job."

The news spread quickly. Various cabinet members, senators, representatives, and lobbyists stopped by to give their goodbyes, as did his own staff members. Most kept looking about as if nervous someone might see them with the fallen star. Finally, box in hand, followed closely by security, he walked quickly to the entrance and left the site of so much personal glory.

Out front he caught a one-person floater and told the automated machine to take him to the StarMacs on the way to his apartment. They joined the line of floaters flying above the streets crowded with less expensive butanol-powered wheeled cars. Most floaters were nuclear powered, but public ones like this one still used butanol as well.

At StarMacs, another friendly machine served his food. He found an empty table as far away from the noisy serving lines as possible. He relaxed under a climbing plastic ivy while the sound of a gurgling creek played in the background, a tranquil setting to muse about his future over a Big Mac and fried cabbage while sipping a cofftea. Now that he'd resigned from the most powerful political job in the world, what was a political hack like him to do?

He'd miss the excitement. He stared at the plastated meat in his Big Mac. He'd miss the joys of campaigning around the world, such as "First in the World" Australia, where they actually ate real meat. Hard to believe that anyone in this day and age would do that, he thought, and yet he'd found ways to appease the Australians and get their vote, without actually supporting their nasty habit.

He'd miss campaigning at the Great Mall of China and the rest of Asia, at the Blue Whale Aquarium in France-dominated Europe, and in Africa, where the leaders you spoke with in the morning might be in jail or dead that night. In North America, where they tried to placate Utah and ignore Canadian strife, and in the dictatorships and gunfights of Latin America. He'd miss finessing the conservative vote in Islam Nation and buying votes in India. He'd even miss the frozen ghost towns of Antarctica and their single electoral vote.

He'd miss it all.

His TC flashed *Breaking News!* "TC on," he said. Earlier he'd ordered the TC to ignore further reports on the alien, which he knew would be getting around-the-clock coverage. He'd catch up on that later. So it must be some other news.

It was another talking head from WNN. "Visual alerts off, audio alerts only," Toby told his TC. The flashing light in the breaking news headlines irritated him, and there were probably going to be a lot more of them in the near future.

"The Dubois campaign announced that, effective immediately, Campaign Director Toby Platt has resigned for personal reasons. Replacing him is his daughter, Lara Platt, who has worked extensively with her father in various campaigns. Here's what the new director had to say."

The screen switched to a shot of Lara talking into a series of cameras and microphones.

"I've run campaigns with my dad for many years, including the '95 Dubois campaign and the recent primaries, and taking charge won't be a big changeover. Corbin Dubois continues to lead the polls, and with your help, we'll make sure we have another five years. As to me, I've learned from the best, I work for the best, and Dad tells me I'm the best. Two out of three ain't bad!"

Toby heard laughter in the background. Then a voice asked, "Why did your father step down? There are rumors he and the president no longer agree on policy. Is 'personal reasons' code for 'Toby Platt no longer supports the president'?"

Lara grinned, going right to that *trust me, we're the good guys* look she practiced so hard. "Dad's been winning campaigns for decades. He's a legend. And he always took me along. I remember twenty years ago, as a kid whose biggest worry was her hair, getting dragged to campaigns all over the world. And you know what he taught me? He taught me that campaigning isn't convincing people to vote for your guy; it's getting the right guy with the right policies, and letting people see that. And you know what? That's what we've got with Dubois, the right guy with the right policies.

"While my dad and I don't agree on everything, we agree on so much that what's left over fits here in my purse." She opened her purse and pretended to rummage through it. "Yeah, let's see, he still thinks I should be in bed by nine, shouldn't drive, and shouldn't see other guys." There was more laughter.

"More seriously, my dad fully supports the president and his policies, and decided it was time to push the baby bird—that's me—out of the nest so she could fly on her own. He's retiring, and I hope you will all buy his memoirs when they come out. Thank you all."

Toby sat in stunned silence as a talking head ran off facts about his past campaigns. *I support the president and his policies?* How could Lara say this? At some point in the broadcast he'd spilled his cofftea over his food. He continued to eat the soggy fried cabbage.

There was a certain brilliance to what Lara had said. What were the chances that he'd contradict his own daughter in public? Unless he did so, it was official: he supported this president and his policies.

If he didn't, why had he worked so hard to make this man president? Lara had learned well, and he knew who had taught her. He sighed; he'd lost a daughter while creating a campaign aide, and now she belonged to Dubois, just as he had. It turned out Dubois's threat to go after Lara had been a bluff, and he'd stayed with Dubois these last five years for nothing. He wasn't sure if Dubois had promoted Lara because he valued her political skills or if it was part of his revenge against Toby. Probably both.

He had told his daughter that he was going to put her out of a job. In the heat of the moment, when he'd made the threat, he'd forgotten that Dubois had already promised to put her out of a job if he resigned. Technically, as soon as the campaign was over, she'd be "out of a job," at least temporarily. Realistically, she'd be part of the administration for the next five years, if they won reelection, just as he had been during this administration.

So how could he put his daughter out of a job? How could he atone to the world for making Dubois president?

The talking head from WNN was now talking about protests against the attempted shooting of the alien, with replays from various angles. "TC off," he said.

Only one other candidate vied for the job of president, Carl Ajala of Nigeria, the Liberal candidate for president, now meeting with the alien ambassador. The man he and his daughter had spent the past year ridiculing in public while privately planning his political destruction. He'd have to arrange a meeting.

Incoming call from Bruce. "Accept call," Toby said. A screen opened in front of him, with Bruce's grinning face.

"So you finally came to your senses?" Bruce held a ping-pong paddle in one hand and a ball in the other. Toby could hear the familiar sound of ping-pong in the background, out of sight from the TC camera Bruce was facing.

"Are you calling from a tournament?" Toby asked. He didn't have a TC camera handy to transmit his image, so Bruce could only hear him.

"Yep, the collegiate nationals at the Baltimore Convention Center." Bruce began bouncing the ball up and down on his paddle. "I just lost in the final. I'm out in the hallway watching the news. What's going on?"

"I'll fill you in later," Toby said. "How long do you plan on staying in college? You plan on collecting degrees the rest of your life?" Bruce had degrees from the University of Maryland in political science, physics, math, history, physical education, English, and was now working on one in journalism.

"I'll stay as long as they keep paying me to play on the college team. That'll probably be another five years or so, another five degrees. So, do you *really* support this president and his policies, like Lara said?"

"You know the answer to that."

"Then that was her Eth speaking. Or was it? When she said that about you, it must have felt like this." Bruce smacked the ball as hard as he could right at the TC camera he was looking into. Toby flinched. Bruce caught the rebound with his free hand. "You should have left the campaign when I did, back in the primaries. I'm glad I dropped her, she's damaged goods."

"That's my daughter you're talking about." Anger welled up in him before he caught himself. This was Bruce; what did he expect? Bruce was right; Toby should have left the campaign long ago. He'd only stayed because of his daughter. Or was it the lure of power, real or illusory? Suddenly he wasn't sure, and didn't want to think about it.

"No, I'm talking about the drug-popping new director of the Dubois campaign," Bruce retorted. "The Lara I knew disappeared long ago. Someday we'll get her back. Maybe not." Bruce went back to bouncing the ball on his paddle, never missing even though he was looking at Toby. The bouncing aggravated Toby's just-discovered headache.

"That was the Eth you heard," Toby said. He hoped.

"And who chose to take the Eth?" Bruce asked. "Did someone sneak it into her drink or something?"

For a second, Toby was suspicious. Did he know what Lara had done to his drink? No, not possible. Let's not get paranoid.

"Hey," Bruce continued, "what's the alien going to do when he finds out there's not much intelligent life down here, just a bunch of chimpanzees? It's government by, of, and for the chimpanzees!" Bruce liked to point out that a chimpanzee raised in captivity typically had an IQ in the high 60's, about the same as a human five-year old, and about two-thirds of an average human's IQ of 100. Bruce had an IQ of 160, which not only put him in the top 0.01%—one in about 10,000—but also meant that, proportionately, a chimpanzee—or a five-year-old—was closer to the average person in IQ than the average person was to Bruce. As Bruce pointed out at least once a week.

Bruce continued bouncing the ball on his paddle, the steady *ping-ping-ping* pounding into Toby's now searing headache. Toby had discovered Bruce in the 2095 campaign. Despite his youth, Bruce was the most brilliant political strategist he had ever known, and he'd known them all.

Bruce caught the ball and put down the paddle. Toby sighed with relief. "So," Bruce said, "what are you going to do now that your daughter's running Satan's campaign?"

"Not sure yet. I was thinking of calling Ajala."

"That's a bizarrity! You're kidding, right?" Bruce tossed the ball up and swatted it away with the paddle. "I mean, c'mon! Grow a Brodmann! You'd drop Satan to run a cockroach's campaign?"

"And how 'bout you?" Toby asked. "Who do you support?"

Bruce laughed. "Who do I support between Dubois and Ajala? Only a chimpanzee would choose between those two. Besides, what's to choose? You know Ajala has no chance. And since that means you have no place to go to, why don't you come visit me tomorrow afternoon, clear your mind, and we can plan out the future of Toby Platt, world's greatest and most confused political guru?"

As usual, Bruce made sense. Since Bruce lived in Washington D.C., Toby could run a couple of local errands before meeting with Bruce in the afternoon. He guzzled the rest of his cofftea.

He dreaded both errands.

Chapter Eleven
A Political Hack

Wednesday, July 28, 2100

"**W**hy would I hire the man who called my Universal Food Plan 'kindergarten economics'?" asked Carl Ajala, governor of Nigeria, president of the World Food Commission, and the Liberal candidate for president. He sat behind his desk in a dark suit, arms folded in front, a frown on his face. Behind him was a large framed picture of him shaking hands with former President Xu. Nigerian tribal art covered the walls.

The dark-skinned Nigerian spoke slowly with a deep, cultured voice, one that had made him rich doing voiceovers in numerous holograph movies, often as kings and other leaders. Toby had a hard time listening to the man without connecting the voice to that of Hollus the alien in *Calculating God*, the highest grossing movie of all time. The bass voice was his greatest political asset, along with his rock-solid liberal beliefs, where he got points for at least having core beliefs, even if most disagreed with them. Unfortunately, his inflexibility was an eight-hundred pound political albatross around his neck. Plus he surrounded himself with fellow liberal dogmatists rather than political experts. Bruce was right; Ajala had little chance. On the other hand, who would have believed a short, silly-looking monstrosity could have won in 2095?

It hadn't been easy to convince Ajala to see him on short notice. Toby had taken a long-distance floater to the Liberal Headquarters in D.C. Yet, somehow, his heart wasn't completely in it.

On the way in, Toby saw that USE security surrounded the alien ship, which floated above the ground just outside the building. Ajala had told him that Twenty-two was back in the ship, and that the security people had tried cutting into it, with Duffy cursing the whole time. They were unable to scratch the surface. Toby was slightly disappointed the alien was back in her ship; he'd hoped to meet her again.

"You know my background and record," Toby began. "Your campaign is in trouble, and I think I can help." He fiddled with his scarf. "You know I've never been a conservative, and my earliest campaign work was with the Liberal Party. Until a few years ago, I never even worked with a real conservative, only with moderate members of *both* parties. You can look it up."

"I already have," Ajala said. "Are you under the impression that I'm interested in running a *moderate* campaign, one that sacrifices the very principles I believe and run on?" Ajala's voice had risen to a crescendo, like a preacher at the climax of his speech. "These terms—*liberal, conservative*—they are just labels, used to condemn a viewpoint that cannot be condemned by argument. One should never choose their beliefs based on whether they fit comfortably into one of these compartments. And yet, when one makes these choices, they are compartmentalized, packaged and tagged with one of these labels of yours, and it is with these labels that you hope to convince me that you are one of *us*?"

Toby had heard Ajala speak before, always without need of his TC or notes. What he could do with such speaking talent! If the man would only compromise on some issues. Dubois could speak almost as well, but only after hours of painstaking preparation and rehearsal, and reading the text off his TC.

Ajala wasn't through. "Take a step back. Look at yourself. What do you see? To use your labels, you are a man who took a flamboyant nobody conservative with strong friends in low places, and turned him into the president. You took the liberal president, Mr. Xu, a good man, and turned him into a foozle doing commercial endorsements for the latest line of men's clothing. He was the world's fifth president, and the

63

first not to win reelection. Look at him," and he pointed at the picture of Xu behind his desk, "and think about what you did to him and to the world. And you expect my campaign to hire *you*?"

This was not going to be easy. There was no selling Ajala except with the truth. "Yes, I hoped you would hire me to save your campaign," Toby said. "This is an exciting time to be in politics, with first contact and the leadership of the world at stake, and I want to be a part of it. You know what the polls say—your campaign is struggling. Think about what I'd bring. The former campaign director for Dubois changes his mind, realizes that Dubois isn't right for the job, and joins the *Ajala* campaign!"

"Sounds like a publicity stunt." Ajala rose from his desk. "Mr. Platt, I appreciate your coming here, but to be quite blunt, you are a political hack who sells his services to the highest bidder, or in this case, to any available bidder. I'm not bidding. I've heard rumors about why you left the Dubois campaign, and I prefer to assume the best, not the worst. Simply put, mine is a campaign about values, about beliefs, and you do not share those values and beliefs." He paused as he stared at Toby. "Just think about what you are doing! You want to run a campaign in direct opposition to *your own daughter*! That's exactly the type of anti-family message the Dubois campaign—that means *you*—have been trying to stick on us since this campaign began, before we even got out of the primaries."

Toby continued to fiddle with his scarf, eyes now downcast. There was no way to respond to Ajala without resorting to the very type of political double-talk that he wanted to get away from. Ajala was right on every count.

"We may lose on our beliefs to a political huckster like Dubois," Ajala continued, "but I'd rather lose on principles than win by hiring a hit-man whose main attribute is an ability to trick the voters into making winners out of losers."

Well, Toby thought, that was what he should expect. He'd gained respect for Ajala, even if he hadn't gained a job.

The point about his daughter hit him hardest. He was looking to run a campaign in direct opposition to his daughter. Did this say more about him, or his daughter? He didn't want to think about it.

"Mr. Platt," Ajala said as Toby was about to leave, "despite what you've done, deep down I believe you're a good man. Someday we may work together. Just not this time." They shook hands. It was hard not to like Ajala.

Near the front door on the way out, Toby was interrupted. "Excuse me, are you Toby Platt, the campaign director?" asked a teenaged girl, who wore her hair in the new polyhedron fashion, but with a style he'd never seen. The hair was dyed bright green, and shaped into a long tube, about three inches wide, twisted into a knot in the back. Toby recognized the twisted gun barrel image, the symbol for world peace.

She wore a blue business dress with a *Holla fer Ajala!* button, centered under a Hancola logo. Such an awkward slogan was another symptom of an incompetent campaign, Toby thought. The girl looked up at Toby with dark brown eyes and a seriousness beyond her apparent age.

"Yes, I'm a *former* campaign director," Toby said. She had an accent he couldn't place, perhaps a Spanish-Australian mix? No, that wasn't it. "You can read all about me in the memoirs I'm supposed to write now that I'm out of a job."

"Are you going to work for the Ajala Campaign?" she asked. "We need someone to take charge and focus on winning instead of trying to convince Australians to eat wheat instead of meat. We all know what's right, but knowing what's right isn't the same as getting it done. The polls are clear on that."

She went on for several minutes, quoting polls and stats, some of which Toby hadn't heard of. Bruce would have been proud. Wasn't there a rule where you had to be a certain age before you could know the current approval ratings in Bangkok for all the major demographics? Hearing all this from a teenager was somewhat disconcerting. Had he once been like this?

"How old are you?" he asked.

"Why do people always ask me that?" she said. She tilted her head slightly. "I'm seventeen."

"You're right, it's not important," Toby said. "You think they need someone like me here?"

"Well, I may work for the Ajala campaign, but—and please don't tell anyone this—I don't believe they can win. They're going to lose because they won't compromise, and always go with the liberal agenda on every issue, no matter how unpopular. Even if you believe in something, sometimes you *have* to compromise. Maybe we should have found someone else to run."

"Who?" Toby asked. "You don't just wake up one morning and ask someone to run for president of the planet. It takes years of planning and preparation, setting up a worldwide organization, fund-raising, and so on. And you need to be nominated by a major party, and those two spots are taken."

"So you believe most people will only vote for whoever the Conservative or Liberal Parties tell them to vote for? Is there a poll on that?"

Hadn't he once asked the same question, many years ago when he'd first gotten involved in a campaign? Of course, the answer was yes. The masses would vote for whoever the two main parties told them to vote for. It was a law of politics, a law of nature.

"I think people will vote for whoever they think is the best possible candidate, regardless of who they are told to vote for," he lied. "And who are you?"

"I'm Melissa Smith, from Antarctica. I'm an intern here. And *please* don't tell anyone what I said about Ajala!" The girl hurried off.

That, Toby thought with a slight smile, is someone to remember. But now his thoughts turned to his second errand. He fingered his scarf and his heart began to pound as he called a floater to visit his old friend Vinny at the cemetery.

Chapter Twelve
Vinny

Toby stood over Vinny's grave at Germantown Cemetery in Maryland, fifteen miles north of Washington DC. There was no last name, date of birth, or age listed. Nobody had known. The gravestone simply said he died in December of 2066. Toby guessed Vinny had been around fifty, his own age now.

Toby tried to visit the cemetery once a year. It was an uncomfortable place for him, with the graves of his parents, his first wife, Lindy, and of Vinny.

He visited his parents first. Both had died about ten years ago. He stared down at the matching gravestones for a long time. They'd never known how successful he would become. He was glad they hadn't been around when he took over the Dubois campaign.

He moved on to his wife's grave. Had it really been thirty years? She'd died from rare complications during childbirth when Lara was born.

He couldn't remember what she looked like. He pulled up a picture on his TC and stared at it for a few minutes. Lindy had been the second love of his life. Their daughter, Lara, had been the third. Later he'd married Olivia, the fourth love, but somehow she never was at the same level as his first wife and daughter. But his fourteen-year-old son Tyler came out of that marriage, the fifth love of his life. And yet, always in the background, stealing time from them all, was his first and foremost love: politics.

Toby had become eligible to vote when he turned sixteen in 2066. He was already a political hack. The world was a different and simpler place then, he thought, before the rise of the TC, floating cars, and irritating French presidents. He'd volunteered to help that fall at Liberal Headquarters in his hometown of Germantown, Maryland, going in each day after school. His parents had been so proud.

Mayor Jones was from the Liberal Party in a city that slanted conservative. He'd gone moderate in the previous campaign and barely won. He faced a difficult re-election battle. Toby felt part of a team as he joined forces with others to make sure Jones won re-election.

They put Toby to work stuffing envelopes in the archaic practice of sending hard materials directly to voters. That was where he'd met Vinny.

He vividly remembered Vinny's bald head and mottled brown face, clean shaven except at the end. Vinny had said that too much time outdoors had turned his skin a hundred years old.

"The orange one goes on top," said the thin man with the mottled brown face, the worn-out clothing hanging over his frame like a scarecrow. He and Toby sat on opposite sides of a large table. Stacks of flyers and envelopes in front of each. The copy machine's folding and envelope stuffing feature had broken, so the work had to be done manually. Political posters for Mayor Jones covered three walls of the large, dimly lit room, with the fourth wall the glass storefront. It was late at night and still early in the campaign, so the two were alone with the smell of old coffee and stale pastries.

"Does it really matter?" Toby asked. He'd been trying and failing to keep pace with the man, whose fingers sailed over the flyers like a pianist as he stacked, folded, stuffed, and sealed. It contrasted sharply with his old-man's slouching walk.

"Makes a big difference," the man said. "The orange one is the hook. The blue one is the sale. The green one closes the deal and asks for money. We could send these things electronically, but people like something in their hands, makes it more personal. Did you know people are more likely to read an orange or yellow flyer than any other color? That's why that goes on top."

"They study things like that?" Toby asked, wondering if it were true.

"Definitely!" The man grinned. "Paper flyers will always be a part of politics, and as long as that's true, it'll be the subject of science and art. My name's Vinny, and you must be Toby Platt, the new kid. Glad to know you!" He extended his hand and they swapped low fives. "Let me explain how this works."

That's when Toby's real education began. Nothing in the flyers was left to chance. The orange cover letter was directed at the mayor's political base. It focused on wedge issues, twisting the opponent's ideas into a psychedelic nightmare that outraged anyone with common sense, with the mayor's ideas brought in to save the day.

The second page, a friendly, soft blue, personalized the candidate with background info that turned him into something between a saint and a superhero, with a clever mix of heroic deeds he'd done and great ideas he'd use to save humanity and the local voters.

The third page, a pointed green, asked voters for their support, and told of the wonderful things they would get if they sent sums of money to the candidate.

The flyers included flattering pictures in carefully posed candid shots showing the candidate building shelters, ladling soup to the poor, and shaking hands with various celebrities.

"Most voters are registered as either Liberals or Conservatives," Vinny said. "Donkeys or Roosters. Our primary job is to remind the Donkeys who to vote for."

Toby found this troubling. "People vote for whoever we tell them to vote for, just because of their political party? Don't we need to do more than that?"

Vinny flashed him the "you have much to learn" grin that he'd get to know so well. "It's more important that we give them an excuse to vote for their party than we give them an actual reason. The easiest way is to get them mad at the other guy so they vote for our guy. If we do our job, most voters from our party are going to vote for whoever we tell them to vote for. Most of the rest is just showcasing."

"Germantown is half ebony," Vinny explained. Mayor Jones was an ebony, the politically correct term for those of African ancestry. Toby soon learned all about demographics. "To win, Jones needs at least seventy percent of them, to make up for the non-ebony vote, which'll mostly go against us."

"You think," Toby asked, "white people like me won't vote for him, while ebonies like you will?"

"That's the racist truth. And I'm no ebony—like most white guys, you can't see past the skin color. I'm a true white man." At Toby's incredulous look, Vinny flashed white teeth at Toby. "My ancestry's equal parts ebony, white, yellow, and red. When you mix all the colors of light, you get true white. That's me."

The large Hyundai car factory in Germantown had closed a few years before, killing the local economy. It had also led to a major homelessness problem. These problems had helped elect Jones mayor. To be re-elected, Vinny said he needed to show he was fixing the problems.

"People expect their leaders to fix the economy for them," Vinny said. They were sorting another mailing by zip code, since someone had gotten them all jumbled together. "In the short term, economics is all voodoo and luck. Since voters always vote on short-term interests, elections are won when the economy goes your way, and lost when it goes against you and you can't change the subject. Since the economy's falling apart right now, Jones thinks he needs to focus on the homeless problem to change the subject and win the election. He raised local taxes on the wealthy to pay for it. And he's going to lose the election because of it."

"What do you mean?" Toby asked. He'd seen the growing number of homeless over the past few years, although he'd never really looked at them, averting his eyes like most people.

"You don't win elections by helping a small number of poor people who aren't likely to vote, while forcing an equally small number of wealthy but more politically active people to pay for it. It's the right thing to do, and it's the wrong thing to do."

Toby's eyebrows asked the obvious question.

"It's the right thing because the homeless need the help. It's the wrong thing because he's going to lose the election over it, and then things will get a whole lot worse for the very people he's trying to help."

"So to help people, you have to avoid helping them?" It was right about here, Toby later realized, that he entered the rabbit hole of politics, a world far stranger than anything Alice ever encountered.

"Welcome to politics, kid!" Vinny said. "Doesn't mean you don't help them. But only in moderation. Jones has only so much political capital, and he's overspending it, playing to a liberal base that's not large enough. Haven't you seen all the signs and mailings going after Jones for about fifty different things?"

"Nobody believes that garbage!" Toby protested. "Most of it's made-up lies."

"Everyone says they don't take the garbage seriously," Vinny said, "and yet unanswered charges tend to stick. The garbage accumulates."

"So Jones should respond to the garbage?"

"You can't," Vinny said. "That's the whole point of going after Jones on so many things. You can't defend it all, and if you try, the focus of the election becomes your supposed shortcomings, and that garbage begins to smell. There's only two ways to beat it."

"I'm guessing being a great mayor isn't one of them."

"It helps," Vinny said. "But only as a tie-breaker. The rubbish bin of history is full of great leaders who got voted out of office to the latest chump who, with great sincerity, will say and do whatever it takes to win. No, the only response is to attack back with even stronger garbage about the other guy."

"You said there were two ways."

Jones shook his head. "Too late for the other way. To lock up a primary, you have to pander to your base, and that's what Jones did, way too much. Now he's riled up the opposition base, and that's why there's so much anger against him. If he'd stayed in the political center, he'd have still won the primary—incumbents almost always do—but the opposition wouldn't be out for his blood. Instead, he pandered to his liberal base with his homeless shelters, and got himself bagged and tagged as 'too liberal.' His only way out of that box is to spew garbage right back."

"So why doesn't he?"

"If he did," Vinny said, "he'd lose my support, though I'd still probably vote for him. Jones is a good man doing the right things. Just not a very good politician. Leadership isn't about cramming your views down the other guy's throat. It's about compromise and moderation, and he just doesn't get that."

Lessons like these sunk in on Toby during the weeks they were together. Usually they worked at campaign headquarters. Other times they'd work the streets, putting up pro-Jones signs or setting up meetings where they'd promote Jones. Vinny could stand in front of a group and rattle off all the great things Jones had done, beaming such a smile that listeners never noticed when he switched to criticizing the opposition, riling the listeners up and bringing in votes. Vinny never resorted to the type of venom used by Jones's opponents. His arguments were so strong and logical that Toby couldn't imagine Jones losing.

And yet, as election day neared, polls showed Jones trailing. Toby couldn't believe people were so stupid; surely they'd see the light. Jones *had* to win.

Some of the volunteers and staff, such as Vinny, practically lived at Liberal Headquarters. The campaign served food and drinks for the volunteers and staff at mealtimes. While Toby tired of the repetitive plastated cabbage sandwiches and soups, which supposedly mimicked the real taste and texture of meat, Vinny treated each meal as if it were fine French food, often savoring the smell for a moment before dining.

One day Toby asked Vinny what he did for a living.

"I was a history teacher," Vinny said. "Back when teaching was done by real people, instead of those robot things that turn kids into those frightful zombies we call high school graduates. I got laid off when the economy fell apart."

"But what do you do *now*?" Toby asked.

Vinny looked down at the table, stacked full of flyers and envelopes. "I put pieces of paper inside other pieces of paper, and whatever else is needed in the Jones campaign."

"But that's all volunteer work!" Toby exclaimed. "Don't you need to make money to live on? For food and rent?"

Vinny silently stuffed a few pieces of paper inside an envelope before answering. "You know the new homeless shelter on Wisteria Drive? Why don't you come by there tonight, and I'll show you."

Toby didn't have much homework that night, so after he'd finished his volunteer shift at Liberal Headquarters he walked to the shelter, about a mile and a half away. He'd been in his parent's car when they'd driven down Wisteria in the past, but walking it was far different than a quick drive through with the windows up.

At the start of the walk, the streets were lined with businesses: restaurants, retail stores, a laundry, dental and doctor offices, and so on.

Then he came to a residential area, with middle-class houses like his own. As the sun set, he crossed under the very bridge he regularly walked over on his way to school.

On the other side, the houses were smaller, more rundown. It seemed strange that these homes were so close to his, and yet he'd never seen them on foot. Fences were falling down and overrun with weeds. Chipped paint and grime covered the houses. A few dogs barked at him. He held his breath the final block from the overwhelming smell of rot and decay, and finally reached the shelter.

It was surprisingly well kept, compared to the broken-down houses—shacks, he thought—on either side. Two men in grimy clothing were painting the front a fresh white. Toby went in the open front door, passing under the Germantown Homeless Shelter #4 sign.

Inside was one gigantic room, dimly lit by bare bulbs hung from the ceiling. The smell was worse than outside, and Toby only allowed himself short breaths of the pungent air that smelled of urine and sweat. Rows and rows of bunk beds covered the floor, with only a few feet between each. Just inside the door a woman behind a worn-out desk looked up at him.

"I'm trying to find Vinny," Toby said. "I think he works here."

"Don't think anybody by that name works here," she said. "Just a minute." She paged through a notebook. "There's a Vinny at bunk 126A."

After figuring out the numbering scheme, Toby found Vinny lying on a dirty sheet in the bottom bunk in the middle of the room. He was reading a book, with a stack of others next to the bunk. Two small children raced back and forth playing tag. A baby cried nearby. Farther off a man and a woman squared off in a shouting match, with residents of the shelter crowding around to watch.

"*Vinny!*" Toby exclaimed. "I thought you worked here."

Vinny put down the book and sat up. "You asked what I did for food and rent, and now you know. There's not much demand for history majors in this economy. I get my food at Liberal Headquarters and wherever else I can scrounge it. My rent is free, thanks to Jones and his homeless shelters."

Toby looked about. The man and woman were fighting on the floor as others cheered. The crying baby shrieked; its mom lay in bed next to it, holding the baby and staring off into space.

"How long have you lived here?" Toby asked, his heart racing, his shallow breathing more rapid.

"Since it opened earlier this year," Vinny said. "Before that, I was on the streets. You used to walk right by me all the time and never saw me."

Someone was shouting something, but Toby ignored it. "You argued against Jones opening homeless shelters, said he was pandering to his liberal base!"

"It's all a matter of degree," Vinny said. "Tell me, Toby, what do you consider yourself, liberal, moderate, or conservative?"

"If helping the poor makes me a liberal, then I'm a proud liberal."

Vinny tilted his head slightly, giving Toby that knowing grin. "Should the government only focus on the poor?"

"Of course not, just enough—"

"Should the government give nothing to the poor?" Vinny asked.

"*Of course not!*"

"Then you are somewhere in between," Vinny said. "Congratulations. That makes you a moderate." He tapped Toby on the chest. "*Never forget that.*"

A moderate, Toby thought. Somehow it didn't sound very impressive. He knew what liberals and conservatives stood for. What did moderates do? He was an idealist, and wanted to make things better than they were. How could an idealist be anything but a liberal?

"Jones went the liberal route," Vinny continued, "and watch what happens next month in the election. He did the right thing, and he's going to pay for it, like all good leaders eventually do."

The stench—not just from the air—was too much for Toby. He bent over and threw up.

"Welcome to my world," Vinny said as he cleaned up the mess.

Election day arrived. Vinny and Toby manned a booth outside a voting precinct, where they handed out flyers and buttons, and discussed issues with people who came to vote. The conservatives had a similar booth.

At first Toby eyed the conservatives suspiciously. There were three of them. *The enemy.* He was surprised when Vinny went over to chat with them during a lull. After a time Toby joined them as well, and even exchanged political war stories and jokes. He'd heard all of Vinny's, but was fascinated by some of the conservative tales.

So the conservatives were human after all. They simply were wrong on the issues.

Vinny's prediction proved correct as Jones lost the election by ten percent to the conservative challenger, Reginald McGivers. The post-election party at the Jones campaign headquarters was a dreary night as staff and volunteers argued "what ifs" over leftover sandwiches.

Late in the evening Jones himself came by. Toby had seen him at a few campaign events, but it was the first time he knew of that Jones actually came to his campaign headquarters. "A campaign headquarters is no place for a leader," Vinny had once told him.

With his baritone voice, Jones thanked everyone for their help and support, and then left. Toby never saw him again. Liberal Headquarters was cleared out within a day, reopening a month later as a dental office.

Toby visited Vinny regularly at the shelter in the weeks after the election. And then one day there was a "For Rent" sign on the locked door, and the Germantown Homeless Shelter #4 sign was gone. Through a window Toby saw the room was empty, the bunk beds gone. Where was Vinny?

The weather was getting cold, and he worried about his friend. But he was busy with school, and gradually forgot to look for Vinny.

Toby walked over the bridge to and from school each day. One time in December, while walking home, he glanced down while passing over the bridge next to the rundown area near where the shelter used to be. A group of people loitered at the base of the bridge. He looked away and continued walking. A gust of wind hit him, and the overpowering stench of the poor area hit him. He glanced back down again, and realized one of the people below was staring at him.

Vinny!

He raced around the side of the bridge and down the embankment. It was a bittersweet moment; Vinny looked horrible, thin and stooped and holding a thin coat with a broken zipper over himself as he shivered in the cold air. He wore a bright purple scarf around his neck.

"You finally noticed me," Vinny said, to Toby's chagrin. Vinny had been down here all this time, and he'd never seen him. It wasn't completely his fault; Vinny had grown a beard that covered much of his face. It was encrusted with dirt and bits of food.

Vinny's new home was a large cardboard box under the bridge. Inside was a thin blanket and Vinny's books. Seven others also lived under the bridge, each with their own box.

They took a walk together, and passed by where the shelter had been. It was now a second-hand clothing store. Toby checked his wallet, but only had a few dollars. He'd come back the next day with food for Vinny and money from his savings to buy him winter clothing.

When Toby left for school the next morning, he realized with horror that a freezing cold front had moved in, drastically dropping the temperature. With only a scarf, thin coat, and thinner blanket, Vinny must have had a bad night. Toby knew he'd be late for school, but he veered off the bridge to go to the new clothing store. He saw Vinny's cardboard box, but decided he'd surprise him.

He bought a thick coat with a hood, a knit cap, thick socks, and long thermal underwear. He'd get Vinny's shoe size and come back later to get him boots. This was all just temporary stuff; he was determined to talk his parents into letting Vinny move into their guest room. He was already planning out his opening arguments.

He returned to the bridge with the clothing and his school lunchbox, where he'd packed extra sandwiches for Vinny. He knocked on the top of Vinny's cardboard box, breaking off an icicle as he did so.

There was no answer.

"Vinny, you in there?" he asked, dropping the bags of clothing and the lunchbox. Finally he lifted the flap entrance and peeked inside. Vinny lay there, face up, still. Too still.

Toby yanked at Vinny's feet and pulled him out.

"Vinny!" he screamed at the open eyes, all that was visible above Vinny's beard and the purple scarf wrapped around his lower face. Other homeless people exited their boxes and gathered about, shivering in the cold. Someone called paramedics from a public phone.

A woman tried CPR, but gave up after a moment. "He's gone," she said, eyeing the bags of clothing. A siren announced the arrival of an ambulance.

Toby reached down and pulled the dirty scarf free from Vinny. He stared at it for a moment. Then, scarf in hand, he began to run, as fast as he could, in any direction as long as it was away.

He'd been running ever since.

Chapter Thirteen
Moderate Extremists

"The world's greatest and most confused political guru has arrived," Toby said. "So what now?"

Bruce's living room looked like it had gone through the ravages of one too many political campaigns. Flyers and buttons were strewn about along with ping-pong balls on the floor, as if in the aftermath of a hurricane. A poster of Albert Einstein looked down from the wall, white hair flying, with the caption, "*Great spirits have always encountered violent opposition from mediocre minds.*" Toby found the lumpy sofa comfortable, even if he did have to share it with Bruce's iguana, Stupid, who nibbled quietly on processed algae pressed into a reasonable facsimile of a lettuce leaf.

Bruce leaned forward on his squeaky lounge chair. As always, he wore a warm-up suit, this time a faded yellow one with black stripes on the side, covered with equally faded sponsor logos.

"Three options, obviously." Bruce tossed a ping-pong ball back and forth between his hands as he spoke.

"Okay, you've lost me already, and we haven't even gotten past 'obviously.'"

"Option one. You go back to Dubois, grovel, get your old job back, and continue inflicting pain and suffering on the world."

"With your support all the way, no doubt."

"I'm not sure if I'd call it support," Bruce said, still tossing the ping-pong ball back and forth. "I was thinking I'd lead the assassination squad. Wonder what would happen if the director of a political campaign were hit in the back with a ping-pong ball traveling three hundred miles per hour?" He suddenly threw the ball at Toby. Knowing Bruce all these years, Toby was ready and caught it.

He tossed the ball toward the iguana. It dropped the lettuce it was chewing on and looked over the ball. Then it batted the ball back and forth between its front legs. Toby and Bruce watched for a moment. It had a black blotch over its right eye.

"Pretty neat, having a brain that's half cat," Bruce said of his pet. "If only they could genetically enhance humans."

"They could, but it's against the law."

"And it's the people who made it against the law that need the genetic enhancing." Stupid tired of the ball and went back to eating the last of the fake lettuce. Bruce leaned back in his chair, which gave out a drawn-out squeak. Toby grimaced, trying to ignore it.

"I'm leaning toward an option other than assassination by ping-pong ball," Toby said. The poster of Einstein had changed to a picture of Wayne Wallace, the first world president, with the caption, "*Why do I always think 1 m right? Why would I argue something if I thought I was wrong?*"

"Option two. You go back to Ajala, really grovel, and maybe he has an opening for a receptionist. Perhaps in the Himalayas."

"I'll need a bigger scarf," Toby said.

"Or you could stop being an idiot, and take option three."

"Which is?"

"Hey, Stupid!" Toby and the iguana both looked up sharply. Bruce reached into a bag, grabbed another piece of artificial lettuce, and tossed it to the iguana. Stupid stood over it for a moment, licked it several times, then began to eat again.

"Option three," Bruce said. He leaned forward, causing another drawn-out squeak, and Toby almost missed what he said next. "We start a third party, take on the Roosters and Donkeys, and carve them up into entrées for the Australians."

The poster on the wall switched to Winston Churchill, with the caption, *"The best argument against democracy is a five-minute conversation with the average voter."*

"That's a rather big move," Toby said. "You do know the history of third-party challenges?" He tried to ignore the erratic squeaking. Next time he came over he'd bring some oil for Bruce's chair before it drove him crazy.

"Hasn't been a successful one in the fifty years since world government began." Bruce had found another ping-pong ball to toss back and forth. "But before that, where do you think the Roosters came from? They came out of nowhere, and look at them now."

"There's a difference," Toby said. "The Roosters didn't challenge anyone; they just filled a vacuum when the U.S. Republicans fell apart."

When the Republican Party collapsed, they had been taken over by a small group that had long ago followed a minor third-party challenger named Ross Perot. Someone had to fill the political vacuum, and while small in number, they were activists with savvy political leaders. At first they called themselves "Rossters," but that quickly became "Roosters." When the Republican Party was reborn as the Conservative Party and spread worldwide, it took the rooster nickname. Similarly, when the Liberal Party went worldwide, it inherited the donkey symbol from the U.S. Democratic Party.

"Isn't there a vacuum of leadership now?" Bruce asked.

"Not according to the opinion polls," Toby said. "TC, latest polls on presidential race?" He recited the figures the TC showed, which had Dubois ahead worldwide, 46-40%, with 14% undecided. Dubois had dropped about three points due to the alien shootout fiasco, but that was likely temporary.

"That's because voters aren't offered a choice," Bruce said. "Think about it. If you average everyone's political beliefs together, where would they be, conservative or liberal?"

"Neither—they'd be somewhere in between."

"That's called moderate—it was a trick question." Bruce stood and began pacing. "A moderate is a fringe candidate in either party. And

80

that's bubble-brained. Think about it—isn't it surreal that in our current politics, voters tell their leaders that if they compromise too much, they'll vote them out of office, but they'll also vote them out of office if they don't get things done. Maybe we need to teach voters that there's such a thing as compromise?"

The poster had changed to a picture of Thomas Clarke, the world's third president, with the caption, "*Just because you're a politician doesn't mean you have to be stupid.*"

"The strange thing," Bruce continued, "is that when a candidate moves to the center politically, it's news. It should be news when someone moves *away* from the center, where most people should be."

"And yet," Toby said, "most people identify themselves as conservatives or liberals. TC, what are the latest figures on party identification?" The numbers came up on hit TC. "Thirty-five percent conservative, 30% liberal."

"People believe what they've been brainwashed to believe," Bruce said, sitting down again. "And that leaves 35% in between, plus anyone we can counter-brainwash."

"And we're good at that, aren't we?"

"We're the best!" Bruce said. "You know the difference between a lemming and a voter?"

"Voters avoid cliffs?"

"A lemming doesn't think it has a mind of its own. Which is why you can convince voters of almost anything, and they'll think it was their idea. Politics is all about telling people what they want to hear, or convincing them that what you're telling them is what they want to hear." Bruce raised a fist. "Let the brainwashing begin!"

"So what are we supposed to brainwash them to believe?" Toby asked. "To join our merry band of unknown moderates?"

Bruce laughed.

"Didn't know I was a comedian," Toby said.

"You're no moderate. I'm a moderate. You're a liberal who tried so hard to be a moderate that you went conservative. And then you joined Dubois's merry band!"

"Maybe my heart's a liberal, but my head's a moderate. And you were part of the Dubois campaign too."

"Yeah, but I left when I realized he was a brain-damaged maggot who lied about moving to the center, who has no idealism beyond getting elected, who instead of solving problems uses them for political points. That's the short version; want the long version?"

"That's okay," Toby said. "You saw the truth before I did."

The poster had changed to that of former U.S. president John F. Kennedy, with the caption, *"Mothers all want their sons to grow up to be president, but they don't want them to become politicians in the process."*

"I didn't see the truth before you did," Bruce said. "I admitted the truth to myself before you did. You knew what he was like, and what he believed in, when you took over his campaign. You rationalized it, thinking you could lead him to the center, that you could influence Dubois into being a better person, but tell the truth: why did you *really* run his campaign?"

The very question Toby had asked himself over and over for years, with increasing frequency. He had learned from Vinny to grab the political center in the campaigns he ran. Originally, that meant working for the Donkeys, and going as close to the center as he could while still holding on to the left. Then one day he agreed to run a campaign for a moderate Rooster, a candidate for governor of Brazil. They'd won—but afterwards, he'd been blackballed by the Donkeys. And so he began running campaigns for the Roosters. He gained worldwide fame as the main strategist for the winning campaign of David Baxter, now in his second term as the reclusive and ineffective U.S. governor. Then came that fateful call from Dubois . . .

There was no point lying to Bruce. "I wanted to run and win a worldwide campaign."

"And now you have the chance to make up for it."

"What about you?" Toby asked. "You've been hiding at school and playing ping-pong. Why are you so into this suddenly? Something happen at the Nationals?"

"I lost," Bruce said.

"Of course you lost," Toby said. "Look at all the other athletes, and look at yourself! You're like a pebble trying to compete with mountains! Just take the steroids; all pro athletes do. They're perfectly safe."

"Nah, I don't want to put those things in my body," Bruce said, smacking a ball extra hard into his hand. "Let's stick to the subject. Right now we've got a system where the two extremes are loyal to their party instead of what's best for the people in the given situation. Don't you think it's undemocratic for liberals and conservatives to try to force their minority views on the majority?"

"Those are just labels."

"Pretty damn good labels! But what we have are extremists and ideologues forcing their views on the rest of us."

"What's the difference?"

"Extremists start with an idea and take it to a crazy extreme. Ideologues start with the crazy extreme and then rationalize it. Most political party leaders are one or the other."

"Sounds about right." Toby wondered if he was guilty of either.

"We've got a president running for re-election who's perfected the art of ignorance for the masses; we've got a far-left zealot who's a political carcass in a suit running against him; and we've got a galactic civilization out there, watching to see what we do. What do you want to do, Toby?"

The poster changed to Dubois's predecessor, Jing Xu, the man Toby had so successfully dethroned. *"Extremists always have a lot more to say than normal folk because they have a lot more to explain."*

"Will you at least turn off that stupid poster?" Toby asked, wondering if the subject of Xu's quote was a coincidence or if Bruce was controlling which posters and quotes came up. Bruce smiled and leaned back in his chair, which gave out a gut-wrenching squeak.

Jing Xu had been a hard and, at times, nasty campaigner, but he had been a pretty good president. He was a liberal, but a moderate and open-minded one, who actually thought things through rather than mouth campaign dogma. He hadn't deserved to lose.

"Okay, God damn it, I'm in!" Toby said, a flutter of excitement rising inside him. "Now that our merry band of moderates—"

"Not just moderates. Moderate extremists!"

"Okay, now that our merry band of moderate extremists is up to two, what now? We have no staff, no organization, no money, no name recognition, and oh yeah, who do we recruit to run for president? What idiot shall become our human sacrifice, with no chance of winning?"

Bruce pushed his thumb through his ping-pong ball, and tossed aside the broken piece of celluloid. "*You.*"

Chapter Fourteen
A Leader is Found

"*Me?*" The rising excitement inside Toby had reached a crescendo, and his heart threatened to explode. He was supposed to run campaigns, not run himself. The idea had often crossed his mind but only in daydreams, just as one might daydream about flying or meeting aliens, but it was just that—a daydream that would never happen. Like flying or meeting aliens....

It took two hours for Bruce to get Toby to say, "I'll run for president when Dubois and Ajala sing a duet of 'We're together again' on the roof of one of the Twin Towers," and another hour to get him to, "Okay, okay, just turn off that damn poster and stop squeaking your chair." At the time, the poster had a picture of Napoleon Bonaparte, with the caption, "*In politics . . . never retreat, never retract . . . never admit a mistake.*" Bruce turned it off via his TC, revealing that the Einstein picture and quote—"*Great spirits have always encountered violent opposition from mediocre minds*"—was the default mode.

"All you have to do," Bruce said, "is look, act, and sound like a president, and if the voters fall for it, you'll be president."

"Do you really believe that?"

"No," Bruce said. "We'll also need a miracle. I left that out."

Toby shook his head. "You do realize I have a wife and son who might have something to say on this?" His heart still beat like a piston. A very fast piston. And yet he was already adjusting to the idea of being a candidate and perhaps someday running the world. Perhaps the years of daydreaming had prepared him.

"Just a wife and son, huh? I wonder what Lara has to say about that?"

Oops, Toby thought. How could he have forgotten his daughter? Just because she was running Dubois's campaign. . . .

"Besides," Bruce said, "you and Olivia are practically separated, and Tyler lives with her. When's the last time you saw them?"

It had been a while. He'd been staying at hotels for seemingly forever. He did call Tyler at least once a week, but he could do that from anywhere.

"So what now?" Toby asked. "You want to be vice president?"

"No way," Bruce said. "I'd be a heartbeat away from being the most effective and most hated president in history. I don't want to be the head chimp."

"Then I'll hire you as campaign director."

Bruce shook his head. "You couldn't afford me. Not that ten million a year is much these days, but if you want to hire me off the college ping-pong circuit, that's what it'd cost you. If you want a volunteer director, who you'll turn loose so we can make havoc of this race, then you have a deal. But you'll have to do what I say."

"You do remember that I have a little experience myself in running political campaigns? I might have some insight into our plans." Turning Bruce loose in a political campaign, Toby thought, would be like tossing a great white shark into a hot tub full of conservative and liberal online grubbers. Not a bad idea, actually, but there wouldn't be any writers left afterwards to cover the campaign. Someone had to restrain Bruce or he might blow up the planet. Or worse.

"You're the candidate," Bruce said. "Candidates can't see straight. You said that yourself. You need someone on the outside telling you what to do, someone who can keep his eye on the goal, and not worry about minor day-to-day ethical challenges."

"I remember what I said." First Lara, and now Bruce were quoting him. At least he now knew they actually listened to what he said. "What

I told Dubois was, 'I'll tell you what to say, how to say it, what to look like when you say it, and then I'll spin it for the masses.'"

"Sounds about right. When you're on your own, you go all ethical. That's gotta change."

"Sorry, Bruce, but I think I'll keep veto power. I'd like to be the head chimp for a change. You like to quote stuff I've said; do you remember what I told Dubois before his debate with Xu?"

"You told him bringing logic to a public debate is like bringing a neocortex to a laser fight."

"Did I?" Toby didn't remember that one. "What I told him was, 'What does it profit to gain the world if he loses his soul?' I think that's from the Christian Bible."

"We're not going to lose your soul, just lease it out for a while."

"Well that's nice, risking my soul for the good of mankind." Toby decided not to point out that if there was such a thing as a soul, all successful politicians had lost theirs long ago.

"It'll be for a good purpose, and it won't go cheap," Bruce said. "Didn't you also say, 'Never sell your soul to a special interest group until you've calculated the political return'?"

That one Toby remembered. It seemed he'd spent a lot of time thinking about souls when he was with the Dubois campaign.

Time for a compromise, Toby decided. "How's this? You plan and run the campaign, and I'll go along. But I get sparingly-used veto power."

"Great. A wannabe leader who wants to lead. Next you'll be acting all presidential, all grown up and all. It's so wonderful seeing them leave the nest on their own, spreading their wings, taking flight, and falling on their faces."

"Shut up, Bruce, you've got a campaign to run. You might start by raising it from the dead, or rather the unborn. We're two votes, and we'll need about two billion."

"Too bad Tyler's only fourteen and can't vote for two more years." Bruce began bouncing a ping-pong ball on a paddle. Toby grabbed the ball out of the air.

"Bruce, do you ever do anything spontaneously?"

"All the time, but only after I've thought it through."

"Exactly," Toby said. "You've been thinking about this for a while, and I know you have sinister plans for this ridiculously impossible campaign, so why not share them? I already outlined the problems: no staff, no organization, no money, little name recognition, and we can add no strategy to that list."

"Before we get to all that there's a larger imperative," Bruce said. He tossed the paddle aside. "Why do you want to be president?"

"Because—"

"Don't tell me!" Bruce jumped to his feet and pointed at the picture of Albert Einstein. "Tell him!"

"You want me to tell Albert Einstein?"

"No, idiot, think of him as a portal to the world. He represents the public. Tell him why you want to be president. Be spontaneous." Bruce sat down again to another loud, jarring squeak.

Now Toby leaned back in the sofa, ignoring Stupid's squawk as the iguana jumped out of the way. It was such a simple question, one he'd always asked his candidates, but he'd never had to answer it himself. It was a lot easier asking than telling.

"Just say what comes to mind," Bruce said. "We can fix it up later. And I'm recording this for future use."

"The political world is split." Once he started, the words spilled into Toby's head faster than he could say them. "Every five years the two sides duke it out, and we end up with a liberal or a conservative in charge. But that's the view from New York City. The rest of the world isn't liberal or conservative. They don't think that way until we drill it into their heads that they have to make that choice. They just want leaders who will do what's best for all of us, not what some political philosophy says to do. And that usually means finding a solution that's not liberal, not conservative, but a compromise. A moderate solution. Which is where most people are, if we only gave them that choice."

Bruce clapped his hand against his paddle. "Perfect! That's about thirty seconds; later we'll work out a fifteen-second version. But I think we're ready to move to strategy."

"So you have given it some thought?"

"Of course."

So had Toby. "If we're going to start a party in the middle, where most of the voters are, what are the other two parties supposed to do?"

"What do we care?" Bruce said. "Our goal isn't to resolve some sort of conflict with the other parties; our goal is to beat them!"

"Exactly," Toby said. "So now that we're the party of choice for the masses, how do we educate them to this fact?"

"That's the problem, and here's how we're going to solve it."

Toby would have to wait to learn that strategy, as his TC was alerting him to breaking news. The alien was about to give a speech to the world.

Chapter Fifteen
Twenty-two Talks to the Media

"Hello, Earth people." Twenty-two stood on the drawbridge doorway of her spaceship, near the blue Liberal Headquarters, facing a large group of cameras. Dozens of USE security people surrounded the area, all carefully out of the camera's view. Ajala stood behind her.

She'd spent a few minutes wondering about the trees that surrounded them before remembering her sensors said they were made of complex plastics. She examined the grass on the ground and realized it too was artificial. Her sensors showed that they did photosynthesis, just like real plants.

She still wore the yellow vest; it was the only one equipped to protect her. She wondered if the humans had the capacity to color her velvo yellow to match it. Or perhaps they could make her a yellow velvo. She would ask later, but for now, she'd put aside the clashing red velvo for an equally clashing blue one that covered her mouth. If you wore one too long, it became damp from breathing and talking.

Perhaps after she'd been on the planet long enough she'd go native and take off the velvo. She glanced at the camera, and imagined what it would be like to have a few billion beings see her naked mouth. She began to rock side to side, then realized that those few billion were already watching her. She forced herself to be still.

"I am Ambassador Twenty-two," she began. "I am a grod from the star you call Tau Ceti. I am here to observe and learn about your political process. I am told there are two major political parties in your

90

political system. I hope to travel with and observe both of them to learn how your system operates." Once again she wondered about the constant use of the personal pronoun "I," but it seemed the best way to get her message across in this awkward language. Perhaps she should try to vary the way she used the language.

"Someday," she continued, "I hope to welcome your world to the Galactic Union. You have limited local spaceflight to your moon and the planets in your solar system. When you have interstellar flight you will be eligible to join the many other races that make up this great Union." She didn't really think of the Union as being great—a lot of negative adjectives better described it—but the humans would learn that on their own, when the time came. If they got that far. Of course, she wasn't really telling the truth about eligibility rules for joining the Union either; interstellar flight wasn't the only rule.

Several of the press people waved their arms in the air. She looked up, but there wasn't anything to see. She remembered seeing something similar in a video Zero had shown her of a classroom of human children. She aimed her eyestalks toward one large human. "Do you need to go to the bathroom?" There was laughter from the humans. She didn't understand the joke.

The large press person lowered his arm and stepped forward. "Twice security forces have fired on you. Does that bother you?"

What a silly question. "Yes, it bothered me. I do not believe they understood the situation. I hope they will not fire on me again."

A smaller press person with long hair stepped forward. "Will President Dubois allow you to observe his political campaign, after the way you embarrassed him?"

She had no idea. "I hope that he will allow me to observe. I will try not to embarrass him further."

A third press person began to step forward, but the larger first one deftly stepped in front. "Earlier you met with Ajala. Did he agree to your observing his campaign?"

"He agreed to allow this." He also lectured me on the Liberal Party's goals, she thought. It was a difficult concept for her to understand, the way humans grouped together and adjusted their beliefs to match those of their party. She knew that there were other primitive races that did such things, but not on Grodan. She could write next semester's paper on the subject, though she'd have to leave out the fact that she had actually been on a planet outside the Union. Perhaps someday, if Earth were a member, she'd be able to publish her notes.

"The Ambassador and I had a fruitful exchange of ideas," Ajala said, now standing side by side with Twenty-two. "I am looking forward to learning about her race, as she is eager to learn about ours."

The press person with the longer hair stepped forward. "Since our weapons can't hurt you, what's to keep you from conquering us?"

"That's how Dubois thinks," Ajala said. "You saw how he welcomed Twenty-two to our world?"

Twenty-two squeaked in laughter, and tried not shaking too much. Why would she want to conquer a planet? To turn in for extra credit at school? They probably thought her ship was armed and ready to devastate their planet. She did have the hand laser, and she supposed she could use the tractor beam to toss things around a bit. But no point in telling them everything.

"I have no plans to conquer anyone," she said. "I only want to observe your political process. I will start with Ajala. Later I hope that your President Dubois will allow me to observe his activities as well."

"How do we know you're not a spy?" one of the press people asked. She'd lost track of which was which; they all looked nearly alike unless she focused on their differing clothing. She avoided looking too closely, due to the exposed mouths; she knew she was a bit prudish on that.

"I am not a spy." She doubted the humans had anything that could possibly be of any interest other than academic. Like most races, humans were egocentric and couldn't conceive just how unimportant they were in the general course of galactic affairs.

"Will you share your technology with our scientists?" asked the larger one.

"That is against Galactic Union law," she said. "When your planet develops interstellar spaceflight, you will be eligible for membership and access to higher technology."

Nearly all the press people had their arms raised. She decided she'd answered enough questions for now. She looked back at the rows of cameras. "Earth people, thank you in advance for your hospitality. I look forward to learning about you."

Ajala put his arm around Twenty-two's back. "Let's go inside and talk." She followed him back to his office, keeping one eyestalk pointing backwards at the press, which shouted questions—mostly about the Galactic Union—as they followed close behind until they entered Liberal Headquarters. Someday perhaps they'd learn about the Galactic Union.

"That doesn't happen every day," Bruce said. He seemed deep in thought, a ping-pong ball held against his chin. "Wonder if we could get her to observe our campaign."

"That would be exciting," Toby said, "her watching the two of us plan out world conquest. Maybe we should focus on getting the rest of the world to watch us."

"Or get the rest of the world to watch the alien, with us standing side by side, waving and looking presidential."

Not a bad idea, Toby thought. In fact, a great idea. "Why would she want to observe us, when we're a party of two people?"

"Let's remedy that," Bruce said. "A worldwide political campaign starts with a single thought in someone's basement."

Toby scrunched his brow. "Is that something I once said?"

"Nope. I just made it up. And no worldwide campaign ever started in someone's basement. Until now."

"And what was that single thought in your basement?"

"I don't have a basement, and I don't remember what the first thought was," Bruce said. "For historical purposes, I'll come up with something clever later on. Now, let me tell you how we're going to win."

"And I'll tell you why we haven't got a chance. But you go first."

"Sure. But never plan global conquest on an empty stomach." Bruce ordered a spinach pizza and a pair of Hancolas. A few minutes later, Bruce's kitchen completed the order, and they sat down to eat and strategize.

Chapter Sixteen
The Small General From Russia

Thursday, July 29, 2100

The nuclear wars of 2045 and the ensuing economic collapse had devastated much of the world. A century of tsunami-like technological advance became a trickle. Hunger and disease became the norm for much of the world, including United Korea. Russia and Japan marched into the Korean Peninsula with humanitarian aid and helped rebuild the country.

They never left.

In 2091, after forty-six years of cold war, a surprise attack by Japan from the south caught Russian troops in the north off guard. The Japanese surged forward until the Russians made a stand near the Russian-Korean border. With the close proximity of Japan and Russia, the world held its breath as the two slugged it out for seven days.

The crisis seemed to end when Russian troops, faced with the better-armed and seemingly unstoppable Japanese army, retreated back into Russia to the north. Japanese troops pursued, cornering the Russians in the Khrebet Sikhote-alin Mountains. With the Japanese army on one side and the Japanese fleet on the other in the Sea of Japan, the Russian army of 200,000 looked doomed.

Nuclear weapons had been outlawed in 2051, yet most believed that the major world powers, including Russia, had secret reserves to be used as a last resort. If there ever was a time for their use, this was it.

Faced with an impossible situation, General Tarasov called a staff meeting, and announced they had no choice but to surrender their army. In a scene memorialized in the hit 2097 movie *Never Surrender*, General Feodora Zubkov shot and killed Tarasov as he sat at the head of the staff table. Though she was only fourth in command, she took Tarasov's spot at the head of the table. No one protested.

Some thought she would order a nuclear attack. Instead, the diminutive Zubkov ordered an attack down the western side of the mountain against the Japanese army. Under cover of smoke, the troops crept down the mountainside, looking to catch the Japanese by surprise. However, the smoke was too thin, and the Japanese saw them coming. Troops from the south and north converged and devastated the 20,000 Russian troops.

The other 180,000 troops, undetected in the forested mountaintop, had marched north. They broke through thinner Japanese lines into neutral China, marched north around Lake Khanka and into the Changbai Mountains, and caught the Japanese from behind. Two weeks later they reached the 38th parallel, and Korea was once again split in two at the historic divide between North and South. The "Miracle at Khrebet" turned Feodora Zubkov into an international celebrity.

With the huge Russian and Japanese armies facing each other across the divide, with China furious about the Russian incursion on their territory and amassing its own huge army on the China-North Korea border—but not sure what to do with it—and with the Korean people angry at all their neighbors, Feodora thought it amazing that anyone was still alive after nine years.

Now Feodora sat at another conference table, this time with ambassadors and their aides from Russia, Japan and China, with that ignoramus Vice President Persson as mediator. She knew the Korean International Sovereignty Summit was futile, with the participants unlikely to "KISS" and make up. She chuckled at her joke at the summit's acronym. And yet, she thought, there was some argument that talking was better than shooting. Or was it? At least the latter got things done.

A fist-width short of five feet tall, she had to crane her perpetually aching neck to look up at the towering Indian Swede as he spoke down to the representatives in pointless diplomatic talk in the west wing of the United Nations Building, *The Bubble*, home to the world's executive branch and the Red Room. Two of her aides sat next to her.

Feodora secretly liked the nickname the Russians had for her: "Horse." She knew she was ugly. Besides, it was better than what the Japanese called her, the "Mountain Monster." Now a middle-aged 64 years-old with pure gray hair and matching eyes, every morning she still did her two-mile run and one hundred pushups and sit-ups. She'd gained a pound since her army years, and resented it.

Now an "elder stateswoman," her job was to show that the talks were meaningful, even if they were not. As the Russian Ambassador and tactician, she understood that when faced with an intractable problem, her purpose wasn't to find a meaningful solution, but to put off any resolution so that nobody started shooting. As a grubber's online column had famously coined, "experiencialmismeaningfulness" at its best and worst.

She remained convinced the Japanese and Chinese had secret attack plans, which would make all this talk meaningless. She'd rather be in Russia, with the other generals, planning out endless counter-attack scenarios. She was certain it was just a matter of time before there'd be a simultaneous attack from China through the Korean Bay, and from Japan at Tongjoson-Man. Or perhaps the Japanese would surprise them with an attack through Haeju. She had plans in her mind for every Russian platoon for every conceivable attack. Unfortunately, she was no longer the general in charge; she'd been promoted to "ambassador."

Unspoken at the conference was the growing movement in Russia to declare the entire Russian Federation—made up of Russia and fourteen countries near its borders, plus Cuba—as one united country, like the old USSR that had fallen 109 years before. There were even a few supercentenarians still alive from that era. If only the USSR had governed well, who knows what they might have been? There was also the call to add North Korea to the Federation, which she knew went over in China and Japan like a rotting kangaroo carcass in this world of pansy vegetarians.

The conference was turning into the dreariest part of her life, with no end in sight.

"So," Persson said, "in principle, Russia would agree to pull out if Japan pulls out?"

"Only if Japan pull out of the northwest Sea of Japan," Feodora said, as she'd been instructed to do in this subtly planned choreography. "A Japan-free Sea of Japan would be a happy Sea of Japan," she added, unchoreographed. The Japanese ambassador sat up, an angry look on his face, but didn't respond.

"China cannot allow that," said the Chinese Ambassador. "If Japan pulls its fleet, what's to stop the Russians from moving in?"

"We have no interest in Sea of Japan," said Feodora, "but need to keep our options open. Is always better to defend against attack that never come than leave one open to attack that does." It was bad enough defending North Korea from attack, but they also needed to keep a presence to avoid a direct attack on Russia, probably at Vladivostok.

"Japan is willing to relinquish the northwest Sea of Japan," said the Japanese Ambassador, "but only if we are allowed to keep bases at Pohang and Yosu."

"That would be violation of Korean sovereignty," said Feodora, trying not to chuckle outwardly at the irony of holding talks about Korean sovereignty without Korean representatives. "No one wants to violate Korean sovereignty, this is correct?"

Talk about irony, she thought, here have an actual alien ambassador landing outside this very building, and we're squabbling about something halfway across the globe that'll never be resolved in our lifetime unless one side does something unilaterally stupid. She'd spent every waking moment watching the TC newscasts on the alien since the landing two days before. Idiots like Dubois and Duffy made everyone look bad; maybe someday she'd meet Twenty-two and show that not all humans were that stupid. For that audience, she'd even wear her real medals, as heavy and noisy as they were when they jangled about, instead of the holographic version she currently wore over her uniform.

Of course, she also looked forward to finally looking down on a fellow ambassador. She rubbed her aching neck as the towering Persson droned on.

"I will ask President Dubois," Persson said, "to appoint a sub-committee to look into the issues of Pohang, Yosu, and Korean sovereignty. We will reconvene those specific discussions upon receipt of their report. We will now take a lunch, and reconvene in ninety minutes to discuss the reported ceasefire violations on the island of Paengnyong-do, as reported by the Japanese Ambassador."

Feodora fled the room, leaving her Russian aides behind. What a waste of time all this was, she thought. She headed for the Meatie-Veg Cafeteria for lunch, wondering if she'd ever get to make another trip to Australia for some real meat.

To get her mind off the silly talks, she contemplated a new strategy for a theoretical invasion of Japan, involving a northern landing at Aomori, followed by a rapid march southward. Of course, it was theoretical only until the day came when Japan and China played their hand. When that happened, she was determined Russia would be ready to play theirs.

Incoming call from Toby Platt.

What could that be about? She'd met Platt in 2095 when he was campaigning with Dubois in Moscow. She'd heard he'd just quit the Dubois campaign. What could he want with her?

"Accept," she whispered to her TC. Platt's image appeared on her TC.

After brief introductions, Platt got to the point. "How'd you like to be vice president?"

"Strange you ask," she said. "The Russian Conservatives try recruit me to run for president of Russian Federation last year, but I turn them down."

"I'm not talking about Russia. I'm talking about Earth."

Earth? "Mr. Persson might have something to say about that, and so would whoever is running with Ajala."

"Emi Katsuko of Japan."

"Thank you for reminding me . . . that our good friends from across 38th parallel might be brainwave away from presidency." She'd been a Rooster all her life, and yet could barely believe that her party had nominated an idiot like Dubois as president, or that he'd won. Yet who else could she support? The previous president, Jing Xu, wasn't so bad, but he was Chinese, and now a Japanese was running for vice president. They were Russia's mortal enemies, which made them her mortal enemies. Plus, they were liberals, and she really didn't like squishy types. Yet after a few years of Dubois, she'd realized she didn't like conservatives either.

"Since you are no longer with Dubois campaign," she said, "and since you are talking about vice presidency, I'm guessing you now work for Ajala, and he's thinking of replacing Katsuko? It would be great move, but—"

"Nope, that's not it, but you are close. I'm standing outside The Bubble. Can we meet for lunch?"

Bruce had outlined the night before what they needed in a vice president. "The ideal candidate would have a 'tough guy' image, a minimal legislative record that could be used against us, and should be from one of the early regions."

The first election would be in Oceania, Toby had said, so a candidate from there could be ideal. "Oceania's only seven electoral votes," Bruce pointed out. "Even if you get a candidate from Australia and get their four votes, we'd probably lose New Guinea and New Zealand and their votes, since they don't like Australia. Besides, I'd rather a bigger wallop."

The second election would be North America, but they already had Toby for that. Next came Russia and its 40 electoral votes.

"It's not a lot," Bruce said, "but winning there could give momentum in other regions. China's next, with their 159 votes, then United

Europe's 63." They decided they needed someone from Russia, China, or Europe.

"How about General Feodora Zubkov?" Toby said, and Bruce smacked his forehead with his ping-pong paddle.

"Why didn't I think of that?" he exclaimed. "The Mountain Monster! Talk about your 'tough-guy' image—she once called Dubois 'a cold chill in a cold Russian winter.' And she compared liberals to jellyfish but without the jellybone. She'll hurt us in China and Japan, but should help everywhere else."

Toby nodded. "Sounds like a common-sense moderate to me."

They'd taken a floater to New York City that morning to meet with potential staff recruits for the new Moderate Party. They had been delighted to hear that their first pick for vice president was also in town, though that was probably true of many of their choices, since it was capital of the world.

Now they sat at an outside table at the Meatie-Veg Cafeteria, across from what the Japanese called "The Mountain Monster," the legendary Feodora Zubkov, all eighty pounds of her, in full military uniform and holographic medals. Most Russian women appended an "a" to the end of their last name, but not Feodora—"Why not make us wear yellow stars as well?" she'd once said in an interview. From somewhere, mists of fake forest air blew over them. Bruce had discarded the faded yellow warm-ups for a sharper red ones with gold trim. Toby had replaced his green suit with a more conservative gray one—in the fashion sense.

"Hello, dahlings," she said in her deep, almost comical Russian accent when they met. Russia was one of the few places left in the world where English wasn't the first language.

"How go the Korean non-destruction talks?" Toby asked after he'd introduced her to Bruce.

"Like igloo in a room full of hot air," she said. "Did you know Persson more idiot than Dubois? Make president seem like scholar. Hard to believe."

"I know," Toby said. "I've worked with them for five years. Actually, Dubois is smart at some things."

101

"Why not shoot him?"

Toby wasn't sure if she was serious.

"What makes you think we haven't tried?" Bruce asked.

"You aren't going to hurt him much with that ping-pong ball in your hand," she said.

Feodora ordered the brandied corn cabbage, and Toby and Bruce ordered the same out of diplomatic courtesy.

"Ah, the mark of leadership," she said, "following the people to stay in front."

"We figured that if you ordered it, it must be good," Toby said. He'd just noticed the sound of the air vent that blew the mists of forest air over them, and now he couldn't get the sound out of his head.

"I hate brandied corn cabbage," she said. "Tastes like rotting tomatoes. But rest of menu taste like wet dog. I've eaten here before. I think they do it to me on purpose." She stopped and rubbed her neck as her holographic medals silently jangled about.

"Now dahlings, why don't we talk about what you came here to talk about? You're not here to talk about food or Korea or Dubois. You mention vice presidency, yet not for Donkeys or Roosters. What would great Toby Platt and brilliant Bruce Sims want with small general from Russia? Can only mean one thing. Third-party challenge. Doomed, of course. Who in mind for presidency? Someone handsome, I hope?"

Toby and Bruce exchanged glances. "That would be me," Toby said.

"Sorry about the handsome part," Bruce said. "At least you still get the 'brilliant Bruce' part."

"Yes, handsome part missing, and brilliant part suspect," Feodora said. "But Toby still dahling. Maybe you have contacts so I can meet alien ambassador? He's handsome."

"I might be able to arrange a meeting. Actually, he's a she, at least for now. Apparently they go back and forth."

She raised her eyebrows. "Dahling, that's perfect! A woman who become short, handsome man when needed, then back to woman for girl talk. Ah, we'll discuss more later. And now, what is your party? Must be something different from conservatives or liberals. Can't go more right or left, so must be between. So party name either Moderate or Independent Party, or maybe some silly animal name. And you want tough gal like me to bring attention and Russia."

Bruce was smiling. "You figure things out pretty quickly."

"I am general; it is my job to figure out things. You notice medals? They not come from cheap trinket store. Next time I bring real ones and double my weight. Now, why don't you explain to me how you win, and why I should be passenger on your small boat."

Over the next few hours they discussed the election, with Bruce sending detailed maps and plans to their TCs. They had about a month to prepare for eleven consecutive regional elections from all parts of the world, one every week, starting with "First in the World" Oceania. Seventy-seven days of non-stop campaigning.

"We'll travel around the world in eighty days," Bruce said, "with three to spare."

By the time they were through going over Bruce's detailed plans for each continental region, even Toby was convinced they could win. Of course, he knew that all candidates convince themselves they can win, even those that have no chance. The Conservative and Liberal Parties had long ago had their primaries and conventions and chosen their candidates. They had been campaigning all over the world for seemingly forever, and already met in a series of debates. A third-party challenge such as theirs should have been started long ago.

Judging by the familiar irritated look that came over her several times, Toby figured Feodora was ignoring TC calls. When a pair of uniformed men appeared and told her in thick Russian accents that she was needed in the conference at the United Nationals Building, she told them to "be real men" and represent Russia for the afternoon.

"Two of my better aides," she said when they left. "They are very good at not talking."

She had many questions, like a staff sergeant drilling her troops, but Bruce had answers for all, though Toby knew many of their plans were far better on paper than in reality.

"Now, my maybe running mate and campaign director," she finally asked, "what are our actual chances?"

"Some candidates prefer not to know," Bruce said.

"The small general wants to know," she said. "Give nice, round figure."

"Well, if you round off, our chances of winning are about zero," Bruce said.

"That's an increase since yesterday," Toby said. "I like our chances."

"We have zero chance?" she said.

"It'll be like shooting at invisible windmills," Bruce said. "Searching for that favorite speck of sand from your childhood. Trying to win an argument with a sister. Convincing Dubois that the hundred people on the Moon colony should vote. Trying to—"

"I have aide like you," Feodora said. "I almost have him shot, but instead give raise. Okay, I run, but I must explain something first. I do this only for fun, until you prove to me it is real. When you do that, I will campaign for you. Until then, I go back to being small general in Russia and big-shot ambassador in New York."

"Agreed," Toby said, "on one condition. That you will campaign for us in Russia, no matter what the polls say."

"When Japanese asked for conditions in Korea, I blew up one of their battalions," she said. "But for you, I agree. As long as you aren't embarrassment, I will try to win you Russia. In return, you arrange meeting for me with alien ambassador."

"Agreed," Toby said.

"One more thing," she said. "You have staff?"

"We have two," Bruce said.

Feodora looked at him and tilted her head slightly. "I see. You have yourself and Toby. Maybe you should stop trying to fool small general?"

"We're hiring some people this week," Toby said.

"I have two aides that can help you," she said. "They are Russian staff."

"How can they join a political campaign if they work for the Russian government?" Toby asked.

"The people the Russian government would pay for couldn't find haystack sitting on needle," she said. "I pay for these two, so they work for me."

"Do they have any political experience?" Bruce asked.

Feodora leaned back and smiled. "Everyone in Russia is politician."

Chapter Seventeen
An Unexpected Visitor

Friday, July 30, 2100

Back in Washington D.C., Toby and Bruce began the tedious process of setting up a worldwide political campaign. Bruce volunteered to pay for the first month's costs, including a headquarters, a campaign floater, and staff salaries.

"First priority is to raise money before I'm selling carrots on street corners," Bruce said.

There had been a time when presidential and legislative elections were held at the same time, but the two were now separated. The presidency was considered too important for voters to be distracted by other races. One-fourth of the World Congress would be up for election in each of the next four years, and then the cycle would repeat with another presidential election in 2105. Regional elections for governors and other offices were also spaced out, but none were held during a presidential election.

If the Moderate Party still existed next year, they'd have to find candidates to fill hundreds of Senate and House seats, and dozens of governor positions.

They found a five-thousand square foot street-level space for their headquarters in D.C. on Canal Road, a heavily populated area overlooking the Potomac River. Liberal Headquarters was just a few blocks east, with Georgetown University just beyond that. They found it in the morning, Bruce put down a deposit, and by afternoon they were moving into Moderate Headquarters, which Bruce dubbed *The Ranch*. It was all wide open space, no individual offices, just the way Toby liked it. Political campaigns were all about communication, and the last thing needed were walls between workers, even between the candidate and the lowliest volunteer. He soaked it all in, knowing he wouldn't be here that often. Soon he'd be traveling the world, campaigning non-stop.

The two Russian aides, Ivan and Vladimir, were as efficient as Feodora had promised. Ivan had worked in past Russian elections, and so became the office manager, with Vladimir as his assistant. They set about furnishing the place with tables, desks, chairs, and other basic office supplies.

Toby knew they needed to bring in the professionals if they wanted to run a worldwide campaign that would even be noticed enough to be laughed at. Fortunately, he had a decade's worth of contacts. The most famous ones were taken, but they couldn't afford them anyway—and they weren't always the best. Toby knew who the really good ones were, and some were available.

After conferring with Bruce, Toby was about to start contacting the various job applicants when he was smacked in the side of the head by a ping-pong ball.

"Are you forgetting who's the campaign director around here?" Bruce asked. "You've got to let me do my job."

"Old habits are hard to break," Toby said. Having nothing better to do, and with permission from Bruce, he instead set about doing the necessary TC work to make the Moderate Party official, and to declare his candidacy for president of Earth, with Feodora as candidate for vice president.

Incoming Message from Lara Platt.

Toby stiffened at the visual and voice alert from his TC. What did she want?

It was a text-only message. Good, he thought, the last thing he wanted to do was talk to the director of their main opponent. Even if it was his daughter.

"Open message," he said.

Dad, heard what you are doing. Are you trying to embarrass both of us or is this a midlife crisis? You can still come back and co-run campaign. Tell Bruce to get lost.

The bright red letters floated in space, dancing about as the background moved when Toby turned his head and fiddled with his scarf.

He decided not to reply.

After five minutes he stopped shaking and went back to work. But he couldn't get her out of his mind.

Soon the office would be buzzing with activity and dozens of workers, but for now it was just the four of them working late into the night. Toby could already taste the thrill of a new campaign, a glorious battle where, if things went well, he'd make up for the horrible mistake he'd made five years before, and show his daughter who was embarrassing whom. He knew there wasn't any real chance of winning against the sleek Dubois machine or even the rickety Ajala one, but he could always dream. That was the only way to keep fighting in the down-days of a campaign, where little ever went as planned, and the unexpected was expected.

After thirty-four years working on political campaigns, nothing could surprise him.

Until Twenty-two walked through the front door.

Toby looked up at the startled grunts from Ivan and Vladimir. The alien stood in the open doorway, silhouetted by streetlights. Then the door closed and Twenty-two silently shuffled in.

Toby had earlier seen the awkward-looking way the alien walked, where both legs on one side moved forward, and then the two on the other side. He'd looked it up on his TC and found that on Earth, only camels, giraffes, and cats walked that way.

Twenty-two still wore the yellow vest, and now had a matching yellow cloth over her mouth. Her eyestalks looked about independent of each other for a moment, then fixed on Toby as she approached him.

"Are you Toby Platt, who is running for president of Earth?"

"Yes, I am. And may I welcome you to our headquarters."

Twenty-two's eyestalks glanced at each other for a second, then focused back on Toby. "Are you asking a question? You may welcome me to your headquarters."

Bruce stepped forward. "Welcome to the headquarters for the Moderate Party and the next president of Earth. I'm Bruce Sims, director and founder. Our campaign headquarters is your campaign headquarters."

Founder? Toby thought. Shouldn't that be co-founder? Okay, he'd let Bruce have that glory.

Twenty-two looked about, each eyestalk taking in one side of the room. Ivan and Vladimir were frozen against the wall, seemingly braced for action as an eyestalk locked on them for a moment.

"I have learned about Earth's liberal politics from Ajala," Twenty-two said. "I would like to learn more about the process. Ajala said he knew the human who knew more about it than anyone else in the world. He sent me to talk to you, Toby Platt."

Ajala sent her to see him? After Ajala nearly threw him out of his office, that was a surprise. "I would be honored. How did you get here?"

"Ajala had me brought here on a floater. He made sure nobody saw me. Only you two, the driver of the floater, and Ajala know I am here. He did not want the press to know."

"Hopefully you shot the driver," Bruce said. There was a moment of stunned silence.

"No, I did not shoot the driver," Twenty-two said, her eyestalks stiff as they both stared at Bruce. "Should I have?" One of the eyestalks curved and peaked back at Toby.

"He's joking," Toby said. "You'll have to get used to that. Bruce, you might want to tone it down before you instigate an intergalactic incident. Why don't we talk over there, where there are chairs?" He pointed to the front corner.

Toby and Bruce sat down but Twenty-two stood nearby. Toby suddenly realized that the idea of chairs and sitting must be as foreign to the alien as it would be to a turtle.

"What would you like to know?" Bruce said.

"I would like to know about political parties and your two-party system," the alien said. "I do not understand the concept. If there are ten issues, there are 1024 possible permutations. You would need 1024 political parties to handle all the possibilities. Every time a new issue arises the number of political parties would need to double. How does your system handle this with two parties?"

"First off," Bruce said, "put aside any thought that the system is logical. As long as you have that idea, nothing will make sense. Also put aside any thought that the system is designed for enlightened, out-for-the-common-good beings. It's for selfish human bastards."

Twenty-two's eyestalks were absolutely rigid, staring at Bruce as if in utter disbelief, like a cartoon character whose eyes shoot out of his head when he sees something he can't believe. If it was disbelief—hard to tell with an alien creature—Toby wasn't sure if it was because of what Bruce was saying or because he was saying it.

"We're not all selfish human bastards," Toby said. It was a long, ongoing argument between the two.

"Enough to make it effectively true," Bruce said. He pulled a ping-pong ball from his pocket and began fiddling with it. "Now that we've established that our system is irrational and made for self-centered beings that need to be protected from themselves, we can move on to the specifics."

"Why do you change from 'selfish' to 'self-centered'?" Twenty-two asked.

"Huh?" Bruce halted his ball-fiddling.

"You called humans selfish," the alien said. "Then you called them self-centered. I believe you meant the same thing, yet you used different words. Why?"

"That's how humans talk," Toby said. "We find it more interesting to use different words." He noticed that Twenty-two's English skills had improved dramatically.

Twenty-two now focused an eyestalk on Toby, with the other still on Bruce. Toby found this disconcerting. "Even if you mean the same thing?"

"Unfortunately, yes."

"It's the way we talk, chat, gossip, chatter, gab, yak, and natter," said Bruce.

Twenty-two continued staring for a moment, one eyestalk on each, then focused both eyestalks back on Bruce. "Tell me more about the two-party system."

Bruce went back to fiddling with the ball. "It's not really a two-party system, it just works out that way. Humans, in their infinite wisdom—that's sarcasm, in case you don't recognize it—find it more effective in a democratic system to team up together to get things done. For example, those who favor universal free food team up with those who favor abortion rights, thereby increasing their voting power."

"Why don't the ones who favor universal free food team up with those who are against abortion rights?"

"Because they don't."

"That makes no sense."

"And here I thought aliens would be logical!" Bruce said, laughing.

"I am logical."

"Then why are you applying logic when I already told you the system makes no sense?" Bruce said, still laughing. "*That* is not logical!"

The alien stared at him. "What are you doing?"

"It's called laughter," Toby said. "Get used to it—Bruce laughs at a lot of things others don't find funny. You'll also find his opinion of our political system and humanity in general to be somewhat negative, and by somewhat negative, I mean extremely negative."

"Does 'somewhat negative' mean the same as 'extremely negative'? Or is that just another illogical use of the language?"

"One more illogical use of the language for our friendly neighborhood alien!" Bruce said. "But Toby is way too charitable when he said I'm extremely negative toward our political system and humanity."

"What Bruce means is 'yes,'" Toby said. "In the context, which was sarcastic, they meant the same, even though 'somewhat' and 'extremely' normally have different meanings."

"Are you starting to understand the part about not using logic in trying to understand us?" Bruce asked.

"I'm beginning to understand the sarcasm," the alien said. "We have the same thing. But I still do not understand your political system. Why would humans who believe in something team up with others who have a completely separate belief? How do they choose which side of the second issue to team up with? Would not some go with one side, others with another?"

"Nope," Bruce said. "There is mutual self-interest, where one changes his opinion on some issues, or at least pretends to, so he can get others to change, or pretend to change, their opinions on other issues."

"That's wrong!" Twenty-two began rocking side to side. "Why would you have a system that encourages unethical actions? It makes no logical sense!"

"Ah, genuine logical outrage," Bruce said. "It's like a salty sea breeze. Reminds me of Ajala debating Dubois at a UN council meeting. But no, there is no logical sense to it."

"Bruce is just trying to confuse you," Toby said. "It makes sense if you figure certain types of people tend to believe the same type of things. For example, those who are for universal food tend to also be for abortion rights—both are liberal positions."

"Why?" Twenty-two asked.

"If Toby can answer that," Bruce said, "then I'll retire from politics and ping-pong a happy man."

Toby hesitated, then sighed. "Bruce is right, and I spoke too soon. The two issues aren't really related."

Twenty-two took a few steps back. Her eyestalks gave each other a quick glance. Then, with a very human sigh, she stepped back. "Do humans just change their opinions to match what the party tells them to believe?"

"Yes, though few admit it," Bruce said.

"No, though they are accused of it," Toby said.

"You're just saying that to defend humankind's honor," Bruce said. "Ironic you'd lie to defend our honor."

"True," Toby admitted.

Twenty-two stared for a moment. "This whole party concept is faulty. Right and wrong in each issue should be all that counts, not what your party believes. Should not each individual decide things rationally, rather than by what their party says?"

"Of course they should," Bruce said. "But that's logical."

Twenty-two began rocking side to side again. Toby considered jumping in, but realized he didn't have anything to add that Bruce wouldn't jump all over.

"Think of it this way," Bruce continued. "Suppose you want a 'yes' vote on Issue A. You don't care about Issue B. Someone else wants a 'yes' vote on Issue B, but doesn't care about Issue A. You have a better chance of getting Issue A passed by agreeing to vote 'yes' on Issue B, thereby getting the other person to vote 'yes' on Issue A, thereby getting *two* votes for Issue A."

"That is dishonest!"

"Ain't politics great?"

Twenty-two stared at Bruce for a moment. "In your system, two dishonest people who team up together will have more political power than two honest people who do what they believe is right."

"Very good," Bruce said. "You have now graduated from first grade in the wonderful world of Earth politics. But you have a long way to go before you'll spread your wings, my poor caterpillar."

Twenty-two stared at him. "What does a human do if he believes in 'A,' but is against 'B'? And he believes both are important?"

"Usually he changes his opinion on one," Bruce said, "and convinces himself that he did so without any influence from the people and political party that he belongs to, even as his opinions change to match them. And we're really good at convincing ourselves. Of anything."

The stunned silence of a grod was just as deafening as the human kind.

"Do these humans who change their opinions to match their party listen to logic if it contradicts their opinion?"

"Rarely, once these opinions are formed," Bruce said. "Humans have an enormous capacity for strong opinions with little basis in fact. They latch onto any arcane fact or rumor that in any tenuous way justifies their opinions as ammunition that their opinions are valid. And so the ignorance spreads, like a cancer, except in this case there's no cure. And you want to know why there's no cure?"

"Let me guess," Toby said. "Because the masses are chimpanzees?"

"Exactly!" Bruce exclaimed.

"Not everyone is as jaded as Bruce," Toby said.

"The non-jaded ones on the two sides of any issue usually cancel each other out," Bruce said. "So it's us jaded people who make all the decisions, not idealists like you."

"Not always," Toby said. "Only a cynic like you would say that."

"Only an idealist like you would believe otherwise," Bruce retorted.

"We also have political parties in our system," Twenty-two said, cutting off another of their ongoing disputes, "but they are always one-issue and only last as long as the issue is under consideration. A grod may be in many of these parties, each devoted to a different issue. When there is an election, each grod judges on their own which candidates best represents their vision. Since there is usually an office for every major issue, we simply vote for the one we agree with on that issue."

"Sounds like an idealistic system that couldn't possibly work for us," Bruce said. "Now it's my turn to ask some questions. You called yourself fifty-five billion-and-something, and Twenty-two for short. How does your naming system work?"

Twenty-two was silent for a moment. "Long ago, grods were illogical like humans, though in different ways. Then came One. He took control, and forced civilization on us. We owe everything to him."

"I get it," Bruce said. "He became 'One,' and every grod born since has been numbered sequentially, right? And you're number what?"

"You are correct. I am 55,257,461,522. We are informal about our names and usually go by the last two digits."

Makes more sense than our naming system, Toby thought. This seemed a good time to grill the alien about her culture. "I've been wondering about that thing you wear over your mouth."

Both Twenty-two's eyes shot over toward Toby, and the alien rocked back and forth for a moment. "It is my velvo. I had a red one and a blue one; Ajala had this yellow one made for me to match my vest."

"Why do you wear it?" Bruce asked.

Twenty-two's eyestalks looked to the floor. "Civilized grods do not show their . . . mouths in public. It would be embarrassing."

"Sooooo," began Bruce, "to you, this is disgusting?" He stuck his tongue out.

Now the alien's eyestalks stared pointedly at Bruce as she rocked back and forth violently. "Yes. To me that is disgusting. You have no inhibitions about this. Very . . . interesting. May we discuss something different?" She looked back toward Toby. "Ajala said you ran the election campaign of President Dubois. He is a conservative. So you are a conservative also, correct?"

Toby fell back in his chair as Bruce began to laugh. How was he to explain this one?

"No," Bruce said after he'd recovered, "Toby is a liberal trying to be a moderate."

"Am I understanding this properly? This does not make sense," Twenty-two said. "If he is a liberal, why did he run a campaign for a conservative?"

"I think he's been asking himself the same question for five years," Bruce said. "Did I tell you our politics makes no sense? In this case, while Toby's a liberal, or moderate depending on whether his heart or head are talking, Dubois is a conservative who claimed to be a moderate. So they worked together even though they didn't agree on anything."

Toby's hands clenched into fists, but he said nothing.

"This is how your politics works?"

"No," Bruce said. "This is how our politics doesn't work as it bumbles along without causing too many catastrophes. You have to give our system credit that if we vote someone in who causes a catastrophe, we usually vote him out. Eventually."

"You actually give the system credit for anything?" Toby asked.

"It's great at replacing leaders who do stupid things with leaders who will do other stupid things." He began tossing the ping-pong ball from hand to hand.

"It only takes one catastrophe to end a race," Twenty-two said as she followed the ball with her eyestalks. "One of the advantages of joining the Galactic Union is the nuclear web. No race can survive long without it."

"End a race? The nuclear web?" Toby asked, all other thoughts forgotten.

"When a race advances to a level where an individual can cause massive destruction, it is only a matter of time before it happens. The nuclear web is a way to track all nuclear or similar reactions on a planet. Unauthorized usage is caught very early. You will not need this until you are more advanced and develop nuclear weapons."

"We already have," Bruce said. "We're good at such things. We've even blown up a few countries."

"That is not possible," the alien said. "How could a race have nuclear bombs *before* going into space? You do not have to understand nuclear physics to go into space. That is simple rocketry. Your race is only now colonizing your own solar system; you are only barely into space."

"Sorry," Bruce said, "we're precocious."

After another stunned silence, Twenty-two continued. "Normally a race moves into space long before developing nuclear weapons. It is then admitted into the Galactic Union, which sets up the nuclear web. This gives the race time to mature so it understands the foolishness of weaponizing space in a way that can destroy its own world. If you already have nuclear weapons, then I am surprised you still exist. Few races have progressed into space with nuclear weapons. They always destroy themselves."

Now it was the humans' turn for stunned silence.

"Tell me about Earth's military capabilities," Twenty-two asked.

"Sorry, that's not something we can really go into," Toby said.

"Smart," the alien said. "I asked Ajala the same question. He told me all he knew. He believes that grods are far too advanced, and so hiding Earth's military level would be pointless. He is too trusting. Your President Dubois keeps trying to arrest or shoot me. He is too aggressive. Is this another difference between liberals and conservatives?"

"Sometimes," Toby said. "Conservatives tend to be too aggressive, liberals too trusting and willing to talk."

"While us moderates are in between, just right," Bruce said. "The problem with both sides is they're loyal to their party's issues instead of what's right. Moderates try to do what's right for the situation, which is usually somewhere in between. Or we just find the dead center between the two extremes and hope like crazy it's right."

"If Toby is a liberal," Twenty-two asked, "why is he now running for president as a moderate?"

"Do you find that confusing?" Bruce asked.

"Yes."

"Good," Bruce said. "Now you understand."

It was confusing for Toby as well. If he was still a liberal as Bruce claimed, why was he running as a moderate? Or was Bruce wrong, and he was a moderate, as he so desperately wished to be? Just what was he? He wasn't sure anymore. As Ajala had said, they were all just meaningless labels, and yet, as a political person, he was forced to choose. Conservative, moderate, liberal, just what was he? Not conservative, he'd learned that the hard way. There was the whole liberal spectrum to choose from: social liberals, economic liberals, pragmatic liberals, neo-liberals, even conservative liberals. There were just as many or more types of conservatives, and yet where was the spectrum for moderates? Or were they just defined as those between liberals and conservatives?

But hadn't Twenty-two just shown how faulty this thinking was? Was he changing his thinking to match a party's thinking? Was he trying to be a leader by following?

"Do you have reading material about your politics you can recommend?" Twenty-two asked.

"Lots of it," Bruce said. "You can't learn anything that way. Anything you read will make sense, and will have little to do with reality."

"That's not quite true," Toby said.

"Is not the purpose of written materials to put down reality in words?" Twenty-two asked.

"In all cases but entertainment and politics," Bruce said. "Which are really the same. Are you starting to understand?"

"I am starting to see that there is little rational about your political system."

"See?" Bruce said. "You learned that without reading anything. But I can still send you stuff to read. Do you have a thought computer?"

"No I do not. What is that?"

"It's a computer system that's on a chip in our brains, that communicates directly to our brains."

"You put devices in your brain?"

"I take it you do not," Toby said. "Another social difference, like the covered mouths?"

"Yes," Twenty-two said. "It is distasteful to us. Only one with brain damage should need a mechanical device in their brain."

"Skip the reading stuff," Bruce said. "Travel with us, and we'll teach you."

"I will travel with you, with Ajala, and with Dubois, if he allows it."

Bruce turned to Toby. "Can you imagine all the publicity we're going to get? The world's only alien, traveling with us!"

"No," Twenty-two said. "I do not wish to interfere. When I travel with any of the campaigns, it has to be mostly in secret."

"Why?"

"I am just an ambassador learning about your politics. I do not wish to interfere or affect it myself."

"That's fine," Toby said, drowning out Bruce's groan.

"I have another question," Twenty-two said. "How were you, Ajala, and Dubois educated?"

"What do you mean?" Toby asked.

"To become leaders," the alien said. "How many years did you study? What schools? How do you prepare your candidates for office?"

"I think you're about to start shaking again," Bruce said.

"Why?"

"Because we don't do any of that. Our leaders prepare for office by running for office."

Twenty-two stared at him with both eyestalks. "Perhaps you didn't understand my question. How are your leaders educated *before* they run for office?"

"It's not required. Any training would just confuse most of them, and any serious thinking about the issues would handicap them as politicians."

"You do not train your leaders?"

Once again Toby found himself unable to defend the human system of government.

Bruce was laughing and shaking his head. "I can't believe all the time I've spent on campaigns without an inquisitive alien on board. We may lose badly, but it's going to be a hell of a ride."

It was going to be educational for the alien, Toby thought, but even more educational for us. He was already embarrassed, and they'd barely scratched the surface about Earth politics. Our system is what we've made of it, and we're stuck with it. *For now.*

Chapter Eighteen
Extremism in the Pursuit of Moderation Is No Vice

Tuesday, August 17, 2100

The polls for decided voters in Oceania weren't good. But what did Toby expect from countries halfway around the world from the U.S.? He was well known among political types, but to the masses, he was just a name they vaguely remembered hearing somewhere. They'd hoped to start out in the 5-10% range, and weren't even close at 2% or less. The only good news was that about ten percent were undecided.

Oceania	Population (millions)	Electoral Votes	Current Polls Dubois	Ajala	Platt
Australia	37.1	4	46%	42%	2%
N. Guinea	19.2	2	45%	44%	2%
N. Zeal.	7.0	1	61%	31%	1%
Total	63.3	7			

His thoughts were interrupted by an incoming call from Tyler. He smiled as *"Hi Dad!"* was rapidly followed by a single, never-ending sentence where Tyler communicated that school started next week, he was trying out for the table tennis team, could Bruce give him some tips, he was thinking of running for ninth grade class vice president, he liked barbecue cola, and mom had increased his allowance to $150 a week, which he still considered a pittance.

"Don't forget to breathe," Toby squeezed in when the image of Tyler on his TC paused for a second. Toby was fairly certain that most teenage boys did not talk to their dads this freely. Tyler wasn't always that way; sometimes he'd fall into deep funks and not talk to anyone. Of course, Toby thought, that's the norm for teenagers.

Tyler was a bit of a math geek, as well as a non-athletic athlete wannabe. He was big for his age, but clumsy-big. His carrot-red hair matched Olivia's, his mom and Toby's wife. It contrasted sharply with his sister Lara's, whose nearly black hair matched her mother's, Lindy, Toby's first wife. Toby's own thinning reddish brown hair was in the middle, though more on the red side like Lindy.

"Where are you now?" Tyler asked.

"Have you been following the election? Where do you think?"

"In Australia, with Dubois and Ajala?"

"That's where the action is. We'll be landing soon in Canberra, the capital. The Oceania election is next Tuesday."

"Are you going to win?"

"Of course," Toby lied. "Latest polls give us one hundred percent support."

"You used that joke last time," Tyler said. "It's the latest poll from those on your campaign floater, right?"

"I'll have to keep a joke log from now on. Did you hear the one about the one-legged rooster—"

"You told me all your one-legged rooster jokes at Christmas. Is Bruce going to be around any time? I hope he can coach me before the table tennis tryouts."

"If the trials are after November 2, I'll personally fly him out." By then, they'd both be looking for new jobs anyway.

Tyler's face made it clear that was too late. "Tryouts are in October."

"Tell you what," Toby said. "Bruce can't be there to coach you, but did you say you're running for class vice president?"

"Yeah, Jamaal's running for president, and asked me to run with him."

"How'd you like to have Bruce as your personal campaign director? And I'll help—"

"Bruce, running our campaign?" Tyler jumped out of his chair. "Jamaal'll never believe this!"

Toby started to point out that he'd like to help, too, but then stopped. Maybe this was one of those things parents should stay out of. Tyler had worshipped Bruce since they'd met during the previous Dubois Campaign, and he watched all of his tournament matches on TC.

"Hey, Bruce," Toby said after finishing with Tyler, "I've got another campaign for you to run. There's an important local race in Montgomery County, Maryland. I'd like you to run it."

"What?" Now Bruce jumped out of his chair. "I'm doing fifteen things at once here, and I'll have another fifteen after that! Please tell me you didn't just promise me to some hick!"

"I'm afraid I did. Germantown Middle School, kid named Tyler, running for vice president."

"You'll just have to tell him—middle school? Tyler's running?"

"Yep. And—"

"When did you corrupt him?"

"It's been a fourteen-year process. He's also trying out for the table tennis team."

"Perfect!" Bruce said. "Politics is like table tennis. You're deceptive, you go for the kill, and you always put a spin on things. I can't wait to teach him."

"Try not to turn him into you," Toby said.

"I'll get right on it," Bruce said.

It had been a busy few weeks since starting their campaign. Bruce had been a sarcastic whirlwind of motion, hiring staff and recruiting leaders for campaign centers all over the world. Once he had a hierarchy in place, much of the work was done by surrogates, leaving Bruce to work with just Toby and a small staff, where they focused on strategy.

All this cost money. The Roosters and Donkeys were established, with a number of sponsors. When worldwide government began fifty years before, the global soft drink wars were in full swing, they'd quickly moved in on the political need for capital and had been the primary sponsors ever since: the Coke Conservatives and the Hanna Liberals. The two major soft drink companies had a stranglehold on the world politics. If you were a conservative, you drank Coke; if you were a liberal, you drank Hancola. It not only gave the companies built-in customers, but kept other soft drink companies from developing a base, though smaller companies like Pepsi still sponsored sporting events.

Once when campaigning in China with Dubois, Toby had met representatives from a small but ambitious local drink company, Janlibo. At the time, he'd been polite, but even though they were willing to pay well to be a sponsor, it was out of the question as it would conflict with the Coke sponsorship of the Roosters. Janlibo specialized in honey-flavored fruit drinks, but was branching out into the cola business with their new Jancola. When Toby contacted them about sponsoring a Moderate campaign, they were enthusiastic, knowing that while the campaign itself was doomed, they'd get lots of publicity and get in on the ground floor if the Moderate Party ever grew.

Now all their campaign buttons had Jancola logos, which consisted of the name Jancola in a fancy cursive font in purple against an orange background. Bruce even had a special warm-up suit made, purple with yellow trim, with Jancola logos and "Platt for President!" on the back.

The Jancola money wasn't a lot compared to what Toby was used to in his worldwide campaigning with Dubois and the Roosters, but it got them the necessities, primarily rental space and staff around the world, travel costs, some advertising, and the rented campaign floater. And of course, the campaign buttons. Technology may have changed, but no one had ever gotten elected to a major office without buttons, it seemed.

The used ten-seat dragonfly floater was Bruce's new toy. He and the desk situated in front were nearly inseparable as it became the acting worldwide headquarters for the Platt Campaign. Bruce installed thick, dark purple carpet, and had the interior painted light purple, the exterior dark purple. It came with a food and drink bar, showers, and a lounge area in front with a conference table. When they needed to travel, Bruce

123

simply told the floater's computer where they wanted to go, and it took them there. Bruce's feline iguana, Stupid, had taken up residence under Bruce's desk. He had free run of the floater.

Bruce christened the campaign floater *Rocinante*, after Don Quixote's horse. He had the name painted in white on the outside, alongside a cartoon picture of a horse's head. Beneath it he added the words, *"Extremism in the pursuit of moderation is no vice."*

"Why *Rocinante*?" Twenty-two asked after the name's origin was explained. Stupid lay on the alien's head, quietly purring. The alien had secretly hitched a ride with them to Australia, leaving her ship behind in Washington D.C. She'd been splitting her time between the Platt and Ajala campaigns, but few knew her whereabouts. The press and the rest of the world had gone "alien crazy" the past few weeks with seemingly non-stop coverage that mostly consisted of them wondering where she was. Though Twenty-two had given a few short comments now and then, she mostly kept out of sight. Sometimes she would fly her ship out into space, and then return at full speed somewhere on Earth, undetectable by human sensors. Usually she'd just stay at Liberal or Moderate Headquarters.

"The novel *Don Quixote*," Toby explained, "is about chasing an impossible dream. And Quixote does so while riding his horse, Rocinante."

Both of Twenty-two's eyestalks focused on Toby, which he recognized meant she was thinking hard about something. Normally the two eyestalks wandered about, taking in different views. "I think I understand what 'impossible dream' means. Do you believe you cannot win this election?"

"Of course we're not going to win this election," Bruce said. "In fact, Toby and I discussed this recently. Do you know the history of third-party challenges?"

"No," Twenty-two said, now focused on Bruce. "They do not win very often?"

"Almost never," Toby said.

"Which makes this campaign an impossible dream," Bruce said. "Even though most people agree with us on the issues."

Twenty-two's eyestalks split, one on Toby and one on Bruce. "If most people agree with you on the issues, will they not vote for you?"

"It's the curse of the third-party challenge," Bruce said. "Even if a majority of voters agree with you, they think you can't win, so they support someone else rather than waste their vote."

"But why—"

"You are doing it again," Bruce said. "Bringing logic to a political discussion. Toby's a bad influence on you."

Twenty-two was silent for a moment. Stupid began to squirm about on her head, but she ignored him. "Why are you running a campaign you cannot win? This is not bringing logic to a political campaign. This is bringing logic to you."

"And I appreciate your logic," Bruce said. "Sometimes you have to try, and dream, even if you can't win. Read *Don Quixote*."

"I do not understand why you can't win," Twenty-two said. Stupid's tail now hung in front, between her eyestalks. "I do not understand why you would run a campaign you say you cannot win. Tomorrow I will have been on Earth for twenty-two days—just like my name—and I still do not understand humans. I believe I understand iguanas better." She raised three of her four arms and gently lowered Stupid to the floor.

"Neither do we," Bruce said. Twenty-two stared at him, and began shaking slightly. "Someday, if you ever figure us out, give us a call."

With the floater's name, and the cartoon horse head picture painted on it, the Moderate Party now had their mascot: the horse. "Who'd you rather hang out with," Bruce pointed out, "a donkey, a rooster, or a horse? *Giddy up!*"

The *Rocinante*'s computer alerted them that they'd be landing in five minutes.

Toby was not impressed with the *Rocinante*. He was used to traveling in huge, luxurious one-hundred seaters, with private offices and an extensive kitchen. Worse, the *Rocinante* had a faint odor of fish that no amount of cleaning ever reduced, and no air freshener could cover up

125

without becoming overpowering itself. Stupid had gone frantic the first time in the floater, searching every inch of it, trying to find the source of the smell. The odor, and the knowledge that people in their floater had been sticking smelly, slimy fish in their mouths, made Toby nauseous. Sometimes he felt he had to hold his breath until they landed. There were countries, or at least communities, outside Australia that still ate fish, especially in the coastal Asian countries.

Equally bad was the food preparation system, which caused a clicking sound that drove him nuts. He began packing sandwiches in advance to avoid it, but when others used it, he just gritted his teeth.

When Toby was with the Dubois Campaign, they always traveled with a large contingent that he referred to as The Circus: various deputy and assistant campaign directors, including Bruce for a time; pollsters; the press secretary; regular secretaries; ground directors—in charge of coordinating volunteers around the world; fundraisers; researchers; scheduling managers; legal advisors; and the always large security detachment. They'd also had a second huge floater for the press.

Bruce kept their traveling staff small to save money, using TCs to consult with the rest of their staff back at The Ranch and in other campaign centers around the world. Besides Bruce and Toby, only three campaign staff traveled with them: Press Secretary Gene Conkling, and two highly-recommended bodyguards from Nicaragua who called themselves Turk and Crowbar.

Those two kept to themselves, rarely speaking to the Toby or the campaign staff, explaining that it was best they not get personally involved with those they guarded. They were large, husky men, with a slight resemblance, as if from the same mold. Even their wide faces looked similar. The dark sunglasses they always wore on duty seemed a part of their uniform, perhaps so nobody could see where they were looking.

Toby considered Gene to be excellent at his job, but his addiction to hi-cal sweets made him stand out in the crowd. There was a time, Toby had read, when weight problems were common. However, with the advent of no-cal food and the spread of vegetarianism, there were few people around left with this problem, though President Dubois and General Duffy came to mind. Bruce didn't want Gene representing the campaign in public, and often antagonized him by calling him over to discuss "weighty matters." Gene could be a non-stop talking whirlwind on his TC as he worked the major press services all day long. He'd kept Toby booked on numerous talk shows over the past few weeks.

Bruce had brought in several excellent speechwriters. When a speech was needed, Bruce would make a few notes, TC it to The Ranch, and a short time later they'd receive the speech. Sometimes it only needed a few tweaks; sometimes Bruce would slave over it for hours.

Gene was looking off into space, probably examining a document on his TC. "Tomorrow morning, you're on *Good Morning New Zealand*. Then I've got you on three Australian shows, and then we fly out to New Guinea for a rally, with three other rallies in Australia the next day."

"Nothing tonight?" Toby asked.

"You've got the Commencement Dinner," Gene said.

Toby groaned. Every five years the governor of Australia hosted this as the official start of the election season. The candidates were expected to join together and pretend to be friendly partners for the upcoming election. It was a time for smiling and faked graciousness, for friendly humor and proper decorum. In other words, a sham.

"What's on the menu?" he asked.

"Plastated wheat ribs, plus an assortment of appetizers and side dishes. And none of it is no-cal."

"Barbecued?"

"Of course," Gene said. "And quite a dessert bar. Wish I could be there for the avocado pie." He smacked his lips. "It'll be room service for me."

Toby wasn't much for dessert, but anything barbecued had to be good. He wondered if their hosts would also eat the plastated wheat ribs, or go for genuine meat—the thought made him slightly sick. He'd been told that meat tasted almost the same as plastated veggies, though Australian purists got rather animated about that, saying it wasn't the taste, but the texture that wasn't quite right. Someday he was sure the Australians would join the civilized world, but not yet.

A few minutes later Toby watched out a window as the *Rocinante* landed outside their hotel in Canberra. Their campaign was organized and ready to go, and everything was carefully planned out.

But elections never go according to plan.

Chapter Nineteen
Melissa and the Assassin

His name was Marty Reese. *Corporal* Marty Reese, United States Army. He'd watched all three speeches. Right after their arrival in Canberra. First Dubois, who touted the wonderful things he'd done. Then Ajala, who touted the terrible things Dubois had done. And finally Platt, who touted the terrible things both had done. Or something like that. Dubois and Ajala arrived in huge floaters. Platt in a little one.

Reese was certain nobody in the crowd knew of him. Sure, they noticed him. It was hard not to. But after a baleful stare, they would go back to the blithering things people in crowds watching politicians do. Unless someone were to ask them later, "Did you see a man with a missing right arm wearing a fading old-style blue American uniform?" they would never remember him.

Even the army didn't know his real background in the Special Forces. The corporal rank had been a cover for his real work. But an operation during the U.S. occupation of Mexico went bad. His team was killed. He'd lost his arm. They gave him a prosthetic, but returning to active duty was out of the question, against policy. One moment he was an up-and-coming star covert operative. The next he was a handicapped bum. Wandering the streets on a tiny army pension. Even his sometimes-girlfriend in Houston dropped him.

The army had supplied him with an obsolete, low-end prosthetic right arm. It itched and hurt. It never worked well anyway. He could clumsily grab things with it, but that was about all. He'd been right-handed. He learned to do everything with his left arm. He'd finally tossed the fake arm into his storage locker. If he had worn it, its clunky metal parts would set off alarms at security checkpoints everywhere. They'd have confiscated it and held him while it was searched. Probably laugh at the archaic thing. The last thing he wanted was for security to notice him.

He was clumsy, inept, unshaven, and unwashed. When he didn't wear his ragged uniform, he wore worn-out clothes he'd stolen from a charity store. The lowliest people in the streets laughed at him behind his back. He was sure.

How he hated this world. Everybody on it.

He'd killed his supervisors from the Special Forces and Army. He'd decapitated the sometimes-girlfriend from Houston. It wasn't enough. No one noticed.

Reese watched the crowd when Dubois spoke. He saw their rapt attention and the silly blank looks on their faces. If he killed Dubois, how would he be remembered?

He'd followed Dubois around the world. He'd bummed rides on floaters when he could. He'd stolen money for the ride to Australia. As he watched the president from a distance, assassination plans would pop into his head. But who would care if he killed Dubois? Many thought he made a fine but dishonest president. Who cared if the leader lied if he kept the economy going? And kept riffraff like Reese in line?

Killing Dubois would be killing an unloved bureaucrat. Nobody would care.

Reese wanted a president the people loved. One they trusted and cherished as a member of their own family. One who gave them hope. One who seemed to live in that figurative world all presidents aspire to, Camelot.

Then, when he killed that president, the dreams would be blasted. Tears would flow. He'd be remembered. Oh, yes, they'd remember him.

Everyone remembered who killed Lincoln, Kennedy, and Brown. Nobody remembered who killed Garfield, McKinley, and Willard.

Dubois wasn't the one. He was a Garfield, a McKinley, a Willard.

Ajala was loved by his minions. The opposite of Dubois. He fulfilled all of Reese's requirements but one. He wasn't the president. He was well behind in the worldwide polls. Reese would continue to watch the polls, see if Ajala improved. Maybe all that mattered was the perception that he might be the next president. Then Reese could act. But not before.

The third candidate, Platt, had just finished his speech. Reese was irritated at him. Platt would siphon votes from Ajala. He could give the election to the unloved Dubois. He'd keep his eye on Platt. Perhaps do away with him before he caused too much damage. Dubois and Ajala were surrounded by lots of security. There seemed only a pair of guards watching over Platt. Perhaps Reese could kill him without getting caught. Then he could go after Ajala. When the time was ripe.

Reese stared coldly as Platt waved to the crowd. Even caught his eye for a few seconds. He felt a jolt when Platt nodded at him. He breathed heavily, as he often did when he was excited. He'd felt a connection. Maybe this was one to watch. The one to kill.

As Platt spoke, Reese looked about at the crowd. Crowds liked Ajala and Platt. Maybe there was hope. And if either rose in the polls . . . he looked about again. If only they knew, he thought. But they will. They will.

He was hungry and lonely. He looked for a StarMacs.

Melissa was confused. She'd listened to all three speeches from the candidates as they arrived in Canberra. First Dubois . . . thud. While nobody really liked him, he had a razzle-dazzle way of convincing people he was right. Maybe it was that white hair shooting in all directions and the shaking fist as he made his points. Or maybe it was his well-funded ads that were misleading and full of lies. He was like that irritating, eccentric uncle that you gave up trying to argue. And so he led in the polls. The world was full of ignorant people. She would have to do something about that.

Next up was Ajala. She had a love-hate relationship with the man, who she'd only met a few times while traveling the world as a volunteer

131

on his campaign. She loved what he had to say and his refusal to compromise his principles, but she hated what he had to say and his refusal to compromise his principles because they made him almost unelectable. Great leadership meant becoming a leader. His soaring rhetoric and ideas would have dominated in a past world, but funding trumped words in these days of political war. Of course, the funding only meant some people's words were heard more than others'. So it was a war of words, but people tend to believe the words they hear repeatedly until their opinions set. And then they rarely changed. She would have to do something about that, too.

And then there was the new guy, the wild card, Toby Platt, the man who'd made and then rejected Dubois. She'd hated him for years, but now . . . things had changed. But he was almost too quick to give up his principles to get elected. Did he really believe all the compromise and moderate ideas he spoke about? Were his core principles to find the middle in everything? Either he was spineless or he truly believed in listening to the masses and finding that middle area that best represented them. Listening to the masses? That didn't make for great leadership. If she could ever talk to the man, she would do something about that.

She was hungry and lonely. She saw a StarMacs across the street—there seemed one on every corner these days—and she salivated at the thought of a cofftea, the drink of choice by the political class.

She ordered an orange cofftea and a banana muffin from the friendly StarMacs machine. Like all StarMacs, plastic ivy climbed the walls with the sound of a gurgling creek in the background. As she looked about, a voice said, "Wanna to join me?" The voice came from a man in an old-style American military uniform, with one sleeve empty—he was missing his right arm. Why not?

"Sure." She sat down next to the man. She noticed with distaste that he was eating a hamburger—a real one. Australian meat.

He extended his left arm. "Marty Reese. American soldier and political junky."

She smiled. "Melissa Smith, Antarctica girl and fellow political junky. I'm a volunteer with the Ajala campaign."

"Really! You listen to the speeches?"

"All three."

"I guess we agree that Dubois's a massive migraine."

"Don't get me started."

"I'd love to get you started. Tell me about Ajala."

Five minutes later he said, "*Stop!* I give up! I'll vote for him!"

She smiled. One down, several billion to go.

"Don't you think he's too liberal?" asked Reese.

"Liberal? Conservative? Moderate? Those are just silly labels. I think Ajala tries to do the right thing, and usually I think that's what people label as liberal. Liberals stopped slavery, brought the vote to blacks and women, stopped child labor, created the minimum wage, the 20-hour work week, the five-hour workday, workplace safety regulations, social security, healthcare, and universal TCs. Most conservatives opposed these."

"Maybe liberals do some good things, but need conservatives to put the brakes on sometimes, to promote stability and tradition."

"That's why we have moderates." Melissa smiled.

"I'm scared to ask you what you think of Platt."

"Too quick to compromise," she said. "The opposite of Ajala. But at least he's open about his core values, which are to find compromise, and try to define right by the midpoint between two extremes."

"I find his compromising a breath of fresh air," Reese said. "I'm tired of candidates who stick to their party's platform. Like flies in a web."

That's pretty good, she thought. Even Ajala stuck too close to the party line. It was the easiest way in politics, showing backbone by taking the easy way out. Yet Ajala did show backbone in refusing to compromise when it was politically smart. *Damn him!*

"Sometimes these flies need to get swatted," the man continued. "Put down. Don't you agree?"

"What do you mean by swatted?" Suddenly the man sounded creepy. The missing arm only added to the creepiness. Then she mentally swatted herself for having such a prejudice.

"The tree of liberty must be refreshed from time to time with the blood of patriots and tyrants."

"Jefferson said that about the American Revolution. We're not in a revolution. Just a political campaign."

"Same thing. Another campaign. Another loser gets elected. An endless cycle. Only one way to change it. Someone should die. It'd get the attention of voters. Don't you think?"

She wondered if she should alert security. "No one needs to die."

He laughed. "Apologies. Didn't mean that literally. No one's going to die. Except politically."

She brightened. "Ajala's not going to die politically. Unless he starts listening to his political experts, he's already dead. Platt's still a nobody, and so can only go up. So the only one who can die politically would be Dubois. I hope so!"

"If he died, who would care?"

"His family?"

"Politicians don't have real families. His family is his political party. Even they don't care for him. They just want him to win. Someone else needs to die. Someone loved. Someone that would get everyone's attention."

"That's—"

"I mean metaphorically. Of course." Reese smiled. He reached out and patted her hand.

Melissa had had enough. She looked into the distance and let her eyes go blank, pulling her hand away from his as she did so. Then she said, "Sorry, got a call." She pretended to listen intently to her TC, then looked over at the man. "Sorry, they need me. Gotta go." She practically raced for the exit.

Chapter Twenty
The Banquet Surprise

Tuesday night, August 17, 2100

After Toby finished his speech outside the *Rocinante* shortly after their arrival in Canberra, they sneaked Twenty-two into their hotel suite by stuffing her into a large piece of luggage. The alien didn't mind, even said it was "exciting." The suite had three rooms. Toby got a single, while Bruce and Gene shared one room, Turk and Crowbar the other. Twenty-two seemed happy to take up residence in the large living room area, but Toby pointed out that if anyone walked in on them—housekeeping, enterprising news people—she'd be seen. So she took up residence in Bruce and Gene's room, mostly in their closet. Bruce hooked up a video screen so the alien could watch the commencement dinner.

Bruce wore his fancy purple warm-up suit. Toby put on his gray suit and the worn-out purple scarf. He didn't bother with a bolo tie.

"There's no way I can convince you not to wear that thing?" Bruce asked.

"It's my image and political persona," Toby said. "Everyone knows I wear it. Besides, you're wearing a warm-up suit. If you can do that, I can wear my scarf."

"Someday you're going to tell me the history of that scarf."

Someday indeed, Toby thought. He'd never told anyone. It had become part of his mystique, though he'd never planned it that way. Maybe someday he'd write a memoir, and tell the world about Vinny.

Toby had tried talking Feodora into joining them in Australia, but she declined. "You need small general campaigning in land of Big Bear," she'd said. "You can't win without Russia. Besides, if I were in Australia I might have liking for local food, and soon would be big general and big scandal." She admitted she'd once had a taste of kangaroo meat, at the wedding of an Australian immigrant on her staff, and that it had been quite good. "Took many years to forget wonderful texture in mouth. Now plastated food feels like soggy cotton."

They took the *Rocinante* to the Commencement Dinner, which started at eight in the banquet hall at Parliament House, the capital building of Australia in Canberra. Turk and Crowbar wanted to stay with them, but Toby convinced them to stay in the floater for the duration. Over eight hundred attended the dinner. Seemingly every Australian politician was present, from small-town mayors to Australian Governor David Segretti himself.

Toby knew Segretti from the 2095 Dubois campaign. A practitioner of "gotcha!" politics, he'd been instrumental in defeating Xu, whom he'd skewered in speech after speech for past statements. Oftentimes the statements were taken out of context and misleading, allowing Segretti to play his "gotcha" games. Toby had had several violent arguments with the man five years before, but only in his head; being on the same side, he'd never gotten around to confronting him directly. When the Australian campaign ended, he'd forgotten about it.

This time around, of course, Toby knew that Segretti would be gunning for Ajala. He probably had something nasty planned, but not tonight, not at the Commencement Dinner, his quintennial chance to preside over the president of Earth and candidates for the job, all in front of the Australian people.

Segretti, dressed in elaborate yellow robes clasped at the top with a black bolo tie, sat at the head of the elliptical front table. Corbin Dubois, Rajan Persson, and Lara sat, appropriately, to his right; Carl Ajala and his vice presidential nominee, Emi Katsuko of Japan, to his left, both dressed in various shades of blue. Toby sat across from Sagretti, between Bruce and Lara.

Toby noticed that there were no other Australian leaders at the table, not even the vice governor. Segretti wanted the attention to himself. Press people surrounded the front table, broadcasting everything. Toby reminded himself not to pick at his nose or anything else that might be broadcast to the world.

He sat rigidly next to his daughter in her gorgeous red dress, which matched Dubois's broad red tie and Persson's red vest. They hadn't spoken by TC since Lara's text message, and other than a "Hello, Dad" and "Hello, Lara," hadn't spoken here.

Segretti stood up and raised his hands for silence. Looking into the cameras, he said, "Welcome to the start of our great Democratic process. As it always has and always will, we begin here in Australia."

That'll go over well in New Guinea and New Zealand, Toby thought. They were also part of Oceania's "First in the World" regional election.

"The candidates," Segretti continued, "have been campaigning here since before some of them were born." He paused for laughter, but there were only a few nervous giggles. Leave the humor to the professionals, Toby thought. Or at least have a comedian write your material and work with you on the execution. Some politicians are naturally funny; Dubois had that advantage. Some, like Segretti, were not.

Segretti frowned, started to say something, and then changed his mind. He was obviously reading from his TC, though he'd learned to avoid that vacant look that most get when doing so. "Our informed citizens take their responsibility as the first vetters very seriously. Australia has picked the winning presidential candidate in nine of the ten elections, and we're going for number ten. Who will it be? Let's get our first look."

A Dubois and an Ajala impersonator came out from a side door, and went for the front table. Each stood behind the man they were impersonating while a hundred waiters and waitresses served soup to the guests, the two held a fake debate that covered many of the issues in the election. Much of it was the pseudo-Dubois explaining all the extreme things he wanted to do—cut the tax rate to negative imaginary numbers, outlaw food for non-millionaires, and shoot aliens on sight. Each time the pseudo-Ajala would shake his head and say, "You're way too right," and the pseudo-Dubois thought it was agreement rather than a statement of political philosophy. "We agree I'm right!" he exclaimed, with the pseudo-Ajala again agreeing. They covered a number of political issues, many of them ending with the aggressive pseudo-Dubois bullying the cowering pseudo Ajala, who kept giving in.

It was ironic, Toby thought, in that Ajala was the stubborn one who would never alter his views, while Dubois changed with the political winds. But image is everything in politics. Overall, the routine was only so-so. Of course, he thought, it'd be better if there'd been a pseudo-Toby to liven things up!

Finally the two left, and Segretti stood up again. "And now the main course." Once again waiters and waitresses swarmed the tables, placing a plate of food in front of each guest. A baked potato and fried cabbage sat on each plate.

And a huge slab of barbecued kangaroo ribs.

Chapter Twenty-One
To Eat Or Not To Eat

Toby stared down at the meat in front of him. There was no mistaking it for plastated food. There was a time when most plastated vegetables were made to look like real meat, but over a couple generations that became less important. Food that looked like genuine meat had become gross to much of the world. Toby only recognized it as kangaroo meat from his previous trips to Australia, where he'd seen, but never tasted, it.

Gasps echoed around the room. Many of the guests were Australian, and used to meat, but even they knew that this was not what was on the menu.

The smell quickly overwhelmed Toby, a mix of tantalizing barbecue and sickening dead animal flesh. A mixture from hell, Toby thought, feeling nauseous. People ate this stuff?

So what now?

Toby looked up from his plate. Dubois, Ajala, and the others at the table stared down at their plates. Segretti had a huge grin on his face.

"Eat up, my guests," Segretti said. "Our country is watching." He took a deep breath of the fumes from the chopped animal carcasses, and then smiled at the press people, who moved in closer with their cameras as he cut off a bite, stuck it in his mouth, and began to chew with a slow, exaggerated motion.

Ajala was the first to react. He stood and glared at Segretti as he said, "I want to thank you for making it absolutely clear the difference between the immoral—" He pointed a fork at Segretti. "—and the moral." He jabbed the fork into the hunk of meat and held it up. "I will not eat this. What they did to this animal is wrong. What you have done here is wrong. And whoever eats these dead animals is wrong. When I am president, I will return here with an amendment to the world constitution to make sure this never happens again." He flung the meat onto the floor and sat down.

A woman from a back table began yelling, "*Eat wheat, not meat!*" She was led out of the room by security.

Now Dubois stood up. "When in New York, do as the New Yorkers do; when in Australia, do as the Australians do."

"He just lost Italy," Bruce whispered to Toby.

"Or at least Rome," Toby whispered back.

Dubois cut off a piece of the barbeque kangaroo and put it in his mouth. He took a few chews and swallowed. He grinned for the camera, but it was a frozen smile, the type you do when you are gagging but don't want anyone to know.

Dubois began to choke. His face turned red as he fought to keep the meat down. Toby almost admired his old boss for the way he gamely kept it down. Dubois finally swallowed whatever had come up his throat. There was polite applause.

From around the hall came a chant: "*More! More! More! More!*" Dubois tried not to look back. He sat down, but made no attempt to take another bite.

Segretti stood and seemed about to say something.

"My turn," Toby said, standing up. Segretti nodded and sat down. He'd already accomplished his task of drawing Ajala's views on meat-eating out in public, where Australians could see.

"I was told that we would be served plastated wheat ribs," Toby began. "Barbecued, in fact." That drew some laughs. "Now I could give an impassioned speech on morals like my friend Carl. Or I could just dig in, and learn about the wonders of barbecued kangaroo, like my gallantly choking friend Corbin." There was more laughter.

"I'm going to do neither. I'm not going to tell forty-four million Australians that they are wrong, that they are immoral, that they are murderers. They have to judge that for themselves. Like most of the rest of the world, I do not eat meat, and like Carl, I am not going to eat this. Yet, for most of our history, people *have* eaten meat. Were they wrong? I don't know. What I do know is this. I *think* it is wrong. But I'm not going to force the issue on you. If I am president, and the issue goes to the World Court, I will lobby against it. And I will also return here, like Carl, only I won't have a constitutional amendment to ram down your throat. I will have only my powers of persuasion. The final choice will be yours." He sat down.

"Nice, Dad," Lara whispered to him. "You and Ajala just gave us Australia."

Bruce leaned forward and retorted back, "What makes you think he was talking to Australia?"

"Have they moved Canberra out of Australia?" Lara said. "You think anyone outside of Australia's watching a campaign dinner?" The two continued to go at it. Toby felt like the net at one of Bruce's ping-pong matches.

Segretti rose to his feet. "Gentlemen, I am stunned. You are guests in our land, and yet you insult us and call us immoral. Only one of you has shown us respect, and so only one of you deserves the vote of the Australian people, and that is Corbin Dubois." He sat down.

Ajala rose to his feet. "Since we are talking morals, there are other issues of equal importance." He stared down at Dubois, who rose to his feet. "Mr. President, as you choked on that dead animal, a thousand people around the world starved to death. And yet you have continually blocked passage of Universal Food. Perhaps you can explain this to us?"

"Governor Ajala," Dubois said, "I will gladly support Universal Food when you find the funding for it. When you find the incentive for people to work hard when they get everything for free. What you are trying very hard not to say is that you will raise the taxes on our working people to pay for cake for our non-workers. We already give out free health care. Free TCs and TC connection. Free public floaters in the cities. Twenty-hour work weeks. The system can only withstand so much. You, Mr. Governor, are a socialist. What you are pushing for would lead to the downfall of our economic system." He sat down.

"Economic system?" Ajala said. "What economic system is it that starves its own people? Is this economics, or just an economical way to remove liberals from the voting ranks? I suspect there are not that many starving conservatives. Put aside your politics for a change, and side with the people in need!"

"Don't you think you should get in on this?" Bruce whispered. Nodding, Toby rose to his feet.

"Ah, Mr. Platt," Ajala said, "the man who ran the Dubois campaign, and who also opposes Universal Food. Have you ever felt the pangs of hunger, Mr. Platt?"

Toby almost said "yes," but caught himself. Anything he said would be checked out, and he had never really been among the starving. He'd missed meals, but if he were to claim to have felt the "pangs of hunger" for missing a meal, he'd be mocked for it. Except, of course, he was at about two percent in the polls, and so too small a target for most, except perhaps a few late night comedians.

"No, I've never felt the pangs of hunger," Toby said. "Not in the way you mean it, where I didn't know if there was a next meal coming." He faced the cameras.

"A generation ago, after decades of infighting, universal health care was finally passed, and our status as a civilized world went up a notch. And yet, what is now the most common health problem in the world? In a world where food is cheap, hunger is now the prevalent health problem." He turned toward Ajala.

"No, Mr. Governor, I haven't supported Universal Food, not the version you are pushing. The president is right that if you give everything away for free, there's no incentive to work, and the cost is high." He turned to Dubois. "And the governor is right that we who have never felt these pangs of hunger should not be the ones to withhold it from those who do. Food should be a right, but not a lifetime excuse to drop out of the workforce." He faced the cameras.

"Isn't there room for moderation from our government? Let's compromise. Universal Food for those under age twenty-five and those over seventy. For those in between, a one-time six-month waiver, where they'd work for the government ten hours a week, and undergo job training another ten hours. Carl, Corbin, I hope you will join me in this compromise. Or you can spend the rest of eternity arguing about it and never accomplish anything." He sat down.

Dubois stood up. "Fine words, Mr. Platt. A serious candidate for president needs to choose sides, not go squishy and compromise on principles. Now I seem to recall back in our days together that we had another fundamental difference, and that was about Oceania's 'First in the World' status. As everyone knows, I have always strongly supported this. Australians and the rest of Oceania have done this for fifty years, and I hope will do so another fifty years and beyond. The rest of the world relies on their expertise from doing this election after election, and they have never let us down. Their smaller population allows them to get to know the candidates better than can be done in other regions. Perhaps you'd like to share your views, Mr. Platt?"

Toby knew he'd already lost Australia by not completely and unabashedly supporting meat-eating rights. Of course, Australia had never really been his to blow, considering his standing in the polls. He had little to lose—though he had to keep in mind that New Guinea and New Zealand did not allow meat. But what were his chances there anyway?

"Yes, Mr. President, I fondly remember our disagreements on the issue." Toby also remembered Dubois's reasoning on the subject, which had a lot more to do with votes than relying on Australia's expertise. Toby looked into what looked like the largest press camera. "I am against giving any one region preferential treatment over another. It is unfair, unjust, and wrong. If I am elected president, I will ask the world congress to institute a lottery to establish an initial order, and the order of the regional elections from there on will rotate. I believe the people of Oceania will see the justice in this." He sat down.

Ajala, who hadn't sat down, looked to the cameras. "I just want the Australian, New Guinea, and New Zealand people to know that I support their 'First in the World' status one hundred percent. It has served us well, and I will never turn my back on you for this great service." He sat down again.

Toby was a bit surprised at Ajala. He hadn't known Ajala's stand on that issue, but he'd been sure the ultra-moral Nigerian would take the ultra-moral high road, and support rotating elections. Perhaps it was a first crack in Ajala's moral façade?

Toby rose. *"You get 'em!"* Bruce whispered.

"C'mon, Dad," Lara whispered. "Don't you think you should let the *real* candidates debate?"

"Can you two children both shut up?" Toby whispered back, hoping the cameras wouldn't record it. Though if they did, that was fine. *"Let the grownups talk now."* He faced the cameras.

"Why don't we get to the issue that's on all our minds?" he asked. "The issue of Ambassador Twenty-two. I'd like to hear what my esteemed colleagues have to say on that."

Toby sat down. As if on cue, Dubois and Ajala jumped to their feet.

Bruce snickered. *"It's like Mexican Jumping Beans debating each other,"* he whispered.

Dubois spoke first. "From the start, I've recognized the danger of this . . . invasion. And an invasion it is, even if by only one. She travels where and when she wants, and there's no telling what she is doing. She could be scouting for a large-scale invasion." He turned to Ajala. "Perhaps the aliens will give us free food when we're all living in cages."

"From the start," Ajala retorted, "you antagonized the alien, greeting her with firing guns. Do you really fear this single creature? Who has done us no harm, made no threats, and only wants to study us? You want to shoot her; I want to learn from her."

"How can you learn from her when you don't even know where she is?" Dubois said. "I have access to the greatest military surveillance equipment the world has ever known, and we haven't the faintest idea where this alien spy is. Do you?"

"Well, no," Ajala admitted, and suddenly looked uncomfortable.

"I do," Toby said, rising to his feet. He wondered just how many times he'd have to stand and sit before the night was over. His knees were aching and the kangaroo meat smell sickened him. Now that all three were standing, perhaps they could all just stay that way rather than hopping up and down like kangaroos. Well, the living kind, that was.

"And where would that be?" Dubois asked.

"Twenty-two asked me not to say," Toby said. "I believe you are aware that she has spent much of her time with my campaign and with Ajala's. She'd spend time with you except you'd try to shoot her." There was snickering from the other tables.

"Yes, I would," Dubois said. "Though I'd rather she surrender. She's clearly hostile toward our world, and a potential danger. Do you want humans to go the way of the dinosaurs, the Fin Whale, and the American Indian?"

"No," Toby said, hoping that Dubois had just blown the very-much-alive Native American vote—Dubois would likely be hearing from the Navajos in the morning. "I think we should talk with the ambassador, exchange information, and learn from each other. If we are friendly with her, she'll cooperate, and we won't have to worry about what she's doing or where she is."

"Besides," Ajala said, "what's the point of threatening Twenty-two? With their technology, if they want to conquer us, they are going to conquer. I'd rather be their friend."

"I'd rather we stay free," Dubois said. He looked into the nearest camera. "My friends here are well-meaning but soft. What's needed is a firm hand, the same hand I've lent you these past five years. So I say to the alien: *Get off our planet!*"

With that, the dinner hall burst into shouting. It seemed to Toby that the pro- and anti-alien yelling was about equal. To make himself a less conspicuous target, he sat down.

"You know what the sound bite is going to be tonight?" Lara said to Toby, without meeting his eyes. "Did you see the way Corbin looked into the camera when he told the alien to get off our planet?"

"Do you agree with him?" Toby asked.

"What?" She looked up at Toby as if startled. Toby recognized political-think, that mode of mental thought where all that's real is whether or not it helped politically, and all other thinking is left on the cutting room floor. He wondered if she or Dubois had taken any Eth.

"Never mind," Toby said. "Just remember what I said."

"What?" she repeated.

"About your job," he said, feeling a stab to his heart as he said it. It seemed an eternity since he'd told her he was going to put her out of a job, even if he had to "go to hell and back." He got up again, ignoring the pain in his knees, and walked away from the table before she could respond. Bruce followed.

"Great job!" someone said. It was a girl, perhaps seventeen, with green polyhedral hair in a twisted gun barrel design. He recognized her—the Antarctica girl from Liberal Headquarters in Washington D.C. What was she doing in Australia? She wore a *Vote Against the Status Quo! Vote for Ajala/Katsuko* button, with the two lines forming a circle around a Hancola logo. Toby smiled at the slogan; he remembered Lara laughing when he said you sometimes have to take into account a candidate's name when choosing one, or you get stuck with silly slogans like this one.

"You probably don't remember me—I'm Melissa. I think it's great what you are doing," she said. "I disagree with you on most of the issues, but at least you are trying to get things done by compromising. Good luck!" She turned and was gone as rapidly as she'd appeared.

Toby and Bruce hung around the outskirts of the room for a while, talking to the local politicians and guests who'd been seated at other tables. Finally they made their escape and returned to the hotel.

He wondered what Twenty-two, watching from back at the hotel, would think about all this.

Chapter Twenty-Two
Aftermath of the Dinner Debate Down Under

Late Tuesday night, August 17, 2100

"You're going to get clobbered in Australia," Bruce said. "But boy, you sure might pick up everywhere else!"

"You think anyone else was watching?" Toby asked.

Bruce shook his head. "You're getting old and slow-witted, Mr. Former Great Campaign Director. You think the news programs aren't going to replay what happened tonight over and over and over? The whole world's going to see this!"

"Most of those votes are weeks away," Toby said. "How about New Guinea and New Zealand? They don't eat meat."

"Yeah, but they like to vote first. You'll get a bit less clobbered there, but we've planted a seed for the rest of the world."

"Since I'm from the U.S., and Feodora's from Russia, you think we have a chance in those elections?"

"Nope, you haven't got a chance," Bruce said. "You'll get clobbered, filleted, and skinned alive. But we can pretend. If you'd like, we can put you in a political bubble where we tell you you're gonna win, and you never have to deal with reality. You can be a bubble president, like most of our past ones."

Twenty-two had watched the dinner debate, and proclaimed it confusing and irrational. "Both major candidates believe one part of the world should get to vote first? And how they vote influences later voters,

147

which makes no sense. If that is true, how can anyone think it is fair that the law gives some people more influence?"

Bruce had started to say something but was interrupted. "I know," Twenty-two said. "I am looking for logic in your politics. I will try not to make that mistake again."

The newscasts had proclaimed it the "Dinner Debate Down Under." Clips from it ran non-stop, with Toby surprisingly getting equal treatment with Dubois and Ajala. Over and over they played the three of them and their words on meat-eating, on "First in the World," on Universal Food, and on Twenty-two.

Instant polls gave the debate to Dubois, 36% to Toby's 34%, and Ajala's 30%. With voters tired of the long campaign between Dubois and Ajala, Toby was the fresh face.

More important than who won the debate was how it affected voters.

"I'm getting polling results on TC now," Bruce said. He stood still for a moment, then grabbed a ping-pong ball from his pocket and threw it at Toby. "The chimpanzees have spoken!"

The numbers were encouraging. In Australia, it was now Dubois 61%, Ajala 17%, Platt 18%. He'd edged ahead of the unpopular Ajala! In New Guinea, it was Dubois 37%, Ajala 36%, Platt 20%. In New Zealand, it was Dubois 57%, Ajala 26%, Platt 12%. Worldwide it was Dubois 45%, Ajala 36%, Platt 13%.

Incoming call from Zubkov.

"Accept," Toby said, stepping over to the *Rocinante's* TC camera so Feodora could see him.

"Dahling!" said the image of Feodora. "You did wonderful!"

"It wasn't planned," Toby said. "It was supposed to be just a dinner." He should have known from past experience that a political dinner was never just a dinner.

"I could smell wonderful barbecue kangaroo from Russia. I would have eat the dead animal. Ah, I wish I had been there."

"I thought about eating it."

"But you stick with convictions, and make political speech at same time," she said. "That impress me. Now I know campaign real. You campaign in Oceania and North America, and small general join you in two weeks in Russia. After that, we travel together everywhere. Dahling, we can win!"

They discussed campaign strategy for a few minutes. Feodora was going to be on all the Russian talk shows, so they discussed the various talking points. Then she gave him a pep talk about surviving a Japanese ambush in the Russia-Japan war that somehow involved dogs and camouflage umbrellas, and then they disconnected.

Gene had already booked Toby for several talk shows, but after the dinner debate, all the shows were calling him. Toby spent the next week floating from one to another, criss-crossing Australia, New Guinea, and New Zealand, along with numerous rallies and fund-raising events. Over and over he was grilled by the press on his stance on meat and against Oceania's "First in the World" status. He gave the same answers he'd given at the dinner, and whenever possible, changed the subject to his compromise plan on Universal Food. Twenty-two was the other main topic of conversation. Over and over Toby was shown replays of Dubois's now famous "*Get off our planet!*" statement, to which he would shake his head and speak of the value of joining the galactic community. He'd practiced the head shake and rebuttal with Bruce in their hotel room.

Whenever he was asked about the faded purple scarf, he answered, "I look to the future, but the scarf is my link to the past. Where I go, it goes." When pressed, he'd smile and ask what they'd like to discuss, his scarf or Universal Food?

The local newscasters almost universally praised Toby's compromises, even though they condemned his views on meat eating and "First in the World" status. They asked him why he'd chosen this strategy, knowing how it would come off in Oceania. Had he known it would be replayed worldwide?

"It wasn't a strategy," Toby explained over and over. "I was just tired of all the nonsense." It was one of those rare times where truth and strategy matched. Lara, if she'd been speaking to him, might have even praised the bite-worthiness of his explanation.

Dubois and Ajala also blanketed the region. They'd spent years preparing for this, and there seemed a major rally every night at a major city. The Oceania TC newscasts became a non-stop succession of Dubois, Ajala, Toby, and their many surrogates. Toby almost matched them news show for news show, but was badly outnumbered in the surrogates department. The good news for him was that Dubois and Ajala aimed their fire mostly on each other, sometimes even praising Toby—exactly how Toby would have advised them in dealing with a non-threatening, third-party challenge. Dubois was looking for a landslide win, while Ajala just hoped to keep it somewhat close, because he knew he couldn't win in Oceania.

Long before coming to Australia, Toby and Bruce had put the details of their position on their "Platt for President" hubsite, where anyone could access them with their TC. Now their hubsite was overrun with people viewing their proposals, which were mostly detailed versions of what Toby had said at the dinner. They spent time each day discussing and updating some of the details of what was now the Moderate Party Platform.

Toby was especially proud of his Universal Food Plan, which he, Bruce, and others had spent many hours debating. The left wing of the Liberal Party had been fighting for this for decades, but could never get the votes for their more extreme measures. He and Bruce had spent almost as much time debating the acronym: "Short-Term Universal Free Food" (STUFF), "Free Food Foundation" (Triple F), or "Provisional Universal Food Foundation" (PUFF). Toby wanted the more serious Triple F, but Bruce talked him into PUFF.

Perhaps the world would someday adopt a true Universal Food Plan. However, the world was not economically or politically ready, so it was better to work toward it one step at a time, starting with a compromise plan.

Getting the word out was key to winning an election. Dubois seemed best at this. *Stop the Invasion!* and *Get Off Our Planet!* buttons and signs—with the ever-present Conservative Coke logo—sprouted up all over Australia. Campaign by slogan, thought Toby, just as I taught Lara.

A simple, short message, repeated over and over, will usually win out over a more complex, thoughtful one. When it came to political thinking, there were more simple people than complex ones, though he'd never admit that to Bruce.

The Ajala campaign countered with their own buttons and slogans centered over a Hancola logo. The best were *The Galaxy is Watching* and *Universal Food Now!*

The Platt campaign had their own slogans. Toby's favorite was *The Rat, the Doormat, or Platt!*, which labeled Dubois and Ajala in exactly the terms that, deep down, many people thought of them. Another was the one coined by Bruce, *Extremism in the pursuit of moderation is no vice*, as well as the flipped *Moderation in the pursuit of extremism is no vice*, which brought in some conservatives and liberals who thought their candidate too extreme in their methodology. All buttons and signs included the Jancola logo.

They also bought as much ad time as possible, running two different ads. Bruce had worked with an ad agency in putting them together.

The first was entitled "Moderation." The ad opened with a short clip of Dubois's disastrous first meeting with Twenty-two, ending with gunfire. A voiceover with a man's Australian accent said, "He'd shoot the aliens." Then came a clip of Ajala and Twenty-two walking into Liberal Headquarters, arm in arm. "He'd open the henhouse and let a Trojan wolf in." Next was a clip of starving Australian children. "Dubois lets children starve." Then came a shot of the World Bank with a *Closed—out of money* sign in front. "Ajala would give it away for free and bankrupt us all." The ad then showed a clip of Toby at the dinner debate, standing and talking as others listened attentively, and saying, "Isn't there room for moderation from our government?" The ad finished with Toby standing in front of The Twisted Gun at the United Nations Building, saying, "I'm Toby Platt and I approve this message, and hope you will too, because we can no longer afford to have extremists run our government."

The second ad was entitled "PUFF." It opened with a crying child sitting on the ground in front of an empty bowl. The camera backed up to show a dirty, grungy room of crying children, with an Australian flag on the wall. The ad did a rapid series of clips of children and old men and women, all seemingly starving, with clues in each picture to show the various parts of the world they were taken from—flags, famous buildings in the background, pictures on walls, and so on. Then came a voiceover with a woman's Australian accent, "Our children and elderly are starving as the galactic civilization watches. We can solve this problem, but it will take new leaders with fresh ideas. Toby Platt has an affordable plan to solve world hunger. Give our children and elderly a chance." Again Toby came on, holding a child while standing in a room similar to the Red Room, with the world flag in the background. "I'm Toby Platt, and I approve this message because a billion people went to bed hungry last night. I want everyone to go to bed without dinner on election night, and see what it feels like. On election day, eat a good breakfast, be thankful, and remember those hunger pangs when you vote to solve this problem."

The gimmick seemed to work, as "Election Night Hunger Strike" fever swept Oceania and other parts of the world, with news anchors and politicians across the continent saying they'd go hungry that night. Toby, Bruce, and a grumbling Gene skipped dinner as well. So did Twenty-two, though she pointed out that she only ate once a day anyway, usually in the middle of the day, either from food stored in a pouch on her vest or regular human food—with supplements—so it was no hardship for her.

All the "starving" children and other people in the ads were actors, and much of the ads were put together via computer. Toby never stood in front of *The Twisted Gun* or in a Red Room replica.

Dubois and Ajala had their own ads, but aimed their fire on each other. Dubois slammed Ajala over and over for financial ineptness and being out of touch, and painted Nigeria as a hellhole of a nation under Ajala's leadership. Ajala's ads turned Dubois into an uncaring tyrant, and played the clip of the shooting of the alien over and over to the rousing musical accompaniment of *Ride of the Valkyries*. They outspent the Platt campaign on political ads by about 4-1—though, as Bruce kept reminding them, it was not always how many ads you ran, but how you used them. But Toby knew that in elections, a mind-numbing barrage of ads usually overwhelmed quality.

Gene and Bruce had arranged speeches and media appearances all over Australia, New Zealand and New Guinea. Toby had worried that few would show, despite Bruce's smirking assurances that excitement was building for the campaign. By the end of the week, he'd almost lost his voice as he endlessly recited the same basic messages of the campaign.

After a busy week of campaigning by the three campaigns, the citizens of Oceania voted via TC. The world watched and waited.

Chapter Twenty-Three
The Oceania Whitewash

Tuesday, August 24, 2100

"Y ou are moving small sculptures about a checkered square," Twenty-two said, watching Bruce and Toby. "Is this a game?" So Bruce taught Twenty-two how to play chess on the way back to North America on the *Rocinante* after the Oceania election.

The alien picked it up quickly. Toby watched the two go at it, anxiously awaiting the Oceania results. Politics was like chess, he thought; you move your resources around on a checkered world and hope to make it into the endgame.

He thought he had a chance to win New Guinea and its two electoral votes. If he did, voters worldwide would start to notice him. It was all about image. If you looked like you could win, you often did.

"Why did your world government adopt this political system?" Twenty-two asked between moves.

A question that, in his more contemplative moods, never failed to astound Toby, despite his frequent defense of it against Bruce's criticism. How had it happened? The history was clear, but still. . . .

"Remember how surprised you were about us developing nuclear weapons before we were in space?" Bruce said. "Well, that didn't work out very well."

"It probably led to blackmail," Twenty-two said. "A country with such weapons can threaten a country that does not."

154

Toby and Bruce exchanged glances. "It didn't exactly happen that way," Toby said.

"Did a country without nuclear weapons not give in to blackmail?" Twenty-two asked. "You had a nuclear war?"

"Not exactly," Bruce said. "There were two nuclear wars, and three other places that got nuked."

Twenty-two's eyestalks were about as straight as Toby had ever seen them as she stared at Bruce. "Did they not learn from the first one?"

"Two nukes were dropped on Japan in 1945," Toby said. "One hundred years later, in 2045, the Koreas nuked each other, then India and Pakistan had an exchange. Then the rising terrorist group Al-Nahda—'The Awakening'—smuggled nukes into Israel and pretty much took the whole country out."

"And then someone, probably Al-Nahda—they claimed credit—nuked Seattle," Bruce said. "Sneaked them in, probably hoping to wreck the computer industry. That made us rather unhappy, though we caught the ones they planted in L.A., and D.C., and two of the three planted in New York City. A suitcase nuke brought down the Twin Towers again in June, 2045. It's your move."

Twenty-two wasn't looking at the chess board—she never seemed to except to move. They were well into the endgame, with Bruce up a pawn. "What happened to those countries?"

"Let's see," Bruce said, "Russia and Japan went into Korea to help rebuild, and ended up going to war. China went into Pakistan and the U.S. into India, and pretty much rebuilt them in two years, though they stayed another five years after they were no longer needed or wanted. The U.S. and the rest of the world went after Al-Nahda and other terrorists around the world and pretty much routed them. Israel no longer exists, and the survivors relocated to the U.S. in the deserts outside Salt Lake City in New Israel, which hasn't worked out so well—the Mormons are not happy about it. The U.S. rebuilt the Twin Towers in 2049, after cleaning up the radiation mess. And Seattle, well, their software industry moved to Vancouver in Canada, which led to 3-D full-sensory virtual reality, turning Canada into a growing powerhouse until the U.S. invasion in 2071 and the insurgency. Did you get all of that?"

Twenty-two moved a pawn. "Why did they stay in Pakistan and India?"

"Power," Bruce said. "China and the U.S. felt good about themselves for helping out, but if they pulled out, they'd diminish their own prestige. So they stayed, helping out against the will of the ones they were helping. It took a lot of civil protesting, in China and the U.S. as well as in Pakistan and India—plus a resolution from the World Congress—to convince the occupiers that their job was done and it was time to leave." Bruce moved a pawn. "Check."

"You have checkmate in four moves," Twenty-two said. "I do not understand the motives for staying."

"You learn fast," Bruce said. "You remember everything the first time."

"Of course," Twenty-two said. She began setting the pieces up again.

"As to why they stayed, in the immortal words of Robert Heinlein, you just don't grok."

"Grok?"

"It means you don't really understand," Toby said.

"No, I do not," Twenty-two said. "What did your world government do when the nuclear bombs were going off?"

"There was no world government then," Toby said. "That came about because of the nukings in 2045. It started as a private venture, funded by Wayne Wallace, the inventor of the TC and the world's first trillionaire. He bankrolled candidates that would support world government until nearly every country was run by Wallymen. Then a constitutional convention in 2049, and world government in 2050. With Wallace as the world's first president, of course." Surprisingly, there'd been few complaints about Wallace practically buying the presidency. The biggest protests, Toby remembered reading, came about when the USE ordained that countries that had presidents should have their leaders renamed as governors or some other designation. In the U.S., the president became a governor, while state governors became

156

state executives. There'd been a huge march on Washington by pitchfork-carrying protesters, but eventually the issue died down.

Twenty-two's eyestalks glanced at each other, a sign Toby had learned that she was perplexed. "So humans voted for the richest person instead of the best person? Or was Wallace the best person?"

"Nope, he was the richest," Bruce said. "A person votes once, but money votes many times."

"I do not understand that," Twenty-two said. "Money votes?"

"Of course," Bruce said. "Want to play another game?" Twenty-two had already set the pieces up, and made the first move with the white pieces, the king's pawn to the fourth row. She had grown fond of the king's knight opening, and no doubt would be bringing the knight out on the next move.

"He doesn't mean that literally," Toby said. "Money pays for campaigning which gets the votes."

"Same thing," Bruce said.

"Who started the 2045 nuclear bombings?" Twenty-two asked.

"Terrorists," Toby said.

"Why?"

"Because they are terrorists. They had demands that were not being met." Somehow Toby had the feeling he was talking himself into a corner. Bruce was quietly smiling. "Some of the terrorists were even leaders in their own countries."

"Did they have valid demands?" Twenty-two asked.

"Some were."

"Were their valid demands met?"

"Of course not."

"Why not?"

"Because they were terrorists!" Toby exclaimed.

Once again Twenty-two's eyestalks met.

"You don't deal with terrorists, or you just encourage their methods," Toby continued. "The U.S. led the fight against them, and pretty much wiped them from existence. And that put the U.S. in a strong position at the constitutional convention, which is why our political system was adopted."

"Why was the U.S. political system adopted?" Twenty-two asked.

"I told you, because we wiped out the terrorists."

"Did the U.S. political system wipe out the terrorists?"

"Of course not!"

Twenty-two rocked side to side for a moment. "I am afraid I will never grok. Your species needs a nuclear web or you will destroy yourselves."

"Maybe—" Toby began, but stopped when he noticed Bruce looking off into space. "The Oceania results?"

"Yep," Bruce said. "Nothing for us."

Toby pulled them up on his TC.

Oceania	Electoral Votes	Dubois	Ajala	Platt
Australia	4	**65%**	14%	21%
New Guinea	2	**42%**	39%	19%
New Zealand	1	**56%**	30%	14%
Total	7	7	0	0

He hadn't come close anywhere. He'd lost Australia by 44 points, New Guinea by 23, and New Zealand by 42. Not very promising. On the other hand, he had beaten Ajala in Australia—though Ajala had practically given him that. Considering he'd been at about 2% a week before, the results were not bad.

"Will there be a runoff in New Guinea?" Twenty-two asked after Toby put the results on the screen in front so she could see. The alien was nibbling on a hunk of fake lettuce, a vegetable she had taken a liking for. Stupid scurried over and Twenty-two shared a leaf.

"No," Bruce said. "Dubois already won."

"How can Dubois win in a three-way race without getting half the vote?" Twenty-two asked. "Dubois beat Ajala by three points in New

Guinea. Toby received nineteen points. Do not the voters for Toby get a choice between Dubois and Ajala?"

"I know where you're going," Bruce said. "First, put on your illogic hat, and I'll explain."

Twenty-two stared for a moment, then picked up Stupid and put him on her head. "I have put on my illogic hat. Or should I call it my Stupid hat?"

"Okay, then," Bruce said. "Suppose Toby were a liberal, and he and Ajala split the liberal vote, with the same results shown here."

"Then the conservatives get 42%, the liberals 58%, and so the choice of the liberal side wins easily. The choice should be between Ajala and Platt." Twenty-two was stroking the purring iguana with all four arms. Toby found it disconcerting, but Stupid squirmed with enjoyment.

"And yet," Bruce said, "the winner in New Guinea is Dubois, the conservative who loses in a race against either of the other two."

Twenty-two began rocking front and back, waving her arms. Stupid jumped off her head. "An election is supposed to decide the choice of the voters, not the person they least want!"

"I believe your stupidity hat must not be on firmly enough," Bruce said. "Seriously, you are right. One hundred percent, totally, absolutely, unarguably right. But not in human politics."

"So in a race that Ajala should win over Dubois, he loses because someone else with similar views entered the race?" Twenty-two looked like she was about to have a fit.

"Welcome to chimpanzeeland," Bruce said.

"It makes no sense!"

"No it does not," Bruce said. "Do you expect logic from a chimpanzee? In some smaller races, like for city mayor, they do have runoffs if nobody gets fifty percent of the vote, but not in a major race like for president of the planet. That's too important to trust to logic. We may try to recruit a fourth-party conservative challenger to siphon votes away from Dubois. Maybe a fifth-party liberal one to take some from Ajala, just in case."

"Have humans considered dropping this electoral system?" Twenty-two asked. "Going directly by percentage, with runoffs? Not just for three-way races. In your electoral system, it makes no sense to even campaign in countries that will not support you, and so you never get the chance to try to convince them. And if you know a country will support you, you reward them by not going there at all."

"A few people have argued to go to a straight worldwide percentage vote, but there's no real move to change the system," Bruce said. "That'd be too logical. So we only campaign in battleground countries."

Twenty-two stared down at the chessboard. "How can a race that creates such a logical game as chess invent such a political system?"

"Because we're a bunch of simple primates," Bruce said, picking up Stupid. "Another game?"

Once again Twenty-two took Bruce into the end game before losing. Bruce was a very good player, and yet he had to struggle against an alien who had learned the game just a few hours before.

"Play again?" Bruce asked.

"No," the alien said. "I need to practice."

Bruce glanced over at Toby, shrugging his shoulders. "Okay, how do you want to practice?"

Twenty-two stood motionlessly, her eyestalks resting on the top of her head. "I am practicing."

"How?"

"In my head."

Chapter Twenty-Four
A Martyr in Vancouver

Late Tuesday Night, August 24, 2100

T he North American polls were not good. Toby brooded as he looked them over. About 7-10% in each country were undecided, not nearly enough leeway for him to catch up. Getting undecideds was much easier than trying to sway the decided.

North America	Population (millions)	Electoral Votes	Current Polls Dubois	Ajala	Platt
USA	624.6	62	41%	33%	19%
Canada	56.7	6	36%	44%	11%
Mexico	196.5	20	40%	42%	8%
Total	877.8	88			

Even in the United States, his home country, Dubois had him better than two to one. In all three countries, he looked like a kernel of corn between a pair of potatoes. It was going to be a long trek. Destroying windmills would be far easier.

He'd set up a nationwide political network when he'd run Governor Baxter's campaign for U.S. governor. He'd hoped to take advantage of it, but Baxter was a Rooster, and they were not too happy with him anymore. The very people he'd put in positions of power back then were now avoiding his calls, including Baxter.

161

As they flew over the Pacific and approached the west coast of North America, Toby received another text message from Lara. The bright red letters again floated in front of his eyes.

Dad, you did great last week. Without you splitting the vote, we might not have won New Guinea. But we can win on our own. You beat Ajala in Australia, so you can drop out without embarrassment. You've seen the North American polls, you are going to get killed. Come back to Dubois campaign?

He decided to ignore it again, but couldn't seem to put it out of his mind. Why was it so difficult? Why was Lara so difficult?

They landed in Vancouver, Canada, and checked into their hotel. Turk and Crowbar left for the nearest bar. Toby met in his room with Bruce and Gene to review the week's plans.

"You're on several news shows tomorrow," Gene said. "There's a rally in Vancouver Square in the afternoon, then we spend Thursday in Mexico. First thing tomorrow morning, though, is the meeting with Dr. Heilig at Vancouver Hospital."

"You can't get the Canadian vote without her," Bruce said. "Treat her like a Goddess."

"I know," Toby said. "But if we seem too close to her, that could hurt us in the U.S."

In the 2050s, Dr. Mary Heilig had pioneered 3-D full-sensory virtual reality, Full VR for short. She'd surrounded herself with many of the best surviving programmers from the destroyed Seattle, moving them 140 miles north to Vancouver, and created an empire with Virtchy Corporation.

Even the TCs of the 2050s had some capacity for virtual reality, but Dr. Heilig took it to another level. Each year Virtchy came out with a new version until, by the end of the 2060s, Full VR was indistinguishable from reality. It revolutionized the world. No longer did you have to deal with reality. Full VR allowed people to step into their dreams, as real as reality itself.

"*Live the Dream!*" became their rallying cry, and millions, and then billions joined.

Users had their choice of creating their own reality—where anything they could imagine was possible—or enter the rapidly developing Virtchy World. The world of Virtchy, indistinguishable from reality, was "perfect." It was a beautiful utopia without accidents, disease or hunger, a world where nothing went wrong. Anything one desired appeared as needed; trash and other wastes disappeared as they were created.

Of course, many used it for more tawdry purposes. As Bruce once pointed out, the masses can turn any invention into a sex toy.

At first, most people created their own worlds. However, as advanced as Full VR was, it couldn't create realistic people. They looked like people, but if you spent enough time alone in a world populated by virtual people, it became obvious they were not real, more like bad actors in a B-movie. More and more people gravitated toward Virtchy World, where they could associate with real people in virtual mode. It was a perfect world.

Too perfect.

As Virtchy Corporation grew in size and power, the Canadian economy piggybacked and grew until Canada became an economic powerhouse, behind only the U.S. and China. Dr. Heilig became the world's second trillionaire.

To retire to Virtchy World, all one needed were the minimal fees the Virtchy Corporation required for food and a Full VR hookup, which included automatic food intake and waste removal. Food costs were minimal since all the body required was nourishment, no extras, and Virtchy Corporation supplied a simple and inexpensive mix of fats, protein, carbohydrates and vitamins. Two billion living human bodies— with a half million joining every day—soon spent their lives on a bed at a branch of Virtchy Corporation, hooked to machines, while their minds lived out their lives in Virtchy World.

And then came the Lethargia in 2069. The world's economy collapsed as too many people had left the real world workforce to live in the dreamland of Virtchy World. While Virtchy Corporation's stockholders prospered, the rest of the world sank into a worldwide recession.

In an emergency meeting late in 2069, in order to stop the Lethargia, the world government outlawed Full VR. Overnight, Canadian fortunes were lost. Two billion users returned to the real world, many of them broke and ill-equipped physically and mentally to operate outside Virtchy World. With huge unemployment and inflation, the world entered a second Great Depression that would last ten years.

Full VR had been the backbone of the Canadian economy. With no other source of income anywhere near that, and with the depression destroying what little was left of their economy, the Canadian government defied the world government and continued to allow the sale of Full VR on the worldwide black market.

Late in 2071, after Canada ignored repeated demands to stop, the United States invaded with overwhelming force. Within months they destroyed the Canadian armed forces, occupied the major cities, and controlled all major government functions. The Canadian underground fought back. Dr. Heilig became a national hero and a spokesperson for the insurgency. And then she was captured by U.S. forces. She spent the next fifteen years in prison, with subsequent returns afterward for her ongoing protests.

The occupation continued to this day. So did the insurgency.

Turk and Crowbar both complained of headaches the morning following their arrival in Canada. Toby decided he'd have to talk to them later about late-night drinking at bars that illegally served alcohol. However, it didn't seem to affect their efficiency.

Gene stayed behind at the hotel to work out some last-minute logistics about upcoming appearances. Toby, Bruce, and the two bodyguards took the *Rocinante* to Vancouver Hospital to meet with the aging Dr. Heilig. She'd been released just a few weeks before from her latest prison stay, for humanitarian reasons. One hundred years old and slowly dying from a multitude of ailments, former trillionaire Dr. Heilig lived in the hospice wing of the hospital.

From the pained looks on their faces, Turk and Crowbar still suffered from their headaches, but they did so quietly. They entered Heilig's room first, to do the standard security sweep.

"You realize," Bruce said, as he and Toby stood outside the doorway, "that the best security measure against a possible assassin hiding in a hospital room in the hopes that their target might happen to walk in, is to stay dead last in the presidential race so nobody cares enough to try to kill you?" Bruce took a deep breath after the long sentence.

"Then we've done a great job on security so far," Toby said.

"Now remember, no matter what she says, nod and smile, but do not, absolutely do not touch the issue of Full VR with a ten-foot set of crutches. People still remember the Lethargia, and it's a touchy issue."

"Not with a ten-foot set of crutches. Got it."

Bruce glanced inside the room for a moment. "Don't see any killers in there, unless Dr. Heilig's going to jump out of bed and thrash you with a stomach tube."

The silent bodyguards finished their security sweep and motioned for them to come in. An overpowering scent of rose petals assaulted Toby's nose as he entered, indicating that Dr. Heilig's sense of smell must be nearly gone. She smiled as they approached her bed, showing yellowed, crooked teeth that hadn't seen a dentist in decades. Various tubes and wires connected her to beeping machines surrounding her bed. A mountain of blankets covered her, with only her head sticking out, like an emaciated tortoise. Her face was nearly hidden in a forest of wrinkles; for some reason, she'd never had her skin tightened. She was nearly bald, with only a few strands left of willowy, white hair. A somber musical tune played in the background, though the sound was marred by the clicking from one of the machines hooked up to Heilig. On the wall over her bed was a large, scenic picture of an old-style ship at sea, its crew hanging onto rigging as they fought off a storm.

"I've been expecting you, Mr. Platt," she said in a surprisingly strong voice. "Are you here to negotiate U.S. surrender terms?" She stared at him, unblinking, her piercing brown eyes leaving him slightly uncomfortable.

"Not exactly," he said. He turned, indicating Bruce. "This is—"

"Bruce Sims, political maverick and world-renowned smart aleck," she finished for him. "Your underling may wait outside."

Bruce started to say something, but changed his mind. "Call me if you need me." He stepped outside.

"Call me if you need me?" she said. "Are you one of those politicians who can't turn on his TC without an aide holding your cranium?" She continued to stare unblinking. He met her dark eyes for a moment, then looked down.

"He's—"

"We can skip the formalities. You want my endorsement. Why should I give it to you?"

Getting her endorsement would have been huge, but that was not why they were here. Not paying their respects to the Canadian sage would have been political suicide in Canada. Toby was certain she'd endorse Ajala, and then his eight-point lead over Dubois would soar. Dubois probably wouldn't even show up in Canada to battle for its six electoral votes; Mexico's 20 and the U.S.'s 62 were far more enticing. It was Dubois's non-presence that they hoped to exploit, if they could only find a way to defeat Ajala. If they finished second, ahead of Dubois, they might be able to make something of that.

"Dr. Heilig," Toby said, "if you check my record, you know I've been against the occupation as much as you are."

"And yet you ran the campaign for President Dubois, who is completely for it." She clicked her tongue three times in disapproval.

"For that, I apologize," he said. "There needs to be a compromise." Did the woman ever blink? Was it a medical condition or sheer force of character? He took a breath and met her stare.

"Why would I want to talk with you about compromising," she said, "when Governor Ajala wants a unilateral withdrawal of U.S. troops, as well as reinstatement of Full VR as a matter of human rights? Do you agree with him?"

Toby decided to try the personal approach. "May I call you Mary?"

"You may not."

So much for that. "Dr. Heilig, if Ajala were elected president, do you think the U.S. or the world congress would go along with his unilateral withdrawal or his Full VR plans?"

"I'm old, not stupid."

"So you know Ajala can't deliver?" Finally she blinked, and it was as if a weight came off his shoulders.

A bright smile crossed her face. "He'll go to the congress with his plan, and stick to it like a bullcat with a bone. When all others are yelling and screaming at him, he'll keep his cool because he won't understand the situation until he and the shredded bill are thrown out of the Twin Towers."

Toby smiled back. "Then you know a vote for Ajala is pointless. Besides, what are his chances of winning?"

"Better than yours. He was here earlier, and also asked for my endorsement."

"Did you give it to him?"

"What good would that do?"

Toby wasn't sure how to answer that. He was trying and failing miserably to ignore the overwhelming rose petal smell, which had given him a headache. It must have done wonders for Turk and Crowbar with their hangovers.

"Let's review the possibilities," she said. "Ajala wins, and he fights for us and loses, and everything stays the same. Dubois wins, and everything stays the same. Or, in an infinite number of universes, this just happens to be the one where, incredible as it may seem, you actually win. Then you go to congress, and look out over a sea of hostile faces, because they are all members of the Liberal or Conservative Party, and you are neither, and are, in fact, the one who first abandoned the liberals, and then abandoned the conservatives. What do you do then, bake them cookies and hope that'll win their vote?"

Toby wished Bruce were here. He'd love this type of political back and forth. On the other hand, he'd probably so anger her that she *would* try to beat him with a stomach tube. No, this called for logic and diplomacy.

167

"If I were in that position, I would go straight to the people," he said. "Congress may not follow me, but they'll follow the people. They are leaders, and that's what leaders do."

"Nicely put," she said. "And what would your solution be, if not unilateral withdrawal?"

"What do you suggest?"

She was back to her unblinking stare. Dubois would have stared right back, and probably could have matched her, nonblink for nonblink. He was no Dubois.

"I'm glad you asked," she said. She worked her way through the blankets toward the back of the bed, where she sat up, exposing more tubes coming out of her arms and upper body. "Full VR caused unforeseen problems to the world's economy, and sapped the life-energy out of many. It was their choice, and their choice alone. But the world didn't like the consequences, and so outlawed it. There was no thinking about this, it was a knee-jerk reaction to get the problem out of the way. And when we defended the rights of those who relied on Full VR, the U.S. invaded."

She held up one of her tubes. "For many, Full VR was a savior from a lifetime of this." She dropped the tube and waved her hands at the surrounding machinery. "The old and infirm, and the disabled. We helped them live out their lives in paradise, but now they cannot. The world has condemned them to suffering."

She lowered her eyes, to Toby's relief, and reached under her blankets, as if looking for something. Whatever it was, she seemed to find it, then looked up again. "Since the major candidates will not help, and you have no chance, the best way you can help is as a martyr for our cause."

"A martyr?"

"To Canadians, I am a martyr twice over, first for my years in prison for their cause, and now as a prisoner of my body. I am a hundred years old and kept alive by tubes and machines. When you look at me, what do you see?"

Where was she going with this? "I see Dr. Heilig, a Canadian hero."

"Exactly!" she said. "A Canadian hero, but not a world hero. The world does not mourn for old revolutionaries, even when they are sick and dying, and do not care that I could live out my life in Full VR, no longer a prisoner of age and sickness. Another is needed, one who is well known, and yet cut short in the prime of life, with no hope for salvation until the ban on Full VR is withdrawn. Someone like you."

Where was she going with this? She was starting to sound creepy; a chill ran down Toby's spine. He glanced back at the door, wondering if he should call for someone, or just leave.

When he looked back, she was aiming a pen stunner at him. "I don't need to beat you with a stomach tube for this, and I'm afraid your ten-foot crutches aren't going to help you. I suggest you sit down, Mr. Platt, so you don't smack your head on the floor." She motioned at a chair by her bed. He sat. "Your life as you knew it is now over. Millions of people like myself are condemned by our leaders to lives of disability. You will live as we live, and suffer as we suffer. Welcome to our world."

The stunner flashed, and Toby lost consciousness.

Chapter Twenty-Five
Paralyzed

Toby awoke in bed. He stared at the ceiling for a moment, still
half asleep, then tried to sit up.

He couldn't.

He tried lifting his arms, but they too would not move. As the haze of
sleep dissipated, he became aware of what was happening—or not
happening—and began to panic. On top of everything else, he had a
massive headache.

What was wrong with him?

He tried to take a deep breath to calm himself, but couldn't. Unable
to move his head, he shifted his eyes downward, which aggravated his
headache. He could see and feel the tube coming out of his mouth. The
tube went off into a machine on the side of his bed, whose clicking he
now noticed and knew was going to drive him nuts. Artificial
respiration. Shifting his eyes painfully to all sides, he recognized much of
the surrounding machinery as similar to the ones Dr. Heilig had been
attached to. His purple scarf hung over a chair by the side of the bed.
There were other wires and tubes attached to him, but he couldn't see
them clearly without moving his head. On the wall across from him
there was a large picture of an ancient three-mast whaling ship at sea in
turbulent waters, with men in mid-air as they dived off, abandoning the
ship.

Was he in a hospital? It smelled like a hospital, with the antiseptic
scent. Had he been in an accident?

Starting with his toes, he worked his way upward, doing an inventory of what worked and what did not. He quickly realized that he could neither move nor feel anything from his neck down. Above the neck he could feel all too well as his head continued to pound.

Something else seemed to be missing. "TC on," he said with difficulty because of the tube in his mouth. But his TC, for the first time since it had been implanted in him when he was a child, wasn't operating. He was cut off from the world and its information banks.

"Anyone here?" he called out in a whispery voice, all he could manage.

A woman appeared and leaned over him. "You're awake, Mr. Platt?" She was tall and thin, and built like a model. Long blond hair fell over her shoulders and simple white uniform. Her nametag said "Dr. Artaud."

"Where am I, and what's happened to me?" he asked.

Dr. Artaud gave him a seemingly genuine smile. "You are at Vancouver Hospital. You've been unconscious for three days. Do you remember anything from your meeting with Dr. Heilig?"

Memories sluggishly flooded into his brain. "I remember talking to her, and then she flashed a pen stunner at me. That's the last I remember."

"Your bodyguards didn't do a good job checking the room. Dr. Heilig had the stunner hidden in her bed—it should have registered with their equipment. I'm afraid she gave you a full blast, and it's caused extensive spinal damage."

He let that sink in for a moment. But there was something more urgent. "Could you give me something for my headache?"

"I'll put it in your drip." She must mean one of the tubes coming out of the machines on the side and disappearing toward his body, out of his limited field of vision.

A moment later he felt the pounding dissipate, and he could think straight again.

"I need to run a few tests," she said. "Can you feel this?"

"Feel what?"

They went through this several times, but Toby could only assume she was jabbing him with something. He couldn't feel anything. She clicked her tongue in disapproval.

"How bad is it, doctor?"

"Don't worry about that right now, Mr. Platt. The best thing for you now is rest."

For a moment, he considered disappearing into sleep. His head still hurt and he felt woozy. And yet he had a deep-felt urgency, as if there was something he was supposed to be doing. Something important, but he couldn't quite place it.

The election. That's what it was. Shouldn't he be out campaigning? The regional election for . . . North America? Wasn't it a few days away? He had a small chance in Canada, but every moment counted. Where was Bruce?

"I should be out campaigning," he said. "Why can't I get up?"

"Mr. Platt, I'm going to tell you your prognosis. And then you have to promise you'll rest." She leaned over him.

"Mr. Platt, the stunner was set beyond the safety limits, and she gave you a good five seconds or so before anyone stopped her. You were lucky your bodyguards were watching from the door and saw what was happening or you might have died. You've suffered extensive damage to your spinal column. You're paralyzed from the neck down, and will never walk, move your arms, or breathe on your own again."

Chapter Twenty-Six
The End of a Political Career

The masses will not vote for a man in a wheelchair, Toby thought, which is why, a hundred and seventy years ago, Franklin Roosevelt kept his disability a secret. The press was accommodating in those days—and could afford to be when there wasn't a TC in every brain—but no longer. There was no way he could hide his paralysis.

His political career was through. It was as simple as that.

He remembered Dr. Heilig's last words to him before firing the stunner. "Your life as you knew it is now over." He wanted to lash out at her, put his hands on her throat, but he couldn't even roll over. "You will live as we live," she'd said, "and suffer as we suffer. Welcome to our world."

Because of the attack, and despite her age and infirmities, Heilig would be back in prison, though Toby doubted if she would be in the general population. No, not Dr. Heilig, Canadian hero. She was probably in some luxury cell with full TC privileges. Of course, she was nearly as incapacitated as Toby, but she could at least sit up and move around some.

He stared at the sailing ship in the picture on the wall, watching the men in mid-air as they leaped into the stormy waters. Like the members of his campaign when they learned what had happened to him.

"Toby!" It was Bruce.

"About time you showed up." It hurt his eyes trying to follow Bruce as he walked over from the door.

"They didn't exaggerate about you," Bruce said. "You've got more things coming out of you than an octopus." He began pacing back and forth, tossing the ever-present ping-pong ball back and forth between his hands.

"I know that pacing, ball-tossing thing of yours," Toby said. A stab of pain forced him to look up and stare vacantly at the ceiling. "You're planning strategy. As if I'm going to walk out of here and run for president."

Bruce laughed. "Okay, you aren't going to *run* for president, but you can still *wheel* for it."

"Even Twenty-two could tell you that makes no grammatical sense." Mentally, Toby was shaking his head; he could even feel the non-working muscles working. "It's over."

Bruce leaned over Toby. "Franklin Roosevelt did it." His eyes were bloodshot; Toby had an idea of what he'd been doing, or not doing, the last few days.

"Roosevelt hid it from the voters. I don't think you can do that these days."

"Then run as a cripple. You'll get the cripple vote, the victims vote, the anti-crime vote, the bleeding heart vote, and Canada."

"And how about the average mainstream voter? You think they're going to vote for a guy to lead the world who can't even move his head? What are you going to do, get a hospital bed with wheels and wheel me from campaign spot to campaign spot? Have a designated hand shaker for me? And a designated head mover so I can look at the people who come up to shake my designated hand shaker? Oh, and let's not talk about what happens when I need to go to the bathroom." He wanted to shake the tubes sprouting out of him, but all he could do was blink a few times.

"So you're quitting?"

"No, I'm getting out with grace. As much grace as I can while lying on my back like a disembodied head. And yet . . . it's all I know."

The two were silent for a time, something that was rare when Bruce was in the room. Bruce went back to pacing. Toby could only hear it as he stared at the ceiling. He only heard the sound of Bruce breaking the ping-pong ball in his hand. Toby thought about his family, his son and wife in Maryland, and as bad as he felt now, managed to feel worse for not thinking about them sooner. Had they been contacted yet? Did they know what had happened to him or was Bruce keeping a lid on it?

"There is something else," Bruce said.

"There always is when you're around."

"I've spoken to Dr. Heilig. She says they can put you into full-sensory virtual reality. It'll seem as if you were never injured."

"So you want me to be a criminal as well as a cripple?"

"We can use the Full VR images from the system to campaign direct to TC. Nobody will be able to tell the difference."

"Not until Dubois sends the army in to arrest me for illegal use of Full VR. You'll be my accomplice. We can go to jail together, and run for prison president."

"Maybe you should consider Full VR," Bruce said. "It might not be good for the average person, but for the old and infirm, and the disabled, it might not be a bad idea."

"You're starting to sound like Dr. Heilig. Didn't you tell me not to touch this issue with a ten-foot set of crutches? And now I've got this nasty case of conflict of interest."

Bruce began to laugh.

"What's so funny?"

"Your gallows humor. I'm supposed to be the sarcastic one, and you the straight man."

"I like gallows humor. It's liberating."

"I meant that metaphorically. It's not really gallows humor, you're not going to die."

"Oh? Check back with me in fifty years. I'll just lie here and wait.

"You're supposed to be the straight man to *my* sarcasm and jokes!"

"I guess I'm lying down on the job." Toby started to laugh, but it quickly turned into a coughing fit.

"You okay?" Bruce asked as the coughs began to subside.

"I'm perfect," Toby said. "In fact, forget everything I said. Let's run and win."

"Are you serious?"

"Why not? Can I win?"

"Not a chance. But we never had a chance. I thought you knew that."

"No chance? Not even with Full VR, the cripple and bleeding heart vote, and the greatest campaign director in the world?"

"No chance, not even with me. But we can still run and have fun."

"Run and have fun? I want to win!"

"Forget winning. Have you considered becoming a champion of the old and infirm, and the disabled, and argue the case for bringing back full-sensory virtual reality for those who really need it?"

Once again there was silence. Then Toby broke it.

"Get out of here, and don't ever come back." A moment later Toby listened as his friend walked slowly to the door, even heard the smack of a ping-pong ball in his hand—had he gotten a new one out after smashing the previous one? Then he was gone.

They started Toby on rehabilitation. At first he'd approached those sessions with some enthusiasm. However, his enthusiasm dimmed when he realized that all these sessions entailed was for a nameless physical therapist—who seemed no more than a muscular teenager with a lopsided grin on his face—to call out a body part for Toby to try to move. The sessions were futile.

"You said I'll never regain movement from the neck down, right?" he asked Dr. Artaud.

"Right," she said.

"Then what's the point of the rehab sessions?"

"It's better than not trying at all." She quickly left the room.

The next time the therapist came in, Toby told him to get lost.

The stun blast had destroyed both his TC and the brain tissues it connected to. Dr. Artaud explained to him that someday he might be fitted with another TC, but his brain would have to learn to use it. "It'll be like learning a new language," she said.

Toby was horrible on foreign languages. He began to groan, but like the laughter before, it ended in a coughing fit.

"Are you okay, Mr. Platt?"

"Of course I'm not okay!" he cried when the coughs subsided. "Just go away!" He was surprised at his own anger. They could beat Dubois. There had to be a way.

Wayne Wallace won re-election in 2055 despite losing a leg to a would-be assassin. Would they consider a man who couldn't move his arms or legs? What's important in a president is what's above the neck, not below. Were humans so superficial they couldn't see past his disability? He had to make them see.

He stared at his faded purple scarf, still hanging accusingly over the chair by his bed. He thought back to the days of Vinny, when politics was fun and simple.

The world was stuck in this cycle of left and right, like a pendulum that shot back and forth, only stopping at the extremes. Left, with President Xu. Right, with President Dubois. Ajala wanted it to swing left again; Dubois wanted to keep it right a little longer. Only one person had an opportunity to break the cycle, to bring the presidency to the middle, and change Earth politics forever. Only one person. He had a responsibility.

Paralyzed or not, the campaign must go on. He had to talk to Bruce.

"I need an external TC," he repeated for at least the tenth time. Dr. Artaud had brought him one, but it wasn't working.

"I'll try to get another for you," she said.

"I can't run for president from a hospital bed without a TC," he said.

"I really don't think you should be running for president at all, in your condition," she pointed out. She had a nasty habit of clicking her tongue when she disapproved of something, and it was irritating.

"If Bruce were here, he'd have a portable TC for me inside an hour," he said. "Can you get a message to him?"

"You need to rest, Mr. Platt." She left.

He considered his options, but there really weren't any. He was a prisoner until he got a TC or Bruce returned. And he'd told Bruce to never come back.

He stared at the scarf for hours. His eyes hurt from the strain.

Over the next few days, Dr. Artaud brought several portable TCs, but none worked for him. They finally concluded that his brain damage caused this. He'd never use a TC again.

Several long weeks passed. Bruce did not visit.

"Bruce is never coming back."

Startled, Toby pulled his eyes away from the scarf to see Dr. Heilig standing on the other side of the bed, a grim smile on her face. "What are you doing here?"

"I'm here to save you," she said.

"Save me?" he exclaimed, though his voice was still whispery. "You put me here!"

"That I did."

"Shouldn't you be in prison?" he asked. "How'd you get here?"

"I have connections."

"I'm calling the nurse."

"Please don't, at least until you hear me out. I disconnected your call button anyway."

She seemed in much better shape than before, when she'd been the one lying in bed, with tubes and wires coming out of her body. Prison had somehow been good for her.

"What do you want?" he asked.

"Do you remember the last thing I told you before I stunned you?"

"How could I forget?" he said, irritated. "You said my life as I knew it was over. It was."

"No. After that, the very last thing I said. I said, 'Welcome to our world.' Do you remember?"

Why was she parsing what she'd said? How could that be of any possible importance? It was time to call security, get her back where she belonged. She had a way with security—first Turk and Crowbar, and now she'd escaped from a prison cell. They'd probably put her in maximum security this time.

"Now you know what it's like to be old and infirm, and disabled," she continued. "It was at a terrible cost for you, but it had to be done. Now you can see what our government took away from us."

"What do you mean?"

She held up the pen stunner she'd used before.

He started to yell as loudly as he could whisper, but she put her hand over his mouth. "I'm not going to hurt you again. I'm going to free you."

Toby stopped trying to yell, and she removed her hand.

"You can spend the rest of your life lying in bed, a cripple relying on others to take care of you, with all the pain and boredom from that. Or you can become a criminal, and enter Full VR, and be free."

She aimed the stunner at him. He cringed, but there was nothing he could do as it flashed.

It hurt his eyes, but otherwise nothing seemed to happen.

"Now get up," she ordered.

"Huh?"

"*I said get up!*" She slapped him on his chest. He felt it!

He rolled out of bed and stood up. "This is virtual reality?"

"To be specific, 3-D full-sensory virtual reality. Full VR."

Toby stretched his arms and legs for the first time in weeks. He'd lost track of time. "So none of this is real?"

"Not in the least," she said. "You are still lying in bed, paralyzed. Would you rather live in that world? Or this one?"

It felt so real. He examined his hands, and then the room, as Dr. Heilig watched. It was hard to believe, and yet here it was.

Which reality should he choose?

"Have you had enough?" she asked.

"No," he said. "It's not real, but a life lying in bed—that's not real either."

"Do you see what the government has done?" she said. "There are hundreds of millions of people on this world who are in the same situation you and I are in. Under our laws, they are made to suffer. Change the law, and they can live out their lives without pain or disability, and in perfect health."

"There should be an exception to the law," Toby said.

"You may get my endorsement yet." She patted him on the head lightly. "Oh, I don't think you've had a chance to consider all the implications yet of Full VR yet. Here's one." As he watched, Dr. Heilig morphed into Dr. Artaud.

"So you can be anyone you want in Full VR?"

"Yes," Dr. Heilig/Artaud said. "You can be anyone." She morphed into Bruce, then Dubois, then Ajala, and then back into Dr. Heilig. "Pretty neat?"

She held up the stunner. "This isn't real, not here in virtual reality, but it's a handy way to control things. I'm returning you back to reality."

"Not yet—" But he was too late. He was back in the hospital bed, but with his eyes closed. He opened them.

"He's awake!" Bruce's voice said. Toby turned his head, and there was Bruce, sitting in the chair that previously had held his scarf.

He had turned his head—but that was impossible, now that he was back to reality. He was paralyzed for life, so he must still be in Full VR. What type of game was Dr. Heilig playing?

He sat up. "You're not real, are you?"

Bruce stared at him as if he were a rotting pile of meat. "If I listed all the things I thought you might say when you came out of that coma, that wouldn't make the top ten thousand."

"A coma?"

"You've been in a coma for three days, from a stunner Dr. Heilig had hidden."

Only three days? He was sure it had been weeks. But this Bruce couldn't be real anyway. Or could he?

There was a way to check. "Remember when we decided to create PUFF, the Provisional Universal Food Foundation? What were the other two options we considered?"

"Okay, that wouldn't be in my top fifty thousand list of things you'd say. Have you been dreaming in your coma? The doctor said it was possible, but—"

"You're evading the question, so you must not be real." No matter how real Full VR might seem, the computer that ran it would have no way of knowing what they'd discussed in private.

"You wanted to call it Triple F, for Free Food Foundation," he said. "We also considered STUFF, for Short-Term Universal Free Food."

He stared at Bruce, stunned. This was reality. But he was paralyzed for life, and yet he was moving about. It wasn't possible!

"Where's Dr. Heilig?"

"She was taken to prison right after she stunned you, three days ago," Bruce said. "Why?"

He ignored Bruce as he thought furiously. There was only one solution to the puzzle. An unbelievable one.

"We need to see Dr. Heilig."

Chapter Twenty-Seven
Help From Prison

Saturday, August 28, 2100

"So you figured it out," Dr. Heilig said. She was dressed in prison grays, and lay shackled on a prison hospital bed. The doctor verified that she hadn't left the bed in the three days since she'd attacked Toby. All prisoners in hospital beds are shackled by law, he'd explained, but they were pointless in her case. He assured Toby that even if she broke free of her shackles, she couldn't walk on her own, that she'd be dead in minutes if she were not connected to the various machines that surrounded her bed.

"It was Full VR the whole time," he said.

"Of course," she said. "One of my confederates stunned your bodyguards when they were drunk." She clicked her tongue in disapproval. "You should talk to them about their drinking, a nasty habit. When they searched my room, they were under VR via their TCs, and so we were able to hide the stunner. A TC's not designed for VR, and its capability is limited and produces monstrous headaches."

"And so did I," Toby said.

"I didn't stun you," she said. "My Full VR connector was disguised as a stunner disguised as a pen. It is a working stunner—it had to be, to fool anyone—I just didn't use it that way. They thought you were in a coma all this time from my stunning you, when you were in Full VR. The two are indistinguishable, unless you suspect Full VR and look for it. You were in Full VR both when you were disabled and when I came to you and tricked you into thinking I had taken you out of it. I played myself, Dr. Artaud, the physical therapist, and Bruce, using a connector from right here in my prison cell, though they've since found it and taken it away. I studied Bruce's mannerisms in advance—what did you think of my performance?" She paused, smiling when Toby didn't answer. "With Full VR, you were able to experience what it's like to be disabled, and what it's like for a disabled person to live in Full VR. I hope I've given you a lot to think about."

"You have," Toby said. "And that was a pretty good Bruce you did. But we've lost three days on the campaign trail."

"Which is better than losing the weeks you lived in Full VR," she said. "We speeded things up for you with some time perception changes."

"It still only gives us four days to campaign, including election day."

"How many electoral votes did you win in Oceania?" she asked, a grin crossing her face.

"Zero."

"Canada has six. You have my endorsement."

With Dr. Heilig's public endorsement—made from prison—Toby shot up in the Canadian polls. New numbers put Toby tied with Ajala for the lead at 33%, with Dubois at 30%. His rise had come mostly at the expense of Ajala, who had been leading at 44% before, and from undecided voters.

He'd also moved up some in USA and Mexican polls. In USA, new polls had Dubois at 40%, Ajala 29%, and Platt 23%. Ajala still led in Mexico with 41%, with Dubois at 37%, and Platt at 13%.

"Provisional Full VR" became part of Toby's stump speech and ads. Bruce didn't like using the word "provisional," since they already had a "Provisional Universal Food Foundation," and because he thought the word showed indecisiveness, but Toby liked it. It had a moderation feel to it. Under his new plan, Full VR would be legal for those whose lives would otherwise be significantly disadvantaged, with a doctor's signoff.

They would become regular features in hospices and retirement communities, and for the disabled.

Campaign contributions had shot up after the "Dinner Debate Down Under," and with Heilig's endorsement, they went up even more. They could now afford more ads throughout North American and the rest of the world. Meanwhile, Gene had a full schedule throughout the continent for Toby over the next few days, with nearly non-stop news programs, speeches at rallies, and fundraisers.

"You should spend more time unconscious," Bruce said of their rising fortunes.

"You are alive!" Twenty-two had exclaimed when she first saw Toby after his apparent coma. Originally, the alien was going to split her time evenly between Toby and Ajala in North America, but Toby learned that she, along with Bruce, had stayed at his bedside throughout much of his ordeal. She had finally left for a short visit with Ajala, returning immediately when she heard Toby was awake. Toby had had only two arms to defend against the avalanche of four arms and two eyestalks that grabbed and hugged him, to Bruce's merriment.

Soon they were on their way to a fundraiser in Mexico City, to be followed by a rally and a speech, both in commemoration of the tenth anniversary of Mexican Liberation Day. Toby and Bruce sat opposite each other at the table in the *Rocinante*. The alien stood next to them.

Turk and Crowbar sat in the back, red-faced from the rather blunt dressing down Bruce had given them for getting fooled by Dr. Heilig, and about their off-duty drinking, which had left them vulnerable to her plot. But they had decided to retain their services. As Bruce pointed out with a straight face, you'd have to be as smart as he himself was to avoid being outwitted by Heilig, and people that smart don't come along very often.

"What is a fundraiser?" Twenty-two asked.

"Running campaigns is expensive," Toby said. "A fundraiser is where you get much of the money."

"It's where you get a bunch of rich folk together," Bruce said, "look them in the eye, and ask for their money."

Twenty-two had an eyestalk on each of them. "So rich people influence elections with their money? This is where you explain how money votes?" The alien picked up Stupid and put him on her head. "I am afraid I will need my stupid hat."

"Good move," Bruce said.

"Yes, rich people do have more influence," Toby said. "But remember, money doesn't vote. People vote."

"And if you believe that," Bruce said, "I've got a nice flying saucer in Washington D.C. I'd like to sell you."

"You want to sell my spaceship?" Twenty-two asked.

"That was a joke," Toby said. "I think."

"Only the part about selling your spaceship was a joke," Bruce said. "Not the part about money not voting. It does."

Both of Twenty-two's eyestalks were on Bruce. Stupid began to purr.

"Yes, that does need explaining, doesn't it?" Bruce pulled a ping-pong ball out of his pocket and began tossing it up and down. "We only brushed on that subject last time."

Toby realized he'd been fiddling with his scarf since the fundraising discussion began. He wondered if Twenty-two had noticed human nervous habits—scarf fiddling and ping-pong ball tossing. Then he noticed that the alien was slowly rocking side to side. Touché, he thought; what was it about raising money for an election that put everyone on edge?

"To start off with," Bruce said, "There are two types of politicians. Honest ones and dishonest ones"

"I'm looking forward to learning where I stand," Toby said. One of Twenty-two's eyestalks glanced at Toby, giving his feet a look-over, then returned to Bruce.

"Honest politicians," Bruce said, "get funding from those who support their policies; dishonest ones change their policies to get funding." He caught the ping-pong ball and returned it to his pocket.

"Unfortunately," Bruce continued, "the dishonest ones are usually more successful."

"If records of who gave money to candidates were public," Twenty-two said, "then voters would see this."

"The funding is public," Bruce said. He pulled the ping-pong ball back out and began tossing it in the air again. Toby realized he was fiddling with his scarf again.

"Do not voters see which candidates are dishonest?" Twenty-two asked.

"When they choose to," Bruce said. "Usually they base this on their party affiliation."

"Please explain."

"It's quite simple," Bruce said. "If you are a conservative, then the Liberal Party candidate is dishonest. If you are a liberal, then the Conservative Party candidate is dishonest."

Twenty-two began squeaking, which Toby recognized as grod laughter. She was not really the laughing sort, but when she laughed, she went all the way.

As Bruce tossed the ping-pong ball up, Twenty-two leaned forward and swatted it across the floater with one of her eyestalks. "I've been wanting to do that." Toby was impressed; the alien's eyestalks were like extra appendages, as strong and sturdy as an arm, not the soft, wimpy eyestalks of Earth creatures like snails. Stupid jumped off her head and retrieved the ball, returning it to Bruce, who took it from his mouth. Toby wondered if there was a bit of dog in Stupid.

"I should teach you to play table tennis," Bruce said to the alien.

"Which type of candidate are you?" Twenty-two asked.

"Having no chance of winning is a liberating influence," Toby said. "Also, while half the voters think Conservative Party candidates are dishonest, and the other half think the same of Liberal Party candidates, they don't know yet what to make of us Moderates."

"Yes, all one of you," Bruce said. "They all got together and voted 1-0 to be an honest candidate, against my advice."

After a bit more squeaking, Twenty-two asked, "If you will not change your policies to match the rich people, how will you convince them to give you their money?"

"Armed robbery," Bruce said.

"Really?"

"He's joking again," Toby said. "You may never figure out our politics, but eventually you'll figure out Bruce's sense of humor. When you do, explain it to me."

"You did not answer the question," Twenty-two said.

"The first lesson," Bruce said, "is that most rich people donate their money to oppose someone, not to support someone. The most successful fundraisers are when you get a bunch of people together who hate the person you're running against. They'll barely notice your candidate, as long as he mouths slogans that vilify the opponent."

Bruce tossed the ping-pong ball down the floater's corridor and watched Stupid fetch it. "The second lesson is that once you get these rich people together, if you promise them something—access to the candidate, a position in the administration if we win, and so on—they'll sell their children into slavery to raise money for you."

"He doesn't mean that last part literally," Toby said.

"Only because we're against slavery, for the most part," Bruce said. "Do you want to see a fundraiser in action, and see how we convince rich people to give money to people who won't necessarily support their policies, and have no chance of winning anyway?"

"Yes."

"Watch and learn."

Chapter Twenty-Eight
Fundraising with Gangsters

Sunday, August 29, 2100

T he fundraiser, with a million-dollar admission fee, took place at a luncheon at the Vaz, the palace of Mexico City Mayor and alleged gangster Fernando Vasquez. Twenty-two turned down their invitation to come with them, not wanting to affect the election by her public presence with them. Bruce linked his TC to the video screen in the *Rocinante* so she could watch the fundraiser live, from Bruce's perspective.

The Vaz, one of the Seven Wonders of the Modern World, had been built at the height of the Eth trade. U.S. forces destroyed it during the invasion. After the withdrawal in 2090, Vasquez rebuilt it at twice the previous size, officially from profits made from his butanol consulting business. Butanol, the winner over ethanol in the decades-long biofuel sweepstakes as oil supplies dwindled, was made from cellulose, grown in various forms mostly in the heartlands of the U.S., China, Russia, and South America. Little was grown in Mexico. Many old-style floaters, ground-based vehicles, and various industries still used butanol. Politicians who questioned the source of Vasquez's fortune had a tendency to disappear.

From its mile-square base to the many spires that sprouted toward the sky, every inch of the Vaz shouted luxury. The entire outer surface was gold plated, with jewels embedded every few yards. Silent fireworks exploded from the highest spires twenty-four hours a day, with colorful sparks showering down like fireflies. Holly bushes with red berries—real plants—surrounded the palace. It had an indoor basement soccer stadium, art museums, and staging areas for opera and orchestra.

After landing the *Rocinante* outside the palace, where it was taken away by valet parking attendants, they approached the palace on foot in the oppressive heat.

"That's a lot of gold, jewels and fireworks," Toby said.

"It looks like someone with jaundice and chicken pox having a seizure," Bruce said. "I heard the central spire is 666 feet tall, but Vasquez won't let people measure it."

They were each given a one-seat floater at the entrance, and left the oven temperatures outside for the frosty air conditioning inside. Toby and Bruce floated down the extravagant hallways slowly in the chair-sized objects, gazing in wonder at the works of art on the silver-plated walls.

Eventually they reached the central hall, the site of the fundraising luncheon. They were early, so there weren't a lot of people yet in the surprisingly small hall. Overhead was the original Sistine Chapel ceiling, bought and transported to Mexico after the Vatican City Bankruptcy in 2073, during the Third Great Depression.

"Toby!" Fernando Vasquez, grinning widely, extended his hand. He was built like a heavyweight pro wrestler, all solid muscle, about six and a half feet tall, with squinting, coal-black eyes. His shaved head glistened with sweat despite the cool temperature. He wore a blue bathrobe, with a "V" monogrammed over the heart, over golden pajamas.

Toby shook Vasquez's huge hand with both hands, a trick he'd learned long ago to make a recipient feel particularly special. "How are you, Fernando?" They'd known each other for years from past campaigns. As before, Vasquez's perfumed breath didn't quite cover the slight scent of rot.

"For once, we're on the same side." Vasquez's voice was a bit hoarse. He moved closer and slapped him on the back; Toby fought to keep his balance. "And this must be Bruce?" He extended his hand.

Bruce shook hands, but Toby saw how he kept his arm locked, keeping Vasquez at a distance. Smart move; he'd have to practice that one.

"Sounds like you've been talking a bit," Toby said.

"You wouldn't believe it if you saw it," Vasquez said. "There's this girl with weird green hair who came by this morning for something, and we've been in the back all day, arguing politics. You have got to meet her, she's a walking political encyclopedia."

"She's just using her TC," Bruce said.

Vasquez shook his head. "It takes time to use a TC, and she never stops, never breathes, never inhales. She's relentless!"

"I hope she's a moderate," Bruce said.

"I think she's liberal," Vasquez said. "But I'm not sure. There were just too many words for me."

"When do we get to meet this maelstrom?" Toby asked.

Vasquez glanced over his shoulder at a doorway. "She followed me around all morning, wouldn't let me escape. I finally got her together with Georgie Sanchez, my accountant, who thought he knew something about economics. Last I saw, he was drowning."

"Will she be at the luncheon?" Toby asked.

"Let me see." Vasquez's eyes went vacant for a moment as he checked his TC. "No, I don't think so, but I'll put up the million for her, and put her at your table. Hey, it says she's from Antarctica!"

"You don't have to—" Toby began. Then his eyes went slightly wide. Melissa, the girl from Antarctica?

"Guests are coming in fast," Vasquez said, "so why don't you mingle while I check on the food?" He exited through a side door.

The room was filling up. Just when it seemed it had reached capacity, the walls on two sides began to move, enlarging the hall.

Toby fiddled with his scarf as he looked about. He vaguely recognized some of the guests, but wasn't sure. "TC," he whispered, "identify all guests when I approach within six feet." It was time to raise money, or as Bruce would put it, extortion time.

He suddenly realized his neck was bare. He'd unknowingly jammed his scarf in his pocket. It didn't want to be around for this.

Over the next hour, he and Bruce worked the guests, listening to their suggestions while nodding their heads, no matter how stupid the advice was. Everyone knows better than the actual candidate and campaign director, and if either let on that this was not completely true, they'd be in trouble. Toby wondered which would be more sore afterwards, his hand and wrist from shaking hands, or his neck from nodding.

When Vasquez returned, he still wore the gold pajamas, but now with a purple bathrobe. Guests gathered around him as he told stories of the Mexican resistance, all of which featured his own exaggerated heroics.

Then Vasquez announced that lunch was about to be served. Toby and Bruce sat next to each other at the front table, along with Vasquez and others. Vasquez's twelve-year-old son, Marco, sat next to him, a toothy grin exposing a gold front tooth. He wore a purple "Platt for President" baseball cap.

At each spot at the table were platinum silverware and ornate plates covered with sharp warrior images. The plates had small labels identifying them as Aztec, though Toby wasn't sure if they were originals—touched up to restore the ancient images—or duplicates. On each plate was a *Platt for President* button made of silver, with an embedded diamond for the "a" in "Platt."

Toby heard her voice before he saw her. He turned around just as Melissa Smith, she of the green twisted gun barrel hair, sat next to him on his left. She was still talking over her shoulder at a thin-faced, worried-looking man who couldn't have been more than five feet tall, presumably Vasquez's accountant. The man walked around the table and collapsed at the farthest possible seat away from Melissa. She turned to face Toby.

"Mr. Platt!" she exclaimed.

"You sure get around," Toby said. "Washington D.C., Australia, and now Mexico? I thought you were from Antarctica." As they spoke, lunch was served, a bean buffet set on the middle of the table, and vegetable

191

parfaits for everyone. Also, to Toby's surprise, an illegal alcoholic beverage, some sort of wine. Nobody objected.

"I'm with the Ajala campaign, so I go where they go." She glanced at the accountant across the table. "I was supposed to leave this morning, but I stayed to discuss the election with Mr. Vasquez and Mr. Sanchez." Toby wondered if the discussions were two-way discussions, based on what Vasquez had said.

"What were you doing here this morning?" Bruce asked.

"I was here for the Ajala fundraiser."

Bruce and Toby exchanged glances. So Vasquez was covering his bets, doing fundraisers for both of Dubois's opponents. There was no rule against that, but it was considered bad form. Vasquez was making it rather clear that he was only anti-Dubois. Or was there something Toby didn't know?

Vasquez interrupted them by tapping what appeared to be a golden dagger against his glass to get everyone's attention. He stood, as did his son Marco. "I'd like to thank you all for coming here and lowering your net worth for the good of mankind," he began. "Let's face it, a million dollars is a lot of money for normal people—which is why there are no normal people here!" There was some politely forced laughter.

"Every one of you has stepped forward and made their preferences known," he continued. "You've put up your own money for a campaign that's barely gotten started, that half the people on this planet probably don't even know about. That money is gone, as far as you are concerned, but it's an investment. For when this campaign takes off, and Mr. Platt is our next president, every one of us will be knocking on his door, saying 'Hello, remember me?'"

Toby silently groaned. Marco giggled at his dad's side.

Melissa leaned toward him and whispered, "That's the same speech he gave this morning, only it was Mr. Ajala as our next president."

Vasquez went on for a few more minutes as he launched into a diatribe against Dubois that covered just about everything except what Toby knew to be Vasquez's real grievance: an overzealous USE police force, not a good thing for someone in Vasquez's profession.

Vasquez also spoke of loyalty. "You cannot trust a man like Dubois, who sides with the Israelis one day, then with the Mormons when he needs their vote." How had Vasquez known Dubois was going to throw his support to the Mormons? Toby knew about it, since he'd been at the meeting when that decision was made, but as far as he knew, Dubois had yet to go public on this—he'd been holding back on it, presumably as a last-minute surprise. Did Vasquez have inside information?

"There is nothing in this world more important than loyalty," Vasquez said. Then he walked over and stood behind Toby. "I hope all of you have had the chance to meet Toby. Come, shake his hand—preferably his left, since his right is probably a bit worn out from the campaign—and I'm sure he'd love to hear your take on policy and election strategy."

Toby stifled another groan.

"And now I'd like for you to meet the real Toby Platt," Vasquez said as he glanced toward a large screen at the front of the room, snapping his fingers. Toby cringed as the huge, close-up picture of himself appeared. It was large enough that he and everyone else in the room could see crumbs on his worn-out scarf.

What followed was a montage of Toby's silliest moments on the campaign. He knew the late-night shows always did this, but hadn't seen them himself. A "roast" like this was meant in good humor, and was the price one paid for fund-raising, but that didn't make it less embarrassing.

For the next ten minutes he watched himself in his most unguarded moments: chewing with his mouth open; stumbling over words in speeches; accidentally smacking Bruce in the chest while waving his arms during an animated discussion; and other lapses. The ending was a rapid-fire video set to music showing him, Dubois, and Ajala jumping to their feet and sitting down, over and over, at the "Dinner Debate Down Under." Bruce laughed hysterically while Marco went into uncontrollable giggles. Toby found himself smiling even as Vasquez ended the video by calling on "Future President Jumping Bean" to give a speech.

As Toby rose, Vasquez leaned over and whispered, "I hope you have that spot for me on your cabinet. Treasury would be nice." Toby thought his heart skipped several beats. A cabinet position for Vasquez? Was he kidding?

Toby gave his standard stump speech, emphasizing his PUFF plan, and then talking about the glory of Mexican independence. He didn't go into the problems of gun violence, knowing of the accusations against Vasquez in this department. He finished by joking about how he would soon be leaving and they could celebrate another American withdrawal, then sat down.

He whispered in Bruce's ear, "Why does Vasquez think he gets a spot in my cabinet?"

"I may have hinted that," Bruce whispered back. "Since we can't win, we aren't promising anything we have to worry about, right?"

"You hinted—which is a promise to a guy like Vasquez—that he could be my Treasury Secretary?" Toby asked. "Are you out of your mind?" Before Bruce could respond, he said, "We'll talk about this later, after I have you lasered."

Vasquez began to eat, and others joined in. Waiters came by to deliver more food, including a wide variety of plastated foods. Toby liked simple foods, rarely appreciating expensive ones, but the food was the best he'd had all year.

Food seemed to be on Melissa's 17-year-old mind as well. "You know your Provisional Universal Food Foundation is just another way of keeping food from the masses," she said. "It's a watered-down version of what any civilized society should do—feed all its people. How can you justify mass starvation while we eat so well?"

Bruce, on his right, leaned forward. "There isn't mass starvation. That implies a significant percentage of the population, but it's only a few percentage points, ten at most."

Now Melissa leaned forward and stared at Bruce. To avoid the crossfire, Toby leaned back and kept his mouth shut. "Half a billion people went to bed hungry last night," she said, "and millions are starving. If that's not mass starvation, what is?"

194

"When I was a kid and said something my parents didn't like," Bruce said, "they'd send me to bed without dinner. That's not starvation, that's missing dinner."

"Are you really comparing going to bed without dinner for being sassy to missing dinner because there's no food?" Melissa's eyes were on fire. Toby leaned back a bit further in his chair to avoid the flames. "Even those who get enough calories aren't getting enough protein and other nutrition."

"No, but going without dinner doesn't make it mass starvation." Bruce's hand fell toward his pocket; Toby wondered if he'd bring out the ping-pong ball. Somehow tossing a ping-pong ball about didn't fit the current setting. Unless it was one of pure gold.

"It's all about a civilized society," Melissa said, "where people *don't* go to bed without dinner—unless they're acting like little kids, talking nonsense, and need to be punished." She glanced toward Toby. "Maybe you should send your stooge home without supper? Perhaps his mommy could collect all those meals he missed and solve world hunger?"

"Keep me out of this," Toby said, "I'm just enjoying this ping-pong game." He'd been turning his head back and forth to follow the exchange.

"How can we call ourselves civilized," Melissa said, "if we don't follow the Ten Universal Rights?"

"The what?" Bruce asked. Toby also had no idea what these were.

"They are Ajala's new plan for a civilized society." She smiled. "Ajala's going to announce them in a few hours, the ten things any civilized society owes its citizens. Free food. Clean water. Clean air. Health care. Housing. Education. Transportation. Personal beliefs rights. Legal and police protection. And connection to communication networks, which means a TC for everyone."

Ajala was getting smarter, Toby thought. Why hadn't we thought of that?

"For cleaning clocks, his highness ended time paradoxes, like contradictions," Melissa said.

Toby and Bruce both stared at her.

"It's my mnemonic device for remembering all ten items," Melissa said. "The 'For' for 'food,' 'cleaning' for 'clean water,' and so on."

"Cute," Bruce said. "Ajala expects the government to give all of that to all citizens for *free?*"

"Why not?" Melissa asked. "We're already partly there, with health care and other stuff.

"The problem with people like you and Ajala," Bruce said, ping-pong ball now in hand, "is you spend all your time thinking about your destination, but forget about the journey. How the heck are you going to get any of that passed, and where will he get the money? Are you going to double taxes? He goes public with this, he'll get his followers into a frenzy of love, while the commonsense masses—I can't believe I'm calling them that—will vote him off the planet."

"All the great innovators and revolutionaries were 'voted off the planet' at first," Melissa said. "Great spirits have always encountered violent opposition from those with mediocre minds."

Touché, Toby thought; Einstein, right from the poster on Bruce's wall.

"Well," Bruce said, "us mediocre minds have one thing in common. We understand that if you can't pass it, it won't happen, and you end up not just with nothing, but the opposite of nothing—things go negative. How'd you like five more years of Dubois because Ajala goes too far, won't compromise?"

"Children," Toby said, aware that all eyes and ears on the table and surrounding tables were following the discussion, "perhaps it's time to introduce that revolutionary concept known as a compromise. You start with a goal—Ajala's Ten Universal Rights—and work out how to get there. If you can't get there right away, you take the journey step by step, compromising each time to get what's possible at that time. You keep doing this, and eventually you finish the journey."

Vasquez began to slowly clap his hands. "Absolutely brilliant. You with your scarf, her with her hair, and him with his ping-pong ball, you three make a great team. I'm gonna do whatever I can to help you win, and then I can join you as Secretary of the Treasury, and we can work out how to fund these Universal Rights."

Oh brother, Toby thought. What had Bruce gotten him into? Best to nip it in the bud. He'd been hesitant about the fundraiser itself, with a shady figure like Vasquez, but there was no way he was going to put this gangster in charge of the world's money. Vasquez was the tip of a whole iceberg of gangs and violence that ran from Mexico and down through Central America, an issue they'd address when the election moved to Latin America in six weeks—if they lasted that long.

"I haven't really thought a whole lot about cabinet appointees yet," Toby said. "We're a third-party challenge based on ideas. We'll worry about the people to put these ideas in place later on."

Incoming call from Fernando Vasquez. Toby looked up and could see Vasquez's looking at him, a slight smile on his face.

"Accept."

"You're aware that Bruce promised me this position?"

"Did he promise, or just hint at it?" Like Vasquez, he whispered so nobody else could hear.

Vasquez's smile vanished. "I don't play games."

Toby decided that parsing words was not the way to handle Vasquez. "Fernando, are you really supporting me?"

"That is a good question," Vasquez said. "Yes, I support you, even if you are an American. Why? Because I have a lot of money, because I hate Dubois, but mostly because Bruce promised me a place on your cabinet if you win. I don't think you can win, but like I said, I have a lot of money, and I'm covering the odds. Now. Mr. Platt, I want you to look around. There are about two hundred people here, at one million each. You do the math. In return, I expect something, and I don't want hints. If you win, are you going to name me Treasury Secretary, or are you going to stiff me and embarrass me after I already said publicly I'd be Treasury Secretary?"

Toby wished he'd taken some Eth. There were times when the stuff had its uses. But he couldn't make this promise.

"Fernando, I appreciate your help," Toby said carefully, "but I just can't make that promise."

"Then I will make you a promise, Mr. Platt. I like you, but if I have to go to hell and back, I'm going to put you out of this race." The slight smile was back on Vasquez's lips.

Chapter Twenty-Nine
Mexican Liberation Day and the Fly

The rest of the luncheon was a daze as Bruce and Melissa argued and Toby avoided looking at Vasquez as he thought about the man's words. Where had he heard that before?

Then he remembered. It was almost word for word what he'd told Lara when he'd quit the Dubois campaign. Only, coming from Vasquez, it seemed a bit more menacing.

Was it a coincidence, or had someone from that meeting spoken to Vasquez? The only ones possible were Lara, Dubois, Farley, or Persson. Not Persson, he realized; he'd stormed out earlier. He couldn't imagine Dubois or Farley telling something like this to Vasquez. He had a hard time imagining Lara talking to Vasquez either. Could it just be a coincidental choice of words? Plus he knew about Dubois changing sides in the Mormon-Israeli conflict.

Eventually the luncheon ended. Toby publicly thanked Vasquez for his support as the Mexico City Mayor smiled back coldly. Soon they were back in the *Rocinante* and off to the rally.

Twenty-two said she had watched and learned a lot from the luncheon video. "Raising money seems to be important to your political process. Is not your system based on the idea that all voters have equal say?"

"That's correct," Bruce said, "but in politics don't believe everything you see or hear."

"To win an election," Toby said, "you have to keep your eye on the destination. To reach that destination requires money."

199

"Would not the ones with more money have more say than those with less money?"

"Of course," Bruce said. "It's called 'political speech.'" He emphasized each syllable of the two words.

"How is donating money a form of political speech?" Twenty-two asked. "Do they write a message on the currency donated?"

Bruce laughed, and Toby also had to smile at Twenty-two's innocent interpretation. How does one call donating money a type of speech? It made no sense at all.

"According to those who claim money donations are political speech," Toby said, "the money allows them to tell people what they believe."

"Coincidentally," Bruce said, "the ones with lots of money send money—I mean political speech—to the ones who claim that money is political speech."

"But the money is not speech itself," Twenty-two said. "It is simply a means to getting more people to hear one's speech than another's speech. This implies their speech is more important than one who has less money. Does more money make a person's speech more important than another's?"

"No," Toby said, hoping for once to successfully defend the honor of the human political system, "but we value the idea that anyone should be allowed to speak out and give their political views."

"Are all voters considered equal in your system?" Twenty-two asked.

"Of course," Toby said.

"Except some are more equal than others?" Twenty-two asked.

Bruce was in near hysterics. "Twenty-two, you have mastered the intricacies of our politics."

Toby wondered if the alien had been reading George Orwell. The honor of the human political system would have to wait another day.

"A major intricacy of your politics," Twenty-two said, "is that those with money and those who you call 'special interest groups' have more say than others, and you humans see nothing wrong with it."

"There's nothing wrong with legally taking money from special interest groups," Bruce said. "It's almost impossible to win an election without doing so. What's wrong is the very fact that special interest money *is* legal. The masses can't see the distinction, and think it's hypocritical for someone to call for an end to special interest money while taking it himself to get elected. That's why they are chimpanzees."

"We can call it biped politics," Twenty-two said, gently rocking side to side. "A moment ago Toby said that to win an election, you have to keep your eye on the destination. Isn't the journey to that destination, the political process where candidates show they are worthy of the destination, more important than the destination itself?"

"In theory, yes," Toby said. "In practice, the ones who win are the ones who do whatever maximizes their chances of reaching the destination, which is winning the election." He was sounding like Bruce, he realized.

Twenty-two twisted her head side to side, an awkward motion on her thick, essentially neckless frame.

"What are you doing?" Toby asked.

"Something I learned from watching humans, though it is not easy for a grod. I am shaking my head back and forth to show my disagreement and disappointment. We grods also have candidates for leadership who think more of the destination rather than the journey that shows they are worthy of the destination. Unless they hide it well, they are not elected."

"That's true for us as well," Toby said. "And what are you doing?"

Bruce was contorting his body side to side. "Something I learned from watching Twenty-two. I'm voicing my surprise by shaking side to side. Of course we vote out those who are too obvious about *getting* elected rather than *showing* they should be elected. But our stomach for this type of thing is way off the charts."

Mexican Liberation Day commemorated the tenth anniversary of the withdrawal of U.S. troops from Mexico on August 30, 2090, twelve years after the Eth Invasion. Before the invasion, Eth had spread to the world, allowing its users the freedom to act in their own best interests, with ethics no longer a consideration. At the height of the Eth craze, scholars thought it could mark the end of civilization. According to numerous scholarly papers at the time, a politician or corporate leader willing to use Eth had a huge advantage over one that did not, and so by the theory of political and corporate evolution, Eth users tended to dominate all branches of government and large companies, which would make its illegalization a rather unlikely event.

What the scholars did not take into account was the ultimate selfishness of an Eth user in a position of power, who realized it was to their benefit to outlaw Eth for others—while keeping their own stash. The World Congress declared it illegal in 2076.

Mexico dominated the Eth trade, and like Canada with Full VR, refused to close down Eth production and exportation. In 2078, the U.S., which had occupied Canada seven years earlier, invaded Mexico. They overran all the main cities, destroyed all Mexican military bases, and declared victory in four weeks. Then began the Eth Eradication Program, where they divided Mexico into a grid, and searched it, block by block, in the greatest police action in the history of mankind. The U.S. vowed to complete the task in one year.

Twelve years, 153,000 U.S. and 376,000 Mexican deaths, and roughly thirty trillion dollars later, with the Eth trade cut in half, the U.S. declared victory and pulled out.

Over three hundred thousand came to the Mexico Liberation Day rally, held in Toltec Square outside Mexico City on Monday afternoon, August 30, the day before the North American election. Behind heavy security, Dubois, Ajala, and Toby stood near the lectern in front. Dubois and Ajala were surrounded by staff. Toby had only Bruce, with Turk and Crowbar nearby.

Dubois stood behind Toby and put his hand on his shoulder. "You let me down. We were supposed to do this together."

Toby turned around. Dubois stared at him with the cold smile Toby knew so well. It was the first time he'd been on the receiving end.

202

"Come over here for a sec," Dubois said. The two walked a few feet away from the others.

"I couldn't do it anymore," Toby said quietly. "We just don't agree on anything."

"That's why we need to compromise," Dubois said, "like we did five years ago. The point is to win, get in office, and then we can do what we need to do. You can't do that until we're in office."

"That's what you said five years ago," Toby said. "You governed for your base. You've been running for reelection since your first day in office."

Dubois shook his head. "These next five years will be the best yet. Why are you wasting time on a third-party challenge you can't win? You've made your point, you did great in Australia, but your run's over. Have you seen the polls in the U.S. and Mexico?"

"Have you seen the Canadian polls?"

"How many electoral votes does Canada have, six? There's 62 from the U.S., and 20 from Mexico. Canadians just don't breed like the rest of us. Drop it, and come work with me and your daughter."

Lara. Why wasn't she here?

"We were together a long time, Toby, and I can read your mind," Dubois said. "She's back at the hotel, doing the final touches on our plans for the Russian Federation, with a dozen advisors. You should be there, and bring Bruce, if he'll come. Lara's good, but she makes mistakes. We could use your experience."

"Plug it," Toby said, and walked back to Bruce. He should be working with Lara. They were a team. But no more.

"Don't walk away from me!" Dubois said sharply. "You'll be running city council elections after this."

All three candidates gave speeches. Dubois went first, and emphasized how some politicians were soft on crime, would start the slippery slope toward making Full VR legal despite all the problems in the past, and would raise taxes. Surprisingly, he also brought on much booing by bringing up the Eth trade and how it might "come back" if the world didn't stay tough on it. He was probably talking to the U.S. audience.

Toby thought his bringing it up was doubly ironic, both because Dubois used Eth, and because the Eth trade had never gone away, despite official claims by Dubois, and so could not "come back."

Dubois finished with a selective summary of all the things he'd promised to do five years before, and how each had been fulfilled successfully. Bruce made faces at each of the major claims.

"He's dubyaing," Bruce said. "He may have believed some of this stuff five years ago, but there's no way he can still believe it."

Dubois received loud applause along with scattered boos when he was done. Toby remembered that Mexico was one of the few places where Ajala led in the polls—barely—due to Dubois's past support of the American invasion. It had been 22 years ago, and Dubois had just started his political career, but the Mexican media wasn't about to let anyone forget. Yet, as Toby had pointed out more than once, losing Mexico's 20 electoral votes is fine if you get USA's 62.

Ajala went next, and after his standard stump speech, he went after the U.S. for its invasion. The crowd was thunderous in its applause. Then he introduced his Ten Universal Rights. After each item, he shouted to the crowd, "*Don't you deserve this?*" The crowd was loud in its approval.

Toby went last. He, Bruce, and the speechwriters had spent many hours honing his speech. As he walked to the podium, chants of "*Blueshirt go home!*" came from the crowd, the nickname for Americans in Mexico, from the uniform color of American troops. One woman yelled, "*You're taking votes from Ajala!*"

With all the yelling, the person that most caught his attention stood silently near the front of the crowd, staring at Toby. He wore an old-style blue American uniform like the type used in the invasion of Mexico, a surprising wardrobe choice in such a crowd. The man was missing his right arm. Toby met the man's stare for a few seconds, nodded, and went to the podium.

He'd have to win over the crowd. He started with his standard stump speech. He emphasized the importance of PUFF, which was of great value to a country like Mexico, so divided between the rich and poor.

Then he criticized the U.S. for staying in Mexico for so long, while avoiding the question of whether they should have invaded at all over the Eth problem. The crowd loved this part, but Toby knew he suffered from the same malady all moderate candidates face. Mexicans would tend to support the candidate who was most against the U.S. invasion, which was Ajala; the U.S. would tend to support the candidate who was most for the U.S. invasion, which would be Dubois. Perhaps there was a place around the Rio Grande where Toby could find votes.

When he was done, he was surprised by how loud the applause was. "Did you hear that?" he asked Bruce afterwards. "They applauded me as loudly as Ajala!"

"Of course they did," Bruce said. "Applause costs money."

"You're kidding, right?" Toby asked. "You didn't waste money on Mexico, did you?"

"It's not about Mexico, it's about your public image." Bruce waved his arm toward the crowd. "All this will be on tonight's newscasts, and that's what we want people to see."

Toby was skeptical, but if Bruce thought it was worth spending precious campaign money to pay crowd members to cheer for him, that was his call. He wondered how many Bruce had hired, and how many had been hired by Dubois and Ajala.

A fly buzzed next to his face, and he waved his hand at it. The fly flew about in a loop, returning to Toby, who again waved his hand at it, slightly irritated.

Bruce waved his hand in front of Toby's face with blinding speed. "Got 'em!" Bruce then threw the fly against the paved ground. "That shouldn't kill it, just daze it so it'll stop bugging us."

Toby stared at the fly, which now stood quietly on the ground. A fly. A simple fly. It brought back a memory. Could it be?

"TC, get me Phil Farley," he whispered. Soon he had Dubois's Chief of Staff, who was presumably back in New York, keeping things running while Dubois was away. Toby was a bit surprised he took his call.

"I shouldn't even be talking to you," Farley said. "Dubois's pretty angry at you."

"I know, I just spoke with him. Look, Phil, remember a month ago, the last time I was at the Red Room?"

"Sure, Toby, that's the day you got angry and quit."

"I think there's a spy bug there," Toby said. He explained about the irritating fly that had been buzzing about that day. What if it had been a spy device used by Vasquez? It would explain his near quoting of his words to Lara, and explain how he knew about Dubois's upcoming support of the Mormons and betrayal of the Israelis. It would be just like the bravado gangster mayor to have the fly buzz about in the Red Room rather than sit quietly in the shadows. Vasquez had the finances and connections for just such a toy.

Phil listened, but seemed skeptical. "The Red Room is the most secure place in the world," he said. "It'd be impossible for a fly, real or fake, to get inside."

"The fact that one did means it's either a real fly that's really sneaky, or a fake one that's been designed to get past your security. I suggest you do a high-powered sweep."

Farley said he'd take care of it, and disconnected.

And now he had a more distasteful task to take care of. "Bruce, we need to talk."

"I know, I know," Bruce said. "I wish I could play back the recording when I talked to Vasquez, but we were all on no-record." Toby was afraid of that; it was the same feature that kept him and other Dubois aides from ever being able to play back conversations with the President. Toby's TC was also on permanent no-record, so his private TC conversations could not be shared.

"What exactly did you tell him?" Toby didn't think Bruce would lie to him, though he could be tricky with what he actually said.

"All I told him was that anyone who raised as much money as he promised would be thought of when jobs are being handed out. I never even mentioned the cabinet."

"So you thought he might be interested in a sub-cabinet job?" Toby asked. "Perhaps Assistant Secretary to the Undersecretary of the Department of Human Services? Or maybe janitorial services? Or perhaps he could join our technical support, answering questions from stupid campaign aides who mislead wealthy gangsters into thinking they can be my Treasury Secretary?"

"It would be an interesting . . . experience, Vasquez in charge of the treasury."

"And we'd probably experience it from jail," Toby said. "Just be careful from now on. We've reached our quota on gangsters who are out to get me. Which reminds me—how'd you talk me into doing a fundraiser with Vasquez anyway?"

"Probably because we need the money," Bruce said. "If we had enough to hire more security, perhaps fewer hundred-year-old women will kidnap you."

Reese sarcastically clapped as Platt finished his speech. Once again he'd listened to all three speeches. The same old stuff. Platt was definitely siphoning votes from Ajala. His security was still weak. Once again Reese had caught Platt's eye. Once again Platt had nodded at him. As if that would excuse him for his actions. As if that would save him if Reese chose him.

He'd seen Melissa in the crowd. He wanted to talk to her again, touch her hand again. But that would be dangerous. A killer needed to be in the shadows, unseen. Until he struck.

He'd begun his plans. Three of them. One for Dubois. One for Ajala. One for Platt. Three plans for each. Because he was a professional. He'd already made queries. Soon he'd go to Russia for supplies. Then he'd choose. Which fly to swat? It would be the most important choice of his life. It would be the most important choice for the fly as well.

207

Chapter Thirty
A Whirlwind Tour

The rest of Monday and Tuesday—August 31, election day for North America—was a foggy whirlwind for Toby. There had been much more planned, but Toby's hospital stay had forced them to reschedule and compress. Flying from city to city, working roughly from south to north and then west to east, they'd land, Toby would give his stump speech, and then they'd be off for the next one. Puebla, Guadalajara, Torreon, and Monterrey in Mexico, then a quick flight into Texas to do San Antonio, Houston and Dallas. Then west to the Pacific for Tijuana in Baja California, then up the coast: Los Angeles, Santa Barbara, San Francisco, Sacramento, Portland, then a flight over the decimated remains of Seattle and into Canada for Vancouver, Calgary and Winnipeg. The crowds in Canada were noticeably larger and louder than the others, especially in their return to Vancouver.

They flew back into the U.S., with a west-to-east tour planned. The first scheduled stop was at the University of Utah in downtown Salt Lake City. However, after hearing of more Israeli-Mormon rioting near where Toby was scheduled to speak, they cancelled the speech. Much of the rioting came as a result of a speech by Dubois where he condemned the Israelis, until now his allies, and sided with the Mormons. Just as planned so long ago in the Red Room.

"We want to be the party of solutions," Bruce said. "But there's no solution here because both sides are both right and wrong. They hate each other's guts, and their leaders are crazy. There's nothing you or

208

anyone can do here. The fighting will go on forever or until someone nukes the Israelis. Again. Let Governor Baxter deal with it."

Like many past politicians, Toby believed deep-down that if he could just sit down with both sides, he could work out a compromise. Bruce had humored him on this, and even tried to set up a meeting between the two sides that Toby could mediate. Unfortunately neither side would agree to meet unless the other side first met pre-conditions that were the very things that needed to be negotiated. When Toby finally cut off on his TC the shouting representatives from each side, Bruce smirked.

Someday, if he were president, he would find a way to crack this nut. But first, he knew Bruce would say, you'll have to find two leaders who aren't nuts.

As they flew to their next destination, Denver, Toby received a call from Phil Farley from The Bubble, verifying that they had found the spy fly. Their security experts had never seen anything like that sophisticated piece of spyware. He said that whoever created it had a lot of money and resources. Like Vasquez, Toby thought.

Dubois's newly announced support for the Mormon side had increased his lead in the U.S. polls while infuriating the Israelis, who felt betrayed by their former benefactor. Toby had added pro-Israeli statements to his stump speech, but after conferring with Bruce, they took them out.

"What's the point?" Bruce said. "Dubois's going to win the U.S., and if you say anything on the issue, everyone forgets anything else you say. He'll get the Mormon vote, the law-and-order vote, the wealthy, the lemmings swayed by his advertising barrage, and the isolationists who think Twenty-two's going to rape their children. The *Stop the Invasion!* slogan works better here than anywhere else in the world—the U.S. is the most paranoid country in the world, and appealing to their reason is like asking a chimpanzee to study Shakespeare. Ajala will get the Jewish vote, the intergalacticists—say that five times fast—college professors, the poor, and the bleeding hearts. You'll get the scraps left over."

"It's my home country," Toby said. "I'd like to at least compete in it, maybe get some support."

"That's why we're doing this pointless coast-to-coast tour," Bruce said. "Except it's not pointless. It gets you on the news for the upcoming elections, and on issues that'll be important there. Nobody outside the U.S. cares about Mormons and New Israel, so we stay away from those issues."

Twenty-two was watching the riots on video. "This is how humans disagree?" she asked.

"This," Bruce said, "is how chimpanzees work off their energy so the rest of us can solve problems. Protesting is the opiate of the masses."

"Sometimes the 'dumb masses' get things done with their protests," Toby said.

"Yeah," Bruce responded, "and a tribe of chimpanzees could surround and kill a bunch of Mensans, but that doesn't make the chimpanzees right."

"You're really into chimpanzees today," Toby said.

"There's a lot of them out there today," Bruce said, pointing at the rioting video. "So many of them have no understanding of the issues other than what those around them are saying, and those around them are only saying what others around them are saying. It should be the patriotic duty of clueless voters not to vote."

"The voters aren't as clueless as you think," Toby said.

"Do you really want to defend that statement?" Bruce asked.

They worked their way east, at each stop stepping out of the *Rocinante*, giving a speech, then quickly getting back in and taking off for the next stop: Denver, Colorado Springs, Oklahoma City, Kansas City, St. Louis, Chicago, Milwaukee, Detroit, Cleveland, Pittsburgh, Buffalo, a quick run into Canada for Toronto and Montreal, then south to Boston, New York City, Philadelphia, Baltimore, and finally ending in Washington D.C. Toby wished he could have visited more cities in his home country, especially the southeast, but there simply wasn't time. Besides, his voice was nearly gone by the end, despite massive amounts of the age-old cure: tea with honey and lemon juice.

Dubois's favorite slogan, *Stop the Invasion!*, was everywhere. It was Toby's own strategy, the one he'd recommended at his last meeting with

Dubois and Lara. Toby wondered if Dubois had spent as much money on those signs as the entire Platt campaign budget. While flying from city to city, Toby watched the newscasts, and it seemed every newscast had crowds carrying the signs in the background. Every few minutes the newscasts were interrupted by the political advertising barrage. Dubois had twice as many ads as Ajala, who had twice as many as Toby.

Toby spent Tuesday night with his family in Germantown, Maryland, just north of Washington D.C. Outside the house stood several security people, one of the downsides of his entering the race for president. They nodded at Turk and Crowbar, who accompanied Toby. He hadn't been home or spoken more than a few words on his TC with his wife in a couple months since he'd asked her to campaign with him and she'd refused. He expected a frosty reception; it was the price of his chosen profession. He wasn't disappointed.

"Do I know you?" Olivia asked Toby after opening the front door. They'd been married seventeen years. She was small and wispy, with red hair, like Tyler's. She was overdressed, as usual, in a formal white gown that she could have worn in a wedding, as a guest or even the bride. She was the quiet type, perhaps a habit she'd picked up as a librarian, but even more so in recent years.

"You know I've been busy."

"Yes, I've seen it on the newscasts," she said. "Except, weren't you supposed to be running the other side's campaign? The guy who hired you and made you famous and a little less poor?"

"Sorry, I should have consulted you before—"

"You bet you should have!" she slammed the door after him. "Dinner will be ready in ten minutes, if I can get the security people out of my hair." She disappeared into the kitchen.

He wondered what the right word to describe their marriage was. They weren't divorced—not yet. They weren't really separated, since Toby still lived at home—sometimes, though not recently. He was away most of the time, so it was just the requisite separation necessitated by

211

the needs of a political hack-for-hire turned politician. No simple word there.

Bruce had wanted Olivia and Tyler to come on the campaign trail with them, saying it would make Toby look like a "family man." Toby had brought the idea up with her on the TC. She hadn't even given voice to her refusal, just stared at him for a moment, then clicked off.

"Shouldn't you be out campaigning?" It was Lara. The four corners of her black polyhedral hair were each now tipped with a blonde ombré.

"What are you doing here in Maryland?" Toby asked. "I thought you'd be out west campaigning with Dubois."

"You can be a talking head from anywhere."

"But it's better in person. I've always told you that."

"Dad, we're entering the 22nd century! People are used to this type of thing. You don't need to be there physically to make a strong argument."

"You do if you want a personal touch."

She rolled her eyes, bringing a smile to his face. Still the teenaged daughter so many years later. "You run your campaign your way, I'll run mine my way. Or you can drop out and rejoin us, and stop being an idiot."

"A little late for that," he said.

"Yeah, a little late for that." She reached out and felt his scarf. "I'm starting to miss this piece of worn-out garbage." She gave it a yank. "Dad, how did I lose you?"

"You didn't lose me. I lost you."

"Who walked away?"

He gently removed her hands from the scarf and straightened it. "Let's not talk about it. So . . . you'll be joining us for dinner?"

"Sorry, got a talking head thing to do. I'm leaving now. Bye." She gave the scarf a playful yank, and then she was gone.

"Hi, Dad!" Tyler said. At least someone was happy to see him. He wore a yellow warm-up suit with black trim, the same as Bruce often wore. Standing nearby was Hawk, Tyler's new bodyguard, a short and husky man with a crewcut whose eyes constantly moved about while his head stayed still. Toby smiled as he heard the latest on school, the ping-pong team, and the upcoming school election.

"Bruce talked me into running for president," Tyler said.

Toby had asked Bruce to help Tyler out, but hadn't realized they'd already been working together. "I thought your friend Jamaal was, and you were running for VP?"

"He is," Tyler said. "We don't get along anymore."

"What happened?"

Tyler looked away. "We're both running for ninth grade class president, and so we kind of said bad things to each other. The election's in two weeks."

Oh, how Toby sometimes hated politics! Tyler and Jamaal had been best friends since kindergarten. "Does your mom know about this?"

Tyler shook his head.

"I'm rather surprised," Toby said. "Couldn't you and Jamaal find a way to work this out, so you don't have to run against each other?"

The suddenly uncommunicative Tyler shook his head again.

"Why do you want to be class president?"

"I put together a platform," Tyler said. "Do you want to see it?"

"A platform isn't a reason to run for president, son. It's a series of solutions for problems. What problems do you think need to be addressed at your school?"

"Here," Tyler said, sending the platform to Toby's TC. It covered ten topics, such as improving and expanding extracurricular activities, better lunch menus, and an award system for those who achieve high grades and high attendance.

"You don't want to campaign on ten things," Toby said. "Nobody can remember them. You need to focus on maybe three things, and campaign on those relentlessly, until people can't get it out of their heads. In the end, they'll either shoot you or vote for you."

"I know, Dad, Bruce said the same thing, except he said they'd either vote for me or cook and serve me for lunch at school."

Tyler was obviously getting good advice from Bruce. Toby wondered if it would be good public relations if a candidate's son was elected class president. "*Aah!*" he exclaimed, realizing he was thinking like Bruce.

"What'd you say?" Tyler asked.

"Nothing."

"You know something, Dad?"

"What's that?"

"I really want to win this election."

Toby felt a chill run down his spine. What had Twenty-two said about candidates who think more of the destination than the journey?

Olivia called them in for dinner, and they adjourned to the dinner table. Cooking was not Olivia's specialty, and the cabbage and bean pizza was not one of her best. Tyler's face showed he wasn't a fan either. Olivia saved the meal with chocolate ice cream for dessert.

They watched the Joseph Wang show after dinner. For twenty years, the perpetually twelve-year-old title character in the 3-D animated show had mesmerized worldwide audiences with his apparent delinquent behavior as a cover for his true identity as a secret agent. Surrounded by dopey parents straight from central casting, a brilliantly evil and suspicious little sister—whose name was never given—and an unexplained talking dog, Joseph was everyone's hero.

Toby had a surprise for Tyler and Olivia. At nine P.M. sharp, the doorbell rang. Toby stood next to Tyler when he opened the door, and watched as his son's eyes went wide.

Standing before him were Twenty-two and Bruce. In the background were the flashing lights of photographers. Somehow the paparazzi had found them.

Chapter Thirty-One
A Visit from Twenty-two

As they walked up the steps to Toby's house in Germantown, Maryland, Bruce explained the paparazzi to Twenty-two. She'd had some experience with it when she first landed, but the idea that humans would chase famous people around to take pictures and then sell them was a foreign idea. The very act of doing so seemed to her an admission by the photographers that they were inferior to whoever's picture they were taking. Other than One—who was considered superior to all others—no grod would accept such an idea.

She was grateful when Tyler opened the door to let them in. Olivia invited Twenty-two and Bruce into their living room. "Have a seat," she said, motioning toward the cushioned sofa and chairs.

Twenty-two wasn't sure at first if she was actually giving away one of the items of furniture. They would be useless for her; grods didn't have the physical flexibility in their mid-sections to sit down even if they wanted to. Twenty-two didn't really understand why humans sat at all. Why not just stand? Only older or injured grods needed to sometimes lower themselves to the ground to rest their legs. While the others sat, Twenty-two shuffled over and stood next to the sofa, and listened as the humans did what Bruce explained as "small talk." Grods did the same thing, but not nearly to the extent of humans, who could spend hours talking about nothing.

Twenty-two recognized Tyler and Olivia from pictures Toby had shown her. Though she still had problems telling humans apart, their bright orange hair made them stand out, and Tyler was the obviously younger one. Strangely, Toby had said they had red hair, but it was clearly orange. When Twenty-two pointed this out, Bruce had explained that orange hair on a human was called red, just as brown-skinned people were historically called black or ebony, and yellow-haired people were called blond if they were men, blonde with an "e" if they were women. It seemed a complicated and unnecessary code.

But humans were a complicated species. They were intelligent, and yet, when they became emotional, they lost the ability to think rationally. From an evolutionary standpoint, it made no sense; rational thought was most needed in deeply emotional situations, such as when a predator was trying to eat you or a rival was competing for your mate.

They also had weak short-term memories. She'd noted that they often wrote things down, or called up things on their TCs that they'd seen before, as if they truly couldn't keep these items in their memory. Even Bruce, who was teaching her to play chess and apparently was very good, had difficulty keeping track of the pieces if the board wasn't in front of him. Grods had games similar to chess, but the entire games were played in their minds; a board with small sculptures wasn't needed to keep track of the pieces. Humans were as intelligent as grods—more so, in the case of Bruce—but their weak memory skills often made them seem stupid. Or, as Bruce would put it, like chimpanzees.

Knowing that Olivia and Tyler had orange—or red—hair, Twenty-two, using ingredients supplied by Bruce, had died her yellow vest orange, and wore a matching orange velvo. Bruce had helped her with her wardrobe, introducing her to a human tailor, who had made a series of colorful vests and velvos for her. However, while among humans, she doubted she'd wear any of the vests other than the now-orange one with the protective field. It was too dangerous.

She had gotten used to humans leaving their mouths exposed, but could not yet bring herself to do so. She fingered her velvo. There was no logical reason for this modesty, and yet . . . leaving one's mouth out in the open seemed so wrong. She knew it was learned behavior; baby grods had no such modesty.

Of more interest to her was the human ability to work with others. By nature and nurture, Grods valued independence. The idea of a group of grods working together to build a house, run a factory, or to win an election, was both distasteful and foreign to her thinking. Grod science advanced only as fast as individual grods made discoveries.

Perhaps this explained why human technology advanced so much more quickly than the grods' ever did, even though they had been around much longer. How long would it take for them to catch up and surpass grods?

The subject of discussion among the humans came to the election, and Dubois's *Stop the Invasion!* slogan.

"Is there going to be an invasion?" Tyler asked.

"Tyler!" Olivia said.

"It's an honest question," Bruce said. He turned to Twenty-two. "Is there?"

"There is no invasion planned," Twenty-two said. How could there be? She was the only grod who knew about Earth, other than as a point on a map that represented a race that did not yet qualify for Galactic Union membership, and was thereby off limits for any type of contact.

"If there were an alien invasion, could they conquer Earth?" Tyler edged closer on the sofa next to Twenty-two and stared at one of her arms.

A grod warship could destroy the surface of the unprotected Earth in about five minutes, Twenty-two figured. Of course, destroying wasn't the same as conquering. To do that, they could annihilate a few islands, and then blackmail Earth into surrender. That might take a day.

"Humans are a spirited race," Twenty-two said, "and I'm not sure if any alien race could conquer them." She noted that Bruce was smiling and shaking his head slightly.

"There are more alien races than just grods?" Tyler asked.

"There are many," Twenty-two said. "I cannot talk about that until Earth joins the Galactic Union. However, you may touch me."

Tyler's hand had been inching closer to her. Now he reached out and felt one of her arms. "It's smooth."

Soon the discussion moved to Tyler's running for class president, and then to the table tennis tryouts.

"You have a table in the basement?" Bruce asked.

They adjourned to the basement. Bruce and Tyler faced off, warming up by hitting forehand to forehand shots, then backhand to backhand. Bruce gave some tips on technique, guiding Tyler through the proper form for a stronger topspinning forehand, which he called a loop drive. Twenty-two examined a spare paddle, noting the sponge covering with tiny, angled pinholes that exhaled air when struck, putting extra spin on the ball.

"May I play?" Twenty-two asked.

Late Tuesday Night, August 31, 2100

"Damn it!" Bruce was spinning a ping-pong ball on his thumb. They were somewhere over the Atlantic on their way to Russia.

"It's just a ping-pong game," Toby said. Twenty-two, the object of Bruce's distress, was at the far end of the *Rocinante*, no doubt very confused.

"I taught her how to play, and twenty minutes later she beats me! Badly." Bruce caught the ball and pushed his thumb through it. He tossed the smashed ball aside.

"She's not human—"

"You can say that again!"

"—and so her reflexes and coordination are a little better than ours."

"A little?"

"Okay," Toby said, "a lot better. She did say her ancestors snatched small flying creatures out of the air for food. But I bet you can beat her at basketball. Or in a sprint or high jump."

"Yeah, she's about four feet tall. She could barely see over the table." He began nibbling on a pluot—half plum, half apricot. Stupid crawled over and watched with great interest.

"You'll get over it." Toby turned to Gene Conkling. "What's planned when we get to Russia?" Anything to keep his mind occupied as they awaited the North American results.

"Let me give you a rundown." Gene stared off into space, and then recited the scheduled speeches and press events. Normally Bruce would be prepping Toby by now, but he was in a mental funk as he tossed a ping-pong ball up and down and nibbled on the pluot. The speechwriters back at headquarters were already working on his upcoming speeches.

Bruce tossed a piece of the pluot to Stupid, who snatched it out of the air. Bruce got up and stood in front of Gene, who didn't seem to notice him.

"Gene, how many screens do you have open?" Bruce asked. Toby could tell he had several, from the way he was looking side to side, eyes unfocused.

"I've got ones from Russia News Central, from Moderate Headquarters in Russia, a personal spreadsheet with our schedule, and a map of Saint Petersburg."

"Four, huh?" Bruce said. He'd found another of his never-ending supply of ping-pong balls to fiddle with.

"Yep, four," Gene said. "It's about all I can see right now, and—"

"Then you didn't see this coming." Bruce gave Gene a light shove on his chest. Not expecting it, the weighty press secretary fell backward onto a table. There was a *crack* as he hit the table, along with a simultaneous exclamation from Gene.

"Screens off!" Gene cried. His eyes focused and settled on Bruce. *"What the hell was that for!"*

"Okay, I feel better now," Bruce said. "Let's get Toby ready for his next appearance."

Gene glared at Toby as he rose to his feet. Toby sighed.

"Bruce, did you have to do that?"

Bruce's eyes were unfocused and looking off into space—now he was looking at something on his TC. His eyes focused on Toby. "Yeah, I did." He turned toward Gene. "Gene, sorry about that, it won't happen again. The election's getting to me. Let's get to work."

Twenty-two wandered over, an eyestalk on Bruce.

Bruce glanced at her. "Relax, all's well between us, O, Great Goddess of Ping-Pong."

Twenty-two's eyestalks glanced at each other, then focused on Bruce. "Is that a joke?"

"I think it's Bruce's way of accepting that his twenty or so years of training at an Olympic sport was not wasted, because he didn't lose to a mere human or alien, but to an alien with supernatural abilities."

"And from now on, you're the Goddess of Ping-Pong," Bruce said. "We have some more time before we commence filling Toby's head with arcane facts and figures. Let's play chess."

There were a number of briefing papers that Bruce had put together for the next leg of the campaign. Toby hadn't had a chance to look them over until now. He pulled them up and began to read. Many covered the basic talking points that matched up with what Toby said in his campaign speeches. One interesting item he'd sent to all staff was the "Words" memo, which listed the words to be used for describing themselves and their opponents. They were:

Words to describe ourselves: truth, courage, prosperity, humane, liberty, dream, strength, visionary, reformer.

Words to describe opponents: sick, decay, failure, collapse, destructive, pathetic, betray, hypocrisy, waste, corruption, incompetent, bizarre, self-serving, greed, stagnation, disgrace, lie, cheat, steal.

Toby decided he'd have to have a talk with Bruce about the latter list. Politics was a tough game, but he wasn't sure if he wanted get into the name-calling game. For one thing, Dubois had more money, and could put far more attack ads out than he could—usually the only way to win a name-calling fight.

He must have dozed off, as he woke to an agonized scream. His heart racing, he jumped to his feet.

Twenty-two had beaten Bruce at chess.

Just before landing, they received the election results from North America.

North America	Electoral Votes	Dubois	Ajala	Platt
USA	62	**51%**	32%	17%
Canada	6	34%	31%	**35%**
Mexico	20	**46%**	45%	9%
Total	88	82	0	6

They had edged out Dubois to win Canada! It was their first electoral votes. Most of their votes had come at Ajala's expense, who, after getting slammed by Dubois's saturation ads, finished third. Dubois, with his last-minute ad barrage, had come back to beat Ajala by a point in Mexico, while easily winning the U.S. With his seven electoral votes from Oceania, Dubois now had 89 electoral votes to Toby's 6. Ajala was still at zero.

But it was still a long way to the magic 667 needed to clinch the election.

Chapter Thirty-Two
An Expected Invasion

Wednesday, September 1, 2100

Shortly after the creation of the United States of Earth (USE) in 2050, in order to offset United Europe, fourteen regional countries had joined with Russia to form the Russian Federation: Armenia, Azerbaijan, Belarus, Estonia, Georgia, Kazakhstan, Kyrgyzstan, Latvia, Lithuania, Moldavia, Tajikistan, Turkmenistan, Ukraine, and Uzbekistan. Also joining them, from halfway around the world, was Russia's long-time ally, Cuba. Together these countries exercised more political and economic clout than they would have individually.

Their combined population was just over 350 million. However, since all countries got a minimum of one electoral vote, the Russian Federation combined for forty electoral votes. They were a powerful federation as they tended to vote together, usually for the Liberal Party candidate.

Russian Federation	Population (millions)	Electoral Votes
Armenia	3.4	1
Azerbaijan	15.5	2
Belarus	8.2	1
Cuba	10.9	1
Estonia	1.4	1
Georgia	4.7	1

Kazakhstan	19.3	2
Kyrgyzstan	12.6	1
Latvia	2.4	1
Lithuania	3.5	1
Moldavia	4.2	1
Russia	137.2	14
Tajikistan	18.1	2
Turkmenistan	11.1	1
Ukraine	46.1	5
Uzbekistan	51.9	5
TOTAL	350.5	40

The *Rocinante* landed in Moscow early on Wednesday morning, six days before the Russian Federation election the following Tuesday. After taking jet lag pills and checking into their hotel, Bruce explained that, with their victory in Canada and their rise in the polls, they would get more attention—not only from the press and voters, but from nutcases. So there'd be a major increase in security, funded by the world government. The USE Gray Guard would start round-the-clock work immediately. Turk and Crowbar would continue as part of their team, independent of the Gray Guard.

"You won't notice them," Bruce added. "The Gray Guard blends in. See that guy over there?" He pointed at a man sitting in the lounge area, seemingly reading a book. "He's the shift leader. I recognize him from a picture."

With the increased security, Toby realized it would be tricky sneaking Twenty-two into a hotel. The Gray Guard might do whatever it took to protect Toby, but ultimately, they reported to USE. If they saw Twenty-two, they would report it. The news would quickly go to Dubois, and then all bets were off. Toby wondered if Dubois would go so far as to arrest him for harboring an "illegal alien," or whatever charge they could come up with. For now, Twenty-two stayed in the *Rocinante*.

They had just entered their rooms when everyone's TC went off with breaking news. North Korea had formally requested to be admitted to the Russian Federation.

Feodora was full of news when she met Toby and Bruce at the hotel for lunch—cheese sandwiches and salad. "It is done deal, worked out in secret by Russia and North Korea. Russian Federation Parliament will unanimously approve this afternoon. Also, no longer North Korea; now called Kim, after founder, Kim Il-sung."

"Why now?" Toby asked, yawning. What a strange name for a country, he thought. Kim?

Bruce smiled at him. "Must have been a long flight for you."

"At least I didn't get killed at ping-pong and chess," Toby said.

"You must tell me about this ping-pong and chess," Feodora said, nibbling on a plate of vegetables. "Perhaps some other time, when future of world not at stake. You both know debate on Russian Federation as one country or union of countries?"

"Of course," Bruce said. "Russia wants the RF to be one big, happy country, while most of the other countries want to keep their independence."

"Close," Feodora said. "Russia not just want Russian Federation to be one big, happy country. Russia already consider Russian Federation one big, happy country."

"I've heard the argument," Bruce said. "Isn't the whole idea of countries outdated? The whole world is one big, happy country now, minus the happy part."

Feodora nodded. "You are more idealistic than me. Someday the rest of the world see it that way, but not now."

"If the other countries in the RF don't agree they're all one country," Toby said, "then what's Russia going to do?"

"That's why Russia wants North Korea—Kim—to be political issue now," Feodora said. "Russian Federation countries all want Kim in Federation. When China and Japan protest, that unifies Russian Federation. Outside crisis always unites people against outside enemies.

Then Russia makes next big move, call for Russian Federation to be one country."

Bruce was tossing his ping-pong ball up and down. "You realize that if the RF becomes one country, you'll lose electoral votes for the next election?"

"Yes," Feodora said. "As combined country, we have 350 million population, so 35 electoral votes instead of 40. That mean President Dubois and Conservative Party will support it, since conservatives cannot win in Russian Federation. Very blue here."

Toby felt the situation somewhat surreal. He'd just set foot in Russia, and now he was in the middle of historical events.

"How can Russia justify all this?" Toby asked. "It's all just a big power grab for Russia. I mean, it's not the Uzbekistan or the Ukrainian Federation. It's the Russian Federation. Everyone knows which country runs things."

"Let me tell you history of your country," Feodora said. "Before your Civil War, people would say, 'The United States are.' After Civil War, people say, 'The United States is.' It switch from plural to singular, and that's when your country stopped being a collection of states and became one country. Is Russian Federation a country or a collection of countries? Nobody say, 'Russian Federation are.' They say, 'Russian Federation is.' Singular. Because we are one country. Like your Lincoln, we will keep this union together."

"Even if some of those countries object?" Toby asked. He didn't think Feodora's analogy made sense semantically, but it sounded like a good political argument.

"Kim issue will bring Russian Federation together," Feodora said. "Then we persuade them."

"By making an offer they can't refuse?" Bruce asked.

Feodora sighed. "Russia is like ocean tide. It moves in and conquers its neighbors. Then it recedes, and its neighbors go free, but only until the tide comes in again. Right now, tide is coming in. Only this time is purely political. There will be no invasion or threat of invasion by Russia against Russian Federation countries. You have my word."

"And what about North Korea?" Toby asked. "I mean Kim."

"They have been part of Russia since 2045," Feodora said. "Is it not time it be official?"

"Won't China and Japan object?"

"China and Japan will do more than object," Feodora said, sipping her tea. "Tomorrow, in surprise attack, they will invade Russia."

Chapter Thirty-Three
The Russians Hate Everyone

As Feodora predicted, by early afternoon, the Russian Federation Parliament had unanimously approved Kim's admittance. She left to attend meetings, leaving Toby and Bruce to campaign.

The entire Russian Federation was blue territory, and Ajala led the polls in every country. Feodora's presence on the ticket and winning in Canada helped Toby, but he still ran third in every poll. Most people vote based on who is on the top of the ticket, so Feodora's presence wasn't enough. Liberals were for Ajala; those who were against Ajala didn't want to waste their vote on Toby, and so supported keeping Dubois in office. It was the perpetual credibility problem of third-party candidates that Toby and Bruce had to break.

"If we can't find a way to win here, with Feodora on the ticket," Bruce said, "then we're sunk. If Ajala sweeps, then he and Dubois look like winners, and we look like sideshow freaks. And then we go to China, and you know what China thinks of Feodora. Maybe we should have gotten someone from China on the ticket."

Knowing they were probably going to lose China anyway, and that they absolutely needed to do well in the Russian Federation, and not wanting to incur the wrath of their vice presidential candidate, Toby and Bruce had decided to make Kim's admission to the Russian Federation a top priority in their ads and Toby's updated stump speech. Toby had a hard time thinking of North Korea as Kim, but if they wanted to be called that, and wanted admission to the Russian Federation, so be it.

Toby's Provisional Universal Food Foundation was another priority in this socialistic region. That could also get them Cuba, the one country they couldn't campaign in without flying back across the Atlantic. They'd considered a stop there before flying to Russia, but decided it wasn't worth it.

Russia and France were among the few places left in the world where the *English First!* movement had failed. It was a sticky issue; should Russians speak Russian, or join the rest of the world in its common language? A generation before, arguing for English would have been political suicide, but the younger generation had taken to English. Toby was sure that within another generation, Russia would be as Englishized as any other place in the world. But were they ready for it *now*? Dubois, even though he was from France, was for it, while Ajala was against it.

Feodora had given her input on each of these issues, particularly on the Kim issue. On *English First!*, she'd recommended a compromise, arguing for its adoption, but for it not to take effect for twenty years. That way, they would join the rest of the world in its common language, but those who had grown up on Russian wouldn't feel threatened by having it forced on them, while schools adopted it as required curriculum for the upcoming generation.

"These days," Bruce wondered, "why would anyone speak anything other than English?"

"Why would anyone in Russia speak anything other than Russian?" Feodora retorted. "Yet compromise is best. You are always right if you support both sides of an issue." Toby and Bruce wholeheartedly agreed.

She also pointed out a political problem. "Russians hate you because you are an American, one of our long-time enemies."

"Everyone is a long-time enemy of Russia," Bruce said. "Russians hate everyone."

Feodora laughed. "How true."

As usual, Gene had appearances for Toby scheduled all over the Russian Federation, and as usual, the media would cover most of them. That afternoon they were in Moscow and St. Petersburg, followed by whirlwind tours through Estonia, Latvia, Lithuania, and Belarus. Late that night they flew into Ukraine for an early morning speech, after which they'd set off for tours of Kazakhstan and Uzbekistan. The plan was to do three circuits of all the countries in the region.

"Wouldn't it make more sense to spend more time in each country," Toby asked, "rather than spend so much time flying around, since we'll keep coming back to the same countries?"

"Only to a logical mind," Bruce said, which Toby took as a rare compliment. "People tend to see a candidate coming into their country as a big event, and so if we can do it three times in each country, we get their attention three times, and that pretty much sells them. Isn't that what you did with Dubois five years ago?"

It was. Toby realized he was thinking through the fog of exhaustion. There was a reason why a person running for the ultimate decision-making job shouldn't be allowed to make decisions until he was safely in the job.

A ping-pong ball smacked into Toby's shoulder. He looked up. "Whatever you do," Bruce said, "don't get caught in public calling them countries like you just did. To Feodora and a lot of Russians, it's all one big country made up of states that used to be countries, and you need their support. Also, is there any way I can convince you to take off the scarf?"

"Only when you stop wearing warm-up suits."

They also met with Janlibo officials, who very politely but clearly let them know that they felt their product wasn't getting the visuals deserving of the money they were spending on the campaign. From there on, the glass of water he sipped on during campaign stops would be replaced by an orange-tinted bottle of Jancola, with the logo conveniently turned toward the closest media cameras. Toby quickly became sick of the taste, and took to pouring the overly-sweet liquid out and replacing it with plain water.

He also received another text message from Lara: *Dad, we could use you. Dubois will take you back, will back you for president next time.*

He ignored it again.

Between appearances, Toby followed the Kim crisis. At the World Senate, Japan, China, and their allies angrily denounced the move, while Russian Federation countries defended it. As Feodora predicted, the Russian Federation countries were rallying together like a unified country.

It quickly degraded into back-and-forth schoolyard insults. The rest of the world was roughly split on the issue. Soon there would be a vote by the World Senate. If either side refused to abide by their ruling, it could lead to a constitutional crisis, or worse.

As they quickly learned, it was worse. Once again, Feodora had called it.

On Thursday morning, joint Japanese and Chinese forces launched surprise air strikes against Russian forces in North Korea. They quickly defeated the local Russian air forces. Combined, the Japanese and Chinese air forces were stronger than anything Russia could bring in.

By noon, Japanese troops had landed in North Korea, while China invaded to the north, quickly taking the Russian city of Vladivostok. With Japanese forces to the south and east, and Chinese forces to the north and west, and all marching on North Korea, the large Russian army was trapped—a seeming repeat of nine years before.

By Thursday night, it seemed obvious the Russians had been out-maneuvered, out-thought, and out-fought. The Russians needed another "Miracle at Khrebet" to avoid complete humiliation, but it was unlikely the Japanese would fall for the same tactics as before. And now they had the Chinese army to deal with as well.

Despite the invasion, the campaign went on. Throughout their stops in Kazakhstan and Uzbekistan, Toby railed against the Chinese and Japanese invasion.

The only country where Dubois polled close to Ajala was in Uzbekistan, the second largest country in the Russian Federation with 52 million people. Rather than spread his time around, he spent the entire week there, ceding 35 electoral votes while hoping to pull out Uzbekistan's five.

Dubois was in an impossible situation. He needed China's 159 electoral votes—about four times the Russian Federation's. So while he supported the Russian Federation as a single country, he didn't support Kim's admittance, and he couldn't oppose the Chinese and Japanese invasion. His poll numbers plummeted in the Russian Federation, even in Uzbekistan.

Ajala strongly supported the Russian Federation on all issues, and his thunderous denunciations of China and Japan increased his lead in the polls. Toby would need his own "Miracle at Khrebet" just to avoid humiliation. It was looking like a sweep for Ajala.

Amid all this, a smiling General Feodora Zubkov flew to Ukraine to meet with Toby and Bruce.

Chapter Thirty-Four
The Miracle of Osaka

"Russia in big trouble, it seem," Feodora said. The three of them were watching live coverage on their TCs. Within hours, the surrounded Russian forces would either surrender or be slaughtered. Chinese forces had already turned north, taking Khabarovsk, another major Russian city. There was little to stop them from marching through much of southwest Russia.

"I hate to think in political terms at a time like this," Toby said, "but what the hell happened? How could Russia miscalculate this badly? Now Ajala's gonna sweep everywhere, Dubois will take China, and we'll be back to running mayoral elections."

"I think you're completely wrong on this," Bruce said. "After this, nobody's going to hire us to run a mayoral campaign."

"Gentlemen," Feodora said, "Bruce is correct. Nobody is going to hire you to run a mayoral campaign because you will be too busy running world government."

Toby stared at her. Had his vice presidential candidate gone completely mad?

Bruce was a bit more direct. "Are you insane?"

Feodora smiled. "Always have backup plan."

"A backup plan?" Bruce said. "I once played the world champion table tennis player. I was getting killed, but I had a backup plan. I faked an injury and defaulted."

"I have better backup plan," Feodora said. "Russian military big disappointment—many generals with big, cushy desks may soon be working from Siberian igloos, while small general may get demoted from ambassador to old job of supreme commander again. But when military fails, you do next best thing: diplomacy. Tomorrow I meet with Chinese and Japanese generals, and negotiate agreement."

"It seems to me," Bruce said, "that diplomacy works best when you have a hand to play. China and Japan have all the aces, and all you have are deuces. You have nothing to negotiate with."

"You forget the secret to diplomacy," Feodora said with a slight smile. "If only have deuces, make sure deuces are wild."

Feodora studied the inscrutable face of General Kubo, the Japanese High Commander. He looked gleeful, though you had to look closely at his granite face to see it. General Chou of China made no attempt to hide the victorious grin on his face.

"General Zubkov, we agreed to meet with you because of your high standing with the Russian people," Kubo said.

What he means, Feodora thought, is that you humiliated us nine years ago, and now it's our turn. "And I asked to meet with you to work out amicable settlement of Kim crisis."

The two rival generals exchanged glances. Like Toby and Bruce, they thought she was crazy. Many past opponents had thought that, but those that still lived did not hold that opinion.

"It's not Kim," Chou said. "It's North Korea."

"Really," Feodora said. They seemed to expect her to say more, so she didn't.

After an uncomfortable silence, Kubo said. "Let's review the situation. Do you agree, from a military standpoint, that if the Russian troops in North Korea do not surrender, we can destroy them? Is that a fair assessment, General Zubkov?"

Feodora only smiled.

"I'll take that as agreement," Kubo said. "Do you also agree, again from a military standpoint, that we can take out quite a bit of Russian territory, and hold it? That the combined Japanese-Chinese troops are stronger than Russia's, and are in a better strategic position?"

Again, Feodora only smiled.

Chou angered visibly. "We came here at your request, and all you do is grin like a chimpanzee. General Kubo, we are wasting our time here."

Kubo was studying Feodora's face; she stared back, neither backed down. Finally he spoke. "There's something going on that we don't know about. You wouldn't ask to meet with us otherwise. But I have to agree with my colleague that we're wasting time here if all you're going to do is smile at us."

It was showtime, Feodora thought. "General Chou, it is funny you mention chimpanzee. I have friend who also calls others chimpanzees, because he is smarter than almost everyone else. The danger is that when one thinks of others as chimpanzees, one risks not recognizing a smarter chimpanzee."

"Based on what I've seen so far," Chou said, "and using your own analogy, the Russians who brought about this situation are the chimpanzees."

"The question," Kubo said, "is whether there is a smarter chimpanzee. Are you that smarter chimpanzee, General Zubkov?"

Feodora was tempted to screech like a chimpanzee in victory, but restrained herself. "General Kubo, do you know the ten largest cities in Japan?"

There was silence as Kubo stared at her, his granite face now a bit rockier than before. Feodora knew that he knew that somehow, someway, with that seemingly meaningless question, the tables had just been turned.

"I could probably name them," Kubo said.

"Why is this important?" Chou said. Kubo gave him a look, and Chou, who seemed to have more to say, instead leaned back in his chair.

"Choose one," Feodora said.

"Why?"

Feodora only smiled.

After minute, Kubo said, "Osaka."

"Osaka," Feodora repeated. "Is your family from Osaka?" Kubo nodded. "Weren't you worried I would set one off in Osaka?"

234

"No," said Kubo. "That would have been dishonorable."

Feodora scribbled an address on a piece of paper and handed it to Kubo. She'd memorized all ten addresses. "Choose your most trusted aide in Osaka, and have him go to this address. Have him look for closet in basement. Tear down the back of the closet, and he'll find secret compartment. Have him tell you what he finds." She would handle this differently than the Korean Gang of Three in 2045 and Truman a hundred years before that.

Two hours later, they reached an agreement. Chou was reticent, but didn't want to take on Russia without Japanese support. Kubo and Chou agreed to withdraw out of Kim—they no longer called it North Korea—and to support Kim's entry into the Russian Federation.

In return, Feodora pledged Russian support for future Japanese sovereignty over South Korea—she suggested they just call it "Korea"—and for China in its ongoing boundary disputes with Mongolia and Nepal. They also agreed to future meetings to set up a Russia-China-Japan free trade zone.

It had been a short but costly enterprise, she thought, with over fifteen hundred dead for the three countries. There had been many civil wars throughout history with far more deaths to keep a country together; how was that different from a war to bring a country together? It had taken 109 years to put the Soviet Union back together again. It had deserved its prior fate. This time, she thought, let's do it right. She vowed to visit the grave of every soldier who died for all three countries.

It had been worth giving up the location of the hidden nuke in Osaka, even if it meant Japan now had one. Japan's open society had made the smuggling relatively easy. The other nine would remain hidden, and would never be used. She hoped.

"How the hell did you pull this off?" Bruce asked. Already the media was giving nonstop coverage of the agreement, with satellite photos of the Japanese and Chinese troops pulling out. There had been over a thousand Russian deaths in the short struggle, and about half that number for the combined Japanese and Chinese forces.

"It's all about diplomacy," Feodora said.

"You said the secret to diplomacy was to have wild deuces," Toby said.

"Did I say that?"

"Yes!" Toby and Bruce said together.

"Well, if you say so, then I must have. But really, I mostly just smiled at them. That won them over." Despite their persistence, she only smiled and refused to say more.

"I have a question about this war," said Twenty-two. "When these human countries fought, they didn't use nuclear bombs. Why not?"

"Because if they did," Toby said, "then the other side would also use them, and both sides would get destroyed and lose. Whoever uses a nuclear bomb first knows they'll get destroyed in retaliation."

"It's called 'mutual assured destruction,'" Bruce said, "the idea being both sides survive unless one side wants the other side dead more than they want to live."

"So both sides only fight hard enough to maybe win, but not hard enough to make the other too mad, so that win or lose they survive? That is smart; we have same concept. But is there no oversight to make sure the country that is right wins?"

"Whoever wins is always right," said Feodora. "Winners write history books."

When Feodora spoke to the media, she gave Toby full credit for the agreement. "He tell me what to say, what to do. That is why he is running for president, while small general only run for vice president. He may be hated American," and she paused to allow laughter, "but because of him, we have peace. Later, we meet in Osaka to set up free trade agreements between Russia, Japan and China. So we will call what Toby did . . . 'The Miracle of Osaka.'"

Tuesday, September 7, was election day. That night, Toby, Bruce, and Feodora met in her Moscow apartment.

"To Russia's new national hero!" a slightly drunk Feodora said, raising a glass of Russian New Vodka.

"You realize that alcohol is illegal everywhere on the planet?" Toby said, still not quite used to being the toast of the Russian Federation. Of course, his status would change quite a bit when they flew to China later that night.

"You bet it is," Feodora said. "Drink up!"

"To world domination!" Bruce said, holding up his vodka.

Toby raised his as well, and they all drank to celebrate. For they had much to celebrate.

Russian Federation	Electoral Votes	Dubois	Ajala	Platt
Armenia	1	29%	38%	**43%**
Azerbaijan	2	21%	39%	**40%**
Belarus	1	25%	**47%**	28%
Cuba	1	26%	**44%**	30%
Estonia	1	23%	**39%**	38%
Georgia	1	31%	34%	**35%**
Kazakhstan	2	19%	34%	**47%**
Kyrgyzstan	1	17%	40%	**43%**
Latvia	1	32%	**35%**	33%
Lithuania	1	20%	**41%**	39%
Moldavia	1	25%	36%	**39%**
Russia	14	17%	31%	**52%**
Tajikistan	2	17%	41%	**42%**
Turkmenistan	1	27%	36%	**37%**
Ukraine	5	25%	**39%**	36%
Uzbekistan	5	35%	27%	**38%**
TOTAL	40	0	10	30

Dubois had been shut out. Ajala won Cuba, Belarus, Ukraine, and the Baltic states—Estonia, Latvia, and Lithuania—for a total of ten electoral votes. Toby had swept the rest for thirty electoral votes: Russia, Armenia, Azerbaijan, Georgia, Kazakhstan, Kyrgyzstan, Moldavia, Tajikistan, Turkmenistan, and Uzbekistan.

Though Kim was now a part of the Russian Federation, it would vote in the Asian Federation election this time around. Toby was pretty sure he'd win Kim's three electoral votes, but the Asian Federation vote wasn't until week six. It seemed like they had campaigned forever, and yet they'd just finished week three. Week four would be China, followed by United Europe.

"I bet I could win in the U.S. if they ran the election now," Toby said. "Heck, maybe we really can win this thing!"

"Maybe," Feodora said. "But you win here because of this old lady, and you win in Canada because of another old lady. Soon you must learn to win without old ladies."

The electoral count now stood: Dubois 89, Ajala 10 . . . and Platt 36.

Chapter Thirty-Five
A Table Tennis Exhibition in China

Wednesday, September 8, 2100

"**M**aybe you haven't taken a look at the electoral count, or the polls in China and the rest of the world," Dubois said to Lara. They had just arrived in Beijing. "Your dad never looked at these things emotionally; why are you?"

Actually, Lara thought, her dad always did look at these things emotionally. He just never *acted* out of emotion. Maybe Dubois was right; maybe she was acting emotionally? After all, her dad only had 36 votes, mostly from the RF, the most leftist region in the world. After Dubois wins in China, he'd lead 241 to 36, with Ajala at only ten.

"Your dad's winning the RF only takes away from Ajala," Dubois continued. "Let them keep splitting the vote, and we'll have the biggest landslide since Wallace in '50."

"All I'm saying," Lara said, "is that we need to start thinking of my dad as the main challenger. Ajala is through; pretty soon even his followers are going to realize he can't win."

"And you think Toby can?"

Apparently Dubois hadn't learned one of the basic lessons from her dad. "There's no difference between an insurmountable lead, a small lead, or being behind," she quoted him. "In all cases, you find the person most likely to win other than yourself, and aim your fire at that person. An insurmountable lead is only insurmountable if you take out the guy in second place." And, she thought, we have followed this lesson already, taking out Ajala in Oceania and North America, and with Dad's help, most of his support in the RF.

"So you think we should target your dad?"

"He's the one in second place."

Dubois paced back and forth for a moment, then stopped, a grin on his face. "Remind me never to have kids. Okay, put out the word: Toby is the new target. You know everything about him; give every bit of ammunition you have to the ad people, and see what they come up with. We'll destroy him."

"Maybe—"

"Plug the mouth hole, and get to work," Dubois said.

She nodded, but looked away quickly. Like her dad, she could not allow herself to act out of emotion, and targeting her dad was the right thing to do. She left quickly, before Dubois could see the tear running down her face.

Before the roof and famous mural were added, some said the Great Mall of China, one of the Seven Wonders of the Modern World, was the only manmade object you could see from space. But only at nighttime, when the outside lights came on.

The Great Mall ran five hundred miles alongside the Great Wall of China. The Communist Republic of China planned for it to reach a thousand miles within twenty years, and believed it would someday run the entire 4000-mile length of the wall. A monument to China's rapidly-growing free-market economy.

Or, as the Chinese government claimed, it demonstrated the victory of communism over capitalism.

Every few dozen steps, Bruce looked up at the murals painted on the high ceiling. He thought them a complete waste of money, and yet had to admire the vivid images that depicted Chinese history continuously along the ceiling. It was really a single mural, thirty feet wide, five hundred miles long. The colorful and often graphic illustrations—like most countries, China had a violent and bloody history—started with the ancient Xia Dynasty four thousand years ago. It showed the wars leading to the unification of China and the First Emperor Qin in 214 BC, who started construction of the adjacent Great Wall of China. Then came the two thousand years of the Imperial era, from the Qin to the Qing, then the Republic of China, and finally the rise of Communism and modern China, with pictures that were so blatantly nationalistic propaganda that Bruce had to smile. The final murals showed the creation of the mural itself. How many Chinese artists had it taken to paint it?

Many Chinese said you weren't truly Chinese until you'd hiked the Great Mall. After the 2095 election, he and Toby had done so. Bruce would never forget the last hundred miles as he hobbled along on blistered feet. Toby spent weeks with a neck brace from watching the mural while hiking.

Even without considering the mural, the Great Mall was a wonder, the largest mall in the world by several orders of magnitude. Nowhere in the world could one find such an assortment of merchandise. If it could be found anywhere on the planet, it could be found in the Great Mall of China.

And right now Bruce was searching for a new ping-pong paddle. After losing to Twenty-two, he'd broken Sling, his former partner in table tennis. Now he hoped to find another Trump Maestro Prime.

He felt a bit guilty about taking time off from the campaign, but there were a lot of important decisions coming up. He could make most decisions with a ping-pong ball in his hand, but for the really important ones, he thought more clearly if he had the feel of a paddle in his hand.

Equally important, he needed a paddle for the upcoming table tennis exhibition before the Chinese Communist Party, who had celebrated their 150th anniversary the year before. It had been a surprise invitation, but it would give them a chance to meet with China's leaders, who would have great influence over the election. It had been nearly 130 years since the last "Ping-Pong Diplomacy," which had also been a surprise invitation from China to the U.S. in 1971. It had worked then, so why not now?

The aroma from a plastated fish market made him hungry—was that tuna? Maybe he'd stop by on the way back. Or was that real fish?

He bought a new collar for Stupid at a pet store, which had the latest pet fad: barking snakes, with a dog's brain inside a Burmese Python's body. They let him hold one; it coiled its twelve-foot brown-mottled length about his body, wagging its tail as it excitedly barked at him. He gave it a bacon-flavored snack the storekeeper provided. He wondered if it would get along with Stupid. He'd once had a bullcat, but Stupid had so terrorized it he'd given the poor thing away.

A used floater salesman surrounded by balloons yelled at him as he passed by, promising low interest rates and a long-term maintenance deal that Bruce knew was a scam.

He found a nice deal on a "world" warm-up suit at a Mother Ling's Coverings. Like the world flag, it was green, with the white twisted gun symbol in the middle, surrounded by the 165 stars representing all the countries in USE. It was only as he left that he realized that it would likely be outdated in a few months, if the Russian Federation became one country.

A TC saleswoman filled him in on all the latest advancements in TC technology. When the newest device began reciting poetry, he walked off.

He finally arrived at the table tennis store. Normally he got his equipment free from sponsor Trump, but he didn't have time to wait. On the front wall hung hundreds of rackets. Nearly every brand name was represented. There had once been a Bruce Sims model, a modest seller, but it had been discontinued.

He browsed through the Trump brands, and there it was: a Maestro Prime.

Next he'd need new sponge covering, and again there were hundreds to choose from in numerous bright colors. Best to stick with the familiar; he found two sheets of Spinsey pinhole sponge.

Trump's newest playing shoe was the Firmfoot Adjustable, named for its adjustable traction. Bruce found his size.

He browsed through the rest of the store, with every variety of balls, tables, nets, clothing, racket cases, playing bags, and numerous other accessories. He looked through the latest Trump playing cards, but he wasn't in them this year.

He paid for the items, and began the long journey back to the mall entrance. He didn't feel like fish anymore, and grabbed a Big Cheese from a McBurger instead. For some reason he felt nervous about the upcoming exhibition, and he only nibbled on the sandwich. The plastated beef felt like the sponge rubber on his paddle.

The table tennis exhibition was held at the Hall of Champions Stadium in Shanghai, capital of China since the Beijing Rebellion of 2074. Over 100,000 fans jammed the stadium, with tens of millions watching on TC. Toby sat in a front row seat with other Chinese dignitaries. Feodora had stayed home; Russians were not too popular in China.

Toby was uncomfortably aware that Jing Xu, the previous president and now a high-ranking member of the Chinese Communist Party, sat nearby. A lot of Chinese would, unfortunately, remember that Toby had masterminded Xu's downfall in the election of 2095. A moderate liberal in a country of conservatives, Xu maintained his power through the respect and personal loyalties he'd built up over the years, all handled with great political acumen.

The table tennis exhibition went well. The aftermath did not.

The Chinese, U.S., and Brazilian teams were the best in the world. The U.S. had dominated much of the past ten years, with Bruce often a member of the team. China had emerged on top again only this past year, and seemed to have hordes of up-and-coming stars—a scary thing for the rest of the table tennis world.

The muscled Chinese player, Cheng Tongsheng, the world's #1 player, dwarfed Bruce. They were about the same height, but it was obvious Bruce's refusal to take steroids to build up his body cost him speed and power. But it was only an exhibition, not a real match. The two exchanged topspin smashes and counter smashes, and took turns returning smashes with leaping lobs from the back court, while the crowd cheered in amazement.

The score reached 19-all. The last two points featured Bruce at his most acrobatic, racing down one pummeling smash after another, before Cheng finally pounded a winner to lead, and then executed a delicate, unreturnable drop shot to win the game. The result had been planned out in advance, of course; the best way to get Chinese votes would be to put up a great fight against their champion, then lose very close. Bruce hammed it up after the last point, making a hopeless dive toward the table after the drop shot, then lying on the floor still for a moment before jumping to his feet with a big grin on his face and shaking hands with Cheng.

Then came the surprise Bruce and Toby had prepared. Bruce took the microphone.

"One hundred and twenty-nine years ago, my American ancestors played matches with your Chinese ancestors, and that Ping-Pong Diplomacy began a new relationship between our two countries. Things haven't changed much; the Chinese are still polite, the Americans brash, and once again the Chinese kicked our ass." The crowd cheered.

"Now I propose a new wrinkle on things," he continued. "If Ping-Pong Diplomacy worked between our two countries, why not try it again? Nope, I don't mean between our two countries again; I'm tired of losing." Again, there were cheers along with laughter.

"Back then, we were visitors in your country, and you treated us well, as you are now. Now we have a visitor on our world, an alien. Some think we should throw her off the planet, as Chinese and Americans once thought to do to each other. I propose we challenge her to a ping-pong match. What do you say?" There were shouts of agreement.

"Now, you probably think this is an empty rhetorical gesture to get your support in the upcoming election for Toby Platt. If an empty rhetorical gesture will get your vote, then by all means, that's what it is!" He paused for the laughter to end.

"But this is not an empty rhetorical gesture. This is real, and this is Ping-Pong Diplomacy taken to a new level. You all know of Twenty-two, the grod ambassador. What you don't know is that she's been practicing her table tennis game. She thinks she's pretty good. Now, in a game to twenty-one, it's difficult to beat someone named Twenty-two, but I'm going to do my best. Let's hear it for Ambassador Twenty-two, the undisputed table tennis champion of Grodan!"

To the surprise of nearly all, out waddled Twenty-two.

She grasped the spare racket Bruce had loaned her, the very one she'd used to beat him. Now she stood at the table, as unimposing a figure as could be imagined. With her four short legs, how could she have the mobility required in the sport?

Soon, however, the world's experts were introduced to a new type of table tennis. Where the best players had always focused on acrobatic attacks and spectacular off-table defense, Twenty-two simply stood jammed up to the table and returned everything Bruce sent at her, angling shots side to side, with stunning reflexes and coordination. She didn't need mobility or power; there was simply no way of getting a ball past her. Bruce hammered ball after ball at her, to all parts of the table, but to no avail. Eventually, either he'd miss, or he'd have to slow his shots down for consistency. When he did that, that's when Twenty-two would swat in a shot. Usually Bruce could return that one—the alien didn't have great power—but since she almost never missed, and Bruce sometimes did, the outcome was inevitable.

But this was an exhibition. As pre-planned, Twenty-two did move off the table, where her lack of mobility affected her, and Bruce would hammer ball after ball while she seemingly struggled to return each one. In reality, Bruce hit the ball just close enough for her to reach it. After a few shots, he might hit a winner she couldn't reach. Other times Bruce would put the ball up and let Twenty-two smack in shot after shot until he'd pick one out and counter-smash—which the alien would easily block back, though she let some go by on purpose.

Like the previous match, it went to 19-all, and then the "home" player—Bruce—"won" the last two points in a pair of vicious counter-smashing rallies.

245

After thunderous applause, Twenty-two took the microphone. "I recently learned the story of Ping-Pong Diplomacy. It was a time when humans were alien to each other. Yet they greeted each other as friends. Now a real alien walks among you. Once again Ping-Pong Diplomacy has brought us together. I am told that the foremost matter on everyone's mind right now is the upcoming election. I will not take sides. I am just an observer. Whichever side wins, I look forward to someday welcoming Earth to the Galactic Union. I also plan to train a generation of grods in the intricacies of this wonderful sport of table tennis."

Once again there was thunderous applause. Toby knew this would help his campaign, not only in China, but worldwide. Twenty-two didn't have to take sides; she'd just played an exhibition with his campaign director! Their work here was done, and it was time to go. In less than an hour, Toby had a speech to give in Taipei. They should have no trouble making the flight in the *Rocinante*.

Huang Rui, the governor of China, took the microphone. He was the president of Farmland China, the largest supplier in the world of both Butanol and rice, as well as the richest man in China, and the third richest in the world. Toby slouched back in his chair in the stands, thinking about his upcoming speech, and barely paid attention as Huang went through the usual diplomatic niceties.

"...and so I call upon Toby Platt to answer a few questions." Toby sat up, startled at hearing his name. Huang was gesturing for him to join him.

His TC alerted him to an incoming call from Bruce. He took it, whispered, *"Not now!"* and disconnected.

As he joined Huang in the arena, the governor asked the crowd to be silent during the course of the questioning. In the U.S., Toby thought, if someone said that, he'd get booed out of the stadium, but the Chinese people were obviously a more polite society.

The governor handed him a microphone. Normally Toby projected his voice to a microphone via his TC, but for now, a hand-held one would do. He looked over to the sidelines, where Bruce and Twenty-two

246

watched, and gave them a quick nod. He turned back to face the Chinese delegation.

"I did not realize—" he began, but stopped. Jing Xu and the contingent surrounding him had stood and turned away. Slowly they filed out, sending a message to all those who watched. Toby waited until they were gone, then continued.

"I did not realize I would be asked questions today, but I look forward to them." Most of the remaining top leadership of China sat before him in front row seats. Only now did he notice that several held microphones. Among them were Vice Governor Wang Li, the founder and owner of The Joseph Wang Show, and the voice of the infamous Joseph Wang himself; Chinese Secretary of State Mao Dong, majority owner of the worldwide McBurger restaurant; and Chinese Party Leader Chuan Lijun, whose military industrial complex was the largest in the world. While Wang and the others ran the government on a day-to-day basis, Chuan held the ultimate power as the leader of the Communist Party.

"Mr. Platt," Huang asked, "why did you support Russia over China in the North Korean conflict?"

Huang had gotten right to the point. Toby noted he used the old name for Kim, while calling it a "conflict" rather than a war, which might have implied China had lost a war.

"Mr. Governor, first I want to thank you for asking exactly the question that most needs to be answered. The problem is that it addresses only one small part of the issue. Yes, I supported North Korea's joining the Russian Federation, and if they want to be called Kim from now on, that's fine too. But I also supported China in its boundary disputes with Mongolia and Nepal, and successfully pushed for the upcoming free trade meetings between China and Japan, and China and the Russian Federation. By my count, that's four to one in favor of China."

"I find your math suspect," said Wang Li, his rasping voice a lower-pitched version of the one he used for Joseph Wang.

"Mr. Vice Governor," Toby said, "there's been a lot of math today, mostly in games to twenty-one, plus a little Twenty-two. I'll stick with my four-to-one lead. If you'd like, I'll get back to you later with seventeen more things about China I support, so I can make it 21-1."

"That is an interesting answer," said Mao Dong, "but if we are going to talk about boundary disputes, may I ask why we should support someone from America, with its wars on its neighbors Mexico and Canada?"

"The simple answer to that," Toby said, "is that I am not Mr. America, I am Mr. Platt, candidate for president. I was against U.S. forces going into Canada, while Dubois was for it. The Mexican war, while necessary because of the Eth trade, was completely mishandled."

Chuan Lijun rose to his feet. "Mr. Platt, you ran the campaign of President Dubois, which supported the Canadian occupation. Whatever you may have believed in private, that is the side you supported." Toby felt his face going hot; was he about to be chastised on worldwide TC by the top Chinese leader?

"Five years ago," Chuan continued, "there was peace and prosperity in the world. Now we have conflicts with a belligerent Russia, and the hunger rate rises even as wealthy nations like the U.S. and France become wealthier. Do you believe you made a mistake in running the campaign of President Dubois, the man who replaced President Jing Xu of China?"

Toby knew there had been a split in the Chinese leadership. Many supported Dubois, whose conservative principles matched their own. And yet Dubois had defeated their own Jing Xu. The wounds had not healed. He had thought that Chuan supported Dubois, but from what the Party Leader had just said, that did not seem to be true.

There was only one way to answer such a question; he and Bruce had discussed this very situation before. He looked out at the crowd.

Looking out at them was a mistake. Now he noticed the background murmur of the crowd. Suddenly he felt he could hear every whisper, every chair that creaked as someone shifted his weight, even the sound of 100,000 people breathing, by far the largest live crowd he'd ever spoken in front of. Aware that every eye was on him, he paused to get his thoughts together.

"Mr. Platt?"

He took a deep breath, then stared at the nose of the Chinese Party Leader, blocking out everything else. His mind cleared.

"I am glad you asked that question," Toby said. "At the same time, I've dreaded answering it, but answer it I will. So let me be absolutely clear on this." He held the microphone closer and raised his voice.

"Supporting Dubois five years ago was the worst mistake of my political life. He has been a disaster, a plague on the world. To the Chinese people, and to the rest of the world, I offer my apology."

Any applause Bruce had received during the exhibition was dwarfed by the ear-breaking response to this, despite Huang's earlier request for silence. There were boos mixed in, but it seemed mostly cheers.

There was nothing worse in politics than sticking to a losing argument; there was nothing better than admitting you were wrong. This was especially true in China, which had a long history of forced confessions from leaders who had "failed" in some way, whether in reality or simply from the perspective of new leaders.

Maybe he had a chance in China after all? Could he turn Red China purple?

"Mr. Platt," Chuan said, "what you said is a bird's morning song to my ear. Perhaps the dusk of the Dubois administration will end with the dawn of a bright new one. However, there is an even more important question I must ask, perhaps the most important question in the history of humankind."

Uh oh, Toby thought. He glanced at Twenty-two, who stood by the side of the arena with Bruce. She looked back with one eyestalk, the other focused on Chuan.

"You have been traveling with the alien known as Twenty-two," Chuan said, "who just played a marvelous table tennis exhibition. She has learned much about us during her stay here. But what about our learning from her? Why hasn't she shared her technological skills to better humankind?"

This could be a touchy issue, Toby thought. "She has told me that she is not allowed to share their technology with us until we are a member of the Galactic Union."

"And how do we join this Galactic Union?"

"I'm told a primary membership requirement is interstellar spaceflight."

"Why can't the alien give us the technology for this spaceflight, so that we may join this Galactic Union?"

Circular reasoning, Toby thought; he could almost hear Bruce thinking "*Chimpanzee!*" And yet, to most people, it was a reasonable request.

"If I am elected president," he said, "I will do whatever is needed to expedite our membership in the Galactic Union. You are right, that might be the most important question in the history of humankind, and the answer is: let's work with them and fulfill their requirements. We don't need to cheat."

"It is not cheating to do what is in the best interests of our people," Chuan said. "This Twenty-two should be taken into custody and asked to share her knowledge with the Chinese people, which we will then share with the world."

"You are going to arrest her?" Toby said.

"No," Chuan said. "And I want to be clear that neither China nor I have anything to do with this. However . . . we received a call earlier, and we have an unexpected guest." He turned toward an open doorway that led into the arena.

USE security came jogging out, carrying what appeared to be a rolled up tarp. Behind them strode the massive General Waylon Duffy.

They surrounded Twenty-two as the crowd began to boo. Was Duffy a fool? Didn't he remember what happened the last time he tried to capture Twenty-two?

Apparently Duffy was not a fool. Nobody fired on the alien. Instead, they unrolled the object they carried, and threw it—a net—over Twenty-two, who made no attempt to escape. In less than a minute, she was trussed up and carried away.

"This is outrageous!" Toby cried into his microphone, but it had been turned off.

Chuan heard him. He put down his microphone, and spoke directly to Toby. "It is outrageous. It is also necessary."

Chapter Thirty-Six
The Assassin, the Antarctican, and the Alien

Marty Reese had stalked the three candidates throughout their Russian campaigns. He'd seen Dubois scream *"Stop the Invasion!"* from the steps of the Kremlin. He'd watched Ajala reason with hecklers at Saint Isaac's Cathedral in Saint Petersburg. He'd wondered if Platt really had a chance. He listened as he spoke at the Port of Tallinn in Estonia about his compromise plans for universal hunger and the *English First!* movement.

And then came the North Korean crisis. Where Platt leaped to prominence. The more he saw, the more Ajala looked like a loser. Dubois was going to win. Reese was sure of that. But this Platt fellow was getting popular.

Forget Dubois. Forget Ajala. Perhaps Platt was the one to kill. Or was he? Maybe he should wait a little longer to decide. He breathed heavily a few times. At times like this he could barely breathe.

Reese sat in the back of the upper stands, watching the table tennis exhibition. He again wore his old-style blue American uniform. With the empty sleeve where his right arm used to be. He knew it made him stand out. But he *liked* the uniform. With a small pair of binoculars he watched Platt sitting in a front-row seat with the other important people.

Reese was as surprised as everyone when the alien joined the exhibition. Some of his youthful idealism returned. He wondered what it would be like for humanity to go to the stars. He thought the xenophobic Dubois a fool. Humans were immoral idiots. Watching the alien was like taking a deep breath over a fine wine.

The world seemed split on the alien. Half thought as Reese did. The other half thought it a threat. Reese knew a cure for this. A way to make the alien extremely popular. It had worked for Lincoln, Kennedy, and Brown. The attempt on Wallace had made him even more popular than before.

Perhaps he should kill the alien as well.

When Toby was called out to respond to questions, Reese listened attentively. The man handled himself well. If he continued to gain popularity, he would die. So would the alien that had befriended him. A waste, he thought. But necessary.

When security appeared, all eyes but Reese's were transfixed on the scene. The crowd watched as heavily armed men threw the net over the alien and carried it away. Reese's attention stayed on the crowd. He wanted to see how they'd react. Once again, they were split. Half were cheering, seeming to agree that the alien needed to be taken into custody—no doubt they'd seen Dubois's propaganda. The other half were booing.

He imagined their reaction if the alien and Platt were actually killed.

Melissa had sneaked out of Liberal Headquarters in China for the table tennis exhibition. She'd never been a big sports fan, but this was different, almost history, as the legendary political operative Bruce Sims took on the world's best player. She had good seats near the front as she snacked on salted seaweed, and watched them play.

Of course, only insiders really knew of Sims, often called the brains behind Toby Platt, who in turn had once been called the brains behind Dubois. She'd never been so nervous as when she'd argued with Sims at the Mexico City fundraiser. She'd covered up for her nerves by spewing facts as fast as she could talk, to the delight or horror—she wasn't sure which—of both Sims and Platt.

She was amazed when Twenty-two went to the table and showed her abilities. Had she really just learned to play, as Bruce insisted? Or had

253

the aliens been watching humanity, and learning about the game, allowing Twenty-two to practice before coming to Earth?

Toby's responses to the impromptu questioning session impressed her. He had a knack for giving out punchy, yet informative sentences. Dubois would have responded to everything with slogans, Ajala with a lecture.

She dropped her bag of peanuts when they arrested Twenty-two. She couldn't believe it was happening. Is this the face of humanity they wanted to show the galaxy? Her faced flushed red; she was embarrassed to be human. She flushed further when she realized she had reacted like a stereotypical selfish human, thinking of ourselves first. An innocent being had just been arrested, and her first thought was how it made humans look. *What is wrong with our race?* was all she could think.

She knew Dubois was behind this. She vowed to do whatever it took to defeat him in the election. Who could beat him, Ajala or Platt? Soon she would have to choose.

Twenty-two had been caught completely off guard by the sudden attack. She now realized she'd been overconfident after the two previous attacks. The vest defended against most projectile and energy weapons, as well as knives and fists, but not against being carried away in a net. A military forcefield with a locking mechanism would have provided full protection, but her vest only had a simple protective field.

Removing the vest was also rather simple for the humans. While several burly ones held her down, another pulled it up over her head. They laid her sideways on a bed—a highly uncomfortable position for a grod, who normally always stood—and tied her arms and legs together, leaving her defenseless. Then they tied her eyestalks down as well, so she was unable to even look about the room.

With the vest went her sensor, which would have allowed her to communicate with Zero, and order the ship to come to her rescue.

They also took off her velvo, exposing her mouth. Embarrassing as that was, she realized it was the least of her problems. From her reading of human history, the average human could be as savage as the most deranged grod.

"How are you today?" It was the familiar voice of General Duffy. "The rest of you can go." The guards in the room left, leaving Twenty-two alone with the general. "We found this device in your vest," and he held up her sensor. "I haven't been able to get it to work, but I think the scientists will have a great time studying it."

"Is this standard Earth treatment for visiting ambassadors?" Twenty-two wondered if human science was advanced enough to figure out how the sensor worked. She had no idea. She was no mechanic, and didn't really know the inner workings of the sensor herself. She found it hard to think while this human stared down at her naked lips. She vowed not to forget this, then put it out of her immediate thoughts. Her mind cleared.

"Are you under the impression that you are asking the questions?" Duffy asked. "You're a prisoner of war and will be treated as one."

Bruce would have had fun responding to that, she thought. "I must have missed the invasion. Or have you declared war on Grodan?" That would be a short fight. Actually, she doubted there would be such a fight; Earth couldn't send anyone to Grodan, and Grodan had no interest in a backward planet like Earth that had not even qualified for Galactic Union membership.

"Again, you ask questions." Duffy leaned over her; she could smell his breath, which was highly unpleasant. With their velvos, grods did not breathe on each other. "But I'll answer. On your planet, do you have a home?"

"Yes."

"Suppose you found a stranger in your house. What would you do?"

Twenty-two could see Duffy was about to play a semantics game. "I'd ask the stranger to leave."

"And if the stranger refused to leave?"

"Wouldn't you call the police?" Grods, of course, would handle the problem on their own, with their more independent nature. She'd learned humans were different.

"And if the police arrive, and try to make the stranger leave, but he evades them, and hides somewhere in your house? Why, you'd probably worry about your safety with this criminal in your house."

"I am sure you have a reason for asking these questions."

"Of course. Do you know what this is?" Duffy held up a metal tube, about six inches long and an inch thick. He grabbed one end and it telescoped out to about two feet in length, with one end covered in copper. He held it over her like a club.

Twenty-two gave it a look. "I see Earth has discovered electricity." She recognized it as a torture stick, something she'd read about, but never expected to see. Her two hearts began to beat rapidly.

"Very funny. You'll find out more about electricity shortly. Think about it carefully when you speak with me. I think this is the part where I'm supposed to say I don't want to use this, but to tell you the truth, I do." The general grinned, showing her his teeth, which seemed all gold. Was that a style thing, she wondered, or did they have archaic dentistry on this planet?

"Now, when we first learned of your uninvited presence on our planet, you were asked to leave. You wouldn't. Security tried to arrest you, but you evaded them. You are no different than that criminal who broke into your home. You are as dangerous to us as that criminal would have been for you."

Twenty-two thought back to her time at the university when she'd studied first contacts. She didn't remember a chapter on alien ambassadors about to undergo torture. The whole point of first contact was not to get into that situation. Perhaps a real ambassador would have succeeded, but she was just a college student. A terrified one.

"It's time to get to business," Duffy said, pacing around to Twenty-two's back, where she couldn't see him. "I want to know all about grods, especially anything pertaining to their military strength, spaceflight capabilities, espionage activities, and colonization plans for Earth."

Espionage activities and colonization plans? "High, high, zero, and zero."

"What?"

"I said—" Twenty-two broke off with a high-pitched cry. Duffy had applied the torture stick to her. Time seemed to stop as the excruciating electric charge shot through her body, and she screamed as the agony went on and on and on. . . .

"That was a low setting," Duffy said as he turned the charge off. "Do we have a better understanding now about sarcasm?"

Twenty-two's body involuntarily shook, but she didn't say anything.

"I'll take that as a yes. Now, let's start with Grodan military power. What are their capabilities?"

"We could destroy Earth with the push of a button without ever leaving Grodan," she lied.

Duffy rewarded her with another dose of electricity as she screamed in agony.

"I don't believe you," he said. "I want the truth."

If she backed down now, then he'd shock her after every answer to see if she changed her answer. "I told the truth," she again lied. She felt dizzy and desperately did not want to be shocked again.

Duffy studied her for a moment, and seemed about to ask another question. Then he changed his mind and held up the tube.

"I still don't believe you." He extended the torture stick.

Someone opened the door to the interrogation room. Duffy pulled the stick away from Twenty-two, collapsed it back to its smaller size, and put it in his pocket. He then turned to see who was at the door. Twenty-two was facing the door, and saw who entered.

Corbin Dubois.

Several others that Twenty-two recognized as being Chinese followed. They gathered around Twenty-two.

"Has she told you anything useful?" Dubois asked.

"Not yet," Duffy said.

"Why was the alien screaming?" a Chinese man asked. Twenty-two recognized him as Chinese Party Leader Chuan Lijun. "

"I don't know," Duffy said, "perhaps it falsely expects to be tortured, and screamed in fright? Unlike our enlightened society."

"You know China adheres to international law, and does not allow torture."

"Of course," Dubois said, smoothly interrupting whatever Duffy was about to say. "However, this alien is a prisoner of the United States of Earth, not any particular country. I'm ordering her moved to a more appropriate facility."

"You have that authority," Chuan said. "Where would you like us to send her?"

"You don't need to send her anywhere," Dubois said. "I'll have a security detail here shortly. We're taking her to France."

Twenty-two threw up the contents of her stomachs.

Chapter Thirty-Seven
The Election of Germantown Middle School

"What are we going to do about Twenty-two?" Toby wondered aloud. He'd grown attached to the alien. The idea of that naïve alien in the hands of Duffy made him sick to the stomach, like he'd swallowed a barbecued kangaroo whole.

"What we always do when the bad guys do something bad," Bruce said. "Run attack ads. That's all you can until you actually become president."

It took Bruce forty-five minutes to get the first ads out expressing shock at the arrest of Twenty-two. Video of her tangled in the net and getting carried out were run without commentary until the end; the pictures were worth far more than any words. "This is how our president deals with ambassadors from the stars," flashed on the screen at the end of the ad.

Dubois answered back, claiming that Twenty-two was a security threat and a spy, and was only being "held for questioning." Public opinion split along party lines.

Then, in textbook politics, Dubois changed the subject by unleashing a series of negative, hard-hitting ads—all aimed at Toby.

"Congratulations," Bruce told him. "He now sees you as the main threat, even though Ajala still leads you in worldwide polls."

"It's Lara," Toby said. "Dubois fixated too much on Ajala the last two years for him to do this on his own. Lara's convinced him I'm a real candidate."

"You need to work on your daddy skills."

Three of Dubois's ads were especially effective and widespread. The first simply showed Toby publicly giving his support to Russia against China and Japan in the war. The ad finished with Dubois in front of the world flag and saying, "I support China. I'm Corbin Dubois, and I'm asking you to use your common sense."

The second used statistics to discredit his Provisional Universal Food Foundation. In the ad, an actor dressed in rich business clothing sitting behind a desk said, "The Platt Plan should be called the Platt Planetary Poverty Plan, since we'll all be," and the actor miraculously transformed into a bum sitting in a dark alley, "in the poorhouse if it passes." It finished with Dubois again in front of the world flag and saying, "The numbers don't add up. I'm Corbin Dubois, and I'm asking you to use your common sense."

The third ad was more personal. It showed a collage of Toby alternately praising Dubois during his years as his campaign director, and criticizing him as a candidate, all to the accompaniment of the ancient classic, "The Monster Mash." It finished with a narrator saying, "Which Toby Platt is running for president? The one who supports President Dubois when it's convenient, or the one who opposes President Dubois when it's convenient?" It also finished with Dubois, again in front of the world flag, saying, "In these troubled times, we need our president to do what's right, not what's politically convenient. I'm Corbin Dubois, and I'm asking you to use your common sense."

Toby knew the ads would be effective, and that their response ads wouldn't get nearly as much exposure as the better-financed Dubois. The common sense line was a good one.

The first ad was misleading, though there wasn't much Toby could argue with. He had supported Russia in the war, but he had also supported China in its border disputes with Mongolia and Nepal, and was helping set up free trade agreements with Japan and Russia.

The second one simply lied about the math. The misleading and discredited statistics used were from the Department of Human Services. All the higher officials in the department, unsurprisingly, were Dubois appointees. There was little Toby could do about this—the masses simply had no way of knowing who was right.

Toby couldn't complain about the third ad because it was completely accurate. He fiddled with his scarf, wondering how he could have stood in front of cameras all those times, never really lying, but going so close to the edge in an attempt to win votes for Dubois that, cumulatively, what he said was far worse than lies. As Ajala said, he'd been a political hack.

He suddenly felt worse than he had since the campaign began. His own daughter was behind these ads. Twenty-two was in prison. There was a rising tide of criticism that he was splitting the vote, allowing Dubois to win. And he was behind in Chinese and worldwide polls.

"You look in need of a pep talk," Bruce asked. "Suddenly not feeling very popular?"

"After watching those ads, I feel like a two-faced anti-China scoundrel with a fourth grade math education. I wouldn't vote for me."

"You knew Dubois would use ads like these. He's playing to the simple-minded masses. Why aren't we?"

"Because we're hoping for the intelligent vote?"

"Doesn't exist," Bruce said. "Oh, there are intelligent people out there. I'll even admit, this one time only, that there are more of 'em than I admit to. But there aren't enough of them, and so the ones who decide who's going to be president are the idiots."

"The chimpanzees, right?"

"Now you're talking! Dubois's ads don't matter. You aren't running for president to be a saint. You're running to make a difference, to change the world, to show that one doesn't have to be a babbling liberal or moronic conservative to get elected leader of the world. You are rescuing the planet from the shackles of mindless extremism."

"You should put that in an ad."

"Already did. It's running all over China and half the rest of the world."

"Aren't I supposed to approve all ads?"

261

Bruce grinned sheepishly. "Didn't have time, we had to get this one out. Next time."

"You do that. I'd like to know what I'm saying before I say it."

"Will do. Now about the ads, you want to be a saint? Ajala's already taken that position, and look where that's got him. You want to win, we do what Dubois's doing, and demonize him right back."

Somehow, Toby had thought, deep down, that if he ran as a moderate, he wouldn't have to run a scarred-earth campaign. After all, moderates are supposed to be reasonable people who do reasonable things. Was demonizing your opponent to win an election the reasonable thing to do?

"Do we really need to go to Dubois's level?" he asked.

"His level?" Bruce said. He smacked Toby in the head with his ever-handy ping-pong ball. "Wake up! You know the three laws of any successful campaign! Make 'em hate their guy, love our guy, and hate their guy."

"When did those become the three laws of a successful campaign?"

"Since the beginning of time," Bruce said. "And the nice thing is we don't have to make stuff up about Dubois. Which means we can also follow the fourth law of any successful campaign."

"Which is?"

"Never throw mud at an opponent unless you have more mud."

Bruce hit back with their own hard-hitting ads, but without more financing, Toby knew they were outgunned. When people hear a paid ad give one side of an issue ten times, and the other side three times, they tend to believe the one they heard ten times. Of course, if asked about this, everyone says they listen to both sides equally. As Bruce would point out, this just showed that people were clueless.

Twenty-two's arrest was knocked off the headlines by news of the Great Russian Compromise. Most of the Russian Federation countries were leery of combining into one big country dominated by Russia. Instead, they had broken up Russia.

Russia was made up of over eighty republics, provinces, and other territories. After much back and forth deal-making, Russia agreed to recombine into sixteen provinces. Those sixteen would combine with the other sixteen countries in the RF—including Kim—to make up the thirty-two provinces that would henceforth be known as the United States of Russia, or USR. The Russian tide was moving out.

Toby knew that Feodora had been behind the negotiations. Hopefully, with this behind her, she could more actively campaign. He wished the election rules would allow them to skip China and start campaigning early in Europe, but that wasn't an option. The best they could do was blanket upcoming regions with ads.

They needed to compete in China as well. A bad third-place finish could be disastrous in follow-up regions. Voters were attracted to winners.

Bruce's pep talk had been effective. He'd been faltering, but Bruce reminded him of the differences between himself and Dubois, in policies, ethics, and habitual arresting of alien ambassadors. They might end up using the same campaign tactics, but Dubois didn't even question those tactics—Eth or not—while Toby did. And once in office, Toby could drop the negative tactics and use his five years to show what real leadership was all about.

Assuming he could figure out what that was.

The China regional election wasn't the only election coming up. Tyler's middle school election would take place the same day, both on Tuesday, September 14. He called Bruce over and asked about it.

"We've been talking every night," Bruce said. "He's got the finest campaign director ever to run a school election."

"That would be you?"

"That would be correct. He's got flyers all over the place, he's giving speeches, he's—"

"He's giving speeches? Doesn't that mean each candidate gives a speech to an assembly, and then they vote?"

Bruce shook his head. "You've been out of school too long. Tyler's visiting all the school clubs, every after-school activity, even going to a different home room each morning. Every speech is tailored to the group he's talking to."

"What happens if the groups compare notes?"

"Then we shoot them."

Toby started to respond, then stopped. "I think Tyler's in good hands. Keep me posted. I could get used to being co-president with Tyler. He and I don't do enough father-son things together."

"Like the father-daughter things you did with Lara?"

Bruce smartly left before Toby could respond.

The next few days blurred together as Toby gave speech after speech to polite but unenthusiastic crowds. Often his mind was on other things, such as Twenty-two. Then, while giving a speech in Chengdu on Monday afternoon, the day before the election, things got a little more exciting.

As usual, he was surrounded by security, which did its unsuccessful best to blend in with the crowd—not easy, since none of the security was Asian. A man near the front began yelling in Chinese. Later Toby would learn that the man was demanding Toby's arrest for war crimes for his support of Russia.

Toby knew that the best way to handle most hecklers was to ignore them. So he made a pointed effort to look at others in the crowd as he spoke. So he didn't even see the shoe until it hit him in the face.

The man managed to throw his other shoe before he was tackled. Bruce had leaped to his feet from where he sat behind the podium and knocked the second one away before it hit the now-frozen Toby.

A thrown shoe, historically the worst possible insult in the Arab world, had spread in recent times to the rest of the world—another symbol of a system that was getting less civil every year. Toby knew of a number of candidates for office who had been shoed. But it had never happened to him.

Watching the video, he could barely believe that the tired-looking man with the "deer in the headlights" look could possibly be himself. The constant replays of the incident were devastating, both politically and personally.

Election day couldn't have come soon enough for Toby. He hoped to finish ahead of Ajala. Deep down, there was still a part of him that thought that maybe, just maybe, the silent, intelligent masses would turn out and vote him China's 159 electoral votes.

He and Bruce had decided it wasn't worth overdoing it on the last day in China. So they had a relatively easy day, and Toby even got to mingle with locals. At ten that night, they gathered the crew and took off in the *Rocinante* for Dover, England, their first stop in the upcoming United Europe election. The Chinese election returns would be in later. It was a tense time; they didn't want to be blown out. Bruce kept looking off into space, no doubt trying to get any inside news on the results.

Incoming call from Tyler. What would he be calling about? U.S. Eastern Time was thirteen hours behind, so it must be just after nine in the morning there. Tyler should be at school. "Accept," Toby whispered to his TC. Tyler appeared visually on his TC.

Toby could see dried streaks running across Tyler's face; he'd been crying. His left eye was black and puffy, blood-soaked cotton hung out of one nostril, and his torn shirt was streaked with dirt and sweat. Toby went over to the *Rocinante*'s TC camera so Tyler could see him.

Toby took a deep breath. "What happened?" He recognized the background—Tyler was in the school's office area. It took Toby a few minutes to get the usually talkative Tyler to speak, though Tyler's condition and presence in the office told much of the story.

"Jamaal and I had a fight." The cotton in his nose gave him a nasally voice.

Jamaal? He and Tyler had been best friends. Then he remembered— the two were running against each other for class president. With all the distractions in China, he'd forgotten.

"You two are still running against each other?"

Tyler nodded.

"Okay, start at the beginning. I've got plenty of time."

"Where are you?" Tyler asked, rubbing a tear from his face.

"We're probably somewhere over Mongolia by now, on our way to Europe."

"Can you come home?"

Toby very much wanted to. "You know I can't. I'll be in Europe this week. Back to Asia the following week. Then Africa. The week after that is Latin America, and I think I can take a detour to Maryland before that, say around October 6. Now, are you going to tell me why your best friend punched you in the face, or do I have to call the principal?"

"I only did what Bruce told me to do!"

Toby felt a cold front move through his body. *What had Bruce done?*

The story came in bits and pieces, but Toby finally pieced it together. Bruce had told Tyler to think of things to attack Jamaal on. Having known Jamaal since kindergarten, Tyler had little trouble coming up with a list. With Bruce's help, they'd narrowed it down to three. Tyler put them together in a flyer, made copies, and handed them out and posted them all over school.

It took another threat to call the principal to get Tyler to send a copy of the flyer to Toby's TC. He put Tyler on hold, blanking out his picture on his TC, and replaced it with the election flyer.

The center of the flyer had an obviously darkened picture of Jamaal, a standard method of subliminally—and unfairly—making an opponent look menacing to some. The text surrounding it was in large black letters on a yellow background.

The text above read, "Jamaal Hussein wants to run for president?!!!"

To the left, slightly above center, it read, "His dad spent three years in prison." Toby wanted to throw up.

To the right, slightly below center, it read, "Jamaal flunked Intro to Government last year." He wanted to throttle Tyler. And his campaign director.

Below the picture, it read, "Jamaal says the U.S. could learn a lot from the Arab World." At this point, Toby was too dazed to react.

At the bottom, it read, "Use your common sense. Vote American. Vote Tyler Platt," with the last three words bolded.

It took Toby a few minutes for it all to register. His son was distributing *this*?

Suddenly he felt very, very old. What type of father was he? His daughter had sold her soul for politics, and his son was following in her footsteps. Was this some "like father, like son" cosmic joke?

Finally he took Tyler off hold. "Tyler, please tell me you are on Eth. I'd rather that then to believe you'd do something like this."

"It's just an election flyer, Dad. I didn't think anybody would take it seriously."

"Did Bruce see this?"

"Yeah. He helped put it together." Bruce would need some putting together when he was through with him.

"And what did Jamaal do when he saw this?"

Tyler looked down, perhaps hoping his father would forget about the black eye and bloody nose.

"You knew all this stuff because Jamaal has been your best friend since you could walk. Do you know why his dad went to prison?"

"He had some sort of fight with the Islam World government before he came to the U.S."

What was worse, Toby wondered, ripping into an opponent and knowing your attack is unfair, or doing so out of ignorance?

"When Islam World first united—before you were born—they instituted Sharia law. Do you know what that is?"

Tyler shook his head, still looking down, fiddling with something in his hand. *A ping-pong ball?* Toby stared at it for a moment before continuing.

"Sharia law is the set of Islamic laws. They are rather harsh. When you base a government on religious law, it becomes a very inflexible system, and highly undemocratic because you can't change those laws. Jamaal's dad and many thousands of others protested, and the government put him and many others like him in prison. He was tortured, son, tortured and forced to recant his beliefs. Three years later, the Sharia laws were overturned, and he and the others—those who survived—were released."

Toby gave his son a moment to let all this register, then continued. "Grades on student papers are private. The only reason you knew Jamaal flunked that government intro class is because he confided in you as a friend. Do you think it was fair to use that against him?"

Again Tyler shook his head.

"And the part about the U.S. having much to learn from the Arab world?" Toby asked. "Jamaal has spent a lot of time in the Arab world, and you haven't. Are you saying that we in the U.S. have *nothing* to learn from them, that we're better in every way?"

Tyler suddenly smashed the ping-pong ball in his hand and threw it aside, eyes still down. "*I'm sorry!* I've never been in an election before. I wanted to win, and Bruce thought all this was okay. So did Lara."

"Lara okayed that flyer?" Toby asked in stunned disbelief.

"She said if I did well as president, and as long as I didn't actually lie, nobody would remember or care how I got elected."

The ironic thing, Toby thought, was that Tyler would probably win the election. Bruce once said that attack ads, done well and properly distributed, would always win an election, with two exceptions: if the opponent ran better attack ads, or in an imaginary highly advanced society that never has and never will exist. Middle school probably was not that highly advanced society.

"Tyler, why are you still in the principal's office?"

"Jamaal and I are suspended for three days for fighting. Mom's on her way to pick me up."

"Jamaal's there too?"

"He's with the principal now. He already yelled at me."

"Good. I want you to think things over, and when you see Jamaal— your best friend—do the right thing."

Tyler looked up. "I just wanted to win, like all the campaigns you run."

A great influence he'd been with his son. "Tyler, you don't need to win. All you need to do is try hard and do what you think is right, and I'll be proud of you."

"But you're always so proud when your guy wins."

Toby felt like a ping-pong ball had been jammed down his throat. It took him a minute to get any words out.

"When I run a campaign and my guy wins, I'm not proud—I'm happy. There's a difference. Happy comes and goes, but proud can go on forever."

They talked a little longer. Then Jamaal came out, and Tyler said he needed to go talk to him.

Tyler called back a few hours later to let him know that he'd conceded the election. At the request of him and Jamaal, the ballots were destroyed uncounted. He'd joined Jamaal in tearing down the flyers.

And now, Toby thought, he and Bruce had some serious issues to discuss, which might lead to Bruce getting tossed off the *Rocinante* from two miles up.

Chapter Thirty-Eight
The Torture of Twenty-two

Wednesday, September 15

A picture of Tyler's campaign poster leaked to the press, and quickly became the top news story. Toby released a statement saying he disapproved of the poster and had spoken to his son about it, but that anything else on the matter was private. The press didn't agree. Both Dubois and Ajala were smart enough not to comment on the matter, not wanting to seem like they were bullying a 14-year-old and knowing the press would beat Toby to death on it without their help. They were right.

They received the results of the China election on the way to England, and they were worse than expected. Turnout had been high.

	Electoral Votes	Dubois	Ajala	Platt
China	159	62%	25%	13%
Total	159	159	0	0

"They're not voting for Dubois," Bruce said. "They're voting against Ajala, and against you for what you did in Russia."

"Tyler's poster didn't help," Toby said pointedly. At least it had happened here, where they were going to lose anyway, rather than blowing their chances somewhere else.

Dubois had expanded his electoral count to 248, with Platt still at 36, Ajala 10. Some political pundits were already saying the election was over, blaming it on Platt for splitting the vote, though Dubois had beaten their combined vote in China. Dubois was well on his way to the magic 667, while Toby and Ajala were barely out of the starting blocks.

Toby waited until they had arrived in Dover and checked into their hotel before calling Bruce into his room. He was caressing Stupid when he entered. Toby had put up with a lot from Bruce over the years, but this was the first time he ever completely lost it with his political protégé. In all his professional table tennis matches, it was doubtful Bruce had never faced such an onslaught as the one he now faced.

For once, Bruce didn't talk back. He even took on Tyler's head-down posture as Toby lashed into him. "What were you thinking?" he began. "Are you a chimpanzee?" When Bruce couldn't hold back a slight grin at that, Toby lashed into him even harder. Poor Stupid hid behind the bed, occasionally peeking out. It was a long, enjoyable screaming fit, releasing tensions from weeks of campaigning.

"If you ever again talk to Tyler about anything but ping-pong," Toby said at the end of his harangue, "the next sound you hear will be your head getting drop-kicked off the *Rocinante* over the Grand Canyon."

Bruce nodded, looking genuinely guilty, an expression Toby had never seen on him before. "I messed up badly. It won't happen again."

Toby couldn't understand why he hadn't fired Bruce on the spot. But he was a problem solver, and he'd solved the problem. He knew that Bruce would not make this mistake again, and he needed Bruce in this election. If not for Bruce, he'd be puttering about back home with nothing to do.

Maybe he should fire Bruce, drop out of the election, and go home and putter about, he thought. At least he'd be back with his family.

No, he had a responsibility, a commitment to the election. When it was over, when they were living in The Bubble, he'd make it up to his family.

Living in The Bubble? He'd just gotten clobbered in China, Dubois was soaring ahead all over the world, and he was thinking about turning the Red Room purple?

Soon Gene was going over his schedule with him, and Bruce was filling his mind with facts and figures for his upcoming appearances in England while petting Stupid. Toby barely listened as he wondered about what had become of Twenty-two.

Duffy stepped out of the elevator and followed Ms. Annhart into the large, darkened room where they held the alien. They were deep underground; he could feel the air pressure pushing down on him. The room felt damp and smelled of mold. Cracks ran across the stained cement floor.

They had chained the alien to a metal ring that stuck out of a wall, and tied a blanket over its head and eyestalks. Duffy untied the blanket and pulled it off. The alien's odor, like rotting onions, wafted over him, and he wrinkled his nose. It was one more thing he hated about the alien.

"Welcome to France," he said. "This time there will be no Chinese to intervene."

The alien didn't respond, but its eyestalks focused on him. Duffy thought it looked like a fat slug.

"Ambassador, I've brought in a professional. I'd like you to meet Ms. Annhart, who has a lot of experience in . . . interrogation. She will be our guide over the next few days as together we journey past your web of deceit and get at the truth." He had worked with her before, and she had always gotten results. She always started simple, but she'd get creative when necessary. Different hurts for different squirts.

Ms. Annhart was barely taller than the alien. Her scraggly blond hair fell over a thin, blank face that looked like it had been squashed sideways. She pulled a torture stick and a gluepen out of a satchel, then set the bag aside.

She very deliberately walked over to the alien, as if in slow motion, then stooped slightly so her face was so close that the alien had to pull its eyestalks back to avoid rubbing them against her. Suddenly Annhart's blank face broke out in a dazzling smile, and she stepped back. She may be useful, Duffy thought, but she sure was weird.

"Let's start with your spies and contacts here on Earth," he said. "Who's helping you?"

"Helping me do what?" the alien asked.

Duffy nodded toward Annhart. She ran the gluepen over the alien's thick lips, sealing them. Then she touched the torture stick against its mid-section.

Duffy watched with interest and slight distaste as the alien silently writhed in agony, unable to open its disgustingly over-sized mouth. A human under such torture would stink up the room. Instead a sickly-sweet aroma rose from the alien.

After about fifteen seconds, she pulled the stick back. She ran the gluepen over the alien's lips again, and the glue dissolved. The alien let out a gasping cry, its body heaving.

"That's just a taste," Duffy said. If the alien resisted, he wondered what surprises Annhart had in store.

"Humans can breathe through their nose or mouth," the alien said hoarsely. "I only breathe through my mouth. If you glue my mouth together too long, I'll die."

"Pity," Duffy said. "I find screaming a bit uncivilized and rather loud. Plus, not being able to scream makes these interrogation techniques even more effective—one can't even vent off their agony. Charming, isn't it? Now, who are your spies and contacts on Earth?"

"Why should I tell you anything?" the alien asked, its voice high pitched and shaking. "You cannot afford to let me tell others what you have done. Whether I talk or not, you are going to kill me."

"Yes, but it can be a quick death, or a long and painful one. Like this." He motioned at Annhart, who glued its mouth shut again. The alien tried and failed to squirm away as she applied the stick again.

It took only ten minutes to break the alien. It had a pathetically low tolerance for pain, Duffy thought. So much for its early defiance. He could have done this himself without Annhart.

Soon the torrid tale of Fernando Vasquez, the grod spy, poured out of the quaking alien. Duffy nodded knowingly as he listened; there was always a conspiracy. Once the alien started to talk, everything came out. It told all it knew about grod military strength and colonization plans. It would be a struggle of civilizations, and Duffy was determined that Earth would win. He'd oversee the upcoming military buildup. The grods had to travel great distances to get to Earth. With that advantage, Earth would fight them off. Earth must become a military power in the galactic region, he decided, a force to be reckoned with. Someday, he thought, it will be us colonizing grod planets.

He knew of Vasquez, a vocal opponent of Dubois—it all fit. He read up on him on his TC and found that the Mexico City mayor and alleged gangster was currently in Europe. The surprise was that Vasquez had switched sides. He'd recently run fund-raisers for both Ajala and Platt, but now he was supporting Dubois and funding attacks on Platt. Obviously he was trying to get closer to Dubois to aid his spying for the grods.

Duffy also needed info on the alien's ship, which still floated outside Liberal Headquarters in Washington D.C. Army scientists had been unable to break through the ship's forcefield. He asked the alien how to get in.

"The ship scans for my life signs," it said with the deadpan voice of one who has lost all hope. "It won't open for anyone else."

That will be easy to test, Duffy thought. We'll fly the alien to Washington, get it to open the ship, and then send the scientists in.

It was also time to have a talk with the Mexico City Mayor.

Chapter Thirty-Nine
The Baleine Bleue Aquarium at Dover

T he rise of the French banking system before and during the Depression in the 2070's made them the dominant country in Europe. While other countries in Europe went broke, France prospered, and used their wealth to finance the European recovery, saving it from utter ruin. At first, this was welcomed. It was only afterwards, when people were working again and the standard of living was back to pre-Depression levels, that people realized that France now owned most of the continent. Most Europeans found themselves working for French bosses.

French economic success led to a massive increase in military spending, shoring up French dominance. When rebellions sprang out over much of Europe in the 2080's, the French military moved in and shut them down. The issue was hotly debated by the World Congress, but France increased its overseas financial aid, and the resolution to pull their troops back was defeated in both houses.

According to the World Congress, there was no French occupation of any country in Europe. Meanwhile, French troops patrolled the continent.

There were 30 countries and 64 electoral votes in Europe, a rather small number as it was the only continent besides the RF—now the USR—whose population hadn't gone up drastically the past century.

United	Population	Electoral

Europe	(millions)	Votes
Albania	4.0	1
Austria	10.7	1
Belgium	11.0	1
Bosnia & Herzeg.	2.9	1
Bulgaria	6.6	1
Croatia	4.1	1
Czech Republic	9.9	1
Denmark	5.5	1
Finland	6.2	1
France	79.0	8
Germany	73.5	7
Great Britain	96.8	10
Greece	10.9	1
Hungary	9.4	1
Ireland	5.7	1
Italy	63.6	6
Kosovo	4.7	1
Macedonia	1.9	1
Netherlands	17.2	2
Norway	9.0	1
Poland	34.6	3
Portugal	9.6	1
Romania	19.1	2
Scotland	9.7	1
Serbia	5.9	1
Slovakia	5.2	1
Slovenia	2.0	1
Spain	43.9	4
Sweden	11.6	1
Switzerland	8.7	1
Total	582.9	64

They'd decided to focus most of their appearances in three of the biggest: Germany, Italy, and Great Britain. All three candidates had been running ads in Europe for some time, but as usual, Dubois had more money to spend, and so ran more ads than Ajala, who ran more than Toby. Predictably, Dubois had small leads in the polls over Ajala in all three of these countries, as well as most other European countries, while Ajala held similar leads over Toby. Dubois had his homeland France locked up as well as neighboring Spain, so they'd ignore those two populous countries. Feodora would be campaigning outside the Russian Federation for the first time. At her own suggestion, they had arranged a blitz tour of Europe for her, where she would visit all 30 countries in six days.

French dominance in Europe had led to a twin dynamic. Everybody hated the French. But many supported France politically, since they were their bread ticket. Employees might grumble to others about their French bosses, but when it came time to vote, they generally voted to keep the money flowing to their company—unless they were given a strong reason not to.

To overcome this, Toby and Bruce decided to campaign mostly on economic issues. They knew Ajala's free food campaign would hit a chord in much of Europe, especially in the more progressive northern regions. They hoped they could steal that issue away, both by showing their method was a more common-sense approach, and by arguing that they were more electable than Ajala.

"Remind people every chance that Dubois is one of those hated French," Bruce told Toby. "They may believe French leadership is good for them financially, but in the end, most people vote with their gut, even if it's against their own financial best interests. We want their guts to hate Dubois's guts."

The issues in Europe were pretty much all economic anyway. It was the standard conservative-liberal conflict. Dubois favored low taxes for the wealthy, "trickle-down economics," with the idea that they would invest the money in business, thereby creating jobs. Ajala countered with "whale-spout economics," where low taxes for the poor and middle-class put the money in the hands of the masses, and when they spent it, it spouted up to the wealthy, who would then invest in business, creating jobs. He also argued that "Well-fed people work harder, which improves productivity, thereby improving the economy."

In general, Dubois wanted low taxes and low spending except in security matters; Ajala wanted the reverse. Dubois thought unions had too much power; Ajala thought not enough. Ajala wanted to nationalize some of the larger businesses the French had taken over; Dubois was adamantly against this.

Toby would go for the middle ground on each issue. However, finding that middle ground wasn't always easy. Plus he wasn't comfortable with arbitrarily splitting the difference between Dubois and Ajala, as Bruce urged. Sometimes one side was simply right, or at least righter.

The unexpected wild card in the European race was Vasquez. The Mexico City mayor was now campaigning and fundraising for Dubois, and throwing his own money around in the effort. In a continent where money spoke loudly, Vasquez spoke the language. Toby was fairly sure Vasquez had reached some sort of a deal with Dubois. Very likely, in return for Vasquez's support in the election, Dubois would make policing the Eth trade out of Mexico a lower priority. The problem with hypothetical back-room deals is that you never know for sure.

Meanwhile, there was still no sign of where they had taken Twenty-two. The news media was full of speculation, with most believing the alien was being questioned in a Chinese prison, but nobody really knew. Toby felt helpless; there was nothing he could do to help the imprisoned alien other than blast Dubois over it in speeches.

Their first event in England on Wednesday afternoon was a speech at the Baleine Bleue Aquarium at Dover, one of the Seven Wonders of the Modern World. There was no better place to showcase the hated French financial dominance in Europe than this ultimate piece of corporate extravagance. In 2089 the French had located the English branch of the French National Bank—and its blue whale aquarium—near the famous chalk beaches of Kent County, facing France across the narrowest part of the English Channel. Due to this proximity, it had been the bastion against invasions since ancient times. Many considered its location an insult, a reminder of the French economic victory over the British in the 21st century.

There were really two aquariums, each a mile long, and a quarter mile tall and wide. They paralleled each other, a quarter mile apart, with a huge tube connecting them. The aquariums and tubing were transparent, and the water kept pristine, so viewers could watch the 26 blue whales—each named for one of the 26 regions of France—swim majestically in the aquariums and through the connecting tube as they fed on schools of krill that were pumped into the tanks each day.

Standing between the two aquariums, with what many considered the greatest view in the world, was the English branch of the French National Bank. It, too, was a marvel, modeled after the extravagant Palace of Versailles near Paris. The main design difference was the windowed outer walls, so occupants could stare at the whales all day long.

Toby and Bruce stood outside the bank, watching the most famous of the blue whales, Lorraine, swim through the tubing. She was closely followed by another blue whale, Alsace, and her baby, the 30-foot Picardie, whose birth caused much celebration, both for the spectacle of a baby blue whale born in captivity and because it gave each region of France their own blue whale namesake. Turk and Crowbar stood nearby, apparently oblivious to the whales as they watched anyone who came nearby. Dozens of the Gray Guard nonchalantly lurked about, but Toby barely noticed them anymore.

They had just secured a loan from the bank to help finance their campaign, an irony since they were running against a Frenchman, and Toby would shortly be giving a speech against this very bank's extravagance. Janlibo did their international banking with the French bank, so they had little choice.

Lorraine was a wonder of the modern world herself, a one-of-a-kind horned blue whale. She had been created by American and Japanese geneticists, with their work funded by the French bank. Blue whales are baleen whales, while narwhals are toothed whales. To genetically combine them, scientists had created a blue whale with a narwhal's toothed jawbone, since a narwhal's horn is really an elongated tooth. The result was the still-growing Lorraine, sixty feet long with a nearly twenty-foot horn jutting out of her upper left jaw. She still ate like a regular blue whale, sifting krill from the water with her baleen. The horn tended to sag a bit as it wasn't anchored in the toothed jawbone of a narwhale; a blue whale's jaw bones weren't designed for it.

"Incredible, isn't it? Toby said, breathing in the salty ocean air. He'd been transfixed by the whales since arriving, barely paying attention to the bankers during their meeting. The whales' bluish-gray bodies, almost white on the bottom, were up to one hundred feet in length. Their bodies slowly twisted up and down, using their horizontal tail flukes to thrust themselves forward like lords of the sea.

"What a waste of money," Bruce said. With Toby staring out the windows, he'd dealt with the bankers. "Three hundred million cubic miles of ocean, and so what do the French do? They capture the biggest and maybe brainiest animals on the planet, stick the poor beasts in a cage, and put them on display like carnival freaks. Then they decide that's not enough, and so they bring together the best scientists in the world and breed a carnival freak—a horned blue whale! I hope my taxes didn't fund that research." He suddenly grinned. "The French don't even have the common sense to put their whale aquarium in Wales." Toby groaned at the old joke.

Soon people arrived for the mass rally Bruce had organized. Distracted by the huge whales swimming about him, Toby gave his speech on autopilot, reading the lines off his TC.

He covered PUFF, per usual, then he ripped into Dubois for the arrest of Twenty-two, and demanded to know where she was and what was happening to her. He finished by criticizing the French economic takeover of Europe.

"While Englishmen and other Europeans work hard for a living, the French spend their leisure time and your money building aquariums." Toby gave a sweeping gesture with his arms. "And who sits on the board of directors of the French Bank, the only bank in the world that treats whales better than Englishmen? President Dubois!" He paused for the cheers.

"It's time we sent them home and retake your country!" he shouted. "Where are we sending the whales?"

"*Home!*" the crowd cried.

"Where are we sending the French?"

"*Home!*"

"And where are we sending President Dubois?"

"*Home!*" This last was so loud it hurt Toby's eardrums.

After the rally, they left on the *Rocinante* for London for another rally and two news programs. There was also a speech planned in Wales, and another in Scotland, the breakaway Republic that had seceded from Great Britain during the depression in the 2070s.

On the way to London there was breaking news on their TCs. Ajala was giving an unscheduled speech at the Baleine Bleue Aquarium. Toby's political alarm bells went off.

Ajala started out saying many of the same things Toby had said about the French. He went a lot farther.

"Look at that monstrosity!" he thundered, pointing at Lorraine. "Genetics research is valuable for its medical benefits, but a *horned whale*? What possible benefit is that? There is something wrong when huge sums of money are spent on whale aquariums and whale freaks, all for the benefit of a few rich bankers, when that very money could be used to stop hunger and better mankind!"

"You need to learn to thunder with a cultured voice," Bruce said to Toby.

"The irony," Ajala continued, "is that these whales are owned by proponents of the failed economic system known as trickle-down economics, a system designed to make the rich richer and the poor— well, they barely come into the equation. These whales are a symbol for the far more successful whale-spout economics, where all of us are in the equation. For that symbolization alone, perhaps it is worth having an aquarium full of whales on the coast of England."

281

There was more applause.

"A short time ago," Ajala continued, "Mr. Platt stood right where I stand, and gave a similar speech. He rightly criticized President Dubois and his membership on the board of directors for this symbol of French oppression."

"Uh oh," Bruce muttered. "He's playing the hypocrisy card."

"Oh jeez," Toby agreed. His political instincts were flashing danger.

"If it is wrong for President Dubois to sit on that board," Ajala continued, "then why does Mr. Platt do his banking here? This very morning he secured a loan at this bank. Both of my opponents in this election are in thrall to the very ones who oppress you, and yet they ask for your vote so they may continue this oppression!"

There were thunderous cheers that went on for some time. Finally Ajala continued.

"This morning Mr. Platt said the whales, the French, and President Dubois should go home. I ask you, where should Mr. Platt go?"

"TC off," Toby whispered quickly.

"Brilliant," Bruce said. "We just lost Great Britain."

Soon after landing in London, Bruce disappeared. Normally Bruce was like a moth around a light during Toby's appearances, but he was nowhere around when Toby gave a speech at a rally at Wembley-Thatcher Stadium in London, or for the two media interviews afterwards. Gene said he saw Bruce walk off just before the rally; Turk and Crowbar verified this. Toby called him on his TC, but there was no response.

First Twenty-two, now Bruce. They were dropping as fast as his numbers in the British polls.

Chapter Forty
Bruce Meets the Helpful Zero

B ruce hid behind an artificial tree next to a clearing as he spied on Twenty-two's ship from a distance. After they'd landed in London, he'd sneaked off and taken a floater to Washington D.C. He knew that Toby would have objected to his plans, so he didn't tell him. He'd been ignoring Toby's calls since.

There was enough security surrounding the ship to populate a small country. Bruce's mission was to steal the ship, locate Twenty-two, and rescue her. The whole enterprise seemed like something Feodora might do between tea breaks.

He had an idea. There were numerous recordings of Twenty-two speaking. He pulled up the first one, when she gave a short speech to the cameras after her "welcome" by Dubois.

She'd said, *"I am Ambassador Twenty-two. I come from Grodan, the third planet from Tau Ceti. I am here to observe and learn about your political process. I have learned much today. I look forward to learning more. I will be around. Now I return to my ship."*

After some splicing and snickering at all the uses of "I," he had the message he wanted in the alien's voice. He transferred it to an audio player, and played it loudly on a portable loudspeaker he'd brought.

"Ship, I am Twenty-two. Come here."

The security people about the ship looked up. Because they were looking for the source of the loud voice, they didn't at first see the ship as it rose up above the trees, then moved toward Bruce.

It floated down into the clearing next to Bruce. There were shouts and pointing fingers from the security people, and a contingent of them raced for the clearing.

A sing-songy voice called out. "You are not the great Twenty-two."

This must be Zero, Bruce thought. Twenty-two had told him a little about the ship's computer, though not the apparent high regard it held for her.

"I'm Bruce, and I need your help to rescue her."

"Hi Bruce. Does she need a massage?"

He glanced back at the rapidly approaching security. "Twenty-two has been arrested and is in great danger. If you let me inside I can tell you more. If you do not, those people running toward us are going to shoot me in about ten seconds."

The ship's door began to lower in maddeningly slow fashion.

"Come on!" Bruce yelled. The sound of footsteps grew louder.

"Freeze!" someone yelled.

Bruce leaped for the walkway before it was one-third down, and squeezed through the opening between the door and the ship. Someone grabbed his foot as he scrambled up. He looked for something to grab to pull himself in, but there was nothing but whiteness.

Someone grabbed his other foot. They began to pull him out of the ship. At least they weren't shooting.

Then something from inside the ship—a tentacle?—wrapped around his neck, tightened, and pulled. He wanted to scream, but couldn't with the chokehold on his neck. Slowly he was pulled into the ship.

Then the tentacle let go for a second and wrapped around his chest. "Sorry about that," Zero said. "Grods do not have such delicate necks. My sensors said you were in distress. Is this better?"

"Yes!" he rasped as the tug of war continued, but now the tentacle was clearly winning. A moment later he was pulled mostly into the ship. But the security people still grasped his feet, which dangled out the door.

An electric shock went through him, and he yelped. So did the people holding his feet, who released him. The tentacle yanked him the rest of the way into the ship and the door closed.

284

"Sorry again," Zero said, releasing him. "It seemed the most expedient way to make them let go. I could use my tractor beam, but I might have hurt them. Would you like a cup of tea? My research tells me humans like tea."

Bruce looked about, a bit shaky from the electrocution. The tentacle came out of the featureless white wall that circled the room. Then it disappeared into the wall, leaving no trace and the white room completely featureless.

"No thanks. Can you help rescue Twenty-two?"

"Yes. Do you need a place to sit down? Humans use chairs for that, correct?" A bulge came out of the floor, which quickly stretched into a chair. Toby sat down, resting his arms on the armrests. It was soft and comfortable.

"Twenty-two liked the smell of shiggles," Zero said. "Would you like that too?" A few seconds later the room filled with an intense flowery scent.

"You don't seem that enthused about rescuing Twenty-two," he said.

"I am very enthused about it." The tentacle was back, placing a cup of tea on a table in front of him that hadn't been there seconds before. "I believe I used the correct formula for tea. I hope you like it."

"Then why aren't you asking me what happened?" Bruce stared at the tea, unsure if he should try it.

"Because I only respond to questions, except to give out needed information, to aid in the comfort of my passengers, and in emergencies."

If only people were like that, Bruce thought, Earth would be heaven. "Have they been trying to break into you all this time?"

"If you mean the humans outside, yes. They have shown an interesting arsenal of ineffective weaponry."

"What are they doing now?"

"See for yourself." The white walls became transparent. They were surrounded by the security people, who apparently couldn't see in. Several were yelling at each other, though Bruce couldn't hear them— the ship's walls were soundproofed.

"Can you create a face or something, so I'll have something to talk at?"

"How is this?" A tentacle came out of the wall. Its tip rapidly formed into the face of the famous cartoon character Joseph Wang. "This is the most common face shown on human entertainment programs."

"That'll be fine," Bruce said. He hated the cartoon. "Twenty-two was arrested and is imprisoned somewhere, probably in China. Can you find her?"

"I have already done so with my sensors," Zero said. It seemed strange to Bruce to hear Zero's voice come out of the moving lips of Joseph Wang. "Are you going to try the tea?"

Bruce stared at the glass. What the heck, he thought, if it'll keep Zero happy. He took a sip.

He spat it out reflexively, almost before he consciously tasted the foul stuff. His nose had been stuffed up from his earlier tussle or he would have smelled the putrid liquid.

"Would you like another?" the face of Joseph Wang asked. As Bruce watched, the "tea" he'd spit out disappeared into the floor.

"No thanks. Where is Twenty-two?"

"She is in France, in Val-de-Marne, southeast of Paris."

"Do you have the ability to rescue her?"

"I believe so." The tentacle reappeared, this time holding a pitcher. It refilled his glass, and then disappeared into the wall again.

"Then why haven't you?"

"Why should I?"

"Wouldn't her being arrested be considered an emergency?"

"Why?" The Joseph Wang face looked perplexed.

Okay, he decided, maybe it wouldn't be heaven if people were like this. It was time to take charge. "Do you have any weapons?"

"Twenty-two left a hand laser behind. The tractor beam can be used as a weapon. The ship can be used as a ram."

That should be sufficient. "Take me to Twenty-two."

Chapter Forty-One
They Are Not Worth Our Time

Twenty-two stiffened when the door opened. With the blanket again tied over her head, she couldn't see who it was. However, she recognized the loud, pounding steps of General Duffy, followed by the light pattering of Annhart. She rocked back and forth against her chains as her insides tightened.

"You'll be interested to know that your crony Vasquez has been taken into custody in Berlin."

She wondered what Vasquez would say when Duffy had him tortured. Like her, he'd have to make more things up to satisfy Duffy. Which of his enemies would he "give up" to stop the agony of torture?

He pulled the blanket off her head. "We're leaving for Washington immediately, where you'll give us access to your ship. Annhart is coming along. I'll have a lot of questions for you on the way." The woman gave her dazzling smile.

Twenty-two had worked out an elaborate story involving hidden grod bases on Mount Everest and Antarctica, advanced equipment that spied on Earth's communications, and a country that was collaborating with the grods. She hadn't decided yet which country or people she would name as collaborators.

The ground shook, knocking Duffy and Annhart off their feet. Twenty-two swung against the chains that held her. The support column in the middle of the room began to shake.

"What the hell?" Duffy exclaimed, looking up. The ceiling shook as if there were an earthquake. Parts of it crumbled down. The support column broke apart and fell. This went on for several minutes.

Then the entire ceiling lifted *upwards*. It shot up a ways, then disappeared off the side, leaving a long vertical tunnel to the surface.

Floating above the tunnel was Zero.

The ship dropped down through the vertical tunnel and came to a stop, just above the two staring humans and one relieved but anxious grod.

"How are you, Wonderful Leader?" came Zero's voice.

"I am fine," she said. "You may give me a long massage if you can get me out of here."

"That is a deal, My Idol." Zero's door opened, and a tentacle came out. It grabbed one of the chains holding her and yanked it out of the wall, bringing down a good portion of the wall, which it grabbed and tossed aside. Twenty-two was quickly freed. The tentacle grabbed her and brought her into the ship, and the door closed.

Twenty-two wasn't surprised to see Bruce in the ship. She knew someone had to be telling Zero what to do, and for that she was grateful. The walls were transparent from the inside so she could see out.

"Welcome aboard, Ambassador," Bruce said. "I see Zero has a high regard for you."

Twenty-two was embarrassed, both by Zero's flattery—which she'd never expected anyone else to hear—and by Bruce seeing her mouth. "Zero, turn flattery mode off. Bring me the red velvo."

"Yes, former great one." She quickly put it on.

Despite her embarrassment, Twenty-two couldn't help but add her squeaks of relieved laughter to Bruce's deeper ones. She'd just been rescued from torture, and she was worrying about a flattering computer and an exposed mouth?

"Zero, they took my sensor. Do you detect it?"

"It's in another room higher up." A chunk of material from above came out, showering Duffy and Annhart with more dirt. Then the sensor floated out toward the ship and through the now-opened door, which closed behind it.

"What should we do with those two?" Bruce asked. "Zero could bang them together a few times with those tractor beams."

"Thank you for rescuing me," she said. "I will have a story to tell you and Toby soon. As to them. . . ." She looked out through the one-way transparent walls at Duffy and Annhart. Duffy stood in the middle of the room, hands on his waist. He'd been yelling the whole time, but she'd barely heard him. Annhart cowered in a corner.

"They are not worth our time," she finally said. "Let's go."

They took Zero to the hotel in London that Toby and Bruce were staying at. Within minutes, the floating ship was surrounded by police, news crews, and onlookers. Zero went as close to the hotel's entrance as possible and lowered the walkway door.

Video of the ship floating outside the hotel, and of Twenty-two and Bruce getting off it, were all over the news programs. Toby was watching them when they arrived in his room.

"Why do I have the feeling you have a very long story to tell me?" he asked.

"We both do," Bruce said. "You're supposed to go to a dinner tonight in Nottingham, but tell Gene to cancel. We're not going to win England anyway. And I'm looking forward to hearing Twenty-two's story as much as you are."

They went out of chronological order, with Bruce telling his story first. Toby thought he should fire Bruce for disappearing like that, but knew he wouldn't. Bruce was too valuable. He wished Bruce would at least keep him in the loop, but Bruce was Bruce. It'd be easier to walk to Grodan than get him to change.

"Does this make up for messing up with Tyler?" Bruce asked.

"About one percent," Toby said. "You'll be working that one off for the rest of your life and beyond."

Toby and Bruce were stunned by Twenty-two's story.

"And you let them go?" Bruce said of Duffy. "If I'd known what he did to you . . . I can think of some creative ways to use Zero's tractor beam."

"I wanted to do that as well," Twenty-two said.

"What stopped you?" Toby asked. "For once, I'm in agreement with Bruce."

"You will find this hard to believe," Twenty-two said.

"You think so?" Bruce said. "I just rode a spaceship halfway around the world at speeds beyond imagination, then watched a tractor beam scoop out huge hunks of an underground building to dig a tunnel. I'm ready to believe just about anything."

"If this were on Grodan, I would have killed both of them," Twenty-two said, lowering her voice to a whisper. "But here . . . with humans . . . as an ambassador . . . I wanted to set a good example."

They had to lower a rope to get Duffy and Annhart out, as the underground structure was thoroughly collapsed except for the hole the alien ship had drilled. When he reached the top, Duffy released his fury on his rescuers. They scurried away and brought him a floater before he could carry out his threat of feeding them, in very small pieces, to the horned blue whale in Dover.

Duffy filled Dubois in while he and Annhart flew to Germany. Feeding Vasquez to a blue whale would be far too good for the alien collaborator, now held in a USE facility in Berlin. They'd found the spy fly in the Red Room weeks ago, but had only Toby's rather crazed theory about who had sent it. Now they knew for sure—Vasquez had been spying for the grods.

When Duffy arrived at the USE building, he could almost smell the rat inside, a man who had betrayed all of humanity. By the time he was led in to see the manacled Vasquez, Duffy had worked himself into a frenzy.

"Mayor Vasquez, do you like pain?" the general asked.

"No, I do not," Vasquez said calmly. "No one has told me why I am here. You will be hearing from my lawyers very soon."

"Your *lawyers?*" Duffy scoffed. "You won't be seeing any lawyers. You might not be seeing anything, if I decide to pluck your eyes out for what you've done."

"I have no idea what you are talking about." Vasquez seemed quite calm, Duffy had to give him that. It wouldn't last.

"You are a Grodan spy," Duffy said.

"A *what?*"

Duffy smiled. They always act surprised when you first confront them. He nodded at Annhart. She stepped forward, a torture stick in one hand, a gluepen in the other, and a dazzling smile on her face.

Vasquez talked, and soon Duffy had the whole story, and a list of collaborators. When they were done, Duffy made sure nobody would ever find the body.

"What should we do about Vasquez?" Toby asked. They were on their way to Rome on the *Rocinante*. They had stopped in Switzerland to pick up Feodora. When she saw the horse's head on the side of the *Rocinante*, and they told her that the horse was now the symbol of their party, she found that hilarious, but wouldn't say why. She'd been quite happy to finally meet Twenty-two, but now she snored in the back in her reclined seat.

Bruce was stooped over a chessboard, playing Twenty-two. The alien stood nearby, feeding fake lettuce to Stupid and calling out her moves when needed.

"Wasn't Vasquez the one out to get us?" Bruce said. He moved a pawn. "I moved the king's rook pawn forward."

Twenty-two had both eyestalks on Toby. "Move my rook forward three places." Bruce groaned.

"Yeah, he was," Toby said. "Duffy's going to accuse him of being a grod spy, which is a joke. And then he'll torture him until he tells him what he wants to hear."

"He is guilty of a lot of stuff that he won't be charged with," Bruce said. "He's a well-known gangster, and deserves whatever he gets."

"Didn't you recently arrange a fundraiser with this 'well-known gangster'?" Toby asked.

"Well, yeah," Bruce said. "Sometimes it helps in politics to know people in low places—that's something we learned from Dubois. But Vasquez brought all this on himself. He was spying on the Red Room, hoping to find something to bring Dubois down. Only he spied for himself, not for the 'murderous alien invaders.'"

"Murderous alien invaders?" Twenty-two said. Bruce moved his king one spot sideways and called out the move. "Move my queen forward all the way." There was another groan from Bruce.

"Sometimes torture good." Toby hadn't noticed Feodora getting up. Now she stood over the chessboard.

"Feodora, do you play chess?" Twenty-two asked.

"Of course. I'm Russian." Feodora stared intently at the chessboard for a moment, then said, "Mate in five moves."

"I know," Twenty-two said. "I did not want to—I think the phrase is, 'rub it in.'"

"Ah, diplomacy," Feodora said, shaking her head. "Chess is like war. When game is on, you don't worry about 'rubbing it in.' Diplomacy come after you win."

"But I have already won," Twenty-two said. "He just hasn't seen it yet."

"I'm right here, you know!" Bruce said. "And I do see it. I'm just trying to come up with a good excuse before I concede. I'm thinking getting manhandled and electrocuted by Zero might work."

"Were you tortured?" Feodora's innocent question put Bruce's possible excuse in context.

"You said that sometimes torture is good," Toby said. "I don't agree with that at all. It's an atrocity, and you never get good information out of it."

"Spoken like a true chimpanzee," Bruce said. "Have you fallen for all the liberal propaganda on this? Of course torture sometimes works—if you know when to use it."

"Bruce is correct," Feodora said. "He knows theory. I know in practice."

"But look at what happened here," Toby said, a bit irritated. "Duffy tortured Twenty-two over and over, and all he got were a bunch of lies."

"That's because Duffy is a fool," Bruce said. "People who blindly claim torture never works, and cite examples, aren't thinking clearly. You have to differentiate between information that is immediately verifiable, and the large majority of the time when it is not. It is the latter that consistently gets bad results. Conventional means of persuasion work better in most cases, but not all."

"Twenty-two," Feodora said, "when General Duffy asked you how to get into your ship, you told him Zero wouldn't let anyone in unless it scanned your life signs, correct?"

"Yes. I would have said anything to stop the pain." The alien slowly rocked back and forth.

"If I had been torturing you, I would continue until you told me how to get onto ship immediately. If I did that, what would you have done?"

"I would have told you the password. Zero would have let you in."

"So torture would have worked?"

"Of course."

"You see?" Bruce said. "A person will say anything to stop the pain. But if he knows what he says can be immediately checked, he'll usually tell the truth. That's why torture doesn't work in uncovering information like finding other spies. The captured spy will just turn in whoever he doesn't like, like Twenty-two did with Vasquez. That's why torture rarely makes sense, because you are trying to get information you don't have, and in most cases, you can't immediately verify it when you do get it."

"Vasquez did not seem a nice person when I watched him on video," Twenty-two said. "He was the first person I thought of when I had to give Duffy a name."

"Conservatives," Bruce said, "act like torture often works, when it only works in rare circumstances. They go with 'end justifies the means' thinking, ignoring ethics and basic human rights. They don't see that slippery slope from our values down to those of the very people they would torture. Liberals are adamant that torture never works, which conveniently fits in with their moral beliefs. The reality is in between. But in general, except in an extreme emergency, the liberals are right; torture is just plain wrong."

It all made sense, Toby had to admit. "So what do you all want to do? Make torture legal, maybe under certain circumstances?"

"You don't make torture legal under any circumstances," Bruce said. "If you do that, you are officially sanctioning torture as a policy, which doesn't look too good. Once you sanction torture, then others will do it as well. I'm guessing Feodora and other generals don't want their troops tortured if they are captured. But there are times when torture should be done, even if it's a crime, to stop a disaster."

"If you steal a car to rescue someone from much greater crime—like torture—no one prosecutes," Feodora said. "But stealing car is still crime, even in Russia."

"A lot of people thought Lincoln's Emancipation Proclamation was unconstitutional," Bruce said. "The Supreme Court could have looked into it and ruled on it. Instead, they looked the other way. If there's a nuke in New York City, and we catch the terrorist who knows where it is, nobody's going to prosecute if we torture him to find the location— they'll look the other way. And that is quickly verifiable info, so torture should work. But it still shouldn't be legal."

"Bruce is right that torture should never be legal," Feodora said. "But I have simpler solution. Only do it when the nukes are about to go off, and you have bastard who planted them. And don't get caught."

Both Bruce and Twenty-two found that rather funny.

"How is that different than Duffy?" Toby asked. He didn't think the torture issue was funny, especially this soon after its use on Twenty-two, even if the alien did.

"How is it different?" Feodora asked. "I only torture bad guys."

Twenty-two agreed to go public with the torture story. Gene had arranged several media interviews in Rome. When Toby showed up with

Twenty-two, they were flabbergasted and brimming with questions for the alien. Toby cut them short.

"Twenty-two has a statement to make to the press. She will not be taking questions afterwards."

Bruce had conveniently thought to bring a smaller podium for Twenty-two to stand behind. She allowed the press to take pictures before she began.

She told the story of her captivity and torture, right up to the rescue by Bruce and Zero. It took some time.

"I am the ambassador from Grodan," she said at the end. "I do not believe grods would torture a human ambassador." Then she stepped back and let Bruce take over and tell the rest of the story.

Toby had done a lot of thought on the issue of torture since the discussion on the *Rocinante*. The whole issue was a quagmire. He now knew that, if he were president, he might actually agree to torture, but only in an extremely rare emergency where they faced disaster, and where the info needed could be checked. Of course, he realized, in any emergency case, the info needed could always be checked, since it either allowed them to end the threat—such as finding a hidden nuke—or it didn't.

Under these circumstances, even if it were against the law, he figured most people would agree with the decision to torture. That was a good way to test any torture question, he thought: If he felt he had to keep it a secret from the world, then it probably wasn't the right thing to do. But the circumstances were so unlikely that he might as well assume it would never happen, and not worry about it until it did.

Perhaps he'd just heed the advice of Feodora. Only do it to the bad guys whose nukes are about to go off. But he wouldn't be saying any of this to the press.

Bruce had finished telling his story to the press, and now it was Toby's turn to talk. He stepped to the podium and looked out over the mass of news people and flashing cameras.

"The price of a government sanctioning torture in any circumstances is too high a cost for any civilized society," he said. "Once you set boundaries of when you can torture, those boundaries can be twisted by those who are now sanctioned to do torture. It's a slippery slope, and we should not go down that path. President Dubois believes otherwise. Not only has his General Duffy been torturing the Grodan ambassador, but you will recall that when the Chinese protested the torture, Dubois was the one who ordered she be taken to France. Why do you think he did that?"

Dozens of hands went up. Feeling brave, Toby called on the dark suited man from the conservative World News.

"What would you do if a nuclear bomb is planted somewhere in New York City, and is going to go off in one hour, and you have the terrorist who put it there? Do you torture him or serve him milk and cookies?"

Toby smiled at the predictable question. He and Bruce had prepared for it. "I'm not going to set policy based on an incredibly unlikely situation just so you can have a headline, so my political opponents can have ammunition, and to give some terrorist justification to torture our people. Next question."

Toby spent the next hour answering more questions. Bruce had wanted him to accuse Dubois and Duffy of torturing Vasquez as well, but they didn't really have proof of that. Besides, as Toby pointed out, did he really want to publicly defend Vasquez? The press knew, or would quickly find out, about Vasquez's seedy side, and Toby didn't want to be connected to that. It wouldn't take the press long to find out about the fund-raiser Vasquez had held for him.

Dubois quickly put out a statement that USE does not torture, that enhanced but legal methods were sufficient, that he had no knowledge of any of the events in Twenty-two's story, and that he would launch an investigation. He also said that the alien would not be arrested, but that the alien needed to come in for questioning.

Toby knew that any investigation by Dubois would find nothing, no matter what it found. Internally, there was a chance Dubois might decide Duffy was too much of a liability, in which case the general would quietly be given early retirement, probably after the election.

The good news was the promise that Twenty-two would not be arrested. The alien preferred traveling with them in the *Rocinante*, but it was getting too dangerous for her. Bruce had brought up the idea of campaigning in Zero, but it wasn't large enough. Plus, it would make Toby look like he worked for the alien, playing right into Dubois's *Stop the Invasion!* ads.

Toby had another question for Twenty-two. "You mentioned there was a password that would get anybody into your ship?"

"Yes. I was close to giving it to Duffy."

"In case this happens again, it would be helpful if we had that, so we can rescue you without having to convince Zero of the problem."

"Your ship computer can be a bit dense," Bruce said. "I'm wondering what a highly-intelligent being with a name like 25,257,461,522 would have as a password." Toby was pretty sure Bruce remembered the alien's number without using his TC.

"That is true," Twenty-two said. "You will laugh when I tell it to you. I never thought a password was needed, so I never changed the default password. So the password, in any language understood by Zero, is "password."

The next day, after several joint appearances in Italy, Toby and Feodora parted ways. Feodora had always been popular in Italy, where *Never Surrender*, the movie of her exploits in the Russia-Japan war of 2091, had been a huge hit. Now she moved on with her 30-country European blitz, using her personal floater, the *Solzhenitsyn*. Gene went with her, while Bruce stayed with Toby. They spent the rest of the week campaigning in Germany, Italy, and Great Britain. Twenty-two decided to spend some time with Ajala.

The following Tuesday night they met up with Feodora in Albania, the last stop on her blitz. The polls showed much of Europe too close to call. They'd get the results on the flight to Sarawak, Malaysia, their first stop for the Asian Federation election. Toby was feeling unusually tense, and every squeak, tap, and footstep bothered him. When Feodora began doing pushups and sit-ups on the floor of the *Rocinante*, he put in earplugs, threw a blanket over his head, and went to sleep for the flight.

Chapter Forty-Two
The Layered Wheat Cube of Sarawak

Wednesday, September 22

The results from Europe came in soon after they landed in Sarawak.

United Europe	Electoral Votes	Dubois	Ajala	Platt
Albania	1	**41%**	19%	40%
Austria	1	**38%**	26%	36%
Belgium	1	**36%**	29%	35%
Bosnia & Herz.	1	**48%**	26%	26%
Bulgaria	1	39%	20%	**41%**
Croatia	1	**41%**	24%	35%
Czech Republic	1	**39%**	27%	34%
Denmark	1	**36%**	29%	35%
Finland	1	39%	21%	**40%**
France	8	**68%**	13%	19%
Germany	7	33%	33%	**34%**
Great Britain	10	**36%**	35%	29%
Greece	1	26%	28%	**44%**
Hungary	1	**36%**	30%	34%
Ireland	1	**37%**	36%	27%
Italy	6	34%	31%	**35%**

Kosovo	1	**42%**	26%	32%
Macedonia	1	36%	22%	**42%**
Netherlands	2	**37%**	27%	36%
Norway	1	**41%**	19%	40%
Poland	3	**39%**	23%	38%
Portugal	1	**48%**	27%	25%
Romania	2	35%	28%	**37%**
Scotland	1	30%	32%	**38%**
Serbia	1	**46%**	29%	25%
Slovakia	1	**38%**	25%	37%
Slovenia	1	**41%**	29%	30%
Spain	4	**51%**	26%	23%
Sweden	1	37%	25%	**38%**
Switzerland	1	**38%**	28%	34%
Total	64	43	0	21

The news was mixed. Once again, Dubois had dominated, beating Toby by better than two to one, and pulling farther ahead in the electoral count, which he now led 291 to Toby's 57. Once again, Ajala had been shut out, leaving him still at 10. Dubois was inching closer and closer to the magic 667.

Most of the countries they had won were those neighboring Russia—Feodora's influence. Eleven races had been decided by a point, with Toby winning six of them.

Germany had saved them from humiliation, with Toby getting 34% to edge out Dubois and Ajala, both of whom received 33%. Toby couldn't help but notice the most interesting and, in some ways, most disappointing result—Great Britain. Most of the polls had shown Ajala winning, but Dubois had beaten him by a point, 36% to 35%, with Toby getting 29%. It was a classic case of splitting the vote; head to head, Dubois wouldn't have beaten either of them.

"Ajala must feel like a blue whale just sat on him," Bruce said.

"Don't forget Africa's coming up in two weeks," Toby said. "He'll sweep most of that, and that's 247 electoral votes."

300

"I don't know about that anymore. But forget Europe, forget Africa, let's focus on the Asian Federation and its 178 votes."

The youngest member of the Seven Wonders of the Modern World would soon be octuplets. The Layered Wheat Cube of Sarawak went into operation in 2096, and after four years of success, seven more were planned. When this happened, the Commission on the Seven Wonders of the Modern World might revoke its status; otherwise, it'd become the Fourteen Wonders of the Modern World, with more to come.

The Layered Wheat Cube was a perfect cube, half a mile—2640 feet—on each glass side. A high-rise apartment complex surrounded it on all four sides. Each of the 660 layers or floors of the cube were four feet high, with an artificial dirt floor and bright lighting on top. Packed densely in between were rows and rows of wheat. Not just any wheat, but genetically created dwarf borlaug-15 wheat: short, high yield, high protein, disease resistant, and with a limited root system.

Toby, Bruce, and Feodora toured the cube, with a speech planned afterwards. Turk, Crowbar, and the usual Gray Guard stood about. Toby had written the speech himself, not bothering with their speechwriters, and Bruce only made a few minor changes. Feodora, who seemed deep in thought and unusually quiet that morning, said she agreed with all of it without seeing it, her eyes glazed as she studied something on her TC.

It was one of the easiest speeches to write. What could be a better answer to solving world hunger problems for the world's rapidly growing population and dwindling arable lands than an artificial cube whose yield per area was not just 660 times greater than normal, but because of the controlled conditions, over a thousand times greater?

The "tour" of the cube didn't actually go inside, since it wasn't made with human corridors, and they didn't think it was dignified to crawl on hands and knees in the access tunnels. They followed a tour guide as he pointed out features from the outside, and then showed them the control station next to the cube. Toby enjoyed the fresh wheat scent, a contrast to the ever-present fish smell in the *Rocinante*. It was offset by an irritating background throbbing from the cube that permeated the air.

"It's entirely mechanized," the guide said. "In fact, I'm not just the tour guide, I operate the entire cube. Which really means it's my job to make sure the on/off button stays on, that the daily supplies come in, and to call a technician if an alarm goes off, meaning something malfunctioned. That hasn't happened in six months."

"What's the annual yield?" Toby asked.

"Over 600,000 tons this past year," the guide said. "Enough to feed three million people for a year. And we do it all on just a half mile square of land."

"A quarter mile square," Bruce corrected. "One hundred sixty acres."

The guide looked at him sharply. "It's half a mile on a side, so half a mile of square land."

"Which means the area is a half mile times a half mile, or a quarter mile of land area."

"I don't think so," the guide said, shaking his head and smiling. Toby gave Bruce a smack on the back when he started to respond. Now was not the time to give a math lesson.

"Where does this mathematical wonder get its power?" Bruce asked.

"From the Bakun Hydro Electric Dam on the Balui River. Sometimes the old-fashioned power sources are the best ones. Our vision is to put these cubes up all over the world, wherever there's a cheap source of power. Safety's also a concern—with all the piracy in the South China seas, we don't like to ship the wheat, so we mostly sell locally and to Indonesia and Brunei."

After Toby gave his speech, they returned to the *Rocinante*. Parked next to it was the campaign's new and much larger floater, christened with a bottle of Jancola by Bruce as the *Sancho*. Toby stepped inside for a look. It was jammed with people behind desks, all seemingly hard at work. When they saw him, work stopped as many of them got their first close-up look of their candidate. Toby waved, thanked them for their hard work, and stepped out.

"Who are all those people?" he asked Bruce.

"I hired them."

"What do they do?"

"I have no idea," Bruce said, "I just try to stay out of their way."

There were several other large floaters nearby—the press. A group of them loitered about. When they saw Toby, they raced after him. Toby fled into the *Rocinante*, wondering how he'd get into the hotel without getting swarmed.

There were 21 countries and 178 electoral votes in the Asian Federation.

Asian Federation	Population (millions)	Electoral Votes
Bangladesh	304.1	30
Bhutan	1.4	1
Brunei	1.0	1
Cambodia	61.2	6
Fiji	1.0	1
Indonesia	430.6	43
Japan	121.0	12
Kim	29.7	3
Laos	25.0	3
Malaysia	58.9	6
Mongolia	5.6	1
Myanmar	70.1	7
Nepal	77.8	8
Philippines	238.9	24
Singapore	6.1	1
Solomon Islands	1.8	1
South Korea	41.3	4
Sri Lanka	31.8	3
Thailand	71.8	7
Timor	6.2	1
Vietnam	147.3	15
Total	1732.6	178

Gene and Bruce had put together a "circle" strategy for the Asian Federation campaign. Vietnam, Laos, Cambodia, Thailand, Myanmar, Malaysia, Singapore, Brunei, Indonesia, and the Philippines roughly circled the South China Sea. They represented 113 of the 178 electoral votes up for grabs, so they'd spend the next week rotating through them as they moved from one speech and media event to another, with a couple of side trips to Bangladesh. They knew they'd win Kim's three votes and lose Japan's twelve, so they wouldn't bother visiting those two. The big prizes were Indonesia's 43 votes, Bangladesh's 30, Philippines's 24 and Vietnam's 15. Other than Kim, Dubois had substantial leads everywhere—this was conservative country. They discussed for hours how they planned to win, but it wasn't very promising.

"This all very good," Feodora finally said. She had been listening attentively but mostly without comment. "But around South China Sea, there's bigger problem than calculating base area of big cube. A problem small general need to take care of."

Toby knew what the problem was. They'd even arranged their flight paths off the main shipping routes to avoid the pirates of the South China Sea. How could Feodora do anything about this if the Chinese navy and all the others on the sea hadn't been able to solve the problem in all these years? With anti-sonar and anti-radar siding and 30,000 islands in a million square miles of sea to hide in, the pirate submarine fleet had little problem evading discovery. Sometimes they'd congregate for a joint attack, but afterwards they'd all separate and disappear.

Toby and Dubois had both promised to mobilize the world's fleets and take out the pirates. Dubois had promised this five years ago, only to find that the time and economic cost of doing so was far greater than the actual damages caused by the pirates, with little hopes of success. USE funding was limited, and there was little chance of getting such an expensive bill through the World Congress. Dubois found numerous ways of making the promise again, which generally translated into "This time I mean it!"

Ajala argued that any talk of mobilizing fleets to hunt down the pirates was just politics, that we had no way of finding the pirates. Therefore, until someone comes up with a better way, it's best to just pay off the pirates, which would cost substantially less than the actual damages they caused. Toby thought Ajala's argument made perfect logical sense, and correctly predicted a ten percent drop in the polls for him. Toby decided this was one of those times where you just have to tell people what they want to hear, and later, if elected president, act in the way they wanted you to act, even if you know it is pointless. As Bruce said, "In a democracy, sometimes you have to do what the chimps want."

"So you are going to take care of the pirates?" Bruce asked Feodora. "Maybe run a few of them through with a sword?"

"No," she said. "I've done that, very messy. I find laser more efficient. To answer question, yes, I will deal with problem."

"Just deal with the problem, right," Bruce said. "It's going to take more than wild deuces to solve this one."

"Always use entire hand dealt. When you need more than wild deuces, use joker." She turned to Twenty-two, who was in a corner playing with Stupid. After spending a few days with Ajala in Europe, she'd flown Zero to Malaysia and joined them in the *Rocinante*. "You avoid interfering with human affairs, yes?"

"It is Galactic Union policy. If I got caught, I would be in very big trouble."

"Then I will not ask you to interfere. But I have question. Zero has sensors that located you in France from U.S. Can it locate submarines that are underwater or hidden in underwater passageways?"

"Easily." Twenty-two was nervously rocking side to side. "However, I cannot hunt down these pirates for you. That is something you have to do yourself."

"Agreed. I would not ask you to do something that would interfere."

Where is she going with this, Toby wondered. She always had an angle, and she was making no effort to hide the grin on her face.

305

"I am ordering the Russian fleet into the South China Sea," Feodora said.

"You can do that?" Toby asked, stunned.

She looked off into space. He heard her whisper, "Get me the Kremlin."

They listened as she gave the Russian fleet their new orders. When she was done, her smile brightened. "Sometimes it is good to be Feodora."

"But what's the point?" Bruce said. "The Chinese fleet is just as big and always on the hunt, and they only get about one pirate sub every couple of years. There are at least fifty pirate subs left."

"However, Chinese fleet doesn't have joker." She turned back to Twenty-two. "I need to locate one pirate submarine. Do you agree that the Russian fleet could locate one?"

Twenty-two was absolutely still, both eyestalks on Feodora. "Yes, they could, eventually."

"So it would only be minor interference if you locate one of these fifty pirates for us?"

So that was her game, Toby thought. It was just like Fedora. She'd instigated a war to draw a group of countries together so they'd unite as one country. Now she'd ordered the Russian fleet to move into the South China Sea just to convince Twenty-two to locate a single sub for her!

"It is still interfering," Twenty-two said.

"So was your confrontation with Dubois," Bruce said. "And your broadcast to the world. And the table tennis exhibition. You've been interfering every step of the way. Not that I object."

Twenty-two began pacing. Toby wondered if that was something she'd picked up on Earth, perhaps from Ajala, a regular pacer.

"Those were incidental," Twenty-two said. "I did not give out or use grod technology to intentionally influence anything. I need some time to think about this."

"Could you let me know by morning?" Feodora asked.

"Why morning?" Twenty-two asked.

"So small general can take next step in master plan."

"No," Twenty-two asked, "I mean why would I need until morning to decide? I have all the data I need. Okay, I agree. I will have Zero locate one pirate submarine for you. Do you just need location?"

Even Feodora seemed caught off guard by the alien's sudden agreement. "If possible, find submarine hidden by island. I need to pay visit."

"*What?*" Bruce exclaimed. "Vice presidential candidates do not cavort with pirates."

"If presidential candidate can cavort with alien from outer space, then small general can talk to humans on island."

"Then we're sending Turk and Crowbar with you," Toby said.

"No. I go alone." When Toby and Bruce tried to convince her, she only smiled and shook her head.

"What about the Russian fleet?" Toby asked. "While you're off having adventures, what do we tell them when they show up? The Chinese aren't going to be happy about them in their back yard. We don't want another war."

"Russian fleet in South China Sea," Feodora said, sounding wistful. "Chinese Fleet in South China Sea. I regret I will miss much of the fun."

Toby sighed. They had plans for Feodora to campaign around Asia. They'd just have to schedule around this. "Sometimes, Feodora, you are like a cold breeze in a blizzard."

"In Russia, that is compliment."

The pirates of the South China Sea were once the Taiwanese submarine fleet. When Taiwan, after over a century of actual independence, officially declared its independence from China in 2074 during the Beijing Rebellion, Toby and most others thought China would invade. However, the Chinese leadership, more enlightened than past ones, and struggling with the Beijing Rebellion while mired in the Third Great Depression, restrained themselves. A decade later, no longer feeling threatened, the reunion referendum passed, and Taiwan reunited with China.

However, not all Taiwanese liked the idea. The military, built up for years to defend against a Chinese invasion, had great difficulty accepting the idea they were now part of what they had considered the enemy for so long. Much of the military fractured into splinter groups.

China easily defeated the rebellious Taiwanese army, air force, and surface fleet. The one group they could not get at was the submarine fleet. They became international fugitives.

At first, much of the world was caught up in pirate-mania, and considered the submariners heroes for their brave stand against the powerful Chinese. Every week there'd be another headline of a Chinese ship sunk. Movies were made of their heroics. However, even a submariner needs food, fresh water, and other supplies, including weapons and ammunition. They couldn't just dock somewhere and go shopping.

So they began stealing. Initially, they only took what they needed, and only from the Chinese. As the years went by, they became progressively less picky in their foraging. The honorable sub captains that led the original revolt were soon overthrown by younger, more aggressive rivals. The world, once so enamored with them, turned on them, and demanded they be hunted down. Betrayed and hunted, they spiraled downward until they were, quite literally, pirates.

In the world of pirates, the ones who talked got swords run through them—or lasered—by the ones who didn't.

And Feodora was on her way to them to chat.

Chapter Forty-Three
Pirates of the South China Sea

Feodora landed *Dulcinea*, her rechristened floater, on the barren sand and rock among the outskirts of the Spratly Islands that Zero said was the location of not one, but two submarines. Since the Chinese and other countries had no need to hide submarines next to barren rocks, she could safely surmise they belonged to the pirates. The fact that there were two increased the likelihood of there being high-ranking officers. That could save some time working up the chain of command.

She'd renamed her floater after joining the Platt campaign. The *Solzhenitsyn* seemed a bit too Russian for a worldwide campaign. She'd found it funny that the Moderate Party's symbol was the horse—her secret nickname in Russia. She liked that nickname, but now enjoyed playing Dulcinea, even if she knew she looked more like a skinny Sancho.

Now she stood on what passed for a beach on what passed for an island on what supposedly passed as a submarine base. It was perhaps three hundred yards long, a hundred wide, slanting upwards to a hill in the middle, where a single coconut tree jutted into the air like a flag declaring the island's independence from the world. With nothing in sight to the horizon in all directions, there was little to challenge its sovereignty.

So, she thought, what do I do now? Yell "Anybody home?" Look for a place to knock? Zero said the submarines were on the south side. She'd landed a bit north of that, not wanting to plop down in the middle of a hostile base.

She walked toward the supposed location of the hidden submarine base. Used to the coldness of Russia, she didn't like the hundred degree heat, though the cool, salty ocean breeze made it livable. A pair of crabs scuttled about at the water's edge. Seagulls flew overhead.

"*Halt! Hands up!*"

Three figures in scuba gear stood in the water just off shore, lasers aimed at her midsection. As she raised her hands, more appeared from behind. Soon she was surrounded by scraggly-looking Taiwanese pirates, half of them men, half women, brandishing lasers and looking anxious to use them.

Sometimes, she thought, it is not good to be Feodora.

She knew pirates preferred lasers because they were silent, allowing them to pick off victims one at a time as they captured a ship without alerting the rest of the crew. An old-fashioned rifle or machine gun with bullets was more deadly; a laser needed to stay on you for a few seconds to kill. However, she'd come here to talk to the pirates, not to evade lasers.

"Who are you?" One of the men who'd sneaked up from behind glared with wildly darting eyes that couldn't seem to focus on her. They came out of a face hidden by hair and beard that looked like it hadn't been trimmed, combed, or washed since the submarine fleet left Taiwan sixteen years ago. The ones not in scuba gear were dressed in wildly divergent fashion, as if they wore whatever they'd captured in the latest haul. Tattooed on everyone's left hand was a twelve-sided star, formerly the national emblem of Taiwan.

"I am General Feodora Zubkov. I am here to meet with your leaders on a matter of mutual benefit."

The man's eyes darted back and forth, catching her occasionally in the middle. "Kill her," he said, and turned away.

Feodora braced herself. Her death would be quick and sweet, as she'd always hoped.

"No, wait!" one of the scuba pirates said. She'd pulled off her face mask to show another explosion of unruly black hair. "Don't you know who she is? She's one of the Russian generals who defeated the Chinese in the Kim War. She's the one who defeated the Japanese in the Russian-Japanese War by invading China."

The darting-eyes man turned back. "The Mountain Monster?" The Japanese name for her. It was all a matter of perspective. "In the movie, you weren't short and ugly."

"In movie, I was played by pretty actress. Here I am real, just short, ugly general from Russia."

"How did you find us?"

She fixed her face in an impassive half-smile. "Russia has developed new sensors that can locate hidden submarines . . . with *zero* chance of mistake." She chuckled internally at her joke. "That is why I must see your leader. Otherwise, every one of you will be hunted down and killed."

Darting-eyes man stiffened. "The Chinese have been trying to do that for years."

"The Russian fleet is on its way now, and will hunt every one of you down. And now they will succeed." She felt energized; lying for a good cause was liberating. "But I have better deal for you."

The man's eyes continued to jerk back and forth, less so than before. She had his attention. "I need to know more about this sensor."

She shook her head. "I can only say more to leader of Taiwanese pirates."

There were gasps from several of them. "We are not pirates," the man said angrily. "We are liberation fighters."

"My apologies. I should not repeat the twisted lies given by media. I know the legends of your brave battles with Chinese imperialists. Your cause is just, and I am here to help you." The best way to get on the good side of a crazed madman was to agree with his crazed view of the world.

He nodded. "So you came here, alone, to talk to the leader of the Taiwanese Liberation Front?"

311

She'd never heard it called that. "Yes."

"Then I will take you to meet that leader." He stood up straight and stared down at her from his full five and a half foot height, nine inches taller than she. "You are speaking to him. I am Admiral Jian Lin."

A quick search by her TC identified him as a Petty Officer Third Class when the submarine fleet rebelled, though she barely recognized him from the clean-cut picture on her TC. Somehow in the sixteen years since he'd fought his way up the ranks, and gotten himself declared admiral, or done so himself. She'd heard rumors of what had happened to the original, less aggressive admirals, and they were not pretty.

"Let's adjourn to my office," Lin said. "Don't bother trying to call anyone on your TC; it won't work." Meaning, Feodora thought, they had an infowave scrambler. Fortunately, she'd downloaded the info on the Taiwanese pirates in advance.

They marched her toward the hill and palm tree in the middle of the island. They stopped next to a group of boulders. Lin crouched down and rapped his fist three times on a flat one against the ground. There was a hollow, wooden sound.

A moment later the "rock" opened like a doorway, exposing a sloping tunnel underneath. They went down single file.

She knew where their base was, and now knew the entrance. There was no way they were going to let her live unless they reached an agreement.

The tunnel opened into a huge cavern—the submarine base. Two subs were docked along the surrounding walkway. Several doorways opened into the surrounding rock. Lin led her into one.

His office was a hole in the rocky wall, like a ground squirrel's, but bigger. Lin sat behind a small desk. There was no chair for her, so she stood. Leaning against the wall was a large bulletin board, with news clippings tacked all over.

"I need to know about this new sensor device that you claim can locate our submarines."

She shook her head. "That's a good question so I'm going to evade it. I am here to negotiate, but I am still a loyal Russian." If she appeared too eager, he'd get suspicious.

"I could have you tortured until you talk."

"Yes, and I probably would talk. Then I would have no reason to hold up any agreement we reach, and the Russian fleet will find you as I did, and kill every one of you." She decided to stare him down, and looked into his flickering, evading eyes.

He looked away, and began tapping his finger nervously on his desk. "What do you have in mind?"

"Here is deal." It is good to be Feodora, she thought.

Toby announced the deal he had made with the Taiwanese Liberation Front on worldwide media. The news media spent the next few days showing the Taiwanese submarines, on the surface and escorted by the Russian fleet, as they made the journey north to a Russian base on the Sea of Japan. Toby was declared an "Honorary Admiral of the Taiwanese Fleet."

Of course, Feodora had actually made the deal, but she insisted that he take credit for it. After all, he was at the top of the ticket. Plus, she pointed out, the Chinese and Japanese would go insane if they knew she was behind this, and spurred on by popular demand, would have little choice but to attack. There was little doubt that she was enemy number one in those countries.

The Chinese and Japanese, along with Dubois, were predictably furious at the induction of the Taiwanese submarine fleet into the Russian navy. They demanded the pirates be put on trial, and the Taiwanese submarines delivered to China. Many worldwide agreed with them, but they were the minority—most applauded the solution to the ongoing problem. For several days, the world waited to see if the Chinese and Japanese would launch an attack, but without the provocation of Feodora as the dealmaker, they decided not to attack the massed Russian fleet, now fortified by the fifty submarines.

The irony of the whole thing, Toby thought, was that the cost of hiring the Taiwanese was minimal compared to the overall Russian military budget, and especially when compared to the havoc created by the pirates. While the Chinese and Japanese protested, the rest of the world—especially those bordering the South China Sea—hailed Toby and the Russians as heroes.

"The Russian navy require crew cuts," Feodora said. "The Taiwanese pirates had vowed never to cut or clean their hair until Taiwan was independent from China. So toughest part of negotiation was convincing them to get haircuts. They agreed, but now they refuse to cut fingernails."

The ads from Dubois in Asia were ferocious, slinging up every rumor imaginable to see what would stick. He'd gradually cut back on the *Stop the Invasion!* ads; the public tired of that.

Toby took the same advice he'd always told candidates: never make direct responses to spurious attacks. Those ads often will bring you down in the polls, but you'll go down more if you respond directly and bring attention to them. Instead, respond by counter-attacking. Frame the attack on you in the most favorable way possible for yourself, and immediately launch into a counter-attack. If you harp on whatever your opponent is attacking you on, so will the public.

One Dubois ad attacked Toby for flip-flopping on issues, contrasting his apparent agreement on some issues when he worked for Dubois with his current positions. Rather than rebut them one by one, Bruce put together a response ad where a narrator mocked Dubois for falsely trying to say the very reasons for Toby's leaving his administration—Dubois's bad policies—were flip-flops, when it was actually Dubois who kept flip-flopping. The ad then launched into Dubois's own many flip-flops, such as on the Mormon-Israeli issue.

The only real issue ad from Dubois attacked Toby's—actually Feodora's—solution to the pirate situation. Toby and Bruce decided that didn't need a response; most of the world, and in particular those in the Asian Federation, were on their side.

314

The Platt Campaign launched a number of other ads. With their rise in the polls there had been an increase in fundraising, so they could afford to produce and run more. There were a lot of issues to choose from. Being president for five years gave Dubois the huge advantages of incumbency: the bully pulpit, taking credit for everything good that happens, easier fund-raising since the ones giving the money know he's president, while his rivals only *might* become president. However, Dubois had the disadvantage of a five-year record on issues that could be picked apart.

Bruce practically drooled over Dubois's record.

In the end, Toby had some of Bruce's ads toned down, but if the ads were accurate and fair, he approved them.

The one ad by Dubois that bothered Toby was the family ad. It documented how infrequently Toby saw his wife and son, and pointed out how he'd started up a rival campaign against his own daughter, not the other way around. Every word of it was true. Toby did his best to ignore it, but it felt like a pirate laser through his stomach.

Ajala, rapidly sinking in the polls and now having financial difficulties, had fewer ads, and went almost exclusively positive. It was the smart thing to do: let the two front-runners rip each other apart, and present yourself as a positive alternative.

Toby suddenly realized what he'd just done. For the first time, he'd thought of himself as one of the front runners, just as Bruce had been trying to hammer into him. He knew it was true, but deep down found it difficult to believe. Dubois had started with huge leads in nearly every one of the Asian Federation countries. Now the polls showed them nearly even in country after country.

"*Congratulations,*" said a one-word text note from Lara.

Toby gave speeches throughout the region to the largest and loudest crowds of the campaign. Their internal polling showed that the silent conservative majority was still for Dubois, but that those for Toby were more excited, and therefore more likely to vote. He almost felt sorry for Ajala, now nearly forgotten in the region. His strength would be next week, in Africa, where Toby and Dubois would be left fighting for electoral crumbs.

On election night, Tuesday, September 28, he met Ajala at a dinner held by the Indonesian governor, and the two exchanged pleasantries. "When I am president, there may be a place for you in my administration," Ajala told him. He had discarded the standard suit for a traditional Nigerian robe and matching headdress, both green; what did he have to lose?

"And for you in mine," Toby replied. Ajala didn't seem to be a man whose lifelong ambitions were crumbling; he looked like a huge weight had been taken off his shoulders. Toby felt the reverse.

Melissa was also at the banquet, at Ajala's table. She came over to say hi, and Toby listened to the spirited stat-filled debate she had with Bruce over the captive whales in Dover. Afterward, he couldn't remember who argued what, or much of anything else. His mind was too busy calculating the odds for the various countries in Asia. He'd seen the latest polls. In the two biggest countries, Indonesia and Philippines, with 43 and 24 electoral votes, he and Dubois were dead even.

Soon the banquet ended, and as Melissa shouted a few more whale stats to an overwhelmed Bruce, they left for the *Rocinante*. Then they were on the way to Tanzania. It would be another sleepless night as they awaited results.

Chapter Forty-Four
Tanzania and the Colossus of Bapoto

Wednesday, September 29, 2100

O n the way to Dar es Salaam in Tanzania, they received the results for the Asian Federation election. The biggest prize, Indonesia, was too close to call.

Asian Federation	Electoral Votes	Dubois	Ajala	Platt
Bangladesh	30	44%	11%	**45%**
Bhutan	1	42%	14%	**44%**
Brunei	1	42%	13%	**45%**
Cambodia	6	40%	18%	**42%**
Fiji	1	27%	36%	**37%**
*Indonesia	43	45%	10%	45%
Japan	12	**67%**	29%	4%
Kim	3	5%	23%	**72%**
Laos	3	**41%**	19%	40%
Malaysia	6	34%	10%	**56%**
Mongolia	1	**44%**	39%	17%
Myanmar	7	**39%**	23%	38%
Nepal	8	**45%**	31%	24%
Philippines	24	43%	13%	**44%**
Singapore	1	42%	14%	**44%**
Solomon Isl.	1	33%	33%	**34%**
South Korea	4	**54%**	27%	19%

Sri Lanka	3	40%	19%	**41%**
Thailand	7	42%	12%	**46%**
Timor	1	40%	17%	**43%**
Vietnam	15	39%	21%	**40%**
Total	178	35	0	100

*Too close to call

It was their first continental win. Among the larger countries, they'd pulled out Bangladesh and Philippines both by a point, while sweeping most of the South China Sea countries. But they'd lost Myanmar by a point. The voting contrast in Japan and Kim—voting in the Asian Federation for the last time—was striking; if Toby were to go to Japan, he'd better bring a larger security force. He'd also taken a thumping in Mongolia and Nepal for siding with China in their border disputes. South Korea also showed its displeasure for Toby's support of their rival Kim.

The 43 electoral votes from Indonesia would be huge, and all they could do was wait for the final result. Dubois and Toby tied at 45% each. The initial count had Dubois winning by 47 votes in a country with a population of 460 million and over a quarter million voters. Bruce immediately called for a recount. If they could switch just 24 votes from Dubois to Toby, he'd win.

There was a time, Toby remembered, when recounts and challenges could go on for weeks and even months. With TC voting, there was no real recount, just a computer check to make sure every vote had been counted and was legal.

Five minutes later, the result of the recount was in. By checking all votes against the country's database, the computer recount found 22 votes that had not been counted due to malfunctioning TCs. Since that was not enough to overturn the election, they were discounted. Toby stared at the final numbers for Indonesia:

Dubois	117,634,583	45.442056%
Platt	117,634,536	45.442038%
Ajala	23,598,091	9.115906%

All 43 electoral votes from Indonesia went to Dubois.

"How can Dubois win by 0.000018%, and still get one hundred percent of the electoral votes?" Twenty-two asked. "You can give electoral votes proportionally by percentage. Or you can use your TC technology to allow voters to give their second choice. That allows an instant runoff between the top two finishers. Yet you choose not to do this." Bruce began to answer, but Twenty-two interrupted. "Do not answer. I believe you call that a rhetorical question."

They won an even 100 electoral votes to Dubois's 78, with Ajala again getting shut out. Dubois still held a commanding lead, 369-10-157, and they were running out of time to catch up.

If only we'd had one more speech in Indonesia, Toby thought, one more commercial, one more rally or media event, *anything* to convince 24 voters to switch, it would have been so much closer. The Gods of politics were toying with him.

There were 37 countries and 247 electoral votes in Africa, to be decided on what was known as "Super Tuesday." Because many African countries had joined Islam Nation, it was sort of a mishmash, especially in the north, where neighboring countries almost alternated between the two.

"I've never understood why they call it Super Tuesday," Toby said. "It's only two votes more than India, and less than a fifth of the overall total."

"You want to ask them?" Bruce asked. Toby did not.

Africa	Population (millions)	Electoral Votes
Angola	78.3	8
Benin	47.8	5
Botswana	3.2	1
Burundi	74.0	7
Cameroon	60.8	6

Cape Verde	1.7	1
Central Afr. Rep.	9.6	1
Comoros	4.4	1
Congo	20.4	2
Equatorial Guinea	3.2	1
Eritrea	26.5	3
Ethiopia	275.8	28
Gabon	3.2	1
Ghana	99.6	10
Guinea-Bissau	16.5	2
Ivory Coast	58.0	6
Kenya	112.2	11
Lesotho	1.4	1
Liberia	29.7	3
Madagascar	82.0	8
Malawi	58.2	6
Mauritius	1.7	1
Mozambique	62.8	6
Namibia	2.3	1
New Ghana	7.2	1
Niger	93.0	9
Nigeria	477.3	48
Rwanda	39.1	4
Sierra Leone	19.6	2
South Africa	62.2	6
Sudan	125.3	13
Tanzania	149.3	15
Togo	26.3	3
Uganda	186.0	19
Western Sahara	1.3	1
Zambia	28.5	3
Zimbabwe	26.2	3
Total	2374.6	247

As they approached Dar es Salaam, Toby received an incoming call from Ajala. What would he want? Toby took the call, and Ajala appeared on his TC.

"Congratulations on your solution to the South China Sea pirates," Ajala said. "If I were president, I would make you my Secretary of State."

"I appreciate that, Governor. And I appreciate your willingness to take unpopular stands, even when they cost you votes." Toby noticed he'd said "If." Just yesterday he had said "When I am president."

"However, you will never be my Secretary of State," Ajala continued. "Though I hope you may consider me for your cabinet."

It took Toby a moment for it to register. "Are you dropping out?"

Ajala took a deep breath. "Yes. The voters have sent me a message—I will not be president. I would do well in Africa, but I would be taking votes from you, and making Dubois president. I could not live with myself if I did that."

Ouch, Toby thought. A pointed reminder of who made Dubois president. "You know how I regret what happened in '95. I just wish we could have worked together this time to defeat Dubois, perhaps compromising on some things to gain votes—"

"And that is where we are different, Toby. You compromise, you win, you get things done, but things are never as good as they should be. I rarely compromise, I rarely win, and I rarely get things done. But someday, when I do win, I will make things historically better than you could."

"Fair enough analysis," Toby said, though he wasn't in total agreement. He hoped to do a few historic things himself. Historic didn't have to be liberal or conservative; it could just be *right* "And I was serious about wanting you in my administration if I win."

"I will consider it. For now, I will drown my sorrows in Nigerian whiskey. Did you see I lost to you in the Fiji and Solomon Islands by a point? I vacation at Fiji. They may have lost my business."

Was Toby the only one in the political world who remembered, or cared, that alcohol was illegal? He never would have believed it of Ajala. Perhaps he was speaking metaphorically.

"If I choose not to join your administration—I do not know if I could accept some of your compromises—would I still have your ear?"

"You can call me at any time on any issue," Toby said.

"I appreciate that. In return, I will give you my endorsement. That will win you Nigeria and perhaps other countries. The ten electors from the RF will all go to you, since you finished second in those six countries."

When he was off with Ajala, he broke the news to the others. It was a jubilant time. Nigeria was by far the most populous country in Africa, and its 48 electoral votes almost doubled the next highest, Ethiopia's 28. Suddenly all of Africa was in play. Plus they'd just inherited Ajala's ten votes from the Russian Federation. Now they were "only" down to Dubois by 369-167.

If their situations were reversed, Toby wondered, would he do the same as Ajala? Philosophically, Ajala was in a different situation. When you're off to the left, and you're splitting the vote with someone in the middle, you mostly take votes away from the one in the middle, which helps the one on the right, the one you least want to win. If you're in the middle, as he was, then it's not philosophically as important who wins, the left or right. In this case, character counted. He hoped that if he were in the same situation as Ajala, he too would drop out so the honorable man would win.

If Toby were to win, Ajala would be the perfect Secretary of Agriculture.

None of them had ever been to Dar es Salaam, so it was their first look at the Colossus of Bapoto, one of the Seven Wonders of the Modern World.

It had been fifteen years since the coup that brought General Amri Bapoto to power in Tanzania. It had taken him less than five years to erect the 800-foot statue of himself that stood astride the 300-foot wide mouth of the Dar es Salaam harbor. The statue had a thoughtful look, with a book under one arm. The other arm held a laser aimed at ships approaching the harbor, a rather direct message to behave, or else. The entire silvery-white statue was platinum plated at a cost that must have broken the Tanzanian treasury. The colossus dwarfed its predecessor, the ancient Colossus of Rhodes, which had stood a mere 110 feet tall.

"That is an interesting way to welcome others," Twenty-two said. "Very much like Dubois's welcome to me with many aimed weapons."

"I can smell the arrogance," Bruce said.

"Agreed," Toby said, though all he could smell was the persistent fish smell inside the *Rocinante*. It was the only time he could remember where the two agreed on anything about art. Bruce tended to see such things in functional terms.

"Maybe someday they build smaller one for me," Feodora said.

"Do grods have such monuments?" Toby asked.

"Yes, but only to One." She had told them much, though not all, of the most famous of grods.

"How big are they?"

"The largest is the Moon of One, which circles Grodan. It is only 23 of your miles across, but entire moon is sculpted in the shape of One."

Gene and Bruce had previously worked out a rather simple schedule for Toby and Feodora where they would visit just 15 of the 37 countries, avoiding the countries where Ajala had substantial leads. Rather than a whirlwind tour all over Africa, they'd go to nearly every major city in just those countries. With Ajala dropping out, their African plans had just become a logistical nightmare. Gene and Bruce, and others from The Ranch, were working their TCs, arranging new events all over the continent.

"We're focusing on the big ones," Bruce said between calls. "Nigeria's 48, Ethiopia's 28, Uganda's 19, and Tanzania's 15. If the press picks up our events in those countries, we should do okay in the smaller countries."

"It's fun to watch our minions working hard," Feodora said. Coming from anyone else, it would have sounded arrogant, but from her it came off as complimentary. She had decided to ride with them, and so had arranged for an aide to bring *Dulcinea* to Tanzania. The plan was for her to take her own floater after the planned Tanzania events, and campaign separately from Toby so they could cover more ground.

For much of Africa, the twin problems of abortion and overpopulation were the key issues. Much of Africa outlawed or frowned on abortion, leading to more population pressures. To solve the problem, some countries were enforcing a "two-child rule" to stabilize populations. Some of the more populated ones had resorted to a near draconian "one-child rule." This had previously been done successfully in China and semi-successfully in India.

Dubois had strict yet simple positions on these. Abortion was wrong, but if the government needed to restrict births, and punish those who broke such restriction laws, it had that right.

Ajala's position was the exact opposite. He was pro-choice on abortion, but felt any restriction on family size was wrong.

Toby was also pro-choice. He believed a two-child policy might be necessary, but that a one-child rule was too much. However, there was little to be gained by going public with any of these views. On issues like these, no matter what policy you adopted, people were far more likely to vote against you for a position than for you. Instead, they'd focus their campaigning on increasing wheat production. Introducing layered wheat cubes to Africa and PUFF were to be a major part of his stump speeches in Africa.

Tens of thousands showed up for Toby's speech that afternoon at Bapoto Square. As he expected, he received his greatest ovation when he spoke of PUFF and the layered wheat cubes. Hungry people were more interested in the nuts and bolts of putting food on the table than fancy words about economics or other arcane polices.

Feodora also gave a short address. She spoke like a pro, Toby thought, watching her punctuate her contralto voice with fist pumps. Sometimes she walked among the crowd while talking, often disappearing in the forest of taller people, giving security a major headache.

"Good performance?" she asked afterwards.

"Excellent," Toby said.

"Someday you explain what prancing about in front of people and yelling slogans has to do with leadership."

"Will do."

Bruce told them to hurry as they had another engagement coming up, so they left quickly for the *Rocinante*.

That's when General Bapoto, seemingly out of nowhere, stepped in front of them, surrounded by scarlet-uniformed guards.

Every one of them had a gun pointed at them, most at Toby.

Turk, Crowbar, and the Gray Guard security quickly surrounded Toby, guns pointing back. But more scarlet men poured in—Bapoto's Red Guard—and soon the sea of red greatly outnumbered the Gray Guard.

"You are under arrest," Bapoto said.

Chapter Forty-Five
For Fifteen Electoral Votes

"Put your weapons down," Toby ordered his security. He wasn't sure if they'd follow his orders, but they did. He had no doubt they'd give up their lives for him, but it was pointless when you're outnumbered three to one and surrounded.

He turned to Bapoto. "General, what's going on?"

Bapoto's chest full of medals jingled on his royal purple uniform as he laughed. Unlike the tall, svelte athlete that overlooked the harbor, the real Bapoto was nearly as short as Feodora and at least two hundred pounds overweight, almost as wide as he was tall. His polyhedral black and purple striped hair went straight up, adding a foot to his height. Such polyhedral hair was a recent fad among women, but this was the first time Toby'd seen it on a man. The stripes looked ridiculous, like a big piece of children's candy.

Bapoto snapped his fingers, and a chair was laid behind him. He fell back into it, and spent a moment catching his breath.

"We'll get to that," he finally said. "Shackle these three, and disarm and put their security in a holding area."

The Red Guard quickly followed the orders.

"I'm surprised and disappointed you don't know what's going on," he said. "I've put out an arrest warrant for Mr. Dubois and all those who work with him, for crimes against humanity."

"Really?" Bruce asked.

Bapoto looked Bruce up and down. "Did you give your underling permission to speak?"

"He always has permission to speak."

Bapoto nodded toward one of the Red Guard. The husky woman nodded toward two others, who grabbed Bruce from behind, holding his arms back. The husky woman put her weight into an uppercut to the stomach. They released Bruce as he fell to the ground, clutching his stomach and groaning. Then he glared at Bapoto through gritted teeth.

"He did not have *my* permission to speak," Bapoto said, "and underlings do not speak in my presence without that."

Toby stared down at Bruce. "What exactly are you charging us with?"

"I think that would be obvious. Dubois's crimes against humanity are well documented. You ran his campaign in 2095, and have worked with him since, which makes you a criminal as well." He glanced down at Bruce. "This worm also helped elect Dubois, and now works with you, so he's just as guilty." He turned to Feodora, who had smartly decided to remain quiet. "And this is the 'Mountain Monster.' The Japanese have a warrant for your arrest, and offer a bounty." He turned to the husky woman. "Put these dirtballs in our dirtiest prison cell. Tomorrow they will be tried, and if I decide the charges are true, they will be put to death."

The Red Guard took them to a cement prison cell that was as dirty as Bapoto asked for. They were surprised and disappointed to find Gene and Twenty-two there. The Red Guard had broken into the *Rocinante* and arrested them as well. They had taken Twenty-two's sensor.

Twenty-two had earlier ordered Zero to hide in the ocean while they were in Tanzania, and planned to keep the ship nearby just in case. With Toby, Bruce, Feodora, Gene, and Twenty-two all locked up, there wasn't anyone to bring Zero to rescue them, and without the sensor, Twenty-two couldn't call the spaceship. Their TCs were blocked as well, presumably by an infowave scrambler.

"We're not exactly giving the ambassador a good impression of humanity, are we?" Bruce said. The four humans sat against the wall while Twenty-two stood. The darkened cell smelled of old urine. A

327

faucet from a grimy sink continuously dripped, causing Toby to grit his teeth. He knew he wouldn't be getting any sleep that night.

"There is good and bad," Twenty-two said.

"Hardly," Bruce said, gesturing at the walls of their prison. "Any wild deuces or jokers, Feodora?"

"Not this time, I'm afraid."

"Well, Twenty-two," Bruce said after they'd stared at the walls for a while, "you've been in prisons in China, France, and now Tanzania. Any burning questions on humanity you'd like to ask? We're not going anywhere, so now's your chance."

Twenty-two tilted her body slightly sideways. "There is something I have been wondering about for several weeks, which I believe is an issue here in Africa. Both humans and grods have elections where the majority decides who will be elected. I have been studying human demographics, and noticed that some groups increase in population much faster than others. The Mormon population in North America has a much higher birth rate than the Jewish population, and so they have far more Mormon voters than Jewish voters. African countries with rapidly growing populations also rapidly increase their electoral votes."

"That," Toby said, "is why Dubois, a big New Israel supporter, flip-flopped and supported the Mormons."

"And before you comment," Bruce said, "yes, it's dishonest, and yes, voters notice the flip-flop, and yes, they still voted for him if he supported their views. There's an art to the flip-flop, where you completely change your views and act like nothing special happened."

"My question," Twenty-two said, "is why a group gets more political power simply by breeding more?"

Now Toby was confused. "How else would you do it? A majority is a majority. If a group increases its numbers, you still have to count every vote."

"Why?" Twenty-two asked. "Do you believe that a higher breeding rate implies better political judgment, which should be rewarded with more voting power?"

"How else would you do it?" Toby asked.

"To start with, should birthrates not be controlled by the government?" Twenty-two asked. "Otherwise, you will overpopulate your world, and everyone loses."

Now Bruce looked surprised. "Your government controls who has children?"

"Of course. Everyone has a quota of two. If more are needed, increased quotas are randomly given out."

"So what," Bruce asked, "do you do if a grod reaches her quota, and becomes pregnant? Or do grods have children like humans?"

"The process is similar," Twenty-two said. "Any offspring beyond the quota is terminated."

"Ah," Bruce said, "abortion on demand."

"No, only abortion for those beyond the quota, and for birth defects. Why would someone abort a baby if it is inside their quota, unless there is a birth defect?"

"Oh, boy," Bruce said, "I'd like to sic you on a few million self-proclaimed ethicists!"

"How do humans avoid overpopulation if the government doesn't control birthrates?"

"We don't," Toby said.

"Then you are doomed," Twenty-two said.

"Glad that's cleared up!" Bruce said. "So grods allow abortion only for birth defects and to uphold the quota for offspring?"

"That is correct."

"Humans have a slightly different and more complex view on this," Toby said. "I'll let Bruce explain."

"You see," Bruce began, "abortion is one of the biggest issues splitting people apart politically, mostly because people bring religion into the equation. Many people believe that human life begins at conception, and so all abortion is murder."

"They believe a clump of a few cells is a human being?" Twenty-two asked.

"Humans don't handle continuity questions very well," said Bruce, "and so many can't see the difference between the beginning and the end of a pregnancy—and since it ends with a baby human, they believe it must have started with one, even though an embryo, at least in the early stages, has no more consciousness or awareness than a potato."

"I'm a Christian," Gene said. Toby was surprised—Gene got things done, but rarely spoke up on issues. He'd had no idea Gene had religious views.

"So you believe in supernatural beings?" Bruce asked.

Gene ignored Bruce. "Like a lot of others, I believe that human life begins at conception, and so abortion is murder. If you kill that 'clump of cells,' you kill what is, and will be, a human being."

"How can it both be and become a human being?" Bruce asked.

"That's just semantics," Gene said.

"No, it's logic," Bruce said. "That clump of cells either is, or is not, a human being. Which is it? Is there a sliding scale as it becomes more and more human, and it becomes a human at some point in its development?"

"It's a human being," Gene said. "It simply hasn't developed all the way yet. What do you think it is?"

"Let's look at what it actually is," Bruce said. "We'll even advance that clump of cells a few months. Let's say that embryo is the size and intelligence of a mouse, though I'm guessing a mouse is smarter than an embryo of similar size. For the sake of argument, let's assume they are, roughly, the same intelligence. Then the only difference between them is that one has the *potential* to become something much more intelligent."

"And if you kill that *potential*, you have killed a human being," Gene said.

"Provisionally agreed," Bruce said. "But a human woman can have a baby every nine months for roughly thirty years, if they choose. That's forty babies each. Yet, on average, they choose to have only two or three; we'll say three. So by not having a baby every nine months, they have killed 37 human beings!"

"But those 37 never existed!"

"Doesn't matter," Bruce said. "I've already shown that it is the *potential* that is key, and you've agreed that if you kill that potential, you've killed a human being."

"So we should round up all the women that don't have 40 babies and try 'em for murder?" Toby asked.

"Exactly, if you are against abortion," Bruce said.

"You realize your entire argument is silly?" Gene said.

"Only because it is prefaced on your supposition that abortion is murder," Bruce said. "Since you agree that the conclusion is silly, then the premise, that abortion is murder, is silly."

"Oh, come on," Gene began. "By your logic, why don't we allow abortion right up until birth? Imagine that last-minute rush to abort a nine-month-old baby before it has the temerity to get born and ruin everyone's plans!"

Bruce was shaking his head. "Humans have such great difficulty with sliding scales. They always think in black and white. Suppose embryos didn't grow for the first four months after conception, and they then instantly grew to baby size. Do you think there'd be this abortion debate? No, because abortion would then be accepted until the size increase. Because it's instead a gradual process from conception to birth, some people can't bring themselves to set a time where abortion is okay, and so decide it's always wrong. Nonsense."

"And it is wrong, because it's murder," Gene said. "But I'll agree it is a moral judgment based on my religion."

"If abortion is murder," Bruce said, "what should happen to the woman who has the abortion?"

"I'd rather go after the one who performed the abortion."

"Really?" Bruce shook his head with a laugh. "Then the woman who just committed pre-meditated murder goes free?"

Toby considered Bruce's arguments. They seemed logical. At the same time didn't it justify infanticide? After all, a baby doesn't have adult human intelligence, and so could be considered just a "potential" human being. At what point does an embryo or baby become a human, with the full human rights? These were arguments that philosophers and logicians had argued for centuries, and it wasn't about to get settled here.

Toby tuned them out for the next hour as they argued back and forth—Gene often sputtering, as he simply didn't have Bruce's knack for debate—while Twenty-two listened in rapt attention. Ultimately, Gene's argument seemed to come down to a religious one, that human life was sacred, even as an embryo, and so abortion was wrong. Toby was pretty sure that Gene wasn't the only Christian who would squawk with outrage at Bruce's argument, and yet it made sense to him. After all, few people thought a woman who had an abortion should spend years in prison for it, so how could it be true murder?

It seemed rather surreal to argue about abortion while sitting in a dark, dirty prison cell, but what should he expect? You can put a group of political people together anywhere, and eventually they'll talk issues.

"Dahlings, this all very informative," Feodora said. She'd been quiet since the debate began. "I do not believe a debate on abortion in prison ever solved the abortion question. Perhaps we discuss our defense at trial tomorrow? So we look good before they kill us?"

Gene seemed startled. "They're really going to kill us?"

"Of course," Feodora said.

After a moment, Gene sighed. "I'm still not sure why we were arrested. What exactly does Bapoto have against Dubois?"

"Oh, he has nothing against Dubois," Feodora said. Toby and Bruce were nodding their heads. "Many people are starving in Tanzania, from overpopulation and poor economic policy. Bapoto can either blame himself or blame someone else. He blame Dubois."

"And with control of the Tanzania media, what he says is all that gets out. It's a dangerous country to be associated with a perceived or made-up enemy."

"And you brought us here because?" Toby asked.

"For the best of reasons," Bruce said. "Fifteen electoral votes."

Chapter Forty-Six
The Trial and the Cat

The trial was a sham. The three judges, with General Bapoto presiding, sat on a raised dais before an empty room other than the five shackled and gagged defendants and two dozen of the Red Guard.

Bapoto himself read the charges. For Toby, it was a long recitation of Dubois's "crimes," with Toby guilty by association. Many of the accusations had a kernel of truth, though greatly exaggerated through the fog of poor reasoning and bias. Bruce's guilt was also by association during the time he worked on Dubois's election. Gene's guilt was the most tenuous, since he had never worked with Dubois. However, since Toby was guilty by association with Dubois, that made Toby a criminal, and so by association, Gene was guilty as well.

He also read a long list of Feodora's supposed crimes in the Russia-Japan war in 2091. It read as if it were straight from her Japanese accusers. There was no mention of crimes by Twenty-two.

They were not allowed to give a defense.

"I have given these charges much thought and consideration," Bapoto said. "Which is why no defense is needed, since I will act on your behalf if I find you deserving. However, after balancing the evidence from both sides, I find Toby Platt, Bruce Sims, and Gene Conkling all guilty of crimes against humanity. For these crimes, they will be beheaded at nine A.M. tomorrow. I find Feodora also guilty of crimes against humanity. However, I do not believe this court has jurisdiction, and so she will be handed over to Japanese officials tomorrow morning immediately after the beheadings."

Toby wondered how much the Japanese were paying him.

"I find the case of the alien Twenty-two most enticing," Bapoto continued. "This alien—I don't know whether to call it a him, her, or it—shall be held for further questioning. Do my colleagues concur?"

The two judges at his side nodded their heads. If they did not, no doubt they would lose them.

"Then the sentences shall be carried out as ordered. As to the matter of the so-called Gray Guard and the other security people with them, they will be shot, immediately after the beheadings." He rapped his desk with a gavel.

Toby wanted to protest, and could tell Bruce had even more to say, but couldn't because of the gag. The Red Guard pulled them to their feet.

As they were being led out, the lights went out.

Everything seemed to move in slow motion as the dim outlines of the Red Guard threw their prisoners to the ground and looked about. The only light came through several large windows high along the walls. As they watched, one by one something from outside blanked them out. When the last one was covered, they were left in pitch darkness.

"Lock the door!" Bapoto yelled. But he was too late. Toby heard the main door open, and through a dim ray of light that came through it, could see shouting figures charging into the room. Something about their heads was malformed, as if they were beaked. Then the door closed, and the darkness swallowed them up again.

"Stay down," Feodora said. Somehow she had gotten out of her gag. "Protect your head with your arms."

Gunfire erupted, along with cries of pain. Toby could hear Bapoto yelling, "Get them off me!" One of the Red Guard turned on a handlight, but was immediately shot, and the light extinguished.

After about ten seconds of chaos, the gunfire ended.

"Power on!" a woman's voice called. The lights came back on.

The ground was riddled with the bodies of the Red Guard. Standing over them were perhaps a dozen other of what looked like the Red Guard, but with their shirts turned inside out. They were removing night vision goggles. Standing in front was a young, wispy woman dressed in tight, black clothing, who seemed in constant motion. She paced back and forth, pointing a gun from body to body as she checked if any were alive, while turning her head side to side as if trying to see everything at once.

The five prisoners were unharmed. Feodora was not only free from her gag, but miraculously from her shackles as well. She stood, stretching her muscles.

General Bapoto stood in front of his desk, sputtering and jingling his medals while two of the rebel Red Guard held his arms from behind. The wispy woman approached. A few black lines were drawn on her brown cheeks, like a cat's whiskers.

"*You!*" Bapoto exclaimed. "You were exiled!"

"And now I'm back, Father." She strutted up to him, facing him eye to eye.

"General Paka Bapoto, I presume?" Feodora said. "Also known as 'The Cat'?"

"And you must be General Zubkov," Paka said. "Also known as 'The Horse'?"

Toby thought he knew all about Feodora, but this was the first time he'd heard that nickname. Was she nicknamed after the Moderate Party's symbol?

"I see you have been speaking with my Russian colleagues, General," Feodora said. "We should talk more, but could you free my friends?"

"You may call me Paka," she said as she motioned to one of the rebel Red Guard. Soon Toby, Bruce, Gene, and Twenty-two were out of the shackles and gags.

"And you may call me Feodora."

"And you both can go to hell," the elder Bapoto said. In response, the two guards holding him slammed him against the wall, then propped him back up again.

335

"If you will excuse me, I have something I must do," Paka said.

"If you must," Feodora said.

Paka approached and stood in front of her father. "Father, you look well."

"You look potchy and thin, like a blugging street person."

"That's what I was for the last few years," Paka said. "Palace food will be a wonderful change. You won't be joining us."

She lashed out with a knife Toby hadn't seen. A red streak appeared across the elder Bapoto's throat. The guards released him and he fell to the floor.

Twenty-two waddled over. "He has something of mine." She rummaged through his pockets and found her sensor. "Thank you." She returned to the others.

Paka turned to Toby. "Mr. Platt, General Zubkov, I am honored to have you visit Tanzania. I'm speechless and overjoyed at the presence of your alien friend. After I take care of a few minor matters in regard to this transfer of power from father to daughter, I hope you can be a guest for dinner at the palace tonight. Any enemy of my father is a friend of mine."

The following day, Toby watched as they blew up the Colossus of Bapoto. Charges were laid against each foot. As planned, it fell forward into the harbor. There further charges would break it into pieces, which would be towed ashore so the platinum could be harvested to replenish the Tanzania treasury. Toby figured that if any of the other modern "Wonders" were so destroyed there'd be worldwide protest, but not for this one.

"Silly statue," Paka said. "Took five years to build, ten minutes to set the charges, and ten seconds to blow up. I want something a little more permanent, like a pyramid. The Egyptians had it right. And now there's a vacancy in that 'Wonders of the Modern World' thing!"

Back at the *Rocinante*, Bruce was euphoric over the situation. "You can't pay for this type of shock and outrage!" They were gaining on

Dubois in polls throughout Africa. "I think we need to hire a General Bapoto type as an enemy wherever we campaign. If only they came with warning labels."

"Didn't you see his hair?" Toby asked.

"Good point," Bruce said. "I'm glad Paka took him out of the gene pool."

"But Paka was his daughter, from his genes," Toby said.

"Even a flower can bloom out of manure," Bruce said.

Toby turned to Feodora. "How the hell did you get out of your gag and shackles?"

Feodora shook her head. "A miracle explained is a miracle wasted. If God explained her tricks, would anyone worship her?"

"So you are God now?" Bruce asked.

"If I use magic powers to get out of my shackles, I am a God. If, after lights went out, I rubbed mouth against floor to remove gag, then used teeth to tear keys from where they hung from guard's pocket, then I am no longer a God."

Even Bruce looked stunned.

"You will always be a God to me," Toby said.

Toby had dozens of messages pinging on his TC when the scrambler was turned off. Only a small number of people had access to TC him, or there might have been millions.

There was another note from Lara:

"Dad, I'm so glad things ended well in Tanzania. Tyler said you might visit home before Latin America next week. May I visit at the same time?"

Toby wondered if that message had been approved by Dubois. He doubted if the president wanted his campaign manager vacationing with his chief rival.

He sent a message back inviting her to join them on Wednesday afternoon, October 6, the day after the Africa vote. He hesitated about inviting Bruce, after his actions in Tyler's election, but Bruce did seem truly sorry for that. Tyler's table tennis tryouts were that week, and Bruce could work with him.

The second order of business was winning the African vote. The campaign continued as if there hadn't been a two-day interruption, though Bruce and Gene frantically redid the schedule. Dubois's nasty ads continued, including the attacks on his lack of attention to his family.

Toby taped a new ad where he started off by saying, "I'm sure my esteemed opponent did not intend to lie, so let me correct his misstatements." Then he pointed out that he spoke to his wife and son regularly by TC, and that he'd visited them during the North American campaign, but hadn't been able to since because he was out of the country. He pointed out that the house in Germantown, Maryland, was his legal home, and that he lived there when he wasn't away on business—while leaving out that he was often away on "business" for months at a time. He declared that he was visiting them on Wednesday afternoon, as they'd planned for some time. Finally, he pointed out that attacking an opponent's family life is what one does when the other guy is solving real problems—like the Kim War and the pirate problem—and is gaining in the polls. He emphasized that while he was solving problems, Dubois was out campaigning.

Bruce didn't like the ad, other than the attack at the end. "He's on the attack with his ads, playing to the simple-minded masses, and you want to go defensive?"

Toby agreed, but insisted they run it anyway.

After zipping about Africa for the rest of the week, election day, Tuesday, October 5, finally arrived. As usual, they left for their next destination before the results were in. Feodora traveled separately in *Dulcinea* this time since she'd be going directly to Latin America to campaign. Toby also had a full schedule there, but first they had a more important event scheduled in Germantown, Maryland.

Reese followed the worldwide anger at the arrest of Platt and his entourage. He saw the euphoria when he was released. Many were uneasy with Platt's willingness to compromise. He seemed to lack deep convictions. Yet he was admired. Even loved.

338

Sometimes the world needed a tough guy in charge. That was Dubois. Sometimes the world needed someone more fair-minded. That was Ajala. But Platt? He didn't fit into the red and blue color pegs. He was neither. He was both.

Reese was certain that if the election were run from scratch, Platt would win. But now? His newfound popularity didn't help in the places that had already voted. Now he was far behind.

But he was loved.

Who would the world mourn more, Dubois or Platt? The choice was obvious. He'd chosen Platt weeks before. Yet he hadn't been quite sure of his decision until now. Finalizing the decision took a huge weight off his shoulders. Don Quixote, on his mighty Rocinante, with Dulcinea at his side, would soon meet . . . the Windmill.

Reese already had the supplies he needed. Stolen, or bought with stolen money. Now it was just a matter of finalizing a plan.

Platt had said in an interview he was going home to visit his wife and son on Wednesday. There would be far more security on candidate Platt than his family. Platt had a son, Tyler. He'd be out of school that afternoon. What about the morning? He'd be in school doing a half day until his father arrived.

It'd be a lot easier getting at the son. Tyler. What a nice name. Reese grinned as he made his plans, breathing heavily.

It was time to visit Germantown Middle School in Maryland.

Chapter Forty-Seven
Hostage

Toby was still up at five in the morning on Wednesday as they approached Maryland. He stared out the window at the entourage of security floaters that had surrounded them on all their flights for weeks. After five years of it with Dubois, he was used to it. The Gray Guard once tried to convince them to fly in a more advanced vehicle than the *Rocinante*, and they probably should have. However, they'd grown attached to it, and more important, their followers around the world had romanticized it. To change now would seem to many a sellout, even a betrayal. Instead, they quietly had the shielding upgraded and put in a new, faster engine.

His TC made a light *ping*, as he'd instructed it to do when election results were out. Earlier in the race, he'd relied on Bruce to bring him the election results, but as he rose in the polls, he had become more anxious about it. There was a standing agreement that the person to get results during the night should wake the others, which Toby did.

Most of the results were ready, but not all. They were jubilant at the initial results, which showed Toby up 121-87, with 39 electoral votes too close to call. They knew they had been gaining on Dubois in the polls before voting began, and hoped for a sizeable African victory. They may have gotten their wish.

However, four countries were listed as 50%-50%: Ethiopia, Mozambique, Zimbabwe, and Congo. The big prize was Ethiopia, with its 28 votes. They watched as the recount was tabulated.

After a few minutes, they groaned as Zimbabwe and its three votes flashed for Dubois. Bruce pumped his fist and yelled, "*Yes!*" as Congo's two votes flashed for Toby. Then they groaned again as Mozambique and its six votes went for Dubois. Toby still led, 123-96, as they awaited Ethiopia.

"*No!*" Bruce yelled, slamming a ping-pong ball against the wall, as Ethiopia went for Dubois. Like Indonesia last week, they kept losing the close ones. The final results had Dubois just edging Toby out, 124-123. Even with the ten points Toby had gained from Ajala added in, Dubois led 493-290. Dubois would only need 174 of the 550 electoral votes still to be awarded—less than 32%. It was a somber crew as they headed into Germantown.

Africa	Electoral Votes	Dubois	Platt
Angola	8	**54%**	46%
Benin	5	45%	**55%**
Botswana	1	47%	**53%**
Burundi	7	**55%**	45%
Cameroon	6	44%	**56%**
Cape Verde	1	48%	**52%**
Central Afr. Rep.	1	**51%**	49%
Comoros	1	**52%**	48%
Congo	2	50%	**50%**
Equatorial Guinea	1	**55%**	45%
Eritrea	3	**53%**	47%
Ethiopia	28	50%	50%
Gabon	1	44%	**56%**
Ghana	10	48%	**52%**
Guinea-Bissau	2	**51%**	49%
Ivory Coast	6	48%	**52%**
Kenya	11	**52%**	48%
Lesotho	1	**53%**	47%
Liberia	3	46%	**54%**

Madagascar	8	48%	**52%**
Malawi	6	**51%**	49%
Mauritius	1	49%	**51%**
Mozambique	6	**50%**	50%
Namibia	1	**52%**	48%
New Ghana	1	49%	**51%**
Niger	9	39%	**61%**
Nigeria	48	37%	**63%**
Rwanda	4	**54%**	46%
Sierra Leone	2	45%	**55%**
South Africa	6	**53%**	47%
Sudan	13	**51%**	49%
Tanzania	15	12%	**88%**
Togo	3	46%	**54%**
Uganda	19	**52%**	48%
Western Sahara	1	48%	**52%**
Zambia	3	**51%**	49%
Zimbabwe	3	**50%**	50%
Total	247	124	123

Tuesday night and Wednesday early morning were a busy time for Reese. He brought the needed supplies to Germantown Middle School in a stolen blue floater. He parked it on the fake grass a short distance down the street from the front gate. He wore his cheap prosthetic arm. He looked forward to junking it for his special made version. Plan C.

He made sure no one was watching. Then he awkwardly climbed the fence. His fake arm was useless for climbing.

There were guards next to every door into the school. There were proximity scanners that would prevent him from breaking in or bringing weapons anywhere near. But in the darkness he could move about the grounds. As long as he didn't get too close to the school. He took a long walk around the walls, placing infowave scramblers at each corner. He had a remote control to turn them on. At the right time.

He laid a regular phone set near the front gate by the blue floater. He hid it in the grass. From that he ran regular old-fashioned phone wire under the gate and into the school grounds. He'd stolen the two thousand yards of wire. To match the artificial grass he'd painted the phone set and wire green. He took the wire as close as he dared to the school. He hammered a clasp into the ground over it to hold it in position. Then he ran the wire away from the school. To an out-of-the-way part of the fence that nobody would notice. He drilled a hole in the fence with a small hand laser. He ran the wire through it.

Outside he ran the wire to the street. Earlier he'd located a sewer running underneath it. He'd dealt with bad odors during his years in the army and Special Forces. But nothing like the foul-smelling stench he now faced. He held his breath as he crawled across on hands and knees in two inches of cold water, dragging the phone wire. When he emerged, water and sewage dripped from his clothing. He reeked like a flooded outhouse. He felt like one.

On the other side, he ran the wire to the back yard of a house. Then through several more back yards until he reached the house directly across from the school's front gate. He ran the wire inside. He attached it to a second phone set. The old man and old woman who lived in the house were upstairs. They wouldn't mind. He'd killed them that afternoon and stuffed their bodies in a closet.

Plan B was ready.

He went back and buried several small bombs on the school grounds. They, too, were operated by remote control. He smiled. He was so organized.

He pulled out the paper map of the Washington D.C. and the Germantown area. Once again he examined the line he'd drawn between Moderate Headquarters and Germantown Middle School. He'd placed an "X" at the midpoint between the two. North Potomac. Plan A. He'd use a second stolen floater he'd parked down the street to get there. He'd leave the blue floater behind. Inside the second floater he retrieved the change of clothing he'd left there. And the special-made prosthetic. With a surprise he didn't expect to use. Plan C. The first rule of covert operations is always have backup plans. He was a professional.

His work was done. When the time came he'd send messages to the principal and the police. He'd set off the bombs and turn on the scramblers.

He went back to the house across from the school and took a long, luxurious shower. Then he put on his faded blue American uniform.

Toby spent the morning at The Ranch, going over election plans with Bruce and the rest of the staff. It seemed entire epochs had gone by since they'd rented the place as their headquarters. Toby still remembered that first night after they moved in and how surreal it all felt. And then Twenty-two had walked in the door.

Now the place was surrounded by the Gray Guard, with the inside jammed with staffers and more Gray Guard. The walls and roof had been shielded. It was a good thing they had rented a rather large space, though they'd never dreamed back then that their quixotic quest would turn into a real campaign.

He missed Olivia and Tyler. He'd rather spend the entire day with them, but Bruce thought that this was a good time for the staff to meet for a few hours about upcoming plans, and he wanted Toby there. They normally did this via TC, but it wasn't quite the same. So he'd meet Olivia and Tyler for lunch, and have the rest of the day and night to themselves. No force in the universe would stop that.

Tyler had begged to get the entire day off, but could come up with no excuse to miss his morning classes, and so he was doing a half day.

The morning dragged on as Bruce and the others debated strategy. Sometimes he wanted to yell out, "I'm right here!" as they discussed his various liabilities.

At eleven Toby received a TC call from Stuart Chandler, director of the Gray Guard. Other than exchanging pleasantries, they'd never really met. A longtime military man who still wore a crew cut, Chandler looked as if every muscle in his body stood at attention.

"From the look of your face, there's something really wrong," Toby said. If the man's face were any redder he'd be hospitalized for sunstroke.

"Sir, there's a problem at your son's school. Ten minutes ago all contact with the school was lost—someone's put up an infowave scrambler, so we can't reach the Gray Guard protecting your son or anyone else there. There are reports of explosions. Just before communication went down, we received a message from someone calling himself 'Windmill.' He said he's taken your son hostage at the school."

Chapter Forty-Eight
Three Strikes

Over the strenuous objections of the usually silent Turk and Crowbar, Toby was on the *Rocinante* and on the way to the police perimeter within minutes. The Gray Guard scrambled aboard their floaters on short notice and accompanied him. Bruce and Twenty-two also came along; the alien had never left the ship.

"At least don't fly in a straight line to the school," Turk said. "Take an unexpected route."

Toby himself was at the controls, which were on manual. "Do you really think that's necessary? With twelve Gray Guard floaters surrounding us? In case someone's waiting below on the off chance I might fly overhead?"

"Yes."

"Okay." He swerved off course, closely followed by the Gray Guard ships.

"You realize what you are doing is stupid?" Turk asked. Turk had never spoken to him that way; he'd rarely spoken to him at all. The two had once apologized for not preventing Dr. Heilig's attack, but even then their words had been sparse.

"If you had a family member who was in danger like this, what would you do?" Toby asked. Crowbar had also wandered over and taken off his sunglasses.

"I do have a family member who is in danger," Turk said.

"You mean right now?"

"Yes," Turk said, taking off his dark sunglasses. His eyes were dark and piercing. "Like me, he's doing a job, but someone's making his job dangerous. What do you think *I* should do?"

"You should do what you can to protect your family," Toby said. "That's what I'm trying to do."

"No you're not," Crowbar said. "Going to the school doesn't help Tyler. Your presence doesn't help the police or the Gray Guard."

"You've always tried to do the right thing, from what we've seen," Turk said. "You've always balanced what's needed with the necessary politics. This time you're acting emotionally."

Perhaps they were right, Toby thought. Yet he felt he had to be there. He couldn't sit back at The Ranch and listen to reports. He was Tyler's father, and he had to do *something*.

"I probably am acting emotionally," he said. "But Turk, you said you had a family member who was in danger. Don't you want to go where he is, even if you can't help him?"

"Of course," Turk said. "That's what I'm doing." He pointed at Crowbar. "Didn't you know? He's my brother."

Toby was stunned, but even more, he was embarrassed not to have known. He'd noticed the resemblance between the two when he'd first met them, and yet had never made the connection.

"I'm really sorry, I should have known," he said. "We rarely talk, so I guess my mind was always on other things."

"It's your job to have your mind on other things," Turk said. "That's why we rarely talk to you. Our job is to protect you, not distract you. And this trip is not making our job easier." He and his brother put their sunglasses back on.

Reese watched through an eyeglass from a field in North Potomac. The *Rocinante* and the surrounding Gray Guard floaters went by in the distance. Too far away to shoot down. He'd set up a surveillance camera on Moderate Headquarters. It verified that Toby was there that morning. He'd known that the moment Platt heard the news about Tyler he'd go to the school. What father wouldn't? He'd expected him to go straight there. He hadn't. Instead he took a more circular route. He lost respect for Toby. A true father would have taken the fastest route.

Reese had taken a trip to eastern Russia during the Kim War. There he'd killed a number of Russians to get his hands on an army-issue shoulder cannon. But it was useless from this distance. Nor could he get the shoulder cannon anywhere else with a direct line on Platt. The Gray Guard's proximity scanners made sure no weapon could do that under normal circumstances. Even the air space over Toby during speeches was guarded by Gray Guard floaters.

Plan A hadn't worked. Strike one, he thought. Time to return to the school for Plan B. And if necessary, Plan C. He patted the shoulder of his missing right arm.

A tall, metal fence surrounded Germantown Middle School. By the time Toby got there—with Bruce, Twenty-two, Turk, and Crowbar all at his heels—police had surrounded it with drawn weapons. Frantic parents stood across the street behind red crime scene police tape.

Chandler met him near the front gate, which police had turned into an impromptu headquarters, using the fence and several parked floaters for cover. It was the only place they could look in without clambering over a fence, and so was the logical place. A colorful blend of flowers surrounded the base of the gate; Toby wondered if there was any chance they were real. Fall had just hit the area, and there was a chill in the air.

"How the hell did someone get through security?" Toby asked.

"We have no idea," Chandler said. "There were guards at all the doors and at Tyler's classes, and proximity scanners all around the school. It simply isn't possible. It must have been an inside job."

"Why isn't anyone going in?" Toby asked, trying to ignore the flashing police floaters in the parking lot. Turk and Crowbar had their weapons drawn, Turk a laser, Crowbar a handgun. The Gray Guard had formed a rough protective circle around him, weapons also drawn.

"The message from 'Windmill' said he'd blow up the school if anyone goes on the school grounds," Chandler said, glancing at Twenty-two.

"He said that to prove it, he'd set off some explosions, and witnesses tell us there were explosions on the school grounds about the time we received that message. If the school followed procedure, they went into lockdown. That means the students and faculty are behind locked classroom doors. Until we know more, we don't want to go in. The message was untraceable; whoever did this knew what he was doing."

"Has anyone spoken with this Windmill?"

"He's set up infowave scramblers somewhere inside. No messages are going in or out of the school, and the proximity scanners are blocked. The message said he'd communicate with us soon, though I have no idea how."

As if in answer, a musical tone rang out. Chandler nearly jumped while Turk, Crowbar, and several police and Gray Guard all aimed their weapons at the source of the sound.

Turk found it first, a tiny green phone set hidden in the fake grass, next to a blue floater parked a dozen yards down the street. A green phone line ran from the phone, through the grass, and under the fence and into the school grounds. Nobody had noticed them in the short time they'd been there since their attention was on the school. They'd had no reason to search the area outside the fence.

Chandler took the phone from Turk. There seemed nothing special about it. He motioned for the others to step back. Then he clicked the receive button and said, "Hello?"

Toby leaned in close to listen.

"This is Windmill." There was a long pause. "Who am I speaking with?" The phone was set to speaker mode, so all could hear. The man had a raspy voice and breathed between words.

"This is Stuart Chandler, director of the Gray Guard. Mind telling us what's going on?"

There were several breaths before Windmill continued. "I hold Tyler Platt hostage here in the school. The school is rigged to blow up if anyone tries to enter the grounds or leave the school. Do you understand?"

"Perfectly. Why are you doing this?"

"I have certain . . . demands. But I will only make them to Toby Platt. May I speak with him?"

Toby looked up sharply. How did Windmill know he was here?

"Stay back," Turk said. "Let me see the phone." Chandler handed it to him. Turk examined it, then deftly pulled it apart and examined the inside. "It looks clean." He put it back together and handed it back to Chandler.

"Twenty-two, could Zero sense what's going on in there, and rescue my son?"

Twenty-two ambled closer to the phone, which she examined with her sensor. "Yes," she said in a low voice. "I've called Zero; it should be here in a minute. Zero should be able to detect any weapons in the school and grab them with its tractor beams. It can also grab anyone holding a weapon."

"I haven't got all day," Windmill said. "I know Toby is there. If I do not speak with him in the next twenty seconds, I will put a bullet in Tyler's head."

"Give me the phone," Toby said. Chandler handed it to him. Toby whispered, "I'm going to try to stall for time so Zero can get here."

"Who's Zero?" Chandler asked, but Toby ignored him.

"This is Toby Platt," he said into the phone. "You have my son. What do you want?"

There were several more breaths. Then the rasping voice came back on. "Mr. Platt. I have followed you around the globe, and finally we get to talk."

"What do you want?"

"Are you standing next to the blue floater? Of course you are; that's where I put the phone. You would have made a great president."

As Toby stared at the phone, everything went to slow motion.

Turk and Crowbar leap between him and the blue floater.

Bruce steps between Toby and the two bodyguards, arms held up as if to protect him.

The blue floater explodes like a huge firecracker, pieces soaring off in all directions.

Turk and Crowbar hurtle through the air over Toby's head as if shot from a cannon, their sunglasses and weapons spinning away.

Bruce slams into Toby, and they fall to the ground.

Shouts and screams and cries of pain.

Toby tries raising himself to his hands and knees. He's surrounded by motionless Gray Guard on the ground.

Toby collapses on his back.

Twenty-two stands over him, looking down.

A man in a faded blue uniform appears, yelling, "I'm a doctor!"

The man leans over him, breathing heavily, and says, "You're still alive. Strike Two." He grins.

The man's right arm falls off. Under the arm is a sword that seems to come directly out of the man's shoulder.

The sword stabs down at Toby's neck, a blur in slow motion.

Something—an eyestalk?—swipes at the sword.

Half an eyestalk shoots past Toby. The sword misses his neck and digs into the ground.

The man raises the sword again as Twenty-two advances on him, pink blood pouring out of the eyestalk stump. She is yelling into the sensor she holds in one of her hands.

The man backs away, then lunges at the alien, who falls backward to avoid the sword.

The man raises the sword over Twenty-two.

Something flashes out of the sky. Toby turns his head and sees a black dot silently swoosh down. The instant of impact between Zero and the one-armed man sears into Toby's memory.

Wind and an explosion like thunder hits Toby.

The world fades out.

Chapter Forty-Nine
Mount Momotombo

Toby awoke to a world of silence and bright lights. A nurse leaned over him, saying something, but nothing came out of her mouth. Then Toby realized the world wasn't silent; there was a constant ringing in the background.

"Mr. Platt, can you hear me now?" The voice, which matched her lips, came from his TC.

"Where am I?" He couldn't hear his voice.

"You are in a hospital, Mr. Platt. You were injured in an explosion and by a sonic boom that gave you a concussion and damaged your eardrums. That's why I'm talking to you through your TC."

Then he remembered the events at the school's front gate. "Tyler!" He sat up, then gasped in pain. The nurse pushed him back down. She turned a knob on a machine next to Toby's bed. He noticed the tube feeding into his arm.

"You are in no condition to get up, Mr. Platt," she said. "You have major internal injuries. They will be operating on you shortly. Until then, you need to go to sleep. I just put something in your fluids that'll do that."

He started to protest, then. . . .

When Toby woke up again, a woman stood over him, and she seemed vaguely familiar. Everything seemed fuzzy.

"Are you awake?" she asked. There was something about that—then he remembered he'd lost his hearing, but it was back. He looked at the woman, and recognized his daughter Lara.

"You've been in an induced coma for three days," she said. "With stimulated growth, you should be pretty much healed now."

He sat up, flinching for a second from the memory of the last time he'd done that, but there was no pain. "What happened?" Now he saw that Olivia and Tyler were there as well, asleep in chairs nearby.

Lara summarized. Marty Reese, the would-be assassin, with a few explosives, scramblers, and wiring tricks, had fooled everyone into thinking he'd taken Tyler and the school hostage. He'd gotten Toby to stand near the blue floater, which was packed with explosives. When he'd survived that, Reese himself came out of the house across the street, pretending to be a doctor.

"I remember him now," Toby said. "I saw him at several campaign events. A man with one arm, always wearing an old American Army uniform."

"Melissa Smith also remembered him. Said she met him in Australia. Said he was creepy, talked about swatting candidates like flies."

He took a deep breath. "Tell me the worst. Don't hold back."

"There's not much good news. Your bodyguards, Turk and Crowbar, are dead. So is Chandler and eight of the Gray Guard. Bruce is in critical condition—Turk and Crowbar were between him and the explosion and took most of the impact, or he'd have died. He lost an arm. And Bruce partially shielded you, or you'd be much worse off. Twenty-two lost her left eyestalk, and the sonic boom from her ship hit her pretty hard. After ramming Reese, the ship picked her up and left, and we haven't seen them since. Or Reese, except for a few pieces left behind."

"And Tyler?"

"Nobody at the school was hurt. They didn't even know what was going on. There was an explosion outside the school, so they went into lockdown in the classrooms. Reese never was in the school."

Toby fell back into the bed and tried to blank his mind out, but couldn't. He'd brought about these deaths and injuries by acting on his emotions instead of his brain. How could he go on?

"No one knows much of anything about this Reese," Lara continued. "He's a former U.S. soldier, but since his discharge about fifteen years ago, he pretty much disappeared. You know what?"

"What?"

"I think Dubois sent him. Or maybe Duffy."

Toby had wondered the same thing. "I don't think so," he said. "As bad as Dubois is, I don't think he's ever used an assassin. He'd rather embarrass someone than kill them. And Duffy, if he wanted me dead, he'd arrange someone from the Gray Guard to do it. No, I think Vasquez sent him, before Duffy arrested him." He told her about the confrontation with Vasquez in Mexico City.

"I just can't believe history can be made or unmade by so-called lone assassins," Lara said. "I've been with Dubois since you left, and he's become paranoid. He's worried about India and Islam Nation, thinks you could win both. I'm sure he sent Reese."

"He's worried about me taking Islam Nation? Then he's gone nutty." Toby could take India, which would give him a temporary lead, but if Dubois was worried about the hyper-conservative Islam world, then he was truly out of touch.

"I've quit the campaign," Lara said.

That was not expected. "What happened?"

"I can't stay on a campaign that might be trying to kill my father. But that's not the sole reason. While you were in your coma, I've had a lot of time to think, and I kept asking myself, 'Is the world better with Dubois or you as president?' The answer was obvious, both on personal characteristics and policy."

"That means a lot to me," Toby said. "But I have to ask something. Did you support him before because of Eth?"

"Dad!" She stood up suddenly. "You can't blame that for anything. I wasn't on Eth when I agreed to run Dubois's campaign. When I made decisions to run ads that went after you, I wasn't on Eth, though sometimes I used it afterwards to soften the blow. No one makes bad decisions because of Eth; they're not on Eth when they decide to take it, and they took it knowing what that meant. Good and bad decisions are made on their own. I made the bad decision to run Dubois's campaign, just like you did five years ago."

Daddy's little girl had really grown up. "You learned all this twenty years faster than I did."

"Dad, you're awake?" Tyler yawned, then shook Olivia. "Mom, he's awake."

Victories in Russia and Asia were sweet, but not nearly so sweet as a true family reunion.

"Because you made a commitment to do so, and because the world needs you," Bruce said two days later, Monday morning, in answer to Toby's question. He could not forget his discussion with Turk and Crowbar on the fateful trip to the school. His misguided actions had led to their deaths. How could he go on? He'd asked himself that question over and over since he'd awoken from his coma.

"You can't drop out because an assassin tricked us," Bruce continued, "no more than a president should resign the first time someone gets killed on his watch. It's part of the job, and you know that. You didn't kill anyone; that Windmill character did, and whoever sent him."

Toby had recovered from most of his injuries, much of it during his second three-day coma of the campaign, though the one in Vancouver hadn't been a real coma. Now he stood next to Bruce's bed. Bruce had been hurt far worse, but should recover from most of his injuries. The one thing Bruce wouldn't recover from was the loss of his right arm in an explosion set, ironically, by a man without a right arm. Soon he'd have the best prosthetic arm made. But his championship table tennis days were over.

"History is made by those who make it," Bruce continued. "Don't let this loser Windmill guy be the one who makes it. Besides, you know Dubois and Duffy must have sent him."

"Lara said the same thing," Toby said. "I just don't think they are the ones. I think it was Vasquez."

"Vasquez? Just because he wants to be on your cabinet?"

"You weren't there when he said he was going to put me out of this race."

With little else to do, the two argued for hours over who sent Reese. They also speculated on Twenty-two, who once again had disappeared, this time by choice, but badly injured.

What they did know was that their extensive campaign plans for Latin America were pretty much gone. The explosion had taken place on Wednesday, five days prior. The election was tomorrow, Tuesday.

"You know what else is tomorrow?" Toby asked. Bruce shook his head. "Tyler's table tennis tryouts."

". . . on some of these issues. Just a little more Ajala, a little less Bruce."

Toby awoke to these words, and realized they had been droning on for some time. He opened his eyes and saw Melissa.

"In Latin America," the Antarctican teenager continued, "you need someone who can give your message, not just in speeches to the masses, but to the leaders, the opinion leaders, so if you get their support—"

"How long have you been here?" Toby asked, rubbing sleep from his eyes.

"What do you mean? We've been talking for a while. Oh—you weren't awake? Sorry. Where was I when you first heard, so I can go over that again and—"

"Stop! In the wise words of everyone who's ever had a conversation with you, *I surrender!*"

"That's what I said to her when we discussed the election earlier," said Bruce as he entered in a wheelchair. "But I learned a lot before my head exploded." Several tubes and wires came out of him and connected with various devices on the back of the wheelchair. "She had some good ideas about Latin America."

"Since you two can't campaign and talk to people, you need someone who can," Melissa said.

"But you're seventeen years old," said Toby.

"Don't let anyone hear you said that," said Bruce. "Sixteen-year-olds can vote. And don't spread this around, and I'll deny it if you do, but this teenager is better than me. She doesn't even need a TC. She's earnest and likeable, and I have to fake it. She talks faster than a speeding bullet. More knowledgeable than a politics professor. Able to quote the demographics of La Paz, Bolivia, and everything else about Latin American in a single sentence. Look, up in the press room, it's a bird, it's a plane, it's Melissa Smith! Strange being from Antarctica who—"

"You've been watching old TV shows in bed," Toby interrupted. He sat up. "Would you like to join my campaign?"

"That's what I've been saying for the last ten minutes. I can argue the moderate position since the election is between that and the conservatives, and so there's no liberal position to argue. After the election, if you win, we can discuss what the moderate position should be. With a little makeup I can appear a little older, and be a talking head on shows all over Latin America, both the mainstream English ones and the Spanish ones. My parents were from Argentina and I'm fluent. Vote por el gran Toby Platt!"

"Where did you learn so much about politics?" Toby asked.

"There's not much else to do in Antarctica," she said. "But there's this site I go to on my TC all the time, PoliticalPeopleParty, and I sometimes spend days there, just debating and arguing, and some of the people are so smart. So—"

"You're hired," said Toby.

She froze for a moment, then flashed her best campaign smile. "Thank you. But I'm a volunteer."

"Then donate your salary to PUFF or some other charity. You are now our Secretary of Explaining Stuff. Get together with Bruce and Gene, work out a schedule, and get down to Latin America and start talking. You're our secret weapon down there."

"Sí, señor!"

On Monday afternoon, over the loud protests of their doctors, they flew to Sao Paulo, Brazil. Improvised hospital beds were installed on the *Rocinante* for Toby and Bruce. Toby was pretty much healed, but the doctors wanted him to spend one more day in bed. They wanted Bruce to spend another week in bed, and restrain from any activities. Bruce agreed, then ignored their advice.

Rather than campaign all over Latin America on the final day before the election, Bruce arranged to have Toby campaign by video. Normally that tactic would never work, but with the worldwide media exposure from the assassination attempt, Bruce thought they might away with it. Election rules stated that candidates must be in the continental region holding an election during the week before the election, but due to his hospitalization, Toby had received an abstention from traveling to Latin America until the final two days. Feodora had been campaigning in Latin America all week.

Melissa was on all the talk shows representing the campaign, still looking seventeen despite the makeup. Several opponents appeared to mock her age with condescending smiles and questions, but after getting steamrolled by the teenager they quickly forgot about her age. Bruce even put together a last-minute ad showcasing the progressive look of a Dubois campaign spokesman as he went from confident to nervous frustration as Melissa spoke. The ad finished with a smooth voice saying, "Is this the best they've got, bested by a teenager?"

On Monday night, hundreds of huge screens were erected in cities all over Latin American. By using screens where possible instead of just TCs, it allowed supporters—and potential supporters—to watch it together in rallies. Plus, talking off a huge screen was more impressive than the shrunken image normally viewed on a TC.

"Is it really worth flying all the way to Brazil if I'm just going to speak from the *Rocinante*?" Toby wondered.

"Damn straight it does!" Bruce said, still flat on his back on the hospital bed aboard the *Rocinante*, with a nurse hovering over him. "We may never get off the ship, but to 885 million Latin Americans—and especially here in Brazil, the big prize—you took the time to visit them despite your injuries. You can't pay for that type of publicity—we should give what's left of Reese's body a big kiss."

Toby spoke to Latin American that night from the side of Bruce's hospital bed in the *Rocinante*. The location gave the best of both worlds: it showed a seemingly robust Toby, ready to take on the job of president despite the assassination attempt. And it showed Bruce, still covered with tubes and bandages, showcasing the extent and aftermath of the attempt. After the address was done and the cameras off, Toby collapsed back into his own bed.

The new stump speech highlighted gun violence, a particular problem in Latin America. Dubois was strongly for freedom of weapons and against gun registration. Ajala had been the reverse, a crusader to ban weapons from private citizens. Once again, Toby and Bruce pushed for a compromise: guns should be legal for home defense, and for recreational purposes at gun clubs, but nowhere else. Those who wanted guns had to register them and pass a short, one-time training course.

Toby thought the speech went well. Legalization of guns, along with abortion, were two issues that would never go away. Sometimes the arguments changed, such as the argument for legalizing guns for hunting, which at one time was considered a valid argument—and still was in Australia.

Bruce and Gene arranged a few interviews for later that night, and for Tuesday morning—election day—talk shows in the three largest Latin American countries: locally in Sao Paulo, Brazil; in Buenos Aires, Argentina; and in Bogota, Columbia. But Toby had other priorities, and insisted they return to the U.S. right after the Columbian talk show host finished gushing over how proud Columbia and the rest of Latin America was of him for visiting so soon after the assassination attempt. They landed in Maryland that afternoon. Melissa, the new media darling, stayed behind to represent them on all the talk shows throughout the day.

Tuesday night Toby was at Germantown Middle School. The school had closed on Thursday and Friday after the attempt, but had reopened, with added security and counselors, on Monday. Now Toby sat quietly on the sidelines, surrounded by Gray Guard, watching his son in the table tennis tryouts. Bruce was also there, in a portable hospital bed with two very unhappy doctors. He wouldn't be able to coach, but at least he could watch. For the night, he tried to put away his worries about the election and Twenty-two, and was partially successful.

Tyler didn't make the team—he made first alternate—but vowed to do so the following year. They went out for ice cream afterwards.

On Wednesday morning, they left for India. Toby couldn't fight off the feeling that he was abandoning his family again, leaving them right after such a traumatic time, but with two more major regional elections, there was little choice. Hopefully the election would be wrapped up one way or another in India and Islam Nation, and they wouldn't have to bother with Antarctica. The Gray Guard was in turmoil over their failure to stop the attack, the deaths of eight agents, and the death of Director Chandler. Toby had little trouble convincing them to double the guard over Olivia and Tyler.

Before crossing the Atlantic on their way to India, they had another Latin American errand to run. Toby had spoken with Turk and Crowbar's family by TC. Their parents had flown to Maryland after their sons' deaths, and now joined them in the *Rocinante* as the cremated remains were flown back to Nicaragua. The two had left a will with instructions for their remains. Bruce grumbled about the inefficiency of making a second trip down south. He'd wanted to hurry the parents and the cremation up so they could do the Nicaraguan trip on the way to Brazil on Monday, but Toby threatened to drop him in an active volcano—not an idle threat, considering their destination.

It wasn't until Toby met their parents that he realized that Turk and Crowbar had real names. Of course they did—he'd just never thought about it. They'd gone by their bodyguard names so long he'd taken that for granted.

360

They flew to the shores of Lago de Managua, near Turk and Crowbar's hometown of León in Nicaragua. As per their instructions, they traveled to the northwest shores of Lake Managua and dumped the cremated ashes of Oscar and Fernando Gonzalez into the 4200-foot active volcano and symbol of Nicaragua, the symmetrically cone-shaped Mount Momotombo.

Chapter Fifty
India and the Great Compromise of Sultanpur

Wednesday, October 13, 2100

They did better than expected in Latin America, winning 64 electoral votes to Dubois's 29. People were tired of guns and violence, especially in Central America, where gangsters—like Vasquez in Mexico City, though that was officially in North America—often ruled. Toby won the "Big One"—Brazil, with its 35 votes—55%-45%. The closest race was Argentina, where Toby just edged out Dubois by a few thousand votes. However, in the four countries decided 51-49—Bolivia, Ecuador, Peru, and Venezuela, totaling 18 votes—Dubois won all four.

"Except for Columbia, we could have had a sweep!" lamented Bruce as he broke a ping-pong ball. "We needed those votes. We're running out of continents." Dubois now led 522-354.

Latin America	Population (millions)	Electoral Votes	Dubois	Platt
Argentina	69.4	7	50%	**50%**
Bolivia	27.9	3	**51%**	49%
Brazil	345.9	35	45%	**55%**
Chile	24.2	2	46%	**54%**
Colombia	78.9	8	**54%**	46%
Costa Rica	8.8	1	39%	**61%**
Dom. Republic	19.8	2	38%	**62%**
Ecuador	30.2	3	**51%**	49%
El Salvador	17.4	2	37%	**63%**

Guatemala	51.8	5	36%	**64%**
Haiti	25.1	3	32%	**68%**
Honduras	21.1	2	31%	**69%**
Jamaica	4.3	1	40%	**60%**
Nicaragua	10.9	1	28%	**72%**
Panama	7.4	1	30%	**70%**
Paraguay	16.5	2	**52%**	48%
Peru	55.4	6	**51%**	49%
Puerto Rico	4.0	1	47%	**53%**
Trin. & Tobago	1.3	1	48%	**52%**
Uruguay	4.2	1	**52%**	48%
Venezuela	60.5	6	**51%**	49%
TOTAL	885.0	93	29	64

"India's all or nothing," Bruce said from his new wheelchair on the *Rocinante*. He was tossing a ping-pong ball up and down with his prosthetic right arm, apparently on doctor's orders to develop coordination with the arm and hand, but Toby knew better. "We're down about three percent, but absolutely need those 245 electoral votes to make up for all the ones Dubois got in China, and all the ones he's going to get in Islam Nation."

"So what's the plan?" Toby felt like it was all pre-rehearsed; he knew what Bruce would say, and what his response would be.

"The usual. We'll give speeches, get on the talk shows, and sic Melissa on them. But you know what it's like in India. They buy and sell votes here like the stock market. Except we have the advantage that Dubois broke promises to the political bosses from last time, so he can't play the game this time around. So we can buy votes cheap."

"You know I'm going say no to that," Toby said. "If Dubois were buying, you'd have an argument, but he can't, so we won't. Let's win this fair and square. You've seen how close the polls are. As long as I can stay out of hospitals and prisons, I can put in a full schedule this time around." Toby felt good about taking the so-called risky high road. After

363

his recent brush with death, he saw things a bit differently now. There were more important things than winning all the time.

"Who's more ethical," Bruce said, "the guy who dooms everyone to please his personal ethics, or the guy who sacrifices his ethics for the greater good?"

"Who's more ethical," Toby retorted, "the guy who acts ethically or the one who doesn't?" Toby was the final boss, and he would win this argument. There would be no buying of votes.

"Let's win on the issues," Toby continued. "We can run video of Dubois eating meat in Australia—that'll go over well with the Hindus."

"Actually," Bruce said, "it's beef the Hindus really object to. But I'm sure Dubois eating barbecued kangaroo ribs will be effective. That's offset politically by Rajan Persson, since he grew up in India. Any chance you could replace General Zubkov with General Kadam for your VP, just for a week?"

"He's what, a hundred years old?"

"Just 88, and living at home with his family."

"Fine. You tell Feodora."

"I'd rather not. She'd tear off my other arm."

India's rising technical proficiency led to financial success early in the twenty-first century. India and Seattle—and later India and Vancouver—ruled much of the computer industry. Many fortunes were made.

However, as the rich got richer, and the middle-class more upper middle-class, the poor got poorer. India's historic caste system, which at one point seemed to be dying out, rose again. Amid the rising fortunes and luxury of the upper class, the Dalit—the "untouchables"—became even poorer as discrimination against them rose.

After the nuclear war with Pakistan in 2045, the country was rebuilt, with help from the U.S., and by 2047 the job was done. But who rebuilds slums? The plight of the Dalit and other lower-class castes became still worse. The U.S. finally withdrew their forces early in 2052, though only after nationwide protests in both India and the U.S., and a resolution from the World Congress.

Shortly after the U.S. withdrawal, Raghu Kadam, an untouchable from the slums of Mumbai, led the Dalit in a nationwide boycott in 2052. At first it had little effect as the Dalit made up less than 20% of the population, and their buying power was minimal. However, other lower castes soon joined in, as well as some of the upper class. It brought the economy down.

With the economy in shambles, class warfare broke out in the streets. General Tarang Chatterjee was assigned the task of putting down the insurrection. But the intervention of the army only led to an escalation of violence and the Dalit Rebellion of 2053. At first the Dalit only did random acts of violence, usually against major commercial centers. Whether it was a rebellion or simply terrorism was a matter of interpretation.

The Dalit, with inside help, destroyed much of the Indian air force in the September Surprise of 2053. With the air force no longer policing the skies, the Dalit massed their own army, and marched on the capital, New Delhi. The Indian Civil war had begun.

In March, 2054, the two armies faced each other southwest of New Delhi near Sultanpur National Park among the chirping, squawking, and honking of its famous bird sanctuary. The better-equipped army of General Chatterjee, two million strong, faced General Kadam's poorly-equipped army of four million. The world braced for the bloodiest battle in history.

Instead, under a flag of truce, the two generals met. History does not record whose idea this was, and neither general would admit to it. What's known is the two met for two long days in a tent at Sultanpur. Kadam explained the grievances of the long-oppressed Dalit and other lower castes. Chatterjee, a wealthy member of the upper castes, listened. They reached a compromise.

With a combined army of six million, the two forced their compromise on the Indian government. Essentially "Affirmative Action with a Time Limit," it meant that the lower castes would, for 25 years, be given privileged treatment in government positions and contract services, public funding for schools and other infrastructure, admissions to colleges, and in other aspects detailed in the agreement. The idea had been tried before, called "reservation," but it had been mostly lip service, and not done seriously on a large scale. Effective January 1, 2055, it was also ordained that there would be no favored treatment of any kind after January 1, 2080.

The Great Compromise of Sultanpur saved India. It was memorialized on Mount Bharat, the huge granite mountain artificially created at Sultanpur, and named after the Hindi name for India, Bhārat Ganarājya. Funded by worldwide donations, it was designed to roughly match the famous Mount Rushmore in the United States, only much larger. On it the figures of Generals Kadam and Chatterjee, hands clasped in friendship and agreement, looked down upon New Delhi, as if ready to swoop down if the spirit of compromise were ever forgotten.

"I have no idea where Twenty-two is," Toby said in answer to a question, his voice hoarse from days of campaigning. He was live on News India from their studio southwest of New Delhi, two days before the election. After the dramatic collision between Zero and Reese, Zero had used its tractor beam to load the badly injured alien inside, and then taken off, too fast to track and impervious to human radar and other sensors. There were stories of a huge splash in the Atlantic off the Maryland coast.

He'd already answered numerous policy questions on funding PUFF, on why he was against meat-eating in Australia but wouldn't enforce it, and other issues.

"Why do you want to be president?"

There it was, the toughest question of all for any presidential candidate. A long time ago Bruce had asked him that question, and recorded his answer. Before the interview, Toby had replayed his answer on his TC, made so long ago:

"The political world is split. Every five years the two sides duke it out, and we end up with a liberal or a conservative in charge. But that's the view

366

from New York City. The rest of the world isn't liberal or conservative. They don't think that way until we drill it into their heads that they have to make that choice. They just want leaders who will do what's best for all of us, not what some political philosophy says to do. And that usually means finding a solution that's not liberal, not conservative, but a compromise. A moderate solution. Which is where most people are, if we only gave them that choice."

Since that time, he'd answered the same question numerous times all over the world, but somehow he'd forgotten his original answer, and instead answered in terms of policies geared to the current region. But great leaders don't just push the right buttons based on the political situation.

He looked out the window. Staring down at him from Mount Bharat were the huge faces of Generals Kadam and Chatterjee. One of the Seven Wonders of the Modern World.

Why did he really want to be president?

"While you are thinking about that," the news anchor said, "perhaps you could solve the long-going worldwide mystery of your scarf."

Toby hadn't realized he was fiddling with it. The secret of his scarf and why he wanted to be president—the two were connected.

He turned to the anchor. "I'll answer both questions." He pulled the scarf off and held it up. "This came from a man that none of you have never heard of, but who could have been on Mount Bharat.

"Once there was a man named Vinny."

Bruce sat in his wheelchair, listening on his TC as Toby told the story of Vinny. He had never heard it before—the great mystery of the fading purple scarf was finally out. It was a brilliant political move, he thought. The greatest policies in the world can't bring in as many votes as a great personal story.

It might not be enough. The aging General Kadam had given his endorsement to Toby, closing the gap, but Dubois still had a small lead. The Vinny story should bump him up some, perhaps enough to win, but it was still too close to call. Toby needed some insurance, and that's what Bruce had in mind. He was in another building not far from News

India, looking out another window at the huge, somber faces of Generals Kadam and Chatterjee. What he had planned was quite different in spirit from their great compromise.

They'd worried about the influence of Vice President Rajan Persson in his home country. For some reason, the Indian Swede seemed lackluster in his appearances. While a bit slow in person, he was normally an electrifying speaker, who used his great height and arm span to great advantage as he gesticulated during his speeches. Throughout the Indian campaign, he spoke in a near monotone and barely moved. The Indian press described him as a scarecrow on a windless day.

Toby finished the story, and began to speak of how this related to his wanting to be president, but Bruce had to shut it off; it was time for the meeting. He'd listen to a recording of the rest later.

He manually wheeled himself in, not bothering to put the wheelchair in float mode. Facing him at a table were many of the major political bosses from around the country.

Toby would never know about this meeting.

The extremely old man with the intense stare at the head of the table was the Delhi Lala, leader of the most politically influential of the Indian gangs. He wore an old-fashioned turban, which would have turned curious heads on the street, yet seemed natural on him. He wore simple Gandhi-style glasses, and had a vague resemblance to the famous Mahatma, but the resemblance ended below the neck. The black Stravi suit he wore could have sustained an average Indian for years.

"Thank you for coming to see us," the Lala said.

"Thank you for seeing me again," Bruce said. "How is your family?"

When the formalities were over, he jumped right to the point. "Gentlemen," Bruce began, "five years ago, in this very room, in order to get your vote, President Dubois made you a number of promises. That, along with naming Rajan Persson his vice president, was enough to get your vote. Without that vote, President Xu would have won that election. How has that worked out for you?" They all knew the answer.

"President Dubois fulfilled few of his promises," the Lala said. "He did not name any Indians to his cabinet and government services to

India did not improve. We serve the people, and we thought we best served them with Dubois, but we were wrong." Which, Bruce translated, meant that they couldn't rely on local kickbacks forever if they couldn't bring home government services.

"What do you have to offer for us, and why should we believe you?" the Lala's eyes stared into him. Bruce had to be careful; he didn't want another Vasquez fiasco.

"I can't promise an Indian member of the cabinet. I can promise I will push for one. However, I can promise enough sub-cabinet positions that you'll be in a position to bring in government services yourself—at least an eight percent increase in these services plus inflation." These were things he knew he could swing.

The nice thing about negotiating with the underworld was that they made quick decisions. After talking Bruce up to a ten percent increase, as he'd planned all along, they shook on the deal. The Lala couldn't guarantee India, but he could bring in his political machine, and that was worth a few percentage points. He'd have incentive, because if Dubois won, he'd get nothing.

The irony, Bruce thought, was that in five years they would be our bitter enemy when Rajan Persson ran for president.

"That's a great story," the news anchor said. "What lessons did you learn from it?"

"The lesson from Vinny," he said, "is one I have learned and unlearned several times in my lifetime, and one which I hope I've finally nailed down for good. It's about compromise and moderation. Why? It doesn't matter if you are liberal, conservative, or some other philosophy, you must remember that others believe in their ideals just as much as you do. Forcing your views on them is just as bad as them forcing their views on you."

Toby pointed out the window, and the camera centered on the faces of Kadam and Chatterjee. "Your country almost destroyed itself over differing ideals. What saved it? Only the great fortune of two great visionaries at the right place at the right time. Let's make their vision central to our government."

They left for Pakistan, their first stop in Islam Nation, late on Indian election night, Tuesday, October 19. For once, Toby felt relaxed about the results. Feodora, who had campaigned separately in India, joined them on the *Rocinante*. So did Melissa, who chattered in the background to whoever would listen. While Feodora and Bruce battled forever to a draw on the chessboard, he played three games via TC with Tyler, who'd just gotten out of school. Playing his son was far more fun than with Bruce or Feodora, who took forever to move, and always won easily. With Tyler, they played ten times as many games and still managed to talk between moves. Some said you should make a person earn their victories, but Toby couldn't do that, and secretly lost one of the games.

There was still no sighting of Twenty-two, which worried Toby. He hoped the alien had survived the attack. He vividly remembered Twenty-two's severed eyestalk flying by, and the pink blood coming out of the stump. He hoped Zero was taking good care of her.

"That was a nice story about Vinny," Bruce said after their chess games were over. "I wish we could have used it earlier."

"That might have won you votes," said Melissa. "Especially in Europe. In fact—"

"It just didn't seem right to bring up until now. I hope Vinny wouldn't mind."

"If Vinny were alive," Feodora said, "would he want compromise and moderation?"

"Of course."

"Then, dahling, he would approve."

She was right, as always, Toby thought. "There is something wrong about all the time we've spent working out policies, and yet I may win India because of a story."

"What do you expect?" Bruce said. "We're dealing with chimpanzees."

370

For some reason, Toby felt like he'd been hit in the stomach. "Bruce, the story of Vinny was not for chimpanzees; it was for people, a lesson about compromise and moderation. Don't cheapen it. The masses may be politically ignorant, but they are people with their own ideas and philosophies, and right or wrong, we need to listen to what they have to say. Don't ever call them chimpanzees in my presence again."

Chapter Fifty-One
Twenty-two's Revenge

The results of the India election reached them as they approached Islamabad in Pakistan. Toby had won 53%-47%. With the 245 Indian electoral votes, he now led Dubois, 599-522. However, he knew the numbers were misleading, the lead a mere mirage. Most or all of the 211 electoral votes coming up from conservative Islam Nation would surely go to Dubois, who led the polls in nearly every country. Somehow they had to scrounge up the 68 electoral votes needed to reach the magic 667 needed to clinch the election. Dubois needed 145, but seemed a lot closer to that than Toby was to his goal.

Islam Nation had been created when world government came about in 2050 as a way for Islamic countries to consolidate their power as a voting block. Unlike other continental voting regions, it was a mishmash of countries from three continents, Africa, Europe, and Asia.

Islam Nation	Population (millions)	Electoral Votes
Afghanistan	184.1	18
Algeria	72.3	7
Bahrain	1.8	1
Burkina Faso	82.5	8
Chad	36.6	4
Cyprus	1.1	1
Djibouti	2.6	1
Egypt	175.5	18

Gambia	6.9	1
Guinea	51.2	5
Iran	139.0	14
United Iraq	109.8	11
Jordan	16.2	2
Kuwait	8.5	1
Lebanon	6.2	1
Libya	15.3	2
Mali	82.1	8
Mauritania	12.4	1
Morocco	57.3	6
Oman	5.3	1
Pakistan	494.3	49
Palestine	13.0	1
Qatar	2.0	1
Saudi Arabia	82.9	8
Senegal	48.4	5
Somalia	52.6	5
Syria	55.8	6
Tunisia	16.9	2
Turkey	105.2	11
Un. Arab Emir.	13.5	1
Yemen	110.8	11
Total	2062.1	211

The big prize was Pakistan, with its 49 electoral votes. Bordering it was Afghanistan, with its 18. Across the Gulf of Oman from Pakistan was Oman itself, with a single electoral vote. The three added up to the 68 needed to win the election. In those three countries the polls were too close to call, while Dubois had substantial leads everywhere else. So Bruce had decided that they'd make their last stand in those three. With the momentum from their Indian victory and continued outrage at what had happened in neighboring Tanzania, they could almost feel the polls moving in their favor. He and Gene came up with a grueling week-long

373

schedule for Toby and Feodora that made even the Russian general wince.

"Now I miss basic training," she said, sighing. For the first time since the campaign began, she looked tired.

Despite the desperation of the situation, there was a larger question in everyone's mind: where was Twenty-two?

When Twenty-two awoke, she stood on the floor inside Zero. Several white cables connected her to the wall; she could feel sustenance fluids moving in and out of her. Something was wrong with her vision—her left eye seemed blind.

Then the image came back to her of the sword sticking out of the man's shoulder as it came down on her, slicing off her eyestalk. Then Zero swooping past, ramming the man, and the explosion of wind and sound.

"Are you awake?" Zero asked.

"Yes. Where are we?"

"We are in the Atlantic Ocean, off the coast of the region where you were attacked. Are you comfortable? Would you like something sweet to eat, Exalted One?"

"I'm fine. But I might have something for you to do."

The human who had caused all this havoc—what was his motivation? Without motive, there would be no reason for the attack. Who else had motivation for this, and was willing to use violence?

General Duffy. She was sure of it.

And yet this seemed to go against the Philosophy of One. In all intelligent races, there are three types: the dishonest, the ignorant, and the rest. One said you should seek out the dishonest so you knew who they were, then ignore them. You should seek out the ignorant, and try and change the conditions that led to their ignorance. You should seek out the others, the ones who are neither dishonest nor ignorant, and work with them to find solutions to problems with logic and compromise.

Duffy, with his paranoid beliefs and willingness to torture while publicly denying it, was one of the dishonest. According to One, she should ignore him. But ignoring him allowed him to cause more damage. On Grodan, he would have been found out long ago and imprisoned, unless an individual grod took care of the problem first, as was more likely.

What to do about it?

One also said that those who cannot learn from experience are ignorant and always will be. With a nod of her remaining eyestalk, she made up her mind.

"Zero, can you locate the life signs of General Duffy?"

"I have been tracking him since you first met him. He is currently at what appears to be his home in a location called Merrick, New York."

"Take us there. Make your walls two-way transparent, and make sure human sensors can't detect us."

She caught just a glimpse of Earth's undersea life before they shot out of the water and into the sky. A few minutes later Zero hovered over a large house.

"Break through the roof and pull Duffy out with your tractor beam. Try not to hurt him. Turn on the outside speakers so I can hear what's outside, and he can hear me."

With a thunderous crash, the roof of the house broke into several pieces that were tossed aside, as if a giant unseen hand had grabbed it. A wriggling man in red pajamas rose out of the house and floated under the ship. Duffy looked up and locked eyes with Twenty-two. He screamed.

"Take us up two miles. Go as fast as you can without hurting him badly."

Duffy stopped screaming after the first few seconds, then began to shake, whether from fear or cold, Twenty-two couldn't tell. He never took his eyes off her.

"We're two miles up," Zero said. "Would you like a massage?"

"Not now. General Duffy, are you comfortable?"

Duffy didn't respond, but continued to stare at her as he dangled in the air. His shaking had gotten worse.

"I know you sent that man to kill Toby Platt," she said.

Duffy shook his head. "I don't know what you're talking about. I had nothing to do with it." He stuttered over his words, probably from the cold. Or was it fear?

Twenty-two wondered if Duffy was telling the truth. He was dishonest, but that didn't mean he was guilty of everything he denied. She decided it didn't really matter. He probably sent the assassin, but he definitely had tortured her and lied about it.

"Tomorrow," she said, "you are going to resign your position as a general, and any other positions you have in government. Do you understand?"

Again the general shook his head. "You can't make me do that. Go ahead and kill me if you want. Prove to me you are a barbarian."

The twisted logic of the dishonest, she thought. She hoped not to kill this man. "Zero, on my order, drop him, and follow him down."

"Would you like me to give him a massage with my tractor beams as he falls? He seems tense."

"No massage. General Duffy, you will resign your positions, or fall to your death." To Zero, she whispered, "Be ready to catch him on my order. Try to be gentle." Then, louder, she said, "Release him." Zero did so.

Between the low temperature and the wind chill, Twenty-two wondered if he'd even survive all the way to the ground. Then she noticed his lips were moving, but little sound was coming out."

"Zero, increase volume. What's he saying?"

Stop it! came Duffy's enhanced but cracking voice.

"Catch him," she ordered. Zero slowed the general's fall gradually so as not to hurt him. They came to a stop a hundred feet over Duffy's wrecked house.

"Now do it again." Once again they went two miles into the air, and once again dropped Duffy, who screamed the entire time, and once again caught him one hundred feet above his house. "One more time,"

Twenty-two said. This time the general closed his eyes and gritted his teeth, but was silent the whole way down. After catching him the third time, as they hovered over his house once again.

"Zero, open the hatch and bring Duffy inside."

A moment later the general was inside Zero, held against a transparent wall by a transparent tentacle that came out of the wall.

"General, I don't trust you to resign," she said. "So I am taking a precautionary measure. Zero, lower him so I can reach his head." The tentacle pulled Duffy lower.

Twenty-two moved in front of him. She pulled a device out of one of her vest pockets. She reached up and jabbed him on the top of his head with the device as he grunted in surprise.

"General, I don't normally care what you say or do, but I am not going to allow you to ever use violence again, either yourself or by ordering someone else to do so. I have implanted you with a neural nebulizer. From now on, I can see and hear anything you see and hear. If you resort to violence again, or even threaten it, your head will explode. If you do not resign tomorrow, your head will explode. If you try to remove it, your head will explode. Are you clear on this? Just nod or shake your head; I don't want to hear your voice again."

The general started to say something, stopped and instead nodded.

"Good. And remember—I'll always be watching. If you tell anyone I destroyed your roof, your head will explode. Make up a story about how you were doing home improvements. You are a good liar." And I am learning to be one, she thought. "If I do not have to explode your head, then in one year I will consider removing the device. Zero, put him back."

Soon they were back up in the sky, flying invisibly toward Pakistan, where Zero had detected Toby.

"I am worried about your mental state," Zero said. "Can you explain what you said about a neural nebulizer?"

Zero normally didn't initiate discussions unless forced to, but here it had good reason to. "There is no such thing as a neural nebulizer,"

Twenty-two said. "I made it up. I know that, and you know that, but Duffy doesn't."

She held up the presidential pen Dubois had given to her as a ceremonial gift when she'd first arrived so long ago. "This is my neural nebulizer injection device."

Chapter Fifty-Two
A Secret Tape

When someone knocked on the door of the *Rocinante*, they had no idea it was Twenty-two until the alien waddled aboard. Toby felt like Mount Bharat had been lifted off his back.

They filled her in on the happenings since her disappearance. She was rather vague with her own account, insisting she'd spent the time recovering with Zero at the bottom of the Atlantic Ocean. Where her left eyestalk had been was now just a patch of skin, without so much as a scar.

When Duffy announced his retirement the following day, Bruce questioned Twenty-two, but she insisted she had nothing to do with it. She's a horrible liar, Toby thought.

By Monday the following week, Toby and Feodora had each given a hundred speeches in cities all over Pakistan, Afghanistan, and Oman. Feodora introduced him to a concoction she'd made that kept him from losing his voice, but she warned him he didn't want to know what was in it. He didn't ask.

With the destruction of Israel in 2045, peace broke out in the Middle East, and continued to the present day. Or so the country's leaders claimed. Every few hours they heard explosions in the distance. When they asked about it, they were always told it was construction. It might have fooled Toby, and perhaps even a skeptic like Bruce, but Feodora only shook her head. She displayed for them an amazing ability to identify the type of explosive from the sound alone. Fortunately, after the assassination attempt, the Gray Guard around them had turned into an army, and Toby and Feodora were not allowed anywhere until the new location had been taken apart, brick by brick if necessary.

Toby found campaigning in the region more difficult than anywhere else. The problem, he realized, was that if he said exactly what he believed, he'd lose in a landslide in every country in Islam Nation. A liberal or moderate simply couldn't beat a conservative in the region without falling down that slippery slope of tailoring your message for the audience. He envied Bruce's and Melissa's seemingly natural ability to always stay on message, always answering with what they wanted to say rather than what was asked.

He didn't resort to lying, only avoiding subjects he didn't want to talk about. Politics had made him an expert on evasion, though not as good as Bruce and Melissa. Before this campaign he'd always been more of a behind-the-scenes operator. When the subject of gay rights came up—called "yag" rights in Islam Nation, where even the word "gay" was considered obscene—he'd learned to recite excerpts from the local laws on the subject, and how much he believed in following the law, and then change the subject to the more compatible one of the rights of the lower class.

He could have been more direct, and lectured on "yag" rights. He thought it was silly that in this day and age, the majority in some regions still judged a person by their sexual orientation, but as a candidate for office, he had to take that into account.

Much of the Islamic world had a rigid class system, though not as extreme as it had once been in India. Toby's message of compromise between the upper and lower classes, as symbolized by references to Mount Bharat in India, had taken hold of a certain part of the population in the three countries they were focusing on, all of which were near India's borders. Mount Bharat became a symbol of their campaign, featured in many of their ads.

Three major events occurred that Monday night.

First, Toby received a message from Tyler. One of the players on the school table tennis team had broken a leg. As first alternate, Tyler was now on the team.

Second, Bruce received the latest polls. They were now statistically tied in Pakistan and Oman, and only a point behind in Afghanistan. They were getting killed everywhere else.

Third, Toby received a call from Rahim Aziz, the prime minister of Pakistan, whom he'd met five years before.

"What I am going to tell you is in strictest confidence," Aziz said. "You must not tell anyone the source, nor name my sources. Do I have your word on this?" Toby agreed.

"Vice President Rajan Persson alerted us last night to potential criminal activity inside Pakistan," Aziz said, "at the Islamabad Grand Hotel. An accusation is not enough to get a warrant to bug a hotel room, but the room in question was under the name of the Dubois/Persson campaign. With his permission, we conducted secret surveillance of the room of Dubois's chief of staff, Phil Farley, who I presume you know."

Aziz stopped. He looked like a man in front of a firing squad. What had Farley done?

"You have to promise again," Aziz said, "that you will not reveal my name as your source for what I am about to give you. Nor Persson's name, as he would know it came from me. I must have your guarantee."

"You have my guarantee."

"I am sending you a recording from last night. It is yours to do with as you please. I wash my hands of this, though it will take many washings to clean my soul of what I have seen." He broke the connection.

A moment later Toby received the recording. He watched from the beginning.

The video showed a panoramic view of Farley's hotel room, taken from the ceiling above the bed. At the start, Farley was lying in bed, eyes open, presumably watching something on his TC. There was a knock on the door; Farley answered. It was Dubois.

A few minutes later, Toby watched in growing amazement as Dubois and Farley tore off their clothes. A few minutes later they were rolling about in bed.

Chapter Fifty-Three
The Scarf or the Eth

Toby regretted showing the tape to Bruce. "You have to make it public," Bruce hotly insisted. "It's not a matter of gay rights, it's a matter of truth! Let the people decide."

"What type of president would I be if I get elected from something like this?" Toby paced back and forth on the *Rocinante*, twirling his scarf like a baton. Feodora was at a campaign event in Afghanistan, and Twenty-two had gone with her. Toby had put up a privacy screen so the others up front couldn't hear his discussion with Bruce.

"If you were running the campaign, you know you'd release it," Bruce said. "Dubois would run it. Sometimes the ends *do* justify the means!"

"Once upon a time I would have run it," Toby said, "but not now. We're supposed to be better than they are."

"You know it's not like that." Toby had never seen Bruce so worked up. "You knew when you agreed to run that you'd have to compromise on things you didn't want to compromise on—isn't that what this whole campaign is about?"

"Compromise on opposing points of view, of course!" Toby shouted, his voice beginning to crack. "If the majority of the Islam world is against gay rights, then I'll talk to them about a compromise, but this isn't a compromise—*I can't do this!*"

"*Of course you can!*" Bruce shouted back. "The very fact you showed it to me screams out that, deep down, you want it shown. You knew you couldn't do it, so you showed it to me, hoping I'd talk you into it. At least be honest with yourself!"

Toby stopped pacing. Was Bruce right? No one forced him to show the video to Bruce. He could have deleted it. Instead, he'd shown it to his campaign director. What did that say about his own motives?

"You may be right," Toby said, his voice down to a mere whisper. Bruce slapped a jar of Feodora's throat remedy in front of him. Toby ignored it. "Deep down, I probably do want this shown, so I can win the election and be president. I'm sure you can arrange to leak it to the media so no one can connect it with us. It's all so tempting . . . but it's wrong."

"Of course it's wrong," Bruce said. "If honest politicians run honest campaigns, then only dishonest politicians would win. You know that. This is crunch time. You release that video, you'll sweep the Islam election, and you are the next president. The good that will come from that will overwhelm doing what's necessary to put you in that position."

They were silent for a moment as Toby paced some more. "I'm sorry, I can't do it." His voice was a mere croak, his throat on fire.

"I thought you'd say that," Bruce said. He held up a small bottle. "You know what the right thing to do is, but can't bring yourself to do it. Take one of these." He put the bottle into Toby's hand.

Eth.

Toby realized he was still twirling his scarf. He stopped and looked at the scarf in one hand. Then at the bottle in the other.

One tablet, and he'd be president of Earth. It was that simple. No one would know.

That's not true; he would know, and Bruce would know.

He was Adam at the Garden of Eden, and the snake—or Bruce—was offering him the apple. How had that worked for him?

He stared at the bottle again, then back at the scarf. He handed the bottle back to Bruce. With only a whisper left, he said, "I'm not releasing it." He wrapped the scarf firmly around his neck.

Bruce sighed, his anger seemingly gone. "Okay. But do something about your voice. I need to work on your next speech. I'll let the others in." He stepped through the privacy screen toward the front of the *Rocinante.*

384

Toby was surprised Bruce backed down so suddenly. He gulped down some of Feodora's throat remedy. Soon he'd have another crowd to talk to. He'd lost track of where they were, but Bruce would tell him when they got there.

He was so close to being president. How would he feel later if they lost? Would he spend the rest of his life regretting it? Was it worth throwing all that away to avoid one small transgression?

"Dammit!" Why was he so dizzy? He slammed his fist on the table. Bruce had been right. All his honest babble was just that—babble.

"Have you changed your mind?" Bruce was back.

The wooziness left Toby, and suddenly his mind was clear. Realization hit him on multiple fronts. "I don't know what I was thinking. I'm sending you the tape. Make sure to release it so nobody can track it to us."

"Done."

Toby ordered his TC to send the video to Bruce. "Oh, and Bruce? You think I don't recognize Eth when I take it? You put it in the throat remedy. You're not as smart as you think you are." Already Toby was thinking about certain changes in their platform.

"I'm smart enough. And here's the speech for your next appearance, in Kandahar, Afghanistan."

Chapter Fifty-Four
Bruce's Call

B ruce knew who to send the video to. And yet, he hesitated. Toby would be furious when the effects of the Eth wore off, but he'd get over it. He always did.

"Bruce." Toby had joined him up front. "We need to go over some of the things in this speech."

"What's the problem?" Bruce asked.

"We're in Afghanistan, right?"

"Yes."

"An Islam country, right?"

"Right."

"A conservative country, right?"

"Of course." Bruce didn't like the way this sounded.

"So, how come in Afghanistan, a conservative, Islam country, where we're about to expose the president of the planet as being gay, there's not a word about it in our speech?"

"What's the point? The video speaks for itself. If you go out there and let them know you are for equal rights for gays, or yags as they prefer, that just offsets the video. They may even vote for a gay person who's against gay rights, over a non-gay person who's for gay rights."

Toby was shaking his head. "I don't want to just beat Dubois. I want to crush him. We're switching sides. The huge majority of people in Islam Nation do not believe in yag rights, so neither do we. We're not just going to win, we're going to destroy Dubois so people like him and Ajala think twice before challenging us in five years."

386

This was the man he wanted to put in office? It was like Dubois at his worst. Bruce stared in horrified fascination as Toby reworked the speech.

The real Toby would be back soon. But not soon enough.

"Looks great," he told Toby of the latest addition to the stump speech. "I'll be up front—I need to take care of some stuff while you work on this."

"Of course," Toby said. "Come back when you're done."

He called ahead to let the advance team know that Toby was sick, and they'd have to miss the first appearance in Kandahar. He wasn't letting Toby off the *Rocinante* until the Eth effects were gone.

There was no rush to get to Antarctica, with its small population. So they spent Tuesday night in Muscat, Oman, awaiting results.

"We could have won the whole thing, just like that," Bruce said on Wednesday morning. He had the look of someone who'd won the lottery but missed the deadline and got nothing.

"I'd have ordered your execution as my first act as president," Toby said. "Still, it was tempting. Why didn't you send the video out?"

"If I'd sent that out, you wouldn't have been president," Bruce said. "Some doppelganger who looks like you and sometimes acts like you would have taken the office, but the Toby I want as president would have been dead."

"And after my doppelganger had you executed, we'd both be dead. So you just did the logical thing and saved both our lives."

"Yup." Bruce grabbed another of his endless supply of ping-pong balls and put it in his prosthetic hand, where he now held nine. He rotated the hand about to show that all of the balls were held, not just balanced on top. "I can do eleven with my normal hand."

"Once the Eth wore off, I would have been back to normal."

"If you'd won the election from the Dubois sex video, you'd have fired me. Then you'd have nobody around you could trust to both know the truth and tell the truth."

"So . . . you are the only one I can trust?"

387

"Yup." He stuck another ball in the prosthetic hand, and they all fell to the ground in a bouncing clatter. "*Damn!*" Stupid came racing over, batting at the balls with his front legs.

Toby wasn't so sure about trusting Bruce in all things, not after the promises he'd made to Vasquez and the advice he'd given to Tyler. He'd also heard rumors about him and the Indian underworld. However, he did need him, even if he had to keep him on a short chain, about two inches long. When the Eth first wore off, he'd threatened to cook and feed Bruce to the Australians. And yet, after he finished screaming at him, Bruce pointed out that he'd followed Toby's original, pre-Eth wishes. At the key moment, Bruce did the right thing and didn't release the video. He hadn't dropped the ball.

Maybe Bruce and Lara should get back together. They shared the same "trick Toby into taking Eth" hobby.

The most interesting thing about the whole situation were the actions of Rajan Persson. Toby remembered how Dubois treated him, and it must have been obvious to Persson that Dubois wasn't going to back him for president in five years. So Persson had taken matters into his own hands, and tried to knock Dubois out of the race. If Dubois won, he would pretty much name his successor. If he lost, then he'd be out of the picture, and Persson would be the Conservative front runner for 2105.

Bruce looked up from fighting Stupid for possession of ping-pong balls. "Results are coming in."

A moment later, he had a silly grin on his face.

"We won?" Toby said incredulously. "I'm president?"

"Nope."

Toby's whole body drooped. It was over. "How bad did we lose?"

"You didn't. In fact, you clinched the worldwide popular vote."

"Bruce, I can still have you executed if you don't talk straight. You said I didn't win?"

"It's much better than winning. You won Pakistan and Afghanistan, but lost Oman and the rest. It's a tie."

Bruce still had the silly grin on his face. "How is that better than winning?" Toby asked.

"It's the Satan Scenario," Bruce said. "I can't wait to explain that to Twenty-two! You won 67 electoral votes, he won 144, and so it's all tied up, 666 to 666!"

So it would all be decided by the single electoral vote in Antarctica. He'd have to call Olivia and Tyler and let them know it'd be another week before he could come home.

Islam Nation	Electoral Votes	Dubois	Platt
Afghanistan	18	49%	**51%**
Algeria	7	**64%**	36%
Bahrain	1	**67%**	33%
Burkina Faso	8	**72%**	28%
Chad	4	**62%**	38%
Cyprus	1	**65%**	35%
Djibouti	1	**63%**	37%
Egypt	18	**71%**	29%
Gambia	1	**64%**	36%
Guinea	5	**59%**	41%
Iran	14	**74%**	26%
United Iraq	11	**73%**	27%
Jordan	2	**70%**	30%
Kuwait	1	**65%**	35%
Lebanon	1	**62%**	38%
Libya	2	**74%**	26%
Mali	8	**59%**	41%
Mauritania	1	**66%**	34%
Morocco	6	**61%**	39%
Oman	1	**51%**	49%
Pakistan	49	48%	**52%**
Palestine	1	**70%**	30%
Qatar	1	**71%**	29%

Saudi Arabia	8	**77%**	23%
Senegal	5	**69%**	31%
Somalia	5	**63%**	37%
Syria	6	**69%**	31%
Tunisia	2	59%	41%
Turkey	11	**55%**	45%
Un. Arab Emir.	1	**64%**	36%
Yemen	11	**66%**	34%
Total	211	144	67

Chapter Fifty-Five
The Week the Earth Stood Still

With global warming threatening much of the world in the early twenty-first century, a conglomeration of companies formed the Antarctica Growth and Economic Development Corporation. The AGED Corporation believed that, as the continent warmed, Antarctica would be the next great frontier. With investors flocking to get in on the ground floor of "The Next Big Thing," cities popped up all over the icy continent.

Esperanza, located at Hope Bay in the Trinity Peninsula, just south of South America, became the largest city and the capital of Antarctica. It grew out of three bases: Esperanza Base, founded by Argentina in 1975; Marambio Base, also founded by Argentina in 1969 on Seymour-Marambio Island; and Bernardo O'Higgins Base, founded by Chile in 1948.

At its peak in the mid-2040's, Esperanza was a thriving city of 20,000. Soon it would become "The Great Faux Pas of the Modern World."

The nuclear wars of 2045 kicked huge amounts of dust into the atmosphere, causing a temporary cooling of Earth. This set AGED back several years, but by itself did not deliver the knockout blow. The nuclear wars had the side effect of giving scientists huge amounts of data on the effects on global climate by atmospheric particles. One of the first acts of the newly-formed world government in 2050 was the Sulphur Atmospheric Dust project. Putting sulphur dust ($SO2$) into the atmosphere to block sunlight, as well as iron particles into the oceans to absorb carbon dioxide, brought global warming to a standstill.

It also destroyed the AGED Corporation. The companies that made up AGED pulled their financial backing. Finding themselves living in the middle of the Antarctic icebox, with global warming and continental changes no longer in the future, and with their lifeblood of corporate funding gone, the mass exodus began. Soon Antarctica was a ghost continent littered with ghost towns, of which Esperanza was the largest.

Antarctica retained one major business. Early on, looking for ways to finance the growing colonies, AGED negotiated a 100-year agreement as the recipient of the world's radioactive waste. Incoming waste was packed away in doubly-secure containers and buried as far from civilization as possible, near the Amundsen-Scott South Pole Station. When USE began the process of fighting global warming, AGED protested, and threatened to nullify the agreement. In partial compensation for their losses, USE agreed to fund the relocation of anyone on Antarctica who wished to leave, as well as to grandfather Antarctica in as a USE voting country, despite a population far less than the required one million.

Nobody seriously thought its single electoral vote would ever make a difference.

Due to seasonal residents who came in only during the relatively mild summer season, strict rules were put in place for Antarctica citizenship: one had to be born in Antarctica, or reside there nearly continuously for a period of ten years.

By 2100, five citizens in Esperanza were the only eligible voters left in the frozen ghost towns of the Antarctic.

While Bruce and the rest of his campaign staff spent the next few days creating detailed psychological profiles of the five citizens of Antarctica, Toby went home on Wednesday, October 27. It would be the first time in nearly a year that he, Olivia, Lara, and Tyler would all be home together at the same time.

The candidates and their staffs were invited to an informal dinner at the Esperanza City Hall on the night before the election, Monday, November 1, 2100. That's when the two campaigns would try to convince the Antarctica electorate—all five of them—of the merits of their candidate. Until then, Toby was free.

He'd soon get the full report on the five voters, but he already knew the most important info: Three of the five were Donkeys, while the other two were Roosters. Since it was unlikely a Donkey would choose Dubois over Toby, his election seemed assured. But there was no certainty—you never know how a voter votes until he votes.

Not too surprisingly, one of the Antarctica Five was Melissa Smith. This alone made news all over the world, not that it helped them here.

On Sunday, October 31—Halloween—Tyler dressed as Joseph Wang, the famed cartoon character from the Joseph Wang Show. Toby and Olivia dressed as the dopey parents. Lara dressed as the unnamed "brilliantly evil and suspicious little sister." Tyler felt he was too old to trick or treat, and didn't want the disruption of the Gray Guard swarming over every house they went to, so they went to a masquerade party instead.

When Bruce called him late that night, Toby mentioned their outfits. "You're kidding me!" Toby had no idea what Bruce thought was so funny. "I'm calling you because of Joseph Wang."

"Why would you call me about a cartoon character?"

"I think it's time I fill you in on the Antarctica Five," Bruce said. "Or perhaps Six."

"Six?" That was news. "There are only five, right?"

Being the irritating type, Bruce gave all the background info before he got to the point.

The three members of the Liberal Party were 17-year-old Melissa Smith and her parents Matthew and Melinda. "Based on extensive psychological analysis and personality profiles," Bruce said, "they would jump into the jaws of a great white shark before they would vote for Dubois. You can lock in those three votes."

Ronald Scooter Wang, Jr. and his wife Tyra were the two conservatives. "When someone has 'Scooter' as part of their name, or marries someone with that moniker, we don't need any more analysis," Bruce said. "You can lock in those two votes for Dubois."

"There's a very loud 'however' coming, isn't there?" Toby asked. "Involving Joseph Wang? Can underage cartoon characters vote in Antarctica?"

"You're close. The Wangs have a fifteen-year-old son. His full name is Ronald Joseph Wang, III; he goes by Joseph. We checked; he's the third generation named after Ronald Reagan. And he really is named for the cartoon character Joseph Wang."

Toby began to laugh, but noticed Bruce was not. "He's fifteen, right? You have to be sixteen to vote."

"That's what I've been arguing about all morning with Phil Farley. You know he's running Dubois's campaign now, since Lara resigned? Joseph turns sixteen on Wednesday, the day *after* the election. On Tuesday night, Farley's going to move him to the abandoned city of Dakshin, east of the international dateline. They claim that since it'll be Wednesday there, Joseph will be sixteen, and he can still TC in his vote to Esperanza, where it'll still be Tuesday night and the election still open."

Toby took the deepest breath of his life. "You've got to be kidding."

"Nope. It's all gone to the Antarctica Supreme Court, which is meeting as we speak." Now Bruce was smiling.

"Antarctica has a Supreme Court?"

"Yep. By law, it's made up of the nine oldest citizens age sixteen or older. Since there are only five citizens currently aged sixteen or older, the 'Antarctica Supreme Court' is made up of those five. They'll vote 3-2 that Joseph isn't eligible. Then Dubois will make an emergency appeal to the World Supreme Court, and they'll rule on it."

"What are the chances there?"

"Five of the nine were appointed by conservative presidents, two of them by Dubois. And if they do allow Joseph to vote, and Antarctica is a

3-3 tie, then nobody gets any electoral votes here. Then the entire election is a 666-666 tie, and it goes to the USE Congress."

Bruce didn't need to elaborate on that. With a conservative majority, and five years of shelling out pork projects and earmarks, Dubois would win for certain.

Bruce called again shortly after midnight. As expected, the Antarctic Supreme Court had voted 3-2 that Joseph wasn't eligible to vote. Dubois had already made his appeal, and the case had gone to an emergency meeting of the World Supreme Court, which would meet Monday morning.

"We have two hundred lawyers on the case," Bruce said.

"How about Dubois?"

"About three hundred."

Toby and Lara flew to Esperanza very early Monday morning on a Gray Guard floater, since the *Rocinante* was in Antarctica with Bruce and Feodora. Due to the unique size of the Antarctica electorate, candidates were not required to spend the entire week there. Twenty-two didn't want to take the attention away from the election, so she took a few days off to visit Ajala.

Toby and Lara regaled each other with stories of the campaign, most of them at Dubois's expense. She also told him about the ever-growing split between Dubois and Persson. Toby was tempted to tell her about the video of Dubois and Farley, but he'd promised to keep it a secret. Then Lara shared some important news.

"Dad, I need your help next year. I'm running for the World Congress, from the Maryland district."

For the rest of the trip they planned out her campaign. Poor Bruce had no idea that after running a historic worldwide campaign for president, he was about to move down in the ranks and run a mere congressional race. Toby had always held out hope that, somehow, the two would get back together.

They took the "scenic" route before landing. The shores of Antarctica were beautiful, as blue water met pristine shores. Once they moved inland, it became an overwhelmingly bright and brighter white that went on forever. When they approached Esperanza, a speck in the ocean of white, it reminded Toby of a picture he'd seen of a polar bear hidden in snow on the other pole; all white with a bit of black where the nose was.

The Supreme Court ruling came out shortly after noon. Based on the wording of the law, and in contradiction to what most claimed made common sense, the vote was 5-4 that Joseph Wang could vote. Toby watched the breaking news on his TC.

"You'd think they'd have agreed on one time zone for Antarctica," Bruce said, shaking his head in disgust after Toby arrived. There'd been a move to do so long ago by the AGED Corporation, but the effort had been dropped when they pulled out. The various regions of Antarctica went by whatever time zone their longitude put them at, although unofficially most went by the time zone of their home country. Esperanza, nearly due south of the U.S. east coast, went by U.S. Eastern Time.

"That's it, then," Toby said. "It'll be 3-3, and congress will put Dubois in as president. Are there any more appeals or anything we can do?"

Bruce shook his head. "The Supreme Court has spoken. The next president of Earth will be chosen by a teenager named after a cartoon character."

Chapter Fifty-Six
Esperanza and Hope

T oby had never really understood the term "ghost town" until Melissa took him and Bruce on a tour of Esperanza Monday afternoon. Years of Antarctica winds had reduced the rows and rows of houses circling the town to crumbling ruins. As they moved downtown in the freezing temperatures, it was no better. The remains of the city looked like a smaller version of the nuking of Seattle. The Gray Guard had restored an old Hilton Hotel for the large contingents from the Dubois and Platt campaigns.

"I've seen videos when Esperanza was alive," Melissa said. "My grandparents told stories about it. And then the sponsoring companies left, and so the people left."

"Why did your family and the Wangs stay?" Toby asked.

"Someone has to run the science station and keep the penguins company."

It was early summer in Antarctica, with seventeen-hour days. By December, Melissa told him, the days would be twenty hours long, with twenty-four hour sunshine at the actual South Pole. In July, the height of the Antarctic winter, the nights would be twenty hours in Esperanza, with complete darkness at the Pole.

They got out of the commandeered Gray Guard floater and walked about. Houses creaked under the whistling wind, but otherwise it was spookily silent.

That night, the Smiths and Wangs hosted the election-eve Monday night dinner at Esperanza's town hall. This would be the only real chance to campaign personally with the Antarctica electorate.

Toby had some experience with dinner debates from the famed "Dinner Debate Down Under." That debate had been primarily for the four electoral votes of Australia. This time they were even farther "down under," and it was for president of the world.

He hoped they wouldn't be bobbing up and down again.

Toby, Feodora, and Bruce sat together at the front table. Sitting appropriately to their left were Melissa and her parents; to their right were Joseph and his parents; and opposite them sat Dubois, Persson, and Farley. The press was banned, other than unmanned cameras that broadcast everything live to the world.

Toby had seen the report on Joseph Wang. Chinese-American like his parents, who were originally from San Francisco; tall for his age; home-schooled like Melissa; a good student; a reader of mysteries and, surprisingly, the classics; an excellent skier. Unfortunately, he'd also led a sheltered life, dominated by his parents and their views.

It was a quiet, civil dinner, with no barbecued kangaroo surprises. Melissa and Bruce didn't get into a single argument. Melissa seemed subdued, no doubt knowing that anything she said would have little influence on the Wangs; doubtless they'd argued the issues many times already. Worldwide viewers were likely bored and disappointed.

"The lull before the storm," Bruce TCed Toby.

And then the storm broke. "Toby," Dubois said pleasantly, "didn't you argue against nuclear waste disposal in Antarctica at a news conference in the late 80s, when you were running some governor's race in South America, even though that's Antarctica's main source of revenue?"

"Yes, in the 2088 Argentina governor's race, the dangers of radioactive wastes were an issue, since Argentina is the founding country of Esperanza, the entry point of those wastes. Are you for radioactive wastes in Antarctica?" And the debate was on, with over half the world's population watching.

For two hours, they refought many of the issues of the past eleven weeks: Galactic Union membership, meat-eating, free food, Full VR, Kim and the USR, English First!, China's borders, French banking, pirates, gun violence, gay rights, and others. Dubois argued strongly for his views, while Toby focused on the need to compromise. The vice presidential candidates and campaign directors were mostly quiet. Sometimes Melissa would ask questions, but Joseph silently observed everything. There was no telling what was going on in his head.

The parents asked pointed, partisan questions. However, they were amateurs, and Toby and Dubois had no problem addressing their questions with an answer that turned into a more difficult and pointed question for the other candidate. Sometimes Melissa joined the debate, but even she had nothing that could possibly convince the Wangs to change their vote.

Not once did either candidate raise his voice. Bruce had said that was the most important thing of all, and no doubt Dubois understood that. An angry man rarely looks presidential.

And yet, Toby knew it was all pointless. He looked at the faces of the Wangs, and knew he couldn't convert them. He knew Dubois couldn't convert the Smiths. It would go to the USE Congress, they would select Dubois, and Toby would go down as another losing third-party challenge, one that doomed the Ajala campaign and brought on five more years of Dubois.

In answer to the question of why he wanted to be president, Dubois gave a professional answer that touched on every major issue.

Toby gave nearly the same response he'd given since India, that forcing your views on others is as bad as them forcing their views on you, and that compromise and moderation were the key. He asked if there were any questions.

Joseph glanced at each of his parents, then stood up. What little background whispering came to an end. Everyone wanted to hear what the king-maker had to say.

"I know that everyone thinks I'm a joke," he began. He spoke in a monotone, eyes down. One hand trembled slightly. He's scared out of his mind, Toby thought.

"I've seen the news reports. I'm named after a cartoon character—thanks, Dad." His father looked slightly embarrassed as he shrugged and mouthed the word, "*Sorry.*"

"I can't help my name and my age. But I do know one thing." For the first time he looked at the cameras. "I'm the guy who's going to decide the next president." There was a mass exhalation as people laughed at the unexpected joke.

"So I guess that means everyone's going to listen to me. And I've listened closely to what the candidates said tonight. It really helped me make up my mind." He pointed at Dubois. "I agree with everything he said tonight." He looked toward Toby. "I'm sorry, Mr. Platt, but I had no idea what you were talking about half the time. I think you mean well, but you speak a different language. And look who you surround yourself with. A Russian general known to have committed atrocities in wartime—my parents told me about her. And your campaign director—isn't he the one who thinks most people are too stupid to vote, are like chimpanzees? I've seen reports."

"Actually," Bruce said, "you are right. In the heat of an election race, I do say things like that about voters, because most voters know about as much about the issues as you and I know about brain surgery. If I said you didn't know anything about brain surgery, would you object?"

"So you really think most voters are too dumb to vote?" Joseph asked.

"I would argue that if you don't know the issues, then it is your civic duty *not* to vote."

What the hell is he saying? Voting isn't just a right, Toby thought. It's a responsibility! At least he hadn't said this earlier in public, forcing him to spend the rest of the campaign clarifying that he didn't agree. But at this point, he's not really hurting anything. At best, it's a 3-3 tie and we lose. At worst, it's a 3-3 tie and we lose. It makes no difference anymore.

"Meaning I don't know the issues?" Joseph asked. He shook his head. Then he came over to Toby and extended his hand. "I think you mean well, but I can't vote for you." Toby took his hand and gave a firm shake.

Joseph looked back toward Dubois. "Mr. President, congratulations."

"That pretty much ends it, doesn't it?" Toby watched the Dubois campaign floater leave to take Joseph 1700 miles and four time zones over to the international dateline and Dakshin to vote. It was Tuesday morning. At eight PM Tuesday in Esperanza it would be midnight in Dakshin—the start of Wednesday and Joseph's sixteenth birthday. Melissa went along as a representative of the Platt Campaign to make sure it was all done properly.

"We could always shoot it down," Bruce said.

"Did you notice how many Gray Guard floaters went with them?" It had been a good run, the closest a third party candidate had ever come to winning the presidency.

"It probably wouldn't be good politically to shoot them all down," Bruce said. He was silent for a moment. "You know, a lot's happened during this election."

"Yeah, I'd say! I became a quadriplegic, we battled gangsters, assassins, and pirates, we were imprisoned and almost executed, we went through a war and a coup, and I got stuck listening to you and an alien debate issues for eleven weeks. That's the abbreviated version."

"I don't mean that," Bruce said. "I mean what's happened to me." Suddenly he was tossing a ping-pong ball from one hand to the other. "Look at the stuff I did this campaign. I did strategy based on winning, first, with what's right sometimes a distant second, even tricking you into taking Eth to get you to go along. You don't want to know some of the stuff I did in India and other places! I made promises to a gangster I knew we couldn't keep, and a few other deals you also don't want to know about. I treated Gene like dirt. And the advice I gave Tyler—how could I have done that? I wanted to win so much, and look what it did to me!"

"Nothing that I didn't do as well back when I was with Dubois," Toby said, deciding not to ask about the things he didn't want to know about. "Let's just agree that we'll never do it again. There's more to an election than winning."

"I hope so," Bruce said. Then his eyes brightened. "Though winning will be nice."

"Huh? Is that some sort of joke?" Toby shook his head as he stared at his feet. "You heard what Joseph said. He already congratulated Dubois."

"I don't think you've been paying attention," Bruce said. "As Feodora might say, we still have a joker to play."

Toby looked up. "What do you mean? You think we still have a hope?"

"Definitely. Did you know that Esperanza is Spanish for 'hope'?"

"No, I did not. So you're basing our hopes on the fluke of the town's name? *That's* our joker?"

"Maybe."

As midnight approached, Toby, Lara, Bruce, and Feodora gathered in the *Rocinante*. Toby, Lara, and Bruce planned to fly back to Maryland that night, while Feodora would go back to Russia in the *Dulcinea*.

There was a knock on the door, and there was Twenty-two. "Ajala thought I should be here for historic vote." Toby had to remind himself that while flying from Nigeria to Antarctica may take hours for a floater, for Zero it was just minutes.

"It's midnight," Bruce said soon afterwards. He held a ping-pong ball in each hand. As usual, he'd arranged for the results to be sent directly to him so they wouldn't have to wait for the public announcement that would come a few minutes later. "Results are in."

Suddenly Bruce turned pale. There was a cracking sound as he broke both ping-pong balls. Then he turned to Toby. His lip trembled as he took several breaths. He said something, but it didn't quite come out.

"What—" Toby began, but Bruce interrupted him.

"*We won!*"

Twenty-two shook from side to side. Bruce screamed and systematically pulled ping-pong balls out of a box and threw them at everyone. Feodora doused everyone with Russian New Vodka. Stupid cowered in a corner.

Toby simply sat and took the showers of ping-pong balls and vodka. It simply wasn't possible. They had won.

How had they won?

He finally asked Bruce. "We had a secret weapon, a joker," Bruce said. "Did you forget Melissa went in the floater with Joseph? Do you think *anyone* can withstand Melissa for 1700 miles?"

"So we won 4-2?"

"Nope. 3-2. Joseph must not have voted."

"You mean—you convinced him not to vote?"

"I only suggested it. I think Melissa did the rest."

"You set that up, didn't you?"

"Of course."

"But it's a civic duty to vote! I—I don't want to win this way."

Bruce gave him a professorial stare, literally looking down his nose at Toby. "You'd rather lose because a 16-year-old named after a cartoon character mindlessly voted for the guy his ignorant parents told him to vote for?"

"I'd rather everyone vote, period." Toby began pacing about the floater's purple interior. Never in his life had he gone from such heights of joy to the depths of despair in seconds. Is that how he'd won the election? "It's his civic duty to vote."

"Even if he doesn't know the issues? Even if he's only voting based on slogans, bumper stickers, and attack ads, and because it's how his family always votes? Without thinking about issues and policy or understanding what's at stake? I'd say it's his civic duty *not* to vote."

"He should learn the issues, of course. But if we tell people it's okay not to vote if they don't know the issues, then we're just inviting them to not know the issues so they can avoid voting. *Dammit!*"

"There's an argument there," Bruce conceded. "But I think top priority is to take the time to learn the issues. If you can't bring yourself to do that, then for God's sake, *don't vote.*"

"You're challenging the very foundation of democracy."

"Ignorant voters challenge the foundation of democracy. You want to concede?"

"Toby, we won election," Feodora said. "Now you can use presidency to tell everyone to vote, and everybody wins. Now is not time to worry about this. You have five years to do that. When you do, let me know so I can be in Russia."

Toby couldn't help but smile. "Okay, I'll let it go. But I am going to use this presidency to convince people to vote as a civic duty."

"And to convince them to learn the issues before voting," said Bruce. "We'll make sure they get our side first."

"That, too."

A few minutes later Toby's TC alerted him to an incoming call from Joseph Wang.

"Hello?" Toby said. He was glad TCs did not transmit smell with all the vodka Feodora had poured on him.

"Mr. Platt?" Joseph's face was red, as if he'd been in a violent argument. "I want to explain what happened."

"I saw the result. You didn't vote?"

"I couldn't. It was what Bruce said, about it being your civic duty not to vote if you don't know the issues. A lot of the stuff you said, I'd never really heard that side of things. I wasn't sure what to believe. And then . . . someone convinced me I didn't know the issues."

"Melissa, I presume?"

Joseph nodded. "Have you ever been trapped with her for a few hours? Jeez, she doesn't stop, doesn't let up, not for a minute!"

"Actually, I've had that same experience. You survived?"

"Barely. She's always been like this—now I remember why I avoided her when we were kids!"

"You should have voted. It's a civic duty. A person can't use ignorance as an excuse not to vote. It's just incentive to stay ignorant."

"But Bruce said—"

"Bruce and I just had it out over this. Next time you vote."

"Okay, I will. But you know something? I might have voted for you anyway. The smartest thing Melissa said was that situations change, and someone like Dubois can't change because he's cornered by his political beliefs. You can compromise, and that's why I can trust you as president. Besides, I promised my parents I wouldn't vote for you. But I never said I'd vote for Dubois."

"I'm guessing they didn't take it well?"

"Sure didn't." His eyes brightened. "But you know what? I'll have my diploma next year, just in time for next year's congressional elections. Did you know Melissa was all over the world this past year as a campaign volunteer? She's promised to hook me up somewhere, though I don't know if that's going to work out, since we don't really agree on a lot of stuff. But I'd sure like to get out of Antarctica."

"There's a simple solution," Toby said. "The Moderate Party will be running candidates all over the world next year, and I'd be proud to have you join us as an observer. You don't even have to vote for us." But we're going to try to convince you to, he thought.

Perhaps the Moderate Party would get a new recruit

Epilogue
Inauguration and Revelation

Thursday, January 20, 2101, Noon

"I do solemnly swear that I will faithfully execute the office of President of the United States of Earth, and will to the best of my ability, preserve, protect, and defend the Constitution of the United States of Earth." With those words, Toby Platt became president.

He stood in the shadows of the Twin Towers as the live orchestra played *Hail to the Chief*. He loved that song. Birds chirped in the cool weather. Feodora, Olivia, Lara, and Tyler stood at his side. Most of the World Congress were nearby, clapping and cheering. Even Dubois and Persson clapped politely.

Soon he and Feodora were back in the Purple Room, which had been repainted that very morning. Waiting for him were Bruce, now Toby's chief of staff, and Twenty-two. They had galactic business to attend to.

For the first time, he would sit behind the president's desk. As a special gift, India had sent him General Kadam's desk and General Chatterjee's chair. Toby sank down into the simple, cushioned chair.

It creaked.

"I'm leaving today," Twenty-two said.

"Not before we work out the diplomatic niceties, Ambassador," Toby said. "I want Earth to be a part of the Galactic Union before my first term is over." Hopefully, he thought, there'd be a second.

"That could be a problem," Twenty-two said.

"Is this because of the interstellar space travel requirement?" Toby asked. "You know that's a priority for me."

"That is not the problem," Twenty-two said, "though it is a problem. I would be very surprised if Earth can learn advanced spaceflight technology in five years, ten years, even twenty years. There are certain discoveries you have not made yet. But there is a bigger problem."

"And what is that, Ambassador?"

"She is not an ambassador," Feodora said.

"Huh?" Toby said.

"Ambassadors send reports to home planet," Feodora continued. "They work out relations between their planet and ours. They act diplomatically, and do not get into fights with presidents of planets."

"Maybe Grodan ambassadors are different from ours," Bruce said.

"Feodora is correct," Twenty-two said, her lone eyestalk drooping. "I am not an ambassador."

"*What?*" Toby exclaimed.

"When I arrived and met President Dubois, I could not say, 'I am a college student.' If I had, I would have been treated like . . . a student." She looked up. "My major *is* political theory. I have learned a lot on this school break."

Toby had campaigned heavily on becoming part of the Galactic Union—and he'd just learned his contact was a college kid on vacation!

"Okay," he said. "If you aren't the Grodan ambassador, can you tell us how we can go about applying for Galactic membership?"

"The first part is simple," Twenty-two said. "If you develop interstellar spaceflight, the Galactic Union will detect it, and they will come to you."

"But you said we're more than twenty years away from figuring that out."

"I did say that." Twenty reached into a vest pocket and removed a sheet of old-fashioned paper. She held it up. It was covered with scrawls that looked vaguely like mathematical formulas. "Give this to your scientists. It should help."

"Let me see," Bruce said. "Maybe I can finally make use of those math and physics degrees."

"We have Russian scientists I'd like to bring in on this," Feodora said.

"Bring 'em in," Toby said, leaning back into the creaking chair. "This will be a worldwide Manhattan project, and I'll run it from right here in Manhattan." He wondered if it would cause an international incident if he pitched the Indian chair out the window and replaced it with the nice, quiet one from his old office.

Bruce had sat down on the floor against a wall. "You're kidding!" he mumbled as he stared unblinking at the paper.

"Hopefully that will make up for lying about my ambassadorship," Twenty-two said. "I hope to hear from you in a few years. When you make it to Tau Ceti, contact me. You have my number."

"I'll do that," Toby said. "And then you can introduce us to galactic politics, which must be a lot better than Earth politics."

"No," Twenty-two said, "it is much worse."

Appendix A
A Short Summary of Modern Earth History

2045	Nuclear wars; Korea, India, Pakistan, Israel, and Seattle are nuked; suitcase nuke takes down rebuilt Twin Towers.
2045-2049	Second Great Depression
2049	World Constitutional Convention
2050	World Government created (July 4); Wayne Wallace elected first world president, takes office in 2051; Toby Platt born.
2051	Nuclear weapons made illegal
2052	Dalit national boycott in India
2053-54	Indian Civil War; Great Compromise of Sultanpur
2054	Wayne Wallace loses leg in assassination attempt
2055	Wayne Wallace re-elected as world president
2060	Jim Abrams elected as second world president, takes office in 2061
2065	Jim Abrams re-elected as world president
2066	Toby Platt's mentor Vinny dies
2069	The Lethargia; Full VR outlawed
2069-2079	Third Great Depression
2070	Thomas Clarke elected as third world president, takes office in 2071
2071	U.S. invasion of Canada
2073	Vatican City Bankruptcy
2074	Beijing Rebellion; Taiwan declares independence
2075	Thomas Clarke reelected as world president
2076	Eth declared illegal
2078	U.S. invasion of Mexico
2080	Amaresh Brown elected as fourth world president, takes office in 2081; Great Compromise of Sultanpur agreement expired
2084	China and Taiwan reunited
2085	Amaresh Brown re-elected as world president; General Bapoto takes over Tanzania in a coup
2088	Amaresh Brown assassinated; Vice President Jing Xu becomes fifth world president
2090	Mexico Liberation (Aug. 30); Jing Xu elected as world president

Appendix B
The Seven Wonders of the Modern World

1. ### The Twin Towers in Manhattan
   They are the seat of World Government. The original Twin Towers in Manhattan, USA, were destroyed in a terrorist attack in September, 2001. They were rebuilt, but destroyed again in a nuclear attack on June 12, 2045. They were rebuilt again by 2049. At 4000 feet, well over twice the original height, they are the tallest manmade structures in the world. The North Tower houses the World House of Representatives, the South Tower the World Senate.

2. ### The Vaz Palace of Mexico City
   The Vaz Palace was built in 2091 by Mexican Mayor and suspected gangster Fernando Vasquez. It is the largest palace in the world with a one-mile square base. The entire surface of the palace is plated with gold, with jewels embedded every few yards. It has numerous spires that go a thousand feet into the air, with fireworks displays every hour on the hour. Inside are an indoor soccer stadium, art museums, and staging areas for opera and an orchestra. An earlier Vaz Palace had been destroyed in 2078 by invading American troops during the Eth War.

3. ### The Great Mall of China
   The Great Mall is just over 500 miles long as of 2100, and continues to grow every year. Communist officials in China plan that one day it will parallel the entire length of the 4000-mile Great Wall of China. The roof of the mall has a mural that is also 500 miles long, depicting China's long history from ancient times to the present. Many Chinese said you weren't truly Chinese until you'd hiked the Great Mall. World leaders often make the trek.

4. ### The Baleine Bleue Aquarium at Dover
   The blue whale aquarium was created by the French in 2089, and located in Dover, England, overlooking the French National Bank. It is actually

two aquariums, each a mile long, and a quarter mile tall and wide. They parallel each other, a quarter mile apart, with a huge tube connecting them. The aquariums contain 26 blue whales, each named after one of the 26 regions of France. The most famous of the whales is Lorraine, a genetically created blue whale with the horn of a narwhal.

5. **The Layered Wheat Cube of Sarawak**
The wheat cube is a perfect cube, a half mile on a side, with 660 layers. Each layer is densely packed with genetically created dwarf borlaug-15 wheat, a high yield and high protein version. It went into operation in 2096, with more planned. The cube grows over 600,000 tons of wheat each year, enough to feed three million people annually.

6. **The Colossus of Bapoto in Dar es Salaam.**
[Destroyed on October 1, 2100.]
Construction on the Colossus was completed in 2090 by General Amri Bapoto, then the leader of Tanzania. The 800-foot statue is a likeness of the General, holding a book under one arm, and a laser aimed at incoming ships in the other. The entire surface is platinum plated. It stands astride the 300-foot wide Dar es Salaam harbor.

7. **Mount Bharat and the Generals**
Mount Bharat is an artificially created mountain near New Delhi, India, in Sultanpur, National Park. Carved into the huge granite mountain are the figures of Generals Kadam and Chatterjee, architects of the Great Compromise of Sultanpur in 2054. The two are shown clasping hands in friendship. The mountain is about 1000 feet from base to top.

About the Author

Larry Hodges, from Germantown, MD, was going to be a math professor (bachelor's in math), but science fiction writing and table tennis (yes, ping-pong) sidetracked him, and now he writes (and coaches the latter) for a living. He is an active member of Science Fiction Writers of America with over 70 short story sales. *Campaign 2100: Game of Scorpions* is his third novel, and combines three of his favorite things: science fiction, politics, and table tennis. He's a graduate of the six-week 2006 Odyssey Writers Workshop and the 2008 Taos Toolbox Writers Workshop, and is a member of Codexwriters.com. His story "The Awakening" was the unanimous grand prize winner at the 2010 Garden State Horror Writers Short Story Competition. He's a full-time writer with eleven books and over 1600 published articles in over 150 different publications. He also writes about and coaches the Olympic Sport of Table Tennis, is a member of the USA Table Tennis Hall of Fame (Google it!), and once beat someone using an ice cube as a racket. Visit him at larryhodges.org.

MURDER IN THE GENERATIVE KITCHEN
Meg Pontecorvo
a novella

With the Vacation Jury Duty system, jurors can lounge on a comfortable beach while watching the trial via virtual reality. Julio is loving the beach, as well as the views of a curvy fellow juror with a rainbow-lacquered skin modification who seems to be the exact opposite of his recent ex-girlfriend back in Chicago. Because of jury sequestration rules, they can't talk to each other at all, or else they'll have to pay full price for this Acapulco vacation. Still, Julio is desperate to catch her attention. But while he struts and tries to catch her eye, he also becomes fascinated by the trial at hand.

At first it seemed a foregone conclusion that the woman on trial used a high-tech generative kitchen to feed her husband a poisonous meal, but the more evidence mounts, the more Julio starts to suspect the kitchen may have made the decision on its own.

"With *Murder in the Generative Kitchen*, new author Meg Pontecorvo cooks up and dishes out for you not one, not two, but three original sci fi premises. Enjoy and digest them well!"
—**David Brin**, author of *Existence* and *The Postman*

"*Murder in the Generative Kitchen* by Meg Pontecorvo is a compact little story with a lot to say. Readers will find a fresh take on Asimov's three laws, see a twisted future where vacations are paid for by the courts, and learn that the same old arguments will still be contested long after we're gone."
—**Ricky L. Brown**, *Amazing Stories*

World Weaver Press, LLC

Publishing fantasy, paranormal, and science fiction.
We believe in great storytelling.
worldweaverpress.com